PRAISE FOR
ESTHER M. FRIESNER'S

CHRONICLES OF THE
TWELVE KINGDOMS

MUSTAPHA AND HIS WISE DOG
SPELLS OF MORTAL WEAVING
THE WITCHWOOD CRADLE

"Most original ... should appeal to readers
of all kinds ... She will almost certainly be
one of the more popular fantasy writers of
the next few years."
Science Fiction Chronicle

"Whimsical, inventive, great fun to read"
Peter Heck, *Newsday*

"Highly literate ... told with subtlety and
style ... An example of an exceptionally well
created world. The characters are lifelike and
engaging, civilization and untracked wastes
are neatly balanced, and very little is certain
except that the expected will rarely occur."
The Dragon

"Engaging characters and an intriguing plot"
Library Journal

The Witchwood Cradle

Esther M. Friesner

AVON
PUBLISHERS OF BARD, CAMELOT, DISCUS AND FLARE BOOKS

THE WITCHWOOD CRADLE is an original publication of Avon Books.
This work has never before appeared in book form. This work is a novel.
Any similarity to actual persons or events is purely coincidental.

AVON BOOKS
A division of
The Hearst Corporation
1790 Broadway
New York, New York 10019

Map by John M. Ford

First Avon Printing: March 1987

For my parents, David and Beatrice Friesner, who gave me the freedom to dream and the love and support to help me follow my visions.

AYREE'S TWELVE SISTERS

Menka is the eldest. Athletic and rangy, she loves horses and the simple life.
Wardland: Norm, home of the famous port of Cymweh
Power: to domesticate the swiftest earth-bound creatures; but she especially loves horses
Hairstyle: a long rawhide-tied braid
Tent: plain white
Shield device: a horse rampant, sable, on a field argent
Banner: a simple pennon of white canvas with a black fringe
Fighting style: mounted, first using bolas of her own conjuring whose weights are chunks of star-ice, then an ordinary sword

Shama is as close to ugly as any of the Twelve: Her bitter, catty nature may be to blame.
Wardland: Heydista, famous for lawyers, lawsuits, courts of law, and occasionally justice
Power: to understand the ways of unfeeling things like rocks and minerals
Hairstyle: two braids wound around her ears
Tent: white striped with orange
Shield: bears on a field gules a mailed fist, semé d'or
Banner: a square of red silk horizontally striped with green
Fighting style: mounted, using shurikens; she runs from hand-to-hand combat

Lavah has been under the thumb of her immediate elder sister Shama for too long. Soft-natured, she makes a wonderful toady and tries to ape Shama's catty ways.
Wardland: Leyaeli, kingdom of Bet the Worrier, son of Mil the Perturbed
Power: to work wonders with flowers and herbs (especially the sort that are all show and smell, but have no practical use)
Hairstyle: a fuss of too many curls that are forever getting tangled
Tent: a delicately striped confection of ivory, rose, and dusty blue silk
Shield: bears a rose proper, argent, on a field azure
Pennon: a forked gonfalon striped rose and white
Fighting style: mounted, with a crossbow

Hodah is the ideal fosterer of seedlings, the perfect midwife.
Wardland: Glytch, homeland of Morgeld's evil servant, Tor
Power: centers on the bringing forth of new life
Hairstyle: bound back in a loose ponytail, with two sidecurls
   escaping over the ears
Tent: midnight blue, unadorned
Shield: displays on a field azure an infant warrior, fully armed
Banner: triangular, midnight blue, unadorned
Fighting style: afoot, with a magical silver quarterstaff

Senja is wild, boisterous—even the metalsmith's forge, where
   she shows her greatest talent, is a noisy place.
Wardland: barbarian Vahrd
Power: Senja's skill with metalworking needs no magical
   enhancement
Hairstyle: cut into a short, practical cap of curls
Tent: red, yellow, and green-striped satin, with a gold fringed
   canopy over the doorway
Shield: divided; bears in chief, on a field jaune, a wolf sable,
   eyes rouge, sautant; below, on a field rouge, a dead man
   suspended by one heel, his body pierced with arrows
Banner: a forked gonfalon, striped red, yellow and green, with
   silver bells sewn to the lower hem
Fighting style: afoot, with two swords of her own forging

Lucha is more indolent and luxury-loving than her immediate
   elder.
Wardland: Vair, one of the civilized southern kingdoms
Power: a special skill in games of chance
Hairstyle: long lovelocks gathered at the crown of her head with
   a gemmed golden fillet
Tent: red samite, the canopy and entryway trimmed with silver
   bells
Shield: bears a man's severed head atop a pile of gold pieces, the
   whole on a field sable
Banner: a forked gonfalon, black with silver fringe, and embroidered
   with a sleeping silver panther
Fighting style: afoot, with a curved sword; she collects the heads
   of her enemies

Fortunata is supremely civilized—perhaps as a reaction to her
   two nearest elder siblings—Fortunata prefers study to fighting,
   and always knows the answer.

Wardland: Clarem, seat of the famed university of Panomo-Midmists

Power: musical talent; she patronizes minstrels, and recognizes the importance of the harmonies that bound all magic

Hairstyle: long and straight

Tent: hexagonal, with six alternating panels of blue and white wool embroidered with lifesize portraits of famous women of the Twelve Kingdoms

Shield: bears on a field azure an open book, argent. In chief is the motto: "Here truth shines brightest"

Banner: a cloth-of-silver rectangle stitched with a golden harp

Fighting style: mounted, with a lance, which she uses to keep the battle at bay

Resha, called Resha the Dreamer, is forever wondering what lies on the other side of the Lyarian Sea, the Desert of Thulain, or the eastern forests.

Wardland: distant Sumnerol, closest to the northern wastes

Power: Resha favors those herbs which alter perceptions and thus enhance dreams; through their use, she has become a peerless healer

Hairstyle: two plaits criss-crossed on top of her head

Tent: the dull green of seawater, very small and confining to guarantee her privacy for dreams

Shield: shows a Braegard dragon-ship, argent, on a diagonally slanted field of stripes, azure and vert

Banner: white with the same ship as her shield, vert

Fighting style: afoot, with long and short knives both

Sacchara seems to be sweet-tempered and gets along well with honeybees. She also has a sweet-tooth, and wears loose robes that hide her growing plumpness.

Wardland: Paxnon, where beehives and gardens flourish

Power: to encourage the growth of food crops, especially fruit trees

Hairstyle: long and twisted into a bun at the nape of her neck

Tent: golden silk the color of delicate honey

Shield: on a field or, seven honeybees rampant, gules

Banner: a red silk rectangle with a golden beehive

Fighting style: mounted, with bow and arrows of honey-colored wood

Zabala is an excellent cook, a tireless experimenter in the kitchen, and the perfect partner for Sacchara: Sacchara provides the raw materials, Zabala processes them, and a delicious time is had by all.

Wardland: Malbenu Isle

Power: domestic sorcery

Hairstyle: two pigtails set high on the crown, then braided together until she looks as though she's wearing a hairy heart

Tent: dome-shaped and of white satin, its canopy trimmed with blue and green loops that hold glass windchimes

Shield device: a cookfire, or, on a field gules

Banner: a purple satin triangle bearing a white bowl

Fighting style: afoot, with a morningstar

Asapha, the silent one, never answers back when angry or upset, but goes off to be alone. She almost always wears brown gauntlets embroidered blood-red, though she will fly her hawks bare-handed.

Wardland: Lyf, home of the gaunt gray Kestrel Mountains

Power: Lady of the Birds of Prey, and a patron of archery

Hairstyle: straight, cut to just below the ears

Tent: tiny, bannerless, made of black felt

Shield: sable, divided by a single broad stripe of silver which in turn displays a hawk, sable, a dead nightingale in its talons

Fighting style: afoot, with a spear and a short, single-handed ax; though birds are her best weapon

Basoni, youngest of the Twelve, seems to have avoided the excesses of her elder sisters.

Wardland: Sombrunia

Power: Mistress of the self-shielding spell of invisibility

Hairstyle: long and loose, with the very occasional ornament

Tent: canvas, not silk, striped brown, pale blue, and golden; a small garnet-colored glass bell with a pink tourmaline clapper hangs by the entryway, a cherished gift from her sister Hodah

Shield: a field azure with two bears—one sable, one white—climbing a tree from opposite sides; their paws touch, but their heads are turned from each other

Banner: a white star on a dark blue triangle

Fighting style: mounted, on a small pony, using an ordinary bow; then fights afoot with a sword

PROLOGUE IN PROPHECY

Twelve there be, the fairest;
Ten there be, the blessed;
One lost, and one lost forever,
And one to judge all,
Yet twelve there be, to rule and rest.
Was ever riddle so wrought since the gods were gone?

—"The Chant of the Gateway Beggarman"
from *The Scroll of Oran*, as translated by Beglash the Scribe

An anguished scream tore midnight peace from the halls of Castle Snowglimmer. Witchlight burned cold, luminous, shedding an unsparing brilliance over the smiling corpse upon the bed. Ayree stared at the dead woman and fell to his knees before her—Ayree, Prince of Warlocks, who had hunted the fields beyond the sky and slain creatures too terrible for one nightmare to contain. The silk-hung screens beside the bed he set alight with green fire, then toppled forward as an animal howl burst from him. His white hair fell against the sea-green satin coverlet and his long white hands knotted in it as he sobbed out his grief.

A small hand touched his shoulder. Ayree lifted his head.

"Mother is dead . . . ." The child's clear voice still held a note of questioning, as if she expected Ayree to work some fearsome magic to undo death and prove her wrong.

But Ayree only gazed up into wide eyes as blue as his own and nodded. "Yes, Basoni," he said. "Our mother Charel is dead."

1

In his overwhelming sorrow, he did not think to question why the child was here at this unhallowed hour, so far from her proper bed.

Basoni laughed—a nervous titter, brittle and frightening. "Now I will wake up, won't I? I always do. Even when I have bad dreams, I wake up; dreams of the dark man . . ." Her harsh laugh was gone. The fear in her eyes made Ayree ache with sympathy for this, the youngest and best beloved of all his sisters. "Sometimes I dream you're there, too, Ayree. You and the dark man. Why won't you keep him out? You can do anything. And this dream is so bad, so bad! Take us out of it, Ayree, let me wake up!"

Ayree seized her and took her into his embrace. He stroked her long, golden hair. Already it flowed halfway down her back, and she was only three years old. When she stopped shaking and pressed herself against him, he said, "It is no dream, Basoni."

She pushed away from him, though he still cradled her. "The dark man says that, too! He says that when he comes for me, it's no dream at all. But now I know better. I heard the god speak to Mother, and they talked about him. He is Morgeld."

The face of the witch-king hardened so suddenly that it frightened the child. "Who spoke of Morgeld here? Who was here with her?" he demanded harshly. The dead woman smiled on, and would give her son no answer; Basoni could not.

Basoni felt cold, as if warming magic no longer lined the inner walls of Snowglimmer's ice-hewn magnificence. The shaking came back into her limbs, made her teeth chatter. She was incapable of speech.

Hurrying footsteps came echoing out of Charel's courtyard, a lesser sending of witchlight led a tall young woman into the bedchamber of the sorceress-queen. Basoni saw her through a blur of tears—an older version of herself: Hodah. A shocked gasp escaped Hodah's lips when she saw her mother.

And yet Charel had none of the horror of death on her. Her favorite white satin gown covered her, a brooch of sapphire and pink tourmaline at her breast, little boots of blue-dyed lambskin on her feet. Her fair hair was dressed in elaborate braidings, clasped up in many looped strands by silver pins.

Hodah came nearer. "She looks as if she is dreaming; but she's dead, isn't she, Ayree?"

Ayree's strained face turned slowly to gaze at her. He saw Charel's face in hers, as he did in all his sisters' faces, and traces of their father too—theirs, not his. He rose up, releasing Basoni from his arms. The youngest of the Twelve was still trembling like a startled coney.

"Basoni . . ." Hodah stretched out her arms to the shivering child. Basoni fled to her sister's loving, protective embrace. She had done it many times before, when her sorceress-queen mother was too preoccupied with the great, mysterious magics to comfort a child's small needs. Without consciously knowing it, Basoni had had two mothers all her short life. Now she had only one.

Ayree did not reply to Hodah's question. It needed none. Ayree knew that next she would want to know how Charel had died. So did he.

He held his empty hands out flat above his mother's body and passed into a light trance that lasted less than a minute. The sisters watched, huddling together like sheep surprised by summer lightning.

At last Ayree returned to himself. "She did not die by violence. All magic was taken from her body, and magic was all that kept our mother alive for these many ages."

Hodah dared to touch her brother's sleeve. "But how—?"

Ayree turned away from the bed where the ruined screens still smoldered. He looked to the open balcony where dawnlight was already washing the eternal snows. "She would have borne a son," he said. "A boy. I read his presence within her. Stealing her life-force, he stole his own chance of life as well."

Hodah burst into a torrent of questions. Ayree ignored them, too caught up in fresh grief for his lovely mother's loss to bear speaking. As the questions came louder, faster, more frantically, Hodah let Basoni go, the better to try breaking through the witch-king's shell.

Unnoticed, Basoni fell back into the shadows cast by the bed's huge headboard, the gilded bronze form of a crouching panther with lapis claws and topaz eyes. She glanced behind it to where she and her nearest sister, Asapha, had hidden too long and seen too much.

Four-year-old Asapha was still there, still curled into a mute, frozen ball of fear. Only Basoni knew that she was there. Charel's youngest daughter wondered why she had been able to witness the same horrors and miracles as her elder sister, without such terrible effect.

Perhaps the dark man of her earliest nightmares had unwittingly done some good: Morgeld had inured her to all but the worst fears, made the frightful commonplace by his nightly visitations.

Basoni knelt beside Asapha and tried to rouse her. She overheard Ayree telling Hodah of the Rule of Loss—the payment all witchborn must make for their powers when they conceived or sired children: Males drained magic from the sorceress-mothers who carried them; females drew off the powers of their sires, but Charel might have born a thousand daughters without any loss of magic.

"—could not know what sex her child would be, and so she died."

"And the baby died with her." Hodah's voice was full of yearning.

Basoni knew that she would have to come out from behind the bedstead and tell them about Asapha . . . and more. In the dark, a blade of impossible blue gleamed on the stones. Basoni saw the god's image like a phantom drifting over it—Krisli, Charel had called him, and the name was uttered with so much love that it made Basoni tremble. She saw him again as bitter magic flowed from his body to clothe and compose her mother's corpse. Charel had died in his arms, in the ecstatic moment, and no power on earth would convince the spying child that love had not brought death in its wake.

Charel had loved the god—Krisli, the demigod Inota Battle-lord sired on a fire-spirit—and love had killed her. While Asapha cowered, hands over her eyes, Basoni saw it all. When Asapha dared to peek, beheld her mother already dead, and her spirit fled into terrified silence, Basoni stayed to witness Krisli's last words to his beloved.

I rule the human heart, he had said to the hovering soul, *but you ruled mine, Charel. You thought I came to your bed only to beget the Twelve, the living fulfillment of ancient prophecy. You were wrong. I loved you. Though our daughters someday must ally and destroy my cursed half-brother, though Helagarde will fall to their united powers and Morgeld's death will bring the gods' return, yet what will it matter to me? You are gone.*

Basoni had seen in Krisli's haggard face the gaunt features of the dark man of nightmares. For a fleeting moment she imagined that they were one and the same creature. But there was too much tenderness in the god's look, too little that was cold. And he spoke of love. The dark man had spoken only of possession when his dream-sent whispers terrified a little girl.

The god had bent over Charel's body. *I have killed you,* he had said, confirming Basoni's worst suspicions. *I have killed you as surely as if I struck you down with a sword. If I had known . . . but even my vision has its limits. I foresaw your death, but not that our son would bring it.* Then Krisli wept, and his tears trickled down on the eider pillow beside Charel. They were pale streaks of light, brightness stolen from a clear winter sky, and a ghost formed from the god's tears: The ghost of a sword against the pillow.

I could not know you clung to life by such a tenuous thread, my love. I meant this sword for him, for our son. Now what is it but a gift for the dead and the never born? May your spirit find rest, and his another shell. May the Blue Sword find him, and bring him home.

Then the god was gone. Basoni had crept out of hiding to stare at the token he left behind. The blade blazed blue as the thickest walls of Castle Snowglimmer. When Basoni had come near and closed her hand around the huge hilt, she felt ice. At that moment she heard someone coming, saw the heralding glare of her brother's witchlight. Without a thought, she seized the Blue Sword and dragged it with her behind the bed. Then Ayree discovered Charel's body, and whatever business had brought him to her rooms was forgotten.

In hiding again, Basoni squatted beside her petrified sister and held the god-given blade. She would have to show it to Ayree eventually, have to explain her presence—and Asapha's—soon enough. A dream of the dark man, a frightened awakening, a plea for her nearest sister to accompany her in search of their mother's comforting arms, a stealthy path into Charel's bedchamber . . . and then too much knowledge, too much revelation for a child to grasp. They would all blame her for what had happened to her sister.

Sister.

A visible bloom of warmth filled Basoni's mind. It was not like any light of mortal or magical kindling, but something more.

"Who speaks?" she whispered. Her eyes darted to Asapha, but her lips were still clamped tight.

No name. With life a name; but for me, none. Here I am.

Basoni stared into the blade of the Blue Sword. It held a vision of her mother's body, and the warmth shone from there, where the dead sorceress-queen's hands lay folded over her womb.

"Who—what are you?"

See what I might have been.

Charel's body fell to golden dust. It blew across the empty vistas of Basoni's sight until the glittering grains seemed to multiply, drifting, shaping, spreading across the vision. The unfelt wind that moved it died, and Basoni saw the desert.

A broad highway mostly hidden by the sands cut a faint groove between two rows of worn statues. They were man-shaped, carved with remarkable skill from blocks of garnet. Each distinct face wore an awful look of pain and remorse.

One carved face moved to fill the vision. From the misty borders ringing it, a child's hand touched the blood-red cheek. The sand blew again, and grains of it battered the stone. The child's hand remained, a caress.

The little hand withdrew. A tear trickled silver down the statue's cheek. Age-long stiffened eyelids blinked once, quickly, to flick away the stinging sand. The man of stone was flesh, and free.

I would have freed them all.

The vision was gone from the Blue Sword's blade. Only the feeling of warmth inside remained with Basoni.

"Basoni! What are you doing back he—? Oh!"

Hodah flung her arms around Asapha and called for Ayree to come. She hugged the stiff-limbed child to her and worked what small healing magics she could to release Asapha from the thrall of fear.

In the confusion surrounding the withdrawn Asapha, and Charel's lifeless body, Basoni was ignored.

Ayree had snatched the Blue Sword from her hands before she could speak. Holding it high, balanced across his palms, the Prince of Warlocks sent green fires curling experimentally around the blade. When the sorcerous fires died, the keen edge remained as sharp and whole as ever, though Ayree's fires could blast steel to steam. He made a brief, strange sound in his throat and wheeled away, taking the Blue Sword with him.

Asapha still held Hodah's attention, but Basoni didn't care. The presence was within her again, the warmth bathing her to the bones.

Give me your oath, my sister. In the name of the love that made me and the life I never had, make me a promise. Shelter my kindred, the children who will be born. Shelter them, and swear that no child who lives shall have to live without love. Swear . . .

And in the inmost chamber of her soul, Basoni swore.

Chapter I

THE HUNTER

There shall come a day of gain and loss,
Yet none to read them rightly.
A ring of spells cast by no mortal hands,
No mortal hands to weave a different spell.
Love in the house of death, the ring of fire,
The fire gathered from a dozen lights.
The game is set, the pieces gathered wait,
But to be made or scattered?
I will tell you no more, for the sake of the Queen.

—''The Weirding of the Yellow Witch''
from *The Scroll of Oran.*

Basoni dreamed no more dreams of the dark man after Charel died. Though she was only three, childhood was over for her.

In the three years that followed, she tried to prove that she was not a baby anymore. She turned wild, disobedient, strong-willed. It made no difference. She was still the baby in everyone's eyes, especially Ayree's.

Basoni didn't like that, and she flatly hated it when Ayree hung over her when she was at lessons. Most especially she hated it when Ayree called all his sisters together and ordered them to unite their powers into a spell of his choosing. When the exercise failed—and it failed invariably—he would wear *that* look. And then Ayree would exchange heated words with the other girls, but as he passed down the line his voice grew gentler and gentler, until by the time he reached Basoni, all he would do was pat her on the head and say, ''When you're older.''

So Basoni worked even harder to hone her sorceries, which

made Lavah and Shama exchange overly sweet smiles and loud comments about what a little study-bump their baby sister had turned out to be.

"Worthy to enter the vaults of Tsaretnaidos herself," Lavah mewed, trying to sound like Shama.

It was no competition. Shama was witness of the bitter gibe. "Such studiousness should be encouraged, Lavah, not scorned. Why, Basoni is a model to us all, so eager to obey Ayree." Shama patted Basoni's golden hair in just Ayree's way and added, "Our sweet little baby sister."

"I am *not* a baby! I'm *six!*" she shouted at them. They just giggled. She called them horrid names and ran to her room, her head full of angry thoughts. She wasn't Ayree's ever-obedient worshiper. She would show them all.

In her room she opened a chest of inlaid lacwood and took out her heaviest cloak, whiter than kuroc milk. She fastened it at her throat with an unwieldy silver brooch that had been Charel's. A smooth-cut purple stone gleamed in a silver star, surrounded by a ring of faceted aquamarines. Their pure heaven-blue lights made the central gem take on a sullen glow. She forced the thick pin through the thicker pelt and stood tall.

She was on the brink of great adventure. She would be the first of the Twelve to defy Ayree, for he had forbidden them all to wander from the castle without his express permission. She would steal out of Castle Snowglimmer, using all her skill to baffle the unseen guardians her brother had installed. Once outside, she would travel fast, fast, fast as her nascent magics would take her, to a place that only she and her sisters knew.

Every spring in a sheltered dale near Castle Snowglimmer, Lavah, Resha, and Sacchara would join their magics to create a garden of joys. For spring meant nothing in the northern wastes— no respite from eternal ice and snow—but by uniting their plant-loving powers the three sisters could cheat the endless winter and make the frozen earth bring forth blossoming apple trees, sweet herbs, and the fragrant papery petals of narcissus.

And because no magic can exist and vanish traceless, the frozen remains of trees, herbs, and flowers lay beneath the snow. Basoni meant to go there, dig up a stalk of narcissus embalmed in ice, and bring it home to lay before Lavah and Shama as proof of her disobedience. Let them call her a baby then!

She never knew how well she had learned the lesson of self-shielding until she put it on that morning. If her mother had been alive, Charel would have explained the rule of Precedence of Magics to her youngest child—the rule which states that some mages master one spell above all others, though why, no one can say. Basoni could fasten invisibility around herself more easily than any ordinary cloak. But she hadn't fully realized her power until she turned a corner in the castle corridor and nearly walked right into Tsino, one of the last of the mortal servants left alive in Snowglimmer.

Tsino had been master-tracker to the kings of Sumnerol before he came north to serve Ayree. Master and servant often vanished together, to reappear, in time, with those strange white pelts which never came from any beast in the Twelve Kingdoms. Age had hoarsened Tsino's voice and bent his back, but left his eyesight unmarred, his uncanny ability to scent prey in a shadow untouched.

Basoni stood petrified as the ancient hunter's eyes swept the corridor, rested on her for an endless instant, then moved on. He shuffled off, muttering of ghosts. The hem of his robe trailed over her foot as he passed.

That was the closest she came to capture. At the great gate of icicles it was no trouble at all to slip between the large gaps in the grille. Once through, she whispered a spell that banished footprints.

She ran until Castle Snowglimmer was out of sight, then dropped her shielding spells and took flight for the hidden dale. She dropped caution, too, exhilarated by her small victory over Ayree's vigilance. She was a child who flew, and not a child in the safer skin of a snowbird or a cloud's milky fur. She was not even an invisible child.

If anyone sought her he could not miss her now.

Basoni came to earth on the slope where she and her sisters held their picnics to celebrate spring. The cold was bitter, the sun was a bright glare, and the sky a clean, cloudless blue. Basoni's baby magic doubled the warmth of her fur cloak, then redoubled it. Still her cheeks flamed and her nose began to freeze.

She ran down the brow of the hill, wanting to dig up her proof and be gone. Like any child she lost her footing and slid on her backside, snow getting up under her cloak and into the sleeves of her gown. She picked herself up at the bottom, swore angrily, and dug into the crusted snow.

Under the snow was more snow. Basoni might have used her powers to melt it, but that would mean stealing warmth from her cloak. With wads of flakes turning into icy trickles on her skin, she didn't want to feel any colder, and so she scrambled in the snow like a puppy, mad, wet, cold, and completely indifferent to anything but her task. A long blue shadow fell over her and still she did not look up from her shallow pit until she heard sweet laughter.

"Child, what are you doing here?" Warm blue eyes studied Basoni, red lips formed an indulgent smile. The lady was dressed like a trapper, in a hooded coat of marten skins tied with a woven belt of many colors. From under the dark brown hood, hair as white as the witch-king's framed a lovely face. "You must be frozen!" She knelt in the snow and reached out to stroke the little girl's cheek. Basoni drew back sharply. "Afraid? I won't hurt you. I am Bilka."

"I'm Basoni." She spoke shyly, not used to strangers.

"And what are you, Basoni? One of the snow-spirits?"

"Oh, I'm not a snow-spirit," Basoni said hastily. "I'm a sorceress."

"Indeed?" There was skeptical mirth in Bilka's blue eyes. "Then maybe your spells can help me pitch my tent." She turned her back on Basoni's scowl and climbed the crest of the small hill where her sled waited. It was drawn by a team of broad-padded frostcats, proud in their brass and scarlet leather harnesses, their speckled ivory skins.

Bilka pitched her round, skin-sewn trapper's lodge and set up camp quickly, blithely ignoring Basoni's angry protests that she was indeed a sorceress. As the lady entered her lodge, she lightly said that Basoni might call herself anything she fancied, for children must play.

That was too much. Basoni stormed into the tent and startled Bilka, who was trying to kindle a reluctant fire in the center of the lodge.

Stepping forward, Basoni fixed her eyes on the wood. Bilka gasped as it crackled into flame.

The trapper's daughter uttered a hasty apology, and a gracious invitation for Basoni to remove her cloak and warm herself. She shed her own, revealing a woolen dress the same bright scarlet as her frostcats' harness, a belt of steel discs girdling her waist. There was no more talk of child's play.

Basoni removed her own cloak and let the fire make her warm and dry. Bilka set up a bronze tripod and kettle over the fire, filling it with fragrant dried herbs and snow to make tea. She even brought out a square of candied jican-root and sliced off as much as Basoni wanted, throwing it into the boiling water. It melted, sweetening the tea, the feathery root hairs making yellow swirls on the surface before dissolving entirely.

Bilka drank none of it. "Too sweet for me. I'll brew another pot later," she said.

Basoni didn't notice that no second pot was brewed. It was cozy in the trapper's lodge, and the too-sweet tea made the child yawn. "I am so sleepy," she said, stretching.

"So you should be. Why don't you rest? Nothing's more refreshing than a nap on a pile of pelts."

"I know." Basoni felt a faint pang as she realized that she ought to get the frozen flower and go home—but another yawn smothered that impulse. Basoni told herself that she would only close her eyes for a little while. The furs Bilka spread for her on the hard-packed snow looked *so* attractive . . .

The dark man did not step into her dreams, but they were still dreams of terror. She was alone, stripped naked on a plain of snow. A blizzard's blast lashed her tender skin. She crouched into a ball, too cold to moan, hair growing heavy as hard pellets of ice clung to each strand.

Cold claws dug deeply into Basoni's shoulders, yanking her to her feet, exposing her fully to the gale's howl. "You will not hide from what is mine." An arctic voice numbed Basoni's cheek. Bilka's face was still as beautiful as before, but it swam in the air like a poorly fastened mask.

Then the mask slipped.

Bone-white and empty-eyed, mouth red with blood, the snow-beast leered hungrily. She was the starkness of a winter storm, the cold that kills, the sapping cold that lulls its victims to sleep before fastening itself to their bodies and draining them of life.

Basoni could not speak. The creature laughed and drew the mask back on.

"You will not hide," she repeated. "The storm is mine and you are mine, child of witchcraft. You are a prize, did you know it? Someone will pay me much for you."

The blizzard wavered and began to retreat, revealing the walls of Bilka's lodge. Basoni was no longer naked, but wearing her old gown and cloak, and lying on her side. And she could not move! Though no visible bonds tied her, her hands were clasped together, nails blue with cold, and when she tried to move them apart she heard a chinking sound. The same sensation came when she tried to move her feet.

"You are not mad, little one," Bilka said, smiling at the

astonishment in Basoni's eyes as she tried to part her hands a second time.

"Please . . ." Basoni spoke painfully. Her throat was raw. "Please let me go. My brother is a great magician— Truly! If you let me go, he will reward you—"

The snow-beast laughed. "I will have my reward. My storms will wipe summer itself from the Twelve Kingdoms, and I will feast on the blood and bodies of men and beasts who sleep my frostborne sleep." Bilka's red lips curled back. "My lord Morgeld is a more generous master than your brother Ayree."

Basoni watched as Bilka snatched a small brown pelt from a nearby heap, the head and paws of a weasel still attached to the gutted body. Bilka rubbed the sorry rag against her cheek, and whiteness followed. Ice knit up bones inside an empty skin, glowed blue-white from the dead eye-sockets. Whiskers a web of frost, the transformed ermine poised daintily on its haunches, awaiting his mistress' command.

"To Morgeld, little friend," said Bilka. "To Helagarde, and tell him that I have trapped what he wants."

The ermine chattered its teeth and raked its icy whiskers with its claws, then fell to all fours and scurried from the lodge.

"My pet will reach Helagarde in less than two days," Bilka said. "In the meantime, we can wait."

"My brother will find me before that!" Basoni cried. Her invisible chains clattered on wrists and ankles.

"Will he?" The snow-beast was unconcerned. "Was he able to save you from me? Remember, child, the first mortal witch learned her spells of shielding from a northern storm that covers every sign of man. Whiteness hides more than dark ever can."

Basoni's eyes smarted with tears that she tried to hold back. They slid between her eyelids and Bilka breathed them into frost-flowers on the girl's cheek. Then the snow-beast drew back and sighed.

"You would make a tasty morsel—but I didn't catch you for myself." She gestured, and Basoni's fire crackled blue, burning without heat. The wood was unconsumed, the snow beneath it unmelted. Basoni cursed herself for not having stopped to question where the so-called trapper's daughter had gotten wood in a treeless waste, or why a campfire hot enough to boil tea had done no harm to its snowy bed.

She was still cursing when a huge fur throw landed on her, shutting out the light. A breathing tunnel quickly appeared, Bilka's face at the far end.

"Sleep, if you like; there's nothing else for you to do while I hunt." Then Bilka was gone and there was only the rush of cold air up the tunnel.

Basoni closed her eyes, but not for sleep. She centered all her thoughts on Ayree, opening her self to the outer places, just in case the snow-beast's shielding spell had some flaw to let his questing spirit through. *Here I am! Here I am, my brother. Come!* her soul shouted to his.

No answer.

Eventually she slept, without dreams.

She awoke to hear Bilka's voice—and another. So Morgeld had come. She had slept two days through and he was here to take her. All pretense of dying proudly, silently, and calmly fled her. The child began to cry.

That was when the tone of the two voices grew tenser. A man's heavy footsteps came near the pile of fur covering Basoni. She could just see the tip of a thick leather boot blocking the light.

Bilka shrieked; wind roared beyond Basoni's furs. She heard harsh cries, boots digging into hard-packed snow, and over all the howl of the snow-beast's fury. What could have caused such a falling out between Morgeld and his creature? Instinctively, her hands went up to cover her eyes.

Her hands moved freely apart, past the bounds of the unseen chain once holding them wrist to wrist. Gone also was the one that had shackled her feet.

Basoni had no time to question good fortune. She scrambled up, threw aside the pelt over her, and clapped on her spell of shielding before she was firmly on her feet. Unseen, she raced unseeing for the hide-hung doorway, rushing past the two entangled figures fighting in the center of the lodge. She had seen enough of the snow-beast; she wanted to see nothing of Morgeld. But as she flung back the leather flap, a small white body hurtled through the portal, coming the other way.

Basoni could not help watching as the dog flew past her and leaped for the snow-beast. Snapping and growling, the dog drove into the monster—for Bilka had dropped all disguise. The storm-white hag of the northern wastes had Morgeld pinned to the snow when the dog attacked.

Morgeld? No; not Morgeld at all, but a young and darkly handsome mortal man. His face was twisted with pain, one hand black with frostbite. The dog butted the snow-beast off his master's body and an ice-dagger dropped from her grasp. It dripped blood, and where it cut, flesh froze.

But the white dog would not let Bilka strike again. He had thrown her off his master, and he kept her at bay while the young man seized the creature's dagger.

Wild terror overcame Basoni. She gulped air and ran from the tent, her shield-spell stealing her footprints from the snow.

Later she learned that the man had slain the snow-beast. Menka brought him to Castle Snowglimmer, healing his wounded hand on the way. His name was Mustapha, and his small white dog was a creature of enchantment, having human speech and the ability to take human shape when it pleased him. Too soon they left, pursing adventures of their own.

Ayree never reprimanded her for the folly that nearly ended her life; he didn't have to. The Prince of Warlocks recognized the mark of a broken spirit. From that day onward Basoni was the most obedient of the Twelve. Shame made her so, and a sharp fear of the penalty she had almost paid for her defiance.

Chapter II

THE TREE

"My queen, you wander in gardens you never made and will never truly see."

—"The Envoi of the Condemned Royal Gardener" from *The Scroll of Oran*

The years passed quickly after that, and Basoni studied diligently, until the day came when Ayree stood on the dais before the great throne of Castle Snowglimmer, watching the sparkling remnants of twelve linked firespells tumble from the air in a glittering rain. It had been a wondrous display, made more so by the fact that it was the first time all twelve of the sisters had merged their separate magics successfully.

Basoni smiled up at her brother before falling into a deep curtsey at the foot of the dais steps. She was twenty-two, and she had chosen to mark her coming-of-age in the one way that would most delight Ayree.

"Wonderful," he said. "Magnificent. Perfect." Basoni blushed with pleasure and went back to take her place in the three-deep ranks of her sisters.

"No need to look so pleased with yourself, pet," Shama hissed as Basoni passed. "We had a hand in this, too. It took you long enough to learn how to join your spells with ours. *I* came of age when I was just eighteen."

Basoni did not answer. She had found silence the best way to meet Shama's bitter tongue. From the dais, Ayree spoke: "The time has come. In the name of what was foretold, we must move now."

"Why now, Ayree?" It was Zabala. She was not a warlike

16

soul, and she hated anything that might take her away from her brew-pots and ovens.

"Yes, why now?" Shama demanded. "Morgeld hasn't stirred from Helagarde for years! He's no more threat to the Twelve Kingdoms than a lame turtle."

Lavah's soft hand closed around her elder sister's arm. "Threat or not, Shama, until he is dead, we can never be free. If Ayree says the time is now . . ."

Shama glowered Lavah into silence. "What are *you* in such a hurry to be free of?"

"Lavah is right," said Menka, tossing her thong-tied braid over one shoulder. "I've spent enough years with Morgeld's unmaking hanging over my head. I'm sick of leading half a life! Let it be done with, and let us be released!"

A melodious laugh, low and throaty as a panther's most amorous growl, came from the lady Lucha of Vair. "*I* would relish freedom. We would all put it to excellent use, once obtained. That is"—her eyes lit with lazy amusement as they rested on an angry Shama, a chastened Lavah—"most of us would."

"I would." Hodah's words were a sigh.

Still Shama persisted in her objections. "Why must we rush against Morgeld when he's no immediate danger to us or the Kingdoms? We have lived this long by the rules that bind our blood, and we've only just brought our powers together. What difference will a few more years make?"

"What difference would a century make to you, Shama Bride-biter?" Lucha murmured to herself, the words just loud enough for Basoni to overhear. "You've found it cozy enough, living by the Rule of Loss, even if Lavah's not so pleased with it." In a much louder voice she said, "Are you perhaps afraid to face Morgeld, sister?"

Shama laughed harshly. "Afraid of him? Not even if I were magicless! King Alban of Sombrunia laid him low within Helagarde itself and not one of his dark magics could save him from a mortal man's sword thrust!"

Ayree sank into the great throne. His tunic was the deep blue of an evening sky in the southern lands, sewn with pearls for stars, but his boots were cut high, made for a battle rider. "A mortal man, but no mortal sword," he said. "He is a brave man, a good king, and yet . . ."

"And yet he is not the one," Basoni said softly. Ayree heard her, and he called up an echo that carried her words to every ear.

"His bloodline may destroy Morgeld, but not Alban. So it was prophesied."

"Prophecy!" Shama was never one to let go of an argument. "Then let his bloodline do what it must and leave us out of it. Morgeld is nothing, I tell you! For all we know, he's dead already, and the stink just hasn't been able to ooze out of Helagarde yet."

"He is not dead!"

"He is!"

"He's as *good* as dead, is what Shama means."

"Oh shut up, Lavah. You'd eat a skunk if Shama told you to."

"Can't we let Alban's son kill Morgeld?" Fortunata ventured. "If that's what the prophecy said . . . ?"

Senja shouted, "I want to do it myself! Or why'd I throw out half my life learning to forge good steel! Let me cool it hot from the fire in Morgeld's blood!"

"Senja, you *belong* among those Vahrdish savages you favor. Why don't you just stay there permanently?"

The Twelve were at it again—at each others' throats.

Ayree cupped his face in one hand and let them go on for a time. When he'd had enough, he sliced the air with his arm, creating a peal of magical thunder. The Twelve gazed up at the great throne again, but not all of them looked chastened.

"Alban Stonesword has fathered four sons since he defeated Morgeld and took the lady Ursula of Norm for his queen. But his father, too, had four sons, and Morgeld contrived to kill three, knowing the prophecy concerning the Sombrunian royal house and his own doom. We cannot wait. We cannot risk having Morgeld kill even one of Alban's sons. For all we know, the one he slays this time will be the one who might have killed him. I will not put my faith in luck."

A tree of gold and bronze sprouted from the floor between Ayree's feet, its trunk slender, its branches curling like smoke. Blue leaves with teardrop shapes rustled over half the crown, silver-gray leaves covering the rest. Among the blue leaves, twelve white flowers bloomed, but three swords bristled where the leaves grew gray.

"My sisters, you know this tree," Ayree declared, his slim fingers touching the place where two slightly different colors of bark overlapped each other on the enchanted trunk. "In the ages when the gods still walked with men, our ancestress Ambra planted its seed. Goddess of the Light-in-Darkness, she knew of the long dark falling on these Twelve Kingdoms, but she could not depart without leaving some hope for the children who would come afterward.''

Basoni remembered a witch-child who had not lived to see Ayree's wondrous conjuration of the sacred Tree. In her long years of diligent study and quiet obedience, she had never forgotten the voice of Charel's unborn son, nor the oath she had sworn to her brother never born.

"So Ambra planted the Tree of Second Light in the gardens of a royal palace.'' Ayree spoke on, his eyes on the parti-colored leaves. His sisters knew the tale, but with the Tree before them they listened raptly as it was retold. All knew where that palace lay. It was gone, its gardens swallowed in the sands of the Desert of Thulain. The Older Empire was no more, and only the Tomb of Queen Nahrit stood—empty now—to remind men of what had been.

"In her wisdom, Ambra entrusted its keeping to a simple maidservant, a girl named Saara. Saara's blood held magic, though she did not know it. Elaar the Sea-Witch was her kin, and Ambra, too, but the powers slept in her. For love of the goddess, she tended the Tree. She never knew the mysteries it hid . . . until the day the hero Oran died.

"Saara had always thought the Tree an ordinary plant. But at the moment of Oran's death, light from the Tree flooded Saara's eyes and magic bloomed in her blood. Her bones glowed with so much power that the seven guards Queen Nahrit sent to capture her were instantly burned to ashes.

"She flung her sorcery over her like a cloak and took the shape of seafire that dances on the masts of ships in storms. Out of the flames a dragon's claw emerged and tore the Tree of Second Light from the palace garden. She was the monster—Saara, the Queen's little maidservant—and her wings were cut from sheets of diamond. With the tree in her talons, she flew north over the Opalza Sea and did not land until she felt the wind cold and strong enough to hinder her flight. That was where she landed, and where she raised the icy walls of Snowglimmer, and where she planted Ambra's tree in the heart of her castle, in a place between dreams.

"That tree still grows deep in the hidden places of our castle. It shows by its branches the twin prophecies that were born out of the mouth of the seeress Musa on the day that Janeela, the Silver One, bound Morgeld with sorcery and her life's price.''

Ayree's twelve sisters bowed their heads in a gesture of respect for the mortal woman who had dared to do what the most powerful magicians of her age shrank from attempting. Together they recited the prophecies of the Tree, their heritage:

"By the mortal blood of lost Janeela, mortal hands may doom him. By the twelve silver chains of sorcery that bound him, twelve children of sorcery may destroy him. So Musa the Seeress foresaw, who was of Saara's blood; Musa and Saara, blood of our blood, prophecy of our seeking."

Ayree was silent. He made no move, no gesture to call up a vision, and yet the vision was there. Slabs of purple luminescence cracked the floor of Castle Snowglimmer. Dark Helagarde, Morgeld's fortress, thrust its ramparts up between the witch-king and the twelve sorceresses. The stones of Snowglimmer groaned and rocked underfoot. Asapha's hawk screamed and took wing, flying from the hall in a sparrow's panic.

A bright spear from Ayree's hand struck the amethyst stones, shattering them. The vision died, but a sooty afterimage hung on the air, a curtain through which Ayree's white hair looked gray.

"Morgeld has tried to chop off one branch of Ambra's holy Tree and failed. He has tried to destroy the other and failed again. Will we give him the opportunity to try a third time? He has learned from his errors. Have we done the same? Let magic be the branch of prophecy that ends Morgeld's power and returns the gods! Will you wait for magicless men to cheat us of Morgeld's death? Will you spend your little magics one by one, uselessly? Or will you forge them into a single blade and strike! Strike *now!*"

Cyan lightning leaped from Ayree's right hand. The Blue Sword cut all doubts away.

Eleven voices answered, "*Now!*" Sword, spear, bow, quarterstaff, stars of steel and stars of ice were thrust high, summoned to their mistresses' hands by magic. Glum Asapha gave a hunting hawk's kill cry, and a flight of iron-winged falcons spiraled through the hall, bringing thunder on their pinions. Senja's handforged twin swords licked the air. Even gentle Sacchara raised a battle yell, and Fortunata pounded the butt of her lance against the floor because she had read somewhere that it was the thing to do with lances.

Basoni's silence was lost in the general uproar.

That evening the sisters' quarters were a bustle of battle preparations. All twelve doors were left ajar as the young sorceresses ran from room to room. Resha couldn't find her kit of healing herbs, Fortunata couldn't find her favorite book of military history, Lucha couldn't find her favorite silk rug, Menka couldn't find her chief mount's currycomb, and Zabala couldn't find the right equipment for cooking in the field.

No one could find Basoni.

In his own chambers—once Charel's—Ayree stood on the balcony while familiars in the shapes of winged cats daintily packed his leather bags. A spirit with the face of a kindly grandmother and eight sinuous arms sat mending tears in the warlock-prince's clothes and tent. Powdery snow was falling outside. He allowed it to gather on the railing and froze it where it fell, making fantastic cities in miniature.

"Ayree?" Basoni removed her matchless shielding spell. Two of the winged cats fluttered up, hissing. "How pretty!" she exclaimed when she saw the tiny citadels of snow. Her delight blew them away. "*Ohhh!*" She looked so dismayed that Ayree couldn't help laughing at her. He took her hand affectionately.

"Shall I remake them for you, Basoni? The way I used to conjure toys for you when you were a child?" He raised her chin with two fingers and studied her face with care. Of all his sisters she was the only one who still wore her golden hair loose and uncut, the way he liked best. It cascaded almost to her knees and was very seldom adorned with more than a simple horn comb or a silver flower.

Basoni broke away from her brother's gaze as soon as possible. "If I've disturbed you—"

"I was hoping for some company. Come. If you've finished your packing, share a little mulled wine with me." He waved her toward a table of brass, lacwood, and leather where floating wicks bobbed in an enameled basin of scented oil. The table was Vairish-made, low to the floor and ringed with cushions. Thirteen rose-glass cups were set around it.

Ayree sighed as he sat down. "I hope the others will finish soon and join us."

Basoni giggled as she spread her skirts and knelt on one of the cushions. "I doubt it. It's madness in our rooms. I shut my door and did what you're doing—summoned up a few helpers to tend to my packing."

"Why didn't the others do the same?" Ayree asked, then read the answer in Basoni's look. "Even now they wrangle?"

Basoni sighed and nodded. "For a while, the air was thick with magic in our quarters; too thick."

"So many spells in such close quarters tangle with each other," Ayree agreed. He had seen more than one instance of too many sorceries crossing one another, creating monstrous results. "Menka should've taken charge and made you all wait in turn to use your powers."

"Menka was too busy taking sides while Shama screamed at Lavah about something or other; Resha too, and Senja. Hodah was trying to play peacemaker. While they fought, they dropped their spells and the air cleared. It was all a matter of waiting." Basoni sipped her wine.

"Morgeld is master of waiting." Ayree gazed long into his cup before draining it and pouring another. "I wish your elder sisters had half your patience, Basoni."

"We won't need patience much longer," Basoni said. "Tomorrow we attack Helagarde."

The Prince of Warlocks lowered his empty cup. "No; tomorrow you seal Morgeld in his fortress and keep him there. The attack itself will come . . . later."

"What? But I thought—"

Her distress was not lost on Ayree. "What troubles you, sister? Nothing a little more wine couldn't cure?" His own cup was full again, but not for long.

Basoni shook her head. "I wanted to learn my part in the final spell so that I might practice it."

"Because you are not secure in your powers? Rest easy. All that you must practice—and the rest of the Twelve, too—is bringing your sorceries together; cooperating. I'd say they need the practice in that more than you."

"Then . . . you don't have the spell?"

"I'll find it, never fear!" Ayree finished his wine and helped himself to more, gaining bravado with each cup. "The fulfillment of the prophecy is ours! I want you Twelve to seal Morgeld in his fortress until I find the spell. It can't hide in the old books forever."

Basoni was dismayed. "But why send us to Helagarde before you even have the means to destroy it? What are we to do there, wait for you? For how long? Shouldn't you find the spell first, my brother?"

Ayree's sharp blue eyes narrowed. "And give Morgeld time to slip from his lair? To summon allies? To let the magicless branches of the Tree steal the glory of his doom from *us*?"

She shook her head. "I doubt that imprisoning Morgeld will prevent him from contacting his creatures. He shares the blood of the night-spirits and he rules the shades of those who died in despair. What can keep a ghost in or out?"

Ayree's lip curled. "And since when have you become such

an expert on ghosts? It seems only yesterday you were an infant who ran from the phantoms you saw in every shadow.''

"You aren't listening to what I'm saying, Ayree. The moment we cast our spells against Helagarde, we lose the advantage of surprise. If we could seal Morgeld in Helagarde and then strike him down at once—"

"You will not preach strategy to me! Not even Senja does that.''

"You sound like Senja now.'' Basoni was astonished to hear herself speaking so boldly to Ayree, but something inside her compelled plain talk. His plan was badly flawed—she was convinced of it—and she wondered why her adored brother was so blind to this. "She would be the one to mount a headlong attack against Helagarde without any preparation because that's the way they fight in Vahrd, but—"

"And would you like me better if I acted like Fortunata, then?'' Ayree shouted. "Shall I sit here, forever studying spells, never learning the courage to use them?'' He lowered his voice suddenly. "Is it your own lack of courage that makes you doubt the wisdom of my plans, Basoni? Is that why you would leave Morgeld's doom to magicless hands?''

"So long as Morgeld is destroyed, why should it matter who destroys him, mage or magicless? Ayree, I don't understand . . .''

Anger darkened the witch-king's face. "It is not necessary for you to understand, Basoni. If I didn't know you better, I'd say you were the most rebellious of the Twelve, not the most tractable. Did any of you ever question our mother's commands as closely as you do mine?''

Basoni looked down. "I would never rebel against you, my brother. Not for the world.''

Ayree tried to read truth in her eyes, but she kept them down. He drank deeply before saying, "Then you will prove it: I give you full charge over the Twelve. Tomorrow you will lead your sisters to the shores of the Lyarian Sea. After you have Morgeld pent fast in Helagarde, I want you to find a way to bring all the magics of the Twelve together—constant practice to blend your sorceries so that when I arrive with the final spell, there will be no more of this petty bickering. One stroke of the sword—and death to Morgeld!''

Chapter III

THE MARSH

"Conquer all the lands you desire, my lord, take slaves, burn fields, carry off your plunder—but when you enter a man's home, first wipe your feet."

—"The Farmer's Advice"
from *The Scroll of Oran*

So Ayree's twelve sisters departed from Castle Snowglimmer and descended on Helagarde in a storm of sealing magics. Mounted on clouds and wind, on horseback and dragonback and carpets of silk and air, they swooped down on the amethyst turrets and wrapped Morgeld's castle in a skin of milky fire. When the fire burned away, the shield remained. It was strong, but it would not last forever. Strongest magic was least durable, most selective. Morgeld could not escape his own fortress while the shield endured, but it had no effect on any of his servants. While the Twelve set up their encampment on the Laidly Marshes, they frequently saw dark shapes flitter in and out of the dully glowing spires.

"There's someone outside to see you, Basoni." Hodah pulled back the flap of her little sister's tent and entered unannounced. Basoni looked up from cleaning her shield.

"Ayree!" The youngest sorceress leaped up joyfully, letting the shield tumble to the thick, Sombrunian-made wool rug. "At last!"

"Well . . . no." Hodah looked sheepish. "It's someone else."

Basoni stopped short and stared severely at her sister. Hodah was twirling a sidecurl around her finger and trying to look as though she knew nothing about anything. Whoever this unheralded visitor was, he had clearly made Hodah ill-at-ease.

"Who is it?" Basoni folded her arms across her chest and tried to look severe. Hodah laughed the same way she always had when Basoni, her baby, tried to imitate the grownups. Even though only eight years separated them, Hodah always mothered her, and Basoni believed she always would.

"I think you'd better meet him . . . uh, them . . . for yourself, dear. Really, I'd have gone straight to Menka with this, but she's off helping Senja with her part of—"

Basoni let her arms fall to her sides. "*Them?* We have callers? In the Laidly Marshes?"

"Not we," Hodah said. "You. Specifically."

Ayree's youngest sister made a face. "By name? An envoy from Sombrunia?"

Again Hodah affected total innocence. "Oh, I wouldn't say these . . . petitioners came from your kingdom, love. I think they're more natives."

"Of the worm-blasted *Laidly Marshes?*"

"Don't shout like that, Basoni dear. It makes you sound vulgar. Here, let me smooth down your hair . . ."

With a well-modulated scream of exasperation, Basoni stormed past her put-and-tidy sister and out of her tent. She got up such a fine momentum that she didn't stop until she rammed nosefirst into a brick wall.

Brick walls do not occur naturally on the Laidly Marshes. The small sorceress squeaked with alarm and rebounded, rubbing her nose. The wall undulated and from high above her a gravelly voice inquired, "Did you hurt yourself?"

Basoni tilted her head back to the limit. What she had taken for bricks were really mud-colored scales, and the "wall" was actually the bulky body of the largest demon she had ever seen. If she stood on Menka's shoulders, and Menka balanced atop Senja, she could have come even with the monster's beady little eyes. Lacking those two tallest of the Twelve, Basoni had to tap a gentle levitation spell to rise to the demon's level.

"That shouldn't concern you," she replied. "What's your business here?"

"*Business?*" The creature's words dripped scorn. "A crab's fart for you and your talk of my business!"

The creature's breath was as foul as his manners. He had no head for matters of courtesy, having no head at all: His wattled neck simply went straight on until it got bored and sprouted a few tufts of dirty gray hair with the rough texture of sawgrass. When he spoke, it was as if a sword-cut across his throat were opening and closing, and the bright, wet, scarlet interior of his toothless mouth only added to the effect.

Basoni forgot her sore nose at once. "You will address me with respect, fiend, or you will find yourself wishing you had. Now speak! Why have you come to me?"

"WHY?"

The demon's roar whipped Basoni's short tunic out stiff as a gonfalon in a gale, but her levitation spell was strong. Nothing could move her from her chosen place in the air.

Before she could answer, the sand under the creature's splayed feet began to burp and bubble. Like monstrous naked clams, shucked and sandy, a host of small versions of the huge demon hauled themselves out of the gritty strand. Now Basoni saw what Hodah meant when she had spoken of *them*.

"Look at them," said the large demon, emotion choking him. Viscous drops the color of overripe squash leaked from his eyes. "Poor little tykes. Homeless, now. Orphans of the storm. Cast into a cruel world through no fault of their own and *every* fault of yours! You and your nasty pack of sisters. Oh, woe! Woe!"

The snaggle of small demons huddled around the large one's bulbous knees and began to slobber and whine. Some of the older ones were developing the scales of their guardian and a nice mucky dun color, but the younger they were the more sluglike and translucent their bodies, until the smallest among them was a sight fit to make a serpent lose its lunch.

Prudently Basoni kept her eyes fixed on the senior demon. "What do you mean, it's all our fault that they're homeless? I never set eyes on any of you until now, and I won't pretend I ever wanted to."

"Arrrh," the demon sneered—a neat trick for one without lips. "And what about all *that*? Say all *that* isn't your doing, and die a liar!" His blubbery paw swept the vista of the Laidly Marshes.

The vista of what had been the Laidly Marshes. The vista of what was called the Laidly Marshes. For in truth, there was not much left in sight that was either very laidly or especially marshy. And yes, Basoni had to admit that it was all her doing, if not all her fault.

From her perch in midair, Basoni had an excellent view of what her sisters had accomplished in the seven weeks since they had encamped before Helagarde. Morgeld's hold still dominated the western sea, unchanged by the presence of this small besieging force as it had been unchanged by the ages of the world. But the broad, wide strand of misty, marshy land and the shifting sands that ended in the Lyarian Sea had been transformed. It was Basoni's inspiration, her way of fulfilling the charge Ayree had laid on her to teach her sisters to combine their magics more harmoniously.

"Are you going to deny that—that—abomination is your work?" the demon spluttered. He jabbed a talon at a grove of fruit trees that tapered away into a formal garden planted with frilled tulips and gusts of fragrant sunstorm. Herbs of all sorts covered the ground between the carefully landscaped beds. From farther east twin columns of smoke crept into the clear grey sky. One carried the smell of baking honeycakes, the other brought the music of the forge: hammer and anvil and hot metal's hiss when plunged into cold water.

Traces of each sister's special talents were seen in patches of Hodah's newly sown seeds and tender shoots, Senja's cunningly made metal hives for Sacchara's honeybees, and Lavah's groves where songbirds warbled under the protection of Asapha's hawks. Menka's horses galloped through meadows which once been quicksand bogs and Resha had planted healing herbs where only hollow reeds had thrived. Shama had called to the stones of the earth's heart and they had risen in layers of solid ground to give a firm bottom to the rich soil that was Lucha's gift. Fortunata pored over many tomes to find the proper shapes and boundaries that would make the erstwhile marshes a well-balanced combination of wholesome land, munching the cakes that Zabala baked when she was not domesticating the small wild things of the marshland.

All in all, it was a success from Basoni's point of view, but distinctly unsatisfactory in the demon's opinion.

"Well, Madam High-and-Mighty Sorceress, when you started this little picnic of yours, playing about with our home, what'd you think'd become of *us*, eh?" The monster's grumbles sounded like wet blankets flopping on a line. "Where are we to lure poor fool travelers now you've gucked up our nice quicksands and sloughs? How are they to stumble over the sands, losing more hope every minute, when you've got peach trees cluttering up the dunes and . . . and . . ." For a beast with such small eyes, he did manage to narrow them effectively. "Say, if those cursèd bees are *stingless*, you'll be hearing from my—"

"*Will* you begone?" Basoni stamped her foot. Up in the air it should have made no sound, but the sorceress knew how to call on a cooperative peal of thunder when she wanted one.

The little demons gibbered and meeped, crowding together under their senior's baggy rump. He snarled, spat, and kicked them out from under.

"Begone, is it? Begone to where, I want to know! I hear tell you're the lady thought up this pretty mess, but I happen to know your brother. Why, he and I are just like *that*." The creature crossed two fingers like jointed wursts. "You give us back our Laidly Marshes like they were or I'm telling!"

"You—damned—well—*TELL!*" shrieked Basoni, and she clapped her shield-spell over herself and blinked away. The huge demon stared at vacancy for a while, then cursed and plunged into what little sand was left unoccupied by roses. The junior horrors followed.

Basoni did not unveil until she was inside Hodah's tent with its silken walls of midnight blue and the simple triangular banner of the same color flying at its peak in the sea breeze. The interior was as simple as the outside—a camp bed, a pair of faldstools, a brazier, and an arms-rack attached to the central pole. There Hodah's silver quarterstaff leaned in its socket and her shield bearing the device of a fully armed infant warrior hung from its straps.

Hodah herself was making tea on a tripod over the brazier's coals. "Hello, Basoni. Won't you join me?"

"Demons coming to me with grievances, threatening to tell Ayree about his wicked little sister, the others glaring at me when they think I'm not looking, all the blame, no help, and *you* want me to have a cup of tea!"

"Maybe you're right," said Hodah, retying the sleeves of her loose gown to keep them out of the coals. "Two cups would be better." She passed one to Basoni that was made of thick white clay ringed with a pattern of eversweets, and poured out the steaming drink.

Basoni sniffed. "Mint and oranges. You never forget, do you, Hodah?"

Hodah looked very pleased. "Why should I forget my little sister's favorite tea? It's not as if I have so many important things to be remembering." She filled her own cup.

The tea was brewed exactly as Basoni liked it. Ever since Charel's death, Hodah had taken over the mother's role in Basoni's life, filling the aching void of loneliness with a thousand small affectionate attentions like this. Only in Hodah's company could she relax fully. It was good to have one special person who knew you . . . so well. She felt sorry for her sisters who remained alone.

"I wish Ayree would get here," Basoni said.

Hodah bent over the teapot to see if more water was needed. Her blond hair was caught up in a horsetail bound with blue ribbon, but two curls forever escaped to tickle her cheeks. "So do I. A siege is no battle; not when Morgeld is the one besieged. We're just holding him now, like a pack of boarhounds waiting for the huntsman to come with his spear."

"Ayree will come soon. I know that." Basoni spoke with conviction she only partly felt. "When he does, we'd better be ready to do more than hold our prey."

"After seven weeks, we might be over-ready. Senja's getting restless. So is Menka, and I confess I'm growing weary of doing nothing more than light gardening when I'd rather be fighting. Oh, don't misunderstand, Basoni; your idea to reclaim the Laidly Marshes has been wonderful for bringing all of our powers together. We link strengths and spells almost by habit now, no one's enchantments tangling up with her neighbor's."

"That was the whole point." Basoni frowned. "If my plan's working, what's your complaint?"

"Dear one, while you were in Sombrunia, did you ever see a troupe of traveling players? A *bad* one?"

Basoni thought it over. "There was a fairly bad—no, quite a bad—no, an incredibly awful bunch. Hakiem's Harmonic Histriones. They could turn comedy to tragedy and the other way 'round without meaning to. I never saw a group more in need of rehearsals."

"And I say they probably needed fewer. Oh, Basoni, when a troupe's been together long enough, doing the same dramas over and over again, they can reach the point of perfection. But a point's so small! Soon they rely on rote and routine. Nothing's fresh or new. They grow bored, their gestures and their words turn stale, and soon they're so confident that they know what's coming next, they no longer heed their partners. That's when they make careless slips."

"You're saying that's going to happen to us?" Even as Basoni protested, she knew that her sister was right. Not for the first time she wondered at Ayree's odd battle plan . . . or lack of one. What had really driven her brother to send them all out here in such haste, with seemingly so little preparation for Morgeld's ultimate destruction?

Hodah shrugged. "It could. A siege is the most boring part of any warfare, magical or mortal, and it breeds all manner of ills. If Ayree doesn't find the final spell soon, I'd even consider a charge on Helagarde, just for a change."

"That's a foolish risk and you know it."

"What will we risk?"

Basoni set her empty cup on one knee and ticked off items on her fingers. "Ayree's anger, for one." As his lieutenant, she felt bound to justify her brother's actions. "Letting the foe get an advance look at our tactics, for another. We'd lose the advantage of surprise. Three, we've no concerted battle plan and we might do ourselves more harm than Morgeld. Four, could we maintain the spell containing him to Helagarde while we attack? Five, every battle carries the risk of death. If one of us falls, even wounded—"

"Enough, enough!" Hodah waved her hands in surrender. "The world has truly turned itself on end when a baby sister is wiser than her elders. No wonder Ayree put you in charge. The rest of us are all so old that our brains have dried to peas, rattling around inside our skulls."

"Old!" Basoni leaped up, indignant. Her teacup fell and bounced across the bare earthen floor, cracking when it struck the leg of the brazier. "How dare you call yourself old?"

"I'm thirty," Hodah replied. "If I weren't Charel's daughter and capable of turning backbiters into shrewmice, I'd be called spinster to my face."

"So what? Where's the shame in that?"

Hodah's smile was faint and somewhat sad. "Shame? No. It's something else I feel. I have not lived long for a witch, but I've lived long enough by mortal years. And we are all partway mortal. Yet in thirty years I have never known love . . . None of us have, not even Ayree. Or we've fled it . . . or had it driven away from us."

Love. Basoni was a nightmare-wakened child of three again. Words of love, sounds of love came to her ears out of the darkness in her mother's rooms. And then her mother had died. Basoni did not think it terrible to flee love, but what did Hodah mean by having it driven away?

Hodah was staring into the ash-mantled coals of the brazier. Her eyes were so dark with sorrow that Basoni did not want to pry. At last the wardlady of Glytch rose and took her shield from its peg, gazing with longing at the bright device. "Well, if we are bored by this siege, at least I hope that Morgeld's twice as maddened."

Basoni said, "So do I," but inwardly she wondered whether they expected too much that was human from the man of her vanished nightmares.

Within the seaward tower of Helagarde, Morgeld stood by the lonesome window and rested his crippled hand on the sill. A sword of great power—the Black Sword that had given Alban Stonesword his name—had maimed him in a battle years ago. The wound had healed imperfectly, and not all the arts of Morgeld's night-spirit mother could improve upon its present state. Of course, the powers of elemental night were not best turned to healing. Morgeld would never again wield a sword in that hand.

He must find other weapons.

Gray wool robes were soft as fog around him. The tower walls were so thin that sunlight suffused the round chamber with a thin purple radiance. It was a glow echoed by the amethyst crystal set in a heavy silver necklace that Helagarde's lord held out over the waves in his good hand.

A shadow seeped from the wall behind him. A sheet of blackness kindled eyes that gleamed with swordsteel's hungry brightness. The spirit took the wavery shape of a man in full mail, a duke's device seen in smoky outline on his overtunic. It blotted out the stones.

They are still there. Ayree's twelve cursed sisters are still there.

Morgeld did not turn from the window. "I know, Tor. I know."

What will you do?

"About them? Nothing. Let them stay where they are; I have other things to do. I am sending out the call for three servants such as these god-poor kingdoms have never seen. And when my servants answer my summons, there will be no more talk of the gods' return."

The black shadow burst into the shape of flames. *Servants! I was your servant! You abandoned me to death, and if it were in my power now, I would abandon you!*

Still Morgeld gazed out to sea. "But you cannot abandon me, Tor. You are mine. And you still serve me willingly, after your own fashion, I think."

For vengeance' sake! You won't cheat me of that, my master.

I serve you willingly, as you say, but I won't serve unquestion-
ingly. Nor will I let you close your eyes to present danger. Do
you think your precious servants will answer your call? And will
they answer soon enough? You gamble poorly, my lord Morgeld.
One wager cost you years in bondage, chained by a mortal girl.
A second cost you your hand. This time you dice with prophecy.
You have already lost one round. Gamble wrongly now and it
will cost you your life!

Now Morgeld did turn slowly from the open window: "Loyal
Tor. So much concern for me." His expression was impenetra-
ble. At last he said, "Come."

Where? The shade rippled and blurred at the edges, crumpling
into a ball. The eyes in it looked fully human now, and afraid.

"To my mother's realm." The ball shrank still more. Morgeld
tucked the heavily linked silver and amethyst collar inside his
robes, then beckoned Tor's black spirit with his good hand.
"Don't fear. You go there under my protection."

But why? The shadow's sending was timorous and shaky. *Why*
must we go there at all?

"Why, to find a gift for our besiegers, Tor. A fitting gift to be
swathed in more than one wrapping, and never to be unwrapped
completely until too late. You see, I know Ayree's sisters very
well. I am not quite so thoughtless of my own safety as you
believe. I have tried to undo their threat before, and almost
succeeded. But it seems my ordinary servants are frail, and
unequal to the task I set. Ayree's sisters, on the other hand, are
strong." Morgeld stroked the trembling surface of the ball.
"What do you think I shall do, Tor?"

The black ball suddenly solidified, all trembling gone. It shot
to man height, spread, and for a moment burned itself to the firm
shape and colors of a living human being. Filled with exultation
it cried, *Let them undo themselves, through this gift of yours, my*
lord!

The master of despair inclined his head. "Exactly."

Eagerly the shadow drew nearer. *And what shall the gift be?*

Morgeld smiled. "Love."

Chapter IV

THE PETITIONERS

Over the bog and into the fen,
Here comes a snack from the kingdoms of men!

— "The Lilt of the Smallest Demon"
from *The Scroll of Oran.*

Lucha yawned and stretched on the crocodile divan. The exotic and unwieldly piece of furniture was her worst indulgence while in the field of battle, but by no means her only one. Crouching low to the floor on ivory and ebonwood paws, its beautifully curved and carved black frame cradled a mattress of striped viridian silk. At the foot of the couch, a reptile's wicked grin inlaid of ivory and coral leered at the world. Small rubies rimmed with gold aped the creature's eyes.

Nature's design had been ignored only in the sweep of the beast's tail into an uncrocodilian cushioned fan to support Lucha's head. Given the choice between verisimilitude and comfort, Lucha never had to think twice. Her long lovelocks, fastened at the crown of her head with a golden fillet, tumbled over the headrest's edge. She wore the loosest of Vairish robes, the sort favored by pampered courtesans.

Lucha at ease looked like the human equivalent of the sleeping panther that adorned her black and silver banner, its fringes and forked tail now hanging limp from the pole before her red samite tent. Anyone who didn't know her would assume that she was a lazy, sensual, self-absorbed woman.

In a way, they would be right.

"Asapha, pet," Lucha drawled. "Go and see if the demons have gone yet."

Asapha sat uncomfortably on a pile of the airiest cushions coin could buy, their insides laced with costly oil of hyacinth. Lucha's tent always made her edgy: too many colors and textures, too many smells, and frequently the music conjured up by Vair's guardian lady sounded in too many keys at once.

Music without visible source was unnerving to most mortals. Many kingdoms that otherwise appreciated witcheries punished this one spell remorselessly. It took a sadistic nature, or just a careless one, to fill rooms with musicianless melody without asking the other occupants' permission.

Lucha was no sadist. Neither was she much of a musician. She often accompanied the unseen players of her conjuring on the lute, her chosen instrument, but she had no patience with it, blaming strings, wood, or lutewright for her own misfingerings. The answer then was to smash the worthless instrument to splinters and dangles.

Lucha went through a lot of lutes.

"Why do you care if they've gone?" Asapha asked. Her voice was always rough when she spoke, but she whistled as sweetly as any bird. In the bleak Kestrel Mountains of Lyf where the River Salmlis sprang, there were several clans who did not speak in human tongues at all, but whistled and screamed like hawks. Their voices could span any valley.

"I care because I want to speak with Ayree and I'd rather not look at anything quite so ugly as a demon of the Laidly Marshes. What is worse, I think that this time they've brought their chief to treat with our brother; *The* Demon of the Laidly Marshes, no less, as if he were all the horror this place ever spawned." Lucha yawned again and linked her fingers high overhead, wriggling like a cat in prime sunlight. "*I* like the marshes much better now that we've prettied them down."

Asapha said nothing. She had liked the Laidly Marshes as they were before, but she accepted the need to change them just as she accepted the need to take tasks from her younger sister Basoni's command. All change disturbed, but change would come. The hawkmasters of King Marn taught that those who accepted change were the likeliest to find contentment in their lives.

Fighters and shakers fall young from the sky. Asapha heard Sten's words again so clearly in her memory that she turned deaf when Lucha asked her a question.

"Asapha! I said, what are you going to do after we've ended Morgeld?"

Asapha fingered the brown hawker's gauntlets in her lap. She followed the intricately embroidered pattern of blood-red thread with her eyes, missing not a snag or tie-off. The only time she took off her gloves was when she was forced to visit with her older sisters. Parting with the heavy gloves was like parting with a layer of skin, a special shield between Asapha and the world. Ayree said he understood. So did Basoni. But only Sten really did.

"Bad fortune to talk of victory before," she said tersely.

"Blather. That's only when victory's in doubt. As for me, when this is done I'm going to fly for the southern lands, to sweet, sweet Vair. I shall take up the Council's offer to build me a house near the great bazaar of Ishma." She giggled. "They think it'll be an attraction for trade, to have a lady of sorcery residing right in the heart of that wonderful marketplace. It had better be, because I'll expect a fitting home and it will cost them a few vitrics."

She reached for a dream of the palace she'd demand, empty fingers building spiraling turrets and stonelace-domed plazolets out of air. "And when it is all prepared, then I shall wander through the great bazaar and free as many handsome slaves as I fancy. I will give them each a sack of vitrics and a smile. Then we'll see which of the two they prefer. I shall walk home *very* slowly . . ."

Sten, young to serve the hawkmasters, but wiser than many of them: Asapha saw him before her while Lucha purred on about handsome slaves. His hair dull brown, but his eyes a hawk's new-struck gold. Afoot in the mountains and on horseback in the king's tiny gamepark they had hunted together. Not even Asapha could give her bird to the winds as skillfully as Sten. They had never exchanged more than a few words—but both of them preferred silence.

After Morgeld was gone, after Ayree freed them all of their duty, she would fly with a hawk's wings and come to perch on his bedstead while he slept. He would wake to see a hawk with a woman's face regarding him, but he would not flinch or smile. He would offer her his wrist and she would take it, gripping him to the blood with her talons. The hawk's form would melt from her body, and he would take her love with a silence to bind souls.

"I'll go see if the demons have gone," Asapha said. She stood, pulled on her gloves, and strode to the door flap of Lucha's tent where a trio of silver bells tinkled at the thought of a touch.

"Make sure you come back and tell me," Lucha called from the divan. She extended one arm and plucked a new lute from the air. Asapha heard her hit a clinker in the first chorus of "Willingly" and the usual curse and smash immediately after.

The demons had not gone yet. Ayree's tent, pitched in the middle of the encampment, was besieged by them, although they were the most cap-in-hand bunch of besiegers Asapha had ever seen. They came in all shapes and sizes, none of them pleasing to the eye, many repulsive to the other senses as well. Even the hawkmasters' doctrine of acceptance would have taken a jar if brought nose-to-stench with some of the fiends assembled there.

There were more than marsh-demons present. They had brought backup troops this time, for the dark vastness of the Naîmlo Wood stood fairly close at hand. In fact, the Naîmlo Wood bordered the Laidly Marshes for almost its entire length. Only to the north was it different, where the marshes ended at a treacherous, quicksanded pass into Resha's ward-kingdom of Sumnerol.

Ayree sat on a camp stool, elbow on knee, chin on hand, and appeared to be listening to a long list of complaints as read by the wartiest lump of vileness ever secreted by the sands. Thick-lipped and warted like a gourd, he was a compendium of bluster and blubber, groveling and gravel-colored hide. Here and there he was tufted with coarse hair pushing up between intermittent scales, like weed poking through pavement. Fish, reptiles, and mammals all might have had the joy of claiming kinship with him, if they chose. Oddly enough, none had ever done so. It was said that not even the gods knew the origins of the elemental spirits, and the elementals themselves were at a loss to explain why any creative force would manufacture something as stomach-wrenching as the assorted demons of the Twelve Kingdoms.

The demon addressing Ayree reached the end of his parchment list and let it fall with a cavalier flourish. A smaller demon pounced on it and devoured it, then gave a loud belch redolent of dead fish. The spokesman scowled and slapped his monstrous paw down atop the fiendlet guilty of spoiling his dramatic effect. The resultant squish was very dramatic and effective indeed. Standing behind her brother, Fortunata gagged and ducked inside Ayree's tent. Even the Prince of Warlocks moved his hand up to cover his mouth for a moment.

"Beg pardon," glurped the large demon. He lifted his hind paw and studied what was left sticking to it. Ayree made a hasty gesture and the mess vanished. "Much obliged, sur, I'm sure."

Ayree cleared his throat with difficulty. "Don't mention it. I only wish it were possible to satisfy all of your requests so neatly."

"Wull, 'course it's possible, sur. Now you're here, 'tis. These sisters o' yours, they don't lissun, but you're differnt. You won't leave a poor demon down, now will you, sur? After we's asked you nice an' all?" The monster brought his forepaws together and worried the brim of an imaginary cap between them.

"My sisters have changed your homeland for a good cause, demon. They must—"

"Oh, I know, I know. 'Tis *that* one that they be after." The demon's tusked head lolled toward Helagarde. "But why make me an' mine suffer for't?"

"Aye! Not like we was in league wif t'likes o' *that* one!" squeaked an infant ghoul from the rear ranks. The other terrors skrawked agreement.

"Y'see, sur, we be called Morgeld's children, but that's not true by rights. We'us here before ever 'twas a Helagarde. Wull, we learned to live with it, and we've learned to live with men—"

"Tasty!" someone meeped from the back row. There was a rending sound and some chomping as the monsters' unofficial sergeant-at-arms quelled the out-of-order comment.

"Anyways, we learned to live with much," the chief demon continued once the ruckus died down. "But never once did we have to live with losing what's *home!* Today the Laidly Marshes, tomorrow the Naîmlo Wood, and *then* where d'you expect us to move? 'Tisn't fair. I hear Morgeld's not much of a such for fairness, but I did hope you was differnt, sur."

A slightly green Fortunata emerged from her brother's tent and dabbed cold drops from her forehead with a linen handkerchief, her other hand firm on the spine of a large tome. Ayree looked at her and bit his lower lip. Asapha couldn't tell whether it was a thoughtful mannerism or just a ploy to keep from laughing.

"Well, sister, do your books have any help to give us in this matter?" he asked.

Fortunata adjusted a pair of invisible spectacles—a spell of enhancement to vision—and opened the book. "The Judgment of Canelax *might* show a precedent, although I'd have to return to Snowglimmer to confirm it. There was an incident during the territorial disputes between the kingdoms of Clarem and Norm over the string of islets called Neimar's Necklace. They had been settled by former residents of both kingdoms, and it was decided to clear all squatters off the contested lands until a decision had been reached. However, neither kingdom could offer the displaced persons sufficient land for settlement, so they put them all on ships and sent them off to colonize Braegerd Isle.''

"Braegerd Isle?'' The demon scratched his head, perplexed by Fortunata's monotone recitation. "But . . . there's allus been the barbarian sea-rovers there since forever, ayn't there? Or wasn't they there in them days?''

"Oh, the Braegerd men were there, all right,'' said Ayree. "And I'll wager they didn't take too kindly to having a bunch of mainland colonists dumped on their doorstep.''

"They didn't.'' Fortunata pursed her lips primly. "Nor did the colonists appreciate being shipped off like that. They paid tribute of all their possessions to the Braegerd chiefs, sold themselves into thralldom if they couldn't buy a chief's protection, married their daughters to the battle-lords when possible, and soon became the fiercest breed of sea-rovers the isle had yet produced. They were especially noted for showing no mercy whenever a ship of Norm or Clarem fell to their hands. The pirate raids they staged completely upset the negotiations over Neimar's Neck-lace, and to this day the islets remain uninhabited.''

"Thank you, Fortunata,'' Ayree said. "You realize that all this has been no help at all.''

"To the uneducated, perhaps,'' said the erudite witch. "*I* have no trouble seeing a solution: resettlement.''

"Resettlement? See where that got Clarem and Norm with the islanders!''

"Only because they did not clear matters with the Braegerd men first. However, *we* have representatives of both the Laidly Marshes and the Naîmlo Wood right here before us. Couldn't we cut off a bit of woodland, turn it swampy, and give it to the displaced demons? The Naîmlo Wood is large enough to share, and sharing is often written of as the chiefest virtue. All fiends are brothers under the hide.'' Fortunata waggled a finger at the massed creatures as if she were teaching them their letters.

The demon who headed the delegation from the Laidly Marshes looked bemused. He rubbed his horny head in thought so deep that he did not stop rubbing until he'd worn through a sizable bald patch. Wincing, he stopped and looked over his shoulder at his constituents.

"Wull . . . sounds good to me,'' he said.

"Piss for breakfast sounds good to you!'' skreed a voice from behind. Pine-bark wings crinkled open and a moss-haired goblin lifted himself above the heads of the demonic mob. His scrawny body exuded the slowly mulching rot of the forest floor, with a pinched, scaly face like a pine cone, and green needle teeth. "Says who else it's a good idea, stealing a chunk of our forest? Who says so, that's what *I* want to know? Says a raggle of marsh-slime? Says a pile of sand-droppings and all their gritty kin? Phewt! Grubs and blindworms take the pack of you and shove you into the sea where you belong! Give up some of our nice forest to the likes of you!"

"Oh," said the demon. He sounded chastened. He was not. He spat once, with fiery accuracy—fiery because the monster's spittle turned to blazing plasma in midflight and coated the inhospitable forest demon in a skin of red-gold flame. The unlucky being began as a shriek and ended as a patter of crisp-fried bones on the heads of his former comrades.

The demons of the Naîmlo Wood brushed the blackened splints from their hair, exchanging a few worried looks and a lot of hastily murmured words. Their ranks parted and a very small, insignificant forest fiendlet—a banty-weight horror known to his colleagues as Llew-op-Fish, whose calling was to make deadly woodland toadstools look like succulent mushrooms—sidled up to the demon of the Laidly Marshes.

"Welcome to the neighborhood," he whispered.

"Thank you, Fungus Face," replied the senior demon with all due solemnity, and shook his paw.

"Done!" exclaimed Ayree. Fortunata had fled back into her brother's tent again, not caring to witness any more of the bargainings among demonkind, not even for their academic value. "You will all be settled into your new home as soon as possible."

"Yes, sur," said the huge demon. "How soon's that?"

"After we've defeated—"

"Oh, beg pardon, sur, beg pardon, but that soon's not soon enough. For we're most unhappy, y'see, and we're not all of us as patient as I. 'Twould be a kindness to tell you this, save you a lot of nasty surprises later, but there's some of our blood that've gone all cranky and say they'll take their revenge on your darlin' sisters soon's they try anything against Helagarde or . . . you know who."

Ayree's fists clenched. "Fools . . ."

"So they be, sur. No argument from *me!* But fools can often bollix up a battle better'n trained cavalry. Sometimes the fools *is* the trained cavalry. Fools, aye, but not vicious fools. You neaten things up for us first, make us our new home all nice, and they'll drop their grudges faster'n a minstrel drops his drawers in a lady's beddy-bye."

Ayree drummed his fingers on his knee and frowned. There was a lot of homely truth in what the demon said. The fiends of the Laidly Marshes could not stand against the powers of his twelve sisters, not even if those powers were taken singly. They had been helpless to halt the changes that the Twelve made daily on the once-barren sands.

But it was also true what the creature said about how big a nuisance a pack of disgruntled demons could be.

"Wait here." The witch-king bolted up from his stool and flung light around him, vanishing. The afterglow of his departure sparkled blue and white in the air.

The Demon of the Laidly Marshes stretched out his paw and caught a sprinkling of light. "Purty . . ." He licked off the shining grains, chewed, then hawked up and launched a glob of nonincendiary spittle. "Needs salt," he said apologetically to Asapha, whose brown boots he had spattered.

Asapha strode past the fiendish gourmet and into Ayree's tent. Inside she found Fortunata, who was lying down on Ayree's cot with a damp cloth over her eyes. "Did they go away?" the scholar-witch croaked.

"Still there," said Asapha. She was growing weary of all these questions, and the need to spend so much time surrounded by so many people. Her tent was far removed from the others, a bannerless black pavilion made of felt thick enough to cheat the mountain winters without the use of spells. Inside there was only room for Asapha. For now she liked it that way.

Someday she would see whether she could make room for another.

"What's Ayree going to do about this?" Fortunata wailed, pressing down her eye-soothing compress with the heels of her hands. "He's got the spell we need or he wouldn't have joined us. Why can't we just use it and *leave?* Oh, I am so tired of this awful place! Do you know where Ayree is right now, Asapha?"

"I am here." The Prince of Warlocks spoke, then cast aside the airy cloak of invisibility that had hidden him from his sisters' eyes.

Then three other spells of shielding dropped and Shama, Lucha, and Basoni stood behind their brother.

Asapha stiffened. She disliked crowds, and she especially disliked crowds that sprang out at her. She began to back out of Ayree's tent.

"Asapha, wait. This is work for you, too," the witch-king said.

Shama hurried forward to lay her soft hands on her sister's cheeks and croon, "Yes, darling, don't run away like that. Why, we never get to see you at all, except when we're working together." Asapha tried to jerk her head away from her sister's touch.

"Leave Asapha alone." Basoni did not strike Shama's hands away, but her voice held a note of warning. She stepped up to stand shoulder to shoulder with her nearest sister and felt no resistance when she slipped her hand into Asapha's gloved grip.

"You will not renew your bickerings," Ayree chided. "Not now, not when we are so close to cutting our world free of its pain. I have found the enchantment that will destroy Morgeld and all his works, blast Helagarde to less than ash, and open the pathway for the gods' return."

"The scroll you spoke of?" Even Lucha perked up, and she usually reserved her enthusiasm solely for dreams of cooperative men. Since childhood the Twelve had known of a mysterious scroll hidden somewhere in the lost lands of the Older Empire, a scroll whose bans of wizardry forbade any witch or sorcerer from discovering its hiding place. That remained for a mortal to accomplish.

"No, not that one." The witch-king frowned. The scroll and all it represented reminded him of the second branch of the Tree of Second Light—the disdained mortal branch. "The weirding I have found was gleaned from a book in the vast library of Castle Snowglimmer. Since finding it, I have taken it to those wizards and warlocks wise enough to understand the significance of this discovery. They have all agreed that it may be adapted to our needs. Even Paragore-Tren has said—"

Shama's hand flew up, her brows knotted suspiciously. "Adapted? What's this adapted? I thought you *had* it!"

Ayree began to laugh. "You feel cheated, don't you?" The witch-king's grin faded to a mild, fond smile. "My dear sisters, the years haven't been that kind to any of us. Duty first, lessons, preparations for the final moment . . . I wish there were a way around it. There's none. You know as well as I that some spells spring from the lesson to the lips with little thought and less trouble. Blights and blessings are equally easy. What we have undertaken here is more: It is a spell of unmaking. The gods know how difficult such a spell can be. If used as it stands, the casting I've found would only stop Morgeld for a while, not destroy him utterly. It must be studied and reformed to our purpose. Be glad that this will not take so very long to do."

"Can we help you, brother?" Asapha offered in her strange, gruff voice.

He shook his head. "The actual changing of the spell must be done by one alone. However . . ." He tapped his lips thoughtfully with one finger. "Well, you know I haven't exactly been left alone these days. I've been up to my ears in demonic disputes."

"All my fault." Basoni hung her head. "I was the one who initiated the restoration of the Laidly Marshes. How was I to know what it would stir up?"

Ayree laid his hand on his youngest sister's shoulder. "Any change brings it consequences, especially when it touches matters of nature. You accepted the task from my hands, and you did admirably. I want you"—he indicated the four on their feet—"to follow The Demon of the Laidly Marshes to a plot of land in the Naîmlo Wood and then . . . swamp it."

"Why is Fortunata exempt from this sloppy business?" Shama demanded. "Is she too neat for it?"

"Fortunata will remain in my tent to be my checking power over the spell I've found."

"I thought you had to be left *alone* to do your part. And since when does the mighty Ayree require someone to check his doings?"

The witch-king was losing patience fast. "You have your task, Shama. Your mounts are in tether just behind Fortunata's tent, and your demon guide is patiently waiting for you as well."

"Hmph," Shama snorted when they had left Ayree's tent. "I like *that*. Now he's in a hurry, giving us orders as usual. And for what? To please a pack of demons. There are times I think Ayree's more of an infant than you, Basoni."

"Shama!"

The wardlady of Heydista pursed her lips. "Stop looking at me as if I spat on the Tree. I'm not afraid to speak my mind about Ayree. I have little to lose. You, on the other hand . . . Well, you wouldn't like it if you ceased to be our dear brother's pet, would you?"

"I'm no more his pet than you are! Spill your bile somewhere else," Basoni replied. "We have work to do, and no time to listen to your carping, especially not against Ayree."

"No, of course not. He can do no wrong, can he?" Shama laughed. "Come now, you're spoiled, but you're not stupid. Didn't your ears work in there?" She jerked her thumb at the witch-king's tent. "First he sends us off here from Snowglimmer to wait for his arrival with the spell; then when he does come, the spell's found, but it's not yet ready. He plays a game of stall and bargain, our great brother! He shows the world the illusion of the Twelve united, all ready to destroy Morgeld, when we're far from it. And why? To keep the mortals in their place so that they will make no attempt to snatch the deed from the witchborn.''

Gracefully Lucha interposed herself between Shama and Basoni. ''When you said you weren't afraid to speak your mind, Shama, you led me to believe you had one. If you're so sure Ayree's doing everything wrong, why not tell him? Come along, I'll go with you. He's still in the tent.'' She linked her arm through Shama's and made as if to escort her back into Ayree's presence.

Shama would not budge. Lucha smiled to see the sudden flush of color that dyed her sister's pasty cheeks scarlet. ''So shy, Shama? Or do you just need some time to rephrase your thoughts? You'll have plenty of opportunity while we're swamping the woods. Mud-chucking . . . somehow I think you'll enjoy that sort of work.''

There were no further objections as the four sisters went to find their mounts.

Chapter V

THE BOWER

Sweet love, who wears a hundred faces,
Love, dear master of disguise,
Love, of countless charms and graces,
Love, true father of all lies.

—"The Song of the Lady Myura"
from *The Scroll of Oran.*

Four fine steeds waited at the appointed place. Fortunata's tent was pitched not too far from the Lyarian Sea, and the six embroidered wool panels of the pavilion belled in the ocean breeze. They were Fortunata's pride, the work of her needle, each panel beautified with a full-length portrait in close-stitch of a woman famous for some skill, talent, or virtue apart from birth and beauty.

Then a gust of sea wind bore a sudden stench more potent than any amount of dead fish, and The Demon of the Laidly Marshes was with them. He was coming out of the ground near the horses, looking draggled, for the ground was no longer his beloved, familiar sand, but fertile earth and very heavy. It took a great deal out of a fiend to rise to the occasion through alien soil.

"Peeuw," said Lucha, making useless fanning motions to waft off the demon's odor, made worse by the fact that the horses had been tethered to their places for a while.

There are some things that horses and humans alike simply cannot wait to do. With true flair, The Demon of the Laidly Marshes had chosen the most decorated bit of earth from which to emerge.

"I be ready to lead you where you'd like," the demon said,

44

flicking a few reeking lumps from his shoulders. The sisters dodged despite their dignity. "Got a fine bit o' wood all picked out. Over t' the norther part, where me an' mine can still have the sea close, an' maybe a tidbit or two from Sumnerol in future."

"Tidbit?"

"Tourists," the demon clarified. "Pioneers, like. Folks'll come, once . . . *that* 'un's gone." He jerked his paw in the direction of Helagarde. "Anyways, that's for later. Let's be off." He fell into a rolling waddle heading north, leaving the four sisters to mount up and follow him.

There was no question of using magical means to travel, not when the witchly sisters stood so close to the final battle with Morgeld in both time and space. There was an agreement among the Twelve that dated from their first arrival on the Lyarian strand, long before Ayree rejoined them: They vowed that for the duration of the siege of Helagarde they would not use their powers for small matters, or to accomplish anything that might be done by magicless means.

Brisk and businesslike as always, Menka had decreed, "I don't care what ordinary folk believe or what the minstrels sing. We all know the limits of our powers. There is nothing infinite about magic."

Fortunata had taken that moment to seize an invisible lectern and add, "All that we know is that we do *not* know all there is to know about it."

Menka had given Fortunata a look reserved for the less violent sort of lunatic. "We shall conserve our strength wherever possible," she translated. There was no argument.

When Ayree was informed of their resolution, he approved. Not one of the Twelve took the time to question what she would have done if Ayree had not given their decision his blessing.

As she rode at a comfortable canter away from the encampment, Basoni enjoyed the passing view: the transformations her sisters had accomplished under her guidance.

The groundhugging mists of white and gray were gone, banished by mists of green new grass. A ring of giltsweet trees of Sacchara's planting surrounded the heart of the encampment, each fan-shaped crown just brushing the feathery leaves of its neighbor. Their honeyed fruits crowded the branches, translucent papery shells enveloping the amber meat. Each tree shone like a dragon's hoard in the sunlight.

The Demon of the Laidly Marshes did not pay any heed to the

landscape. His steady rolling pace never changed as he led the four witches through Sacchara's groves to Menka's grasslands. Menka ruled the horse country.

Basoni kicked her feet free of her trailing blue robe and gave her horse both heels, urging him into a short gallop that brought her abreast of The Demon of the Laidly Marshes. The steed was one of Menka's finest, and he overtook the fiend easily as dancing.

"Is it much farther you're taking us?" she inquired politely.

The repulsive creature looked up and registered some surprise to see one of Ayree's fair-faced sisters addressing him socially. "Arrrh . . . no, not such a much farther, as you might reckon it, m'lady. Just over northies a way."

He made vague waving motions with one paw toward an undisclosed goal somewhere ahead and to the right of their path, then twisted his small, glittering red eyes away from Basoni's luminous blue gaze. Like most marsh-demons, he was a literal stick-in-the-mud. Any situation he fancied was improper or extraordinary made him nervous. A beautiful woman speaking to him when it was not a matter of absolute necessity? *Most* improper. He could not stand to have their eyes meet like that for too long. He tried speeding his gait, hoping the young witch would fall back into ranks with her sisters, where she belonged.

Basoni was not aware of the demon's unease. She adjusted her mount's pace to his. Blithely she continued, "Have you been The Demon of the Laidly Marshes long, friend? *The* Demon, I mean."

The creature blinked. *"Friend?"* Only sheer momentum kept him from being shocked to a full stop in his tracks.

"Well . . . if I may call you friend," Basoni said. "And I'd sooner call *you* friend than some of your brethren. At least you seem to know how to conduct yourself. I had quite an unpleasant run-in with another monster . . . fiend . . . relative of yours before my brother came to camp. He was terribly tall, and every inch unmannerly."

The Demon of the Laidly Marshes nodded and fingered his lumpy chin sagely. "No lips?" he asked.

"None worth mentioning."

"Ah. That 'un. Thought himself summat grand on account o' height alone. Not girth nor growth makes the demon, *we* say. He spoke out o' turn to me once, too." His crusty teeth showed, and a little runnel of flame dripped from his gums. "Once."

Basoni decided not to pry further into what had become of the outsized demon. To shift the subject she said, "I apologize for what you and your kin have been going through, but it had to be. Ayree gave me command of the Twelve and told me to give them all something to do together. Clearing up the Laidly Marshes seemed most . . . convenient.''

The demon's chuckle was thick and oily, like a bad cook's soup. Any awe he might ever have had for the beautiful young witch melted away the moment she begged his pardon. But though he no longer feared Basoni, he felt a certain camaraderie for her now.

''Aye, it *were* convenient for you, weren't it? Can't say I blame you overmuch. You and me, m'lady, we're leaders. Got to keep the rabble busied up and out of our hair. Such as we've got, o'course.'' He scraped his scaled pate and grinned at her sideways. ''Oh, politics is sticky business! I didn't come into my high office through family influence, like you. Had to wrest the title from a rival—narsty, scottish piece of fiendkind he was, too. Soon's you and yours set to ruining our nice marshes, we sent for him, and where was he? Drunk as a drone at the Inn of the Virgin's Delight again! So I ups and gives him a drink of summat . . . special. And here I am, The Demon of the Laidly Marshes.''

Basoni's eyes grew round. ''You . . . poisoned him?''

The monster thrust out his chest indignantly. ''Not like it were a hereditary office, m'lady. And not like the others didn't have the same chance to do what I did. We're a free people, we demons, and none of this royal house foolery for us. Every fiend's equal afore the law . . . or will be, once we gets us some laws.''

''Oh, I see,'' said Basoni, who didn't. For one moment she wished she'd been born to the keeping of one of the less courtly of the Twelve Kingdoms—Sumnerol or Lyf, perhaps, or barbarian Vahrd. Sombrunia was too refined to allow its guardian lady the freedom to drop this conversation like a dead mouse and flee back to her sisters' company.

Before she could drum up an excuse for retreat, the demon spoke. ''Now you say you're to blame, m'lady. That's as may be. But you're also going to turn things right for us poor demons again, and that's summat, too. You've a sense of measure, you have; good taste, like.'' He sighed and shook his head. ''More'n I can say for some o' your kinswomen. Look there, for instance.''

''Where?'' Basoni raised herself in the stirrups as she rode. The demon was making motions seaward, with his left paw. There was nothing but grass all around, and the smell of the

Lyarian Sea, and to the northeast the dark fencing of the Naîmlo Wood.

"There. There's where I mean." Again the demon gestured, again Basoni saw nothing extraordinary, although she shaded her eyes and scanned the western horizon intently.

"I think I see some horses . . . but that tall grass is in the way—"

"Ha!" The demon halted and clapped his arms crisscross over his chest, the picture of satisfaction. Coming up from behind, the other three sisters nearly rode him down.

"Why have we stopped?" Shama was still testy. She pulled back on her horse's bridle until the poor thing tongued the bit madly, seeking comfort.

"This is Menka's territory," Lucha said calmly. "We can't swamp this. She'd never have it. Do ride on, Basoni."

Basoni was at a loss to explain the demon's unscheduled stop. "Over there . . ." She pointed to where the golden green grasses, short elsewhere, suddenly reared up into a rippling screen. "He says something's wrong."

"He says?" Shama's eyes slewed around to glare at The Demon of the Laidly Marshes. "You waste our time for a demon's prank?"

"Now do be reasonable, Shama," Lucha drawled. "Why should he want to delay us just for a prank's sake? We're on our way to make him a new home. He'd want to hurry us, not hold us back. Maybe something truly is wrong, something we should know of."

"Something of Helagarde." Asapha's few words were enough.

Unwillingly, Basoni turned her gaze to the southwestern horizon, where Morgeld's amethyst stronghold loomed. She did not relish the sight, yet from the day the Twelve had first thrown their sealing spells over Morgeld's fortress, she had found her eyes drawn to its shadowy turrets. Even when the castle lay far away, it dominated her sight; mastered it the way Morgeld had once mastered her dreams.

It did not comfort her to know that once the amethyst castle had been more fearsome to behold. Songs and tales confirmed Basoni's nightmare memories: of how the souls in Morgeld's thrall had churned the waves at Helagarde's feet to a wild spume, had made the high winds wail with their sorrow.

The castle had shone then with a wicked brightness fed by misery. Basoni knew the old stories of blackly enchanted swords that smiled when they drank the blood of good men. Helagarde was worse than a hundred such swords, and the master of Helagarde was more than worthy of such an awful stronghold.

All that had changed. The empurpled towers no longer glowed brightly. Mariners whose fate or ill-fortune forced them to sail past the violet walls claimed that the stones looked dead somehow; if stone could die.

Basoni's heart beat a little faster with pride. The sword that had robbed Morgeld of a measure of his powers—the sword of blackest stone out of the old legends—that sword had been wielded by Sombrunia's king. Sombrunia, *her* wardland, linked to her life through some magic so ancient that even Ayree could not explain it.

The Demon of the Laidly Marshes interrupted Basoni's reverie. "All the grass so tall over there, it's wrong. It's not natural. Now mind you, I don't have no complaints with some magicked-up changes. But I've been living long enough to say that the wizard what doesn't have no sense of—of—of *style*, like . . . Well, that's all the difference between fairbooth trickery and real enchantment."

Shama's mouth hardened. She pierced The Demon of the Laidly Marshes with a severely critical look. The hapless fiend lowered his head and pawed the short grass at his feet.

"Sorry, m'lady. Speakin' out o' turn like that's not my way. If she's your sister, I guess she's got good reason to throw up all the hidey-blinds she likes, and seawrack take how it all looks. I'll lead you on to where the wood wants swamping."

He started off again on his interrupted course, but Asapha gave her horse a sudden touch of the heels and shot around to cut him off.

"Wait," the wardlady of Lyf said. "We'd better go look."

The four sisters brought their horses together into a line. From their vantage, the blades looked high as the eartips of a full-grown Sombrunian courser. The growth across the rest of the flatland was only hock-deep. The demon was right: There *was* something unsettling about the incongruously tall grass.

Asapha calculated the length of the lissome green palisade. "Five or six horses long, nose to tail, on this side."

Lucha nodded. "And how many deep, do you think?"

Asapha shrugged. "You can't see a thing through the brake. It's thin stalks stretched thinner by Menka's spells. Even from here, I can read the touch of her sorcery in it. The stalks need to grow quite deep to hide anything."

"Menka, who said we were to conserve our powers." Shama seemed to derive a perverse pleasure in catching her eldest sister in violation of one of her own directives.

"Why would she do this?" Lucha posed the question they were all asking themselves.

Basoni suggested, "This could be her way of staying close to her horses. A stand of tall grass is as good as any tent—better, from her point of view."

Shama snorted. "She's got her tent pitched out here anyway!"

"For whatever reason Menka raised this wall, it's here. Perhaps we'd better go back to camp and report—"

A hawk's scream broke from Asapha's lips. Wherever the lady of Lyf roamed, her birds were never far away. Four silvertip falcons plummeted from the sky to her call, but sheared off again as their mistress kneed her mount to a run that bore them both across the field and into the heart of the grassy shieldwall.

The three remaining sisters exchanged a look. The Demon of the Laidly Marshes was fit to be tied. "Got no manners," he grumbled. "Dropping in on a body like that, without no invitation."

Before Basoni or Shama could act, Lucha, too, was gone. She had thrown off her feigned laziness and galloped after Asapha into the tall grass. They saw the thin blades rippling as if storm-tossed, then Lucha rode out again and rejoined them.

"I caught up with her and tried to make her think twice before bolting in there," she said. "So close to Helagarde, how should we know whether this is Menka's creation or the work of something worse?"

"Well?" Shama demanded. "Where is she?"

"In there. She wasn't at all pleased with my holding her back—asked whether I thought she was a fool, not to try sensing whose magic made that wall first. Her hawks tried to rip my hand off her horse's bridle, but not until I took the precaution of reading the signs, too. It's Menka's all right." Lucha sighed. "Asapha's got the subtlety of a swordthrust, but at least she gets things done. Come, sisters. Menka can't be any angrier at four uninvited callers than at one." She put her horse into a trot, Shama's steed following, and quickly reached the point in the green wall where Asapha's horse had broken down a path.

Basoni lingered a moment. "Please wait for us," she told the nonplussed demon. "We won't be long, and maybe Menka will come with us to help make your new marshland."

"If she don't turn you all to toads first," the demon mumbled. But Basoni was already on her sisters' traces.

Asapha had misjudged: The tall grass was more than one horse deep. As soon as she entered that waving green world, Basoni wished that she had ridden once around the perimeter to gauge its true area. Too late, she realized that she had underestimated the grass from a distance. It was far taller than any horse's ears, tall enough so that King Alban's most impressive guardsman, standing on the saddle of one of the king's own stallions, would still be hard-pressed to see over the top.

Asapha's passage had pressed down the stalks, Asapha and Lucha had flattened them even more, but the enchanted stems had an astonishing resilience. Already they were beginning to spring back upright, covering any sign of a pathway. To either side, the untrampled blades loomed high, their tips bending in to weave a canopy of striped shadows overhead.

Basoni encouraged her horse to go faster. She felt a little panic—unreasonable, as all fits of panic were. She had traveled through the worse-than-trackless depths of the Naîmlo Wood many times alone, often afoot. The season-shifting enchantments of its brooding trees did not frighten her, not even as a child. There were places in the Naîmlo Wood where all light from above was blotted out by day as well as by night, other parts of that weird forest where brightness seemed to seep up from the mossy ground at the roots of the ageless trees.

There was no warping of light and darkness here. Tilting her head back, Basoni could see the limpid sky and the sun, bright and familiar through the waving grass stalks. It gave her no comfort. She calmed her fears by telling herself she could always levitate above the grasses; yet something emanating from the core of the grove made her skin chill and prickle under her blue wool robes.

Basoni tried to find the cause of her unease by using all her sensitivities to sift the grass for some sign of alien magic, but it was as Lucha and Asapha had said: Only Menka's spells had been at work here.

When she heard familiar voices not too far ahead, she could have cried out for joy. She gave her horse an uncharacteristically hard dig in the side, startling it into a gallop, and broke free of the high grass.

Asapha, Lucha, and Shama were waiting for her, dismounted. Their horses stood aside, stamping their hooves as nervously as if the ground crawled with young serpents. The sisters stood in a small area of low-growing grass, like that flourishing outside Menka's wall. Between the shoots, dainty orange blooms of firefall sent out their tempting fragrance, but no bees graced the rare flowers.

Basoni could not believe what she saw—or didn't see. She had always had an eye for little things. She slipped from her saddle and knelt to examine the richly perfumed blossoms, each bearing a double ring of stamens heavy with bronze-colored pollen, a squat scarlet pistil shining like a drop of blood. Around the firefalls the grass itself seemed devoid of insect life, the stems unnaturally still.

A falconer's gauntlet thrust itself between Basoni's eyes and the ghostly flowers. She looked up to see Asapha offering to help her to her feet.

As she stood, warmth touched Basoni's heart: a call from one of the others, too kindly to come from Shama. She looked to Lucha, who smiled and pressed a finger to her mouth. Her lips carefully formed the words: *Hush. See what we have discovered.* A hint of sound echoed in Basoni's mind from Lucha's, but only Ayree had the power of soulspeech, to summon with words from afar.

Lucha pulled aside a sweep of the tall stalks.

Flowers in profusion covered a vast, ornate braidwork of grass; rare flowers of every kingdom and every color. In the windless heart of the thicket the sight and scent of so many precious blossoms struck Basoni's senses fiercely, made them throb.

The plaited grass framework over which the flowers ran was taller than a field-tent. It had the shape of a giant's upended basket, with no visible portal. The grasses forming it had been commanded to grow into their twining pattern without cutting, their roots still firm in the soil.

With the step of huntresses, the four witches treaded out a path around the blooming dome and found that it was doorless, windowless, entirely without ordinary means of entry. The silence seemed to grow around them as they walked, smothering the least rustle of their feet in the grass.

In the eerie calm of that place, Menka's groan sounded like the riving of the earth itself.

Metal flashed in the clearing—Asapha's single-headed ax was in her fist. She had left her chosen weapon in her black tent, but it flew to her call as loyally as her birds.

Her sisters did not challenge what she'd done. They had done the same, summoning their fighting gear to hand by magic. Lucha swung her curved sword in slow arcs above her head. Shama juggled three shurikens as casually as if they were rubber balls. She breathed on one and its points puffed into a flame that she alone could touch without being burned. She aimed for the crest of the bower and knew she would not miss.

Basoni tugged her arm down sharply, making her drop the fiery steel star. Shama extinguished the flames with a word before it hit the ground. "Are you mad, Basoni?"

"Are you?" Basoni favored the bow, but now she had her sword drawn, her robes thrown aside. In her brief undertunic her limbs were free for fighting. "Will your spellfires spare Menka? Will burning this bower save her? *See* your target first!" She swung her sword and brought it down in a two-handed stroke against the flowery grass dome.

The braided grasses gave way; no magic strengthened them. Asapha stood at Basoni's side, adding the blows of her ax to the sword's lashing tongue. Standing a little apart, Lucha attacked her section of the wall with her own curved blade. It was easy as chopping field-dried straw.

Heat and a ball of light the color of a lion's eye blasted from the opening. Lucha and Shama staggered back, but Asapha shouted a word and a white hawk of trembling ice crystals swooped from the skies. The creation's talons plunged into the spinning fireball, chilling it out of existence. The hole in the hut's side offered no further opposition as the four poured in between trailing strands of dying flowers.

A hot glare, tawny and powerful, filled the bower. Basoni felt her sword grow warm. Asapha hung back, cowed for a moment. But Basoni never lost a step as she shielded herself with sorcery and walked through the hard glow.

"Basoni, *no!*" Menka's voice reached her with a peculiar echo, as if they both were trapped in a huge bronze flask, surrounded by shadows. Basoni's eyes were still a little dazzled from the barricade she had just passed. Afterghosts of deep blue against a soft blackness almost seemed alive, linking themselves into grotesque shapes.

"Basoni, wait!"

Menka was calling again. But where was Menka in that shifting dark? Wavering tissues of light like the silks of the sea-lords came swimming up at Basoni. She laughed at their fragile beauty and slashed them apart with her sword, striding between the pieces.

"*Basoni!*"

Air clashed into air behind her. The shreds of iridescence came together, unmarked by her swordstroke, and whirled into a band of binding. A second belt of multicolored light slipped into an angled orbit with the first, and a third, and then a fourth. Four spells of imprisonment flew in their eternal circles around her.

"Menka! Where are you? We've come to help you!" Basoni pounded at the racing bands of light with a fist, then with the hilt of her sword, finally with her powers. Nothing touched them. "Let me out!"

When the voices came, they were too sharp. They made lightning dart inside her head. She knew they were the voices of her sisters—Menka, Lucha, Shama, Asapha—but the pain bending her to her knees was too wrenching to let her join individual names to the words tormenting her.

Must we do this? Can't we get her out?

Not now. If we are lucky, later, yes.

If we are lucky?

Bad luck put her there. It might have been any one of us. She was the first, the one who cut—

I tried to stop her. Why in Ambra's name did you come meddling here? Ah, gods!

Do you think you could have overcome something like this alone? You flatter yourself.

Shut up. Join. If what Menka says is true, we must be ready. Basoni also.

Does she know?

She'll know soon enough. Join, I said. It wakes.

Then a roar filled the rainbow prison, wiping out her sister's voices. From the darkness at Basoni's feet, a fearsome being sprang. It was more hideous than any demon Basoni had ever seen, because there was a terrible gleam of cold wisdom in its amethyst eyes. Bony wings stood out from its shoulders—bare bones the color of frost, no skin at all covering them. Manshaped in its fashion, it made inhuman sounds. Its naked flesh was the dappled green and gray of mold.

This fiend was worse than anything the Naîmlo Wood or the Laidly Marshes had ever spawned. It was a creature of the voids where Morgeld walked at his pleasure, a slave of the dark master. Before, Morgeld had tried to break the branches from the Tree of Second Light by sending a snow-beast after Ayree's youngest sister. This time the oldest was his target, a true fiend his tool, his ultimate goal unchanged:

Destroy but one of the Twelve, destroy all.

Strength of a hundred warspells poured from Basoni's lips, drenching her sword with whiteness. She wished for her shield, knowing it could not reach her across the barriers her four sisters had summoned to hold the dark spirit. The creature lunged for her, screaming, and she fended it off with her blade.

It was an inexpert melding of spell to steel. Sorcery shattered from the blade in flakes where it touched the skeletal wings. The fiend wheeled and poised for a second attack. The sound it made was almost laughter.

She can't destroy it! The voices were with Basoni again. They did not pain her so badly now.

One is not enough to destroy it; not even you, Asapha. Don't you think I tried when it first came at me? All I could do was fight a holding battle . . .

You should be grateful we found you.

Gratitude to the chasms! One's not enough, you heard her. Join, *you grubworm!*

My powers are linked the same as yours, damn you. I'm trying!

Ah, gods! One not enough, four more not enough . . . if it will take all the Twelve to kill this monster, how can we summon the others?

One of you must ride . . . must fly back—

Basoni wanted to scream out, *No! Don't leave me here! I can feel Morgeld in this creature's skin! If even one of you deserts me now, he'll have me!* The tear-streaks on her face reflected the whirling rainbows as she crouched to receive the fiend's assault.

Instead of running at her, it vaulted to the highest point of their prison sphere and hovered there, fleshless wings prudently clear of the moving bands of light. Basoni felt a distinct pulling at the blade of her sword and the sensation grew more pronounced. She tightened her hold on the haft, only to feel her arms rising with the blade. She tugged back. Strips of enchantment peeled away and dissolved to nothing, leaving plain metal exposed. She sent ruin flying at the fiend; the spells met a mightier shield than she could penetrate.

She had been born a witch as other children are born to sing or tend sheep or dream. She had not been born with the same powers as every other witch or warlock in the Twelve Kingdoms—no more than common children are all born with the same color hair or eyes. Her chief inborn powers were for defense, not attack. She had learned some spells of destruction as well as the use of common weapons, but her ability to annihilate was not infinite.

She could only stand off the creature for so long. The tug-of

war for her sword was stripping it of her few warspells. Soon it
would be just another blade, magicless against another demon
whose master's powers—even lessened—were still virtually
unstoppable beside her own. The thought of Morgeld made her
fight harder to hold on to the sword. The fiend made a bizarre
noise and the upward pull doubled.

She's losing it!

Sweet Janeela save her!

The chalky wings cut a white line against the rainbow lights.
Basoni closed her eyes and clung to the sword. Sweat mixed with
her tears. She imagined that the metal screeched in agony as its
protective coat of spellcasting was torn away. Though her hands
were aching and stiff, she put her full weight into holding down
the sword.

It shot from her grip-numbed hands, the hilt slick with sweat.
She called out after it, a sob of despair, as it flew at the hovering
demon's heart. The bone-winged thing tumbled lazily aside and
Basoni's blade splintered as it struck the bands of binding surrounding them both. There was hunger in those amethyst eyes as
the monster adjusted the angle of its wings, ready to take its
prey.

Basoni flung invisibility over herself, wondering how long it
would protect her. Their prison was not large. She could not
dodge forever

The creature saw her vanish. This did not disturb it. It
retreated to the heights and began a slow, spiraling descent, its
ghastly wingspan raking only a hair away from the moving walls.
Basoni saw the flying bones come nearer, their clawlike tips
descending to meet her eyes. Weakness seized her as hope
disappeared. She could not even move out of the way—for what?
It would find her at last. Why resist?

In that moment she understood how the *sivrithim*—lost souls—
must feel, caught in Morgeld's snare.

The fiend's right wingtip was a finger's breadth from her eye
when it stopped. In the trance of despair, Basoni thought that
time always seemed to freeze in its most agonizing moments,
bleeding full measure of suffering from its victims. The spell
would break, and she would feel cold bone stab her. The spell
would break soon.

It did not. Basoni felt a small flame of hope. She dared to seek
out the creature's eyes. They were no longer narrowed to a
hunter's sharp gaze, but wide with fear and surprise. Bonds
Basoni could not see clamped themselves to the fiend's wrists, its

ankles, the base of its wings, and held it spread-eagled against the spinning aurora holding them both.

Then the rainbow shell burst apart. Basoni felt real earth under her; she was huddled on the ground, hugging herself, shaking. Her sisters—*all* her sisters, she saw with wonder—were there.

Ayree was there, too.

The fiend squealed, hanging in its unseen shackles in midair, arching its back furiously in an effort to escape. The witch-king regarded it dispassionately. Without taking his eyes from it, he asked, "Are you all right, Basoni?"

"Yes . . . I think . . . yes," she whispered.

Resha knelt beside her, a leather box between her thin knees. Large, deeply shadowed eyes looked out of place in such a sharp-boned face, but her smile softened everything. The wardlady of Sumnerol opened her kit and took out a square bottle whose yellow glass made the contents look like tar.

"This will soothe you." Resha pulled the cork out too roughly; Basoni recognized the brown liquid that splashed out, spotting Resha's white leather trousers.

"No, please." Basoni held up her hands. "Not a dream-draught. I'm all right, I really am."

"If you insist . . ." The healer pounded the cork back in. "Can't cure the healthy of anything but life. It's just as well. We need you to join with us for this." She stood, and hauled Basoni upright with her.

"For what, Resha?"

Ayree was the one to answer. "You will link your powers with the others, Basoni, and destroy this fiend. Practice on the servant what you'll do to the master. I could almost thank Morgeld for this. Go ahead. I will hold him."

The creature appeared to understand what was being said. As the Twelve formed a circle, its struggles grew more frantic. Basoni saw the fleshless wings crack with strain, the heavier shafts begin to wrench free of their sockets. The left wing was weaker. The monster gave a hideous howl as it tore loose from its base and the smaller bones forming it came apart, clattering to the ground.

Ayree quickly slapped a new holding on the fiend's maimed shoulder. "Proceed."

Basoni ignored the rising pulse of power joining power in the circle of Twelve. Her sisters' varied strengths slammed against her, seeking her own, but she could not respond; not now, not seeing what she saw. She leaped from her place in the circle, deaf to the shouts of outrage and confusion assailing her. She seized Ayree's wrist, and with her free hand gestured madly up at her pinioned adversary.

"Look! There, Ayree, where the wing has come away!"

"By Saara's blood . . ."

The witch-king broke free from Basoni's grasp. He cast light from his body so that all might see what he and Basoni saw. The creature revolved slowly in its bonds as the Twelve looked up.

Where the skeleton wing had joined the verdigris body, a patch of naked, healthy, human skin showed through.

"A *sivrith*," the witch-king said. "I have not seen one in . . . Curse Morgeld! He fattens on despair. Hopeless souls and evil men are not enough for him. He sets his traps for good men, too, living men he leads by guile into some shameful deed. And when the victim sees what he has done, he loses faith. He blames himself for Morgeld's snare and submits to Helagarde's lord without a struggle."

"Poor soul," Hodah whispered. "Poor soul, to live captive to such a master."

"Bring him down! Oh Ayree, bring him down!" Basoni's tears were flowing. The other sisters broke the circle to rush together into smaller groups and gabble over the revelation still turning in the air above them. Only Asapha remained aloof, as always.

The monster's struggles had ceased, although it was not dead. Its ugly head hung limply, the amethyst eyes fully shut. Now that she knew what hid inside that horrific shell, Basoni sobbed with compassion.

"Don't cry, little sister," Ayree said softly. He let the captive come slowly to earth. On contact with the ground, all its limbs relaxed, including the remaining wing. "I have undone his bonds, but I can put them on him again quickly, if I must. Which of you will do what is necessary?"

"Necessary?"

"Do what? Kill him? Brother, no! He couldn't help what Morgeld made of him!"

"Peace, sisters," Ayree said. "You know we will not kill him." The Prince of Warlocks looked down at the unconscious creature and mused, "So this is how Morgeld clothes his poor *sivrithim*, in the skins of demons. The lord of Helagarde has given us a great gift. It's not often enough that we can save someone from his service. The books of lore teach that once a *sivrith*'s disguise is stripped off, Morgeld cannot reclaim him.

That is what we must do now. Who would be best to . . . Hodah! Yes, you have the right touch for this.''

Basoni's favorite sister stepped forward until she and Ayree faced each other over the *sivrith*'s supine body. She spared the time to send Basoni a comforting smile before asking, ''What would you have me do? Resha is the better healer . . .''

Four winged cats came to the witch-king's call. With clever paws they raised the wounded creature so that the patch of telltale skin was plain to see. ''Later he will need healing,'' Ayree said. ''What he needs now is you, Hodah. Your hands are strongest among the Twelve to bring forth new life.''

The others set up a low chorus of agreement. Life flourished under Hodah's hands; life when it was youngest, newest, most fragile. Basoni dried her eyes as Hodah began her task.

Gravemold skin peeled away gently but surely. Hodah's mid-wife hands were cautious at first. She had coaxed many new lives into the world, though never a birth like this. Her fingers freed strong, human limbs, a body no longer just manshape, but man's, and finally they lifted off the terrible demon mask of Morgeld's slave. The face revealed was young and handsome. As the last vestige of his former aspect vanished, he opened his eyes and stared at his liberator. In that instant, Basoni saw Hodah jerk backward as if struck by a spear, her face white, and her eyes glowing with the awful light of obsession that Basoni saw in Ayree's whenever he spoke of Morgeld's doom: fearsome intense, burning. It was a gaze that made all other objects invisible.

''The gods bless you, my lady,'' the man gasped.

''Who are you?'' Hodah was shaking.

''I am Galivert.'' Then the man fell into unconsciousness.

Chapter VI

THE GUEST

What can no man read, but every woman?
Every woman.

—"The Echo's Riddle"
from *The Scroll of Oran*

Basoni lay sleepless in her tent, though her battle-weary bones cried out for rest. After the day's events, she'd expected sleep to find her before she found her bed. It was not so. Every time she closed her eyes she saw Hodah removing the demon's skin from the man's body, only this time the transformation she witnessed was not a clean birth. The gray and green hide tore off in ragged, bloody slabs; butcher's work. It was worse than a dream because Basoni knew she was not asleep. She sat up in bed and pressed the heels of her hands against her eyes.

"M'lady?" said a gruff voice outside.

Basoni leaped out of bed, a thin blanket wrapped around her. She pushed her tent flap open so that the garnet-colored glass bell hanging beside it tinkled. The Demon of the Laidly Marshes was waiting for her, his hideous looks made worse by moonlight and the dim, far-reaching glow of Helagarde.

Awkwardly he shuffled his feet. "M'lady, I can wait 'til you've got a robe on."

Basoni held her blanket up carelessly. "Don't worry, I'm not cold." She rubbed one foot with the other. "But I never noticed how damp this ground gets at night. Maybe I should put some slippers on . . ."

"Put some *clothes* on!" the demon bellowed. His vehemence startled Basoni back into her tent. By the time she emerged in more proper attire, tying the belt of her dressing gown, he was still muttering about witches and warlocks having no sense of modesty.

". . . can't control their pinkling bodies, then they might as well learn to *cover* 'em u— Oh. Greetings, m'lady."

"Welcome, friend. I'm glad you've come. I owe you thanks. Will you come in?" She held the tent flap back for him, but he demurred.

"Nothing's owed me, m'lady, and I'm not at home 'midst fineries."

"I owe you everything. Resha told me that it was you who went back to our camp and brought the others."

This flat statement of fact sent the demon into a ballet of discomfort. There was not one physical sign of self-abasement that he missed, from tugging a nonexistent forelock to toeing the soggy ground into a miniature slough at his feet.

"M'lady . . . m'lady, don't put no great meaning onto *that*, now will you? Just a bit o' demonishness, that were; disobeying you, after you said I was to stay where I was. We demons, we don't like getting orders. Break 'em all the time and twice when we can manage it."

Basoni's smile was very warm and amused. "Now why don't I believe you? Could it be the paw tracks we found just outside Menka's bower? You followed us, you saw my plight, and you went for help."

"Went t'get some o' my own kin to see where a smart-mouthed young witchy-girl ends up, *that's* what I went t'do," The Demon of the Laidly Marshes growled. "You couldn't half see my eyes for the tears o' joy that sprung up, watchin' that monster serve you proper. Aye, that were a fiend's fiend, payin' you back for your meddling ways. It were too good a sight t' keep to meself. All blurry-eyed like I was, how was I to know I'us blurting out the whole tale to your thrice-blasted brother Ayree, and not my own underlings?" He thrust his forepaws into absent pockets and kicked up a huge spurt of wet earth, sullenly muttering, "Takin' advantage of me in my infirmary, *that's* what he did, your precious white-shocked brother . . ."

Basoni stifled a grin. She should have known: The Demon of the Laidly Marshes had a reputation to uphold. Doing a deliberate kindness would be his professional ruination, if word got around. She was in his debt; she could at least be discreet.

Tugging the edges of her dressing gown closer together, she tried to look haughty, if only for the poor demon's benefit.

"Hmph. Well. Yes. I should have known better than to waste thanks on one of *your* kind," she said.

The look of gratitude on the demon's ugly face was almost pathetic.

Basoni continued, "I assume you're here for a reason? Besides keeping me awake, I mean."

"Aye," the demon said. He pawed the sandy soil a third time. The four small trenches his taloned toes left behind filled with water until by moonlight they looked like streaks of mercury. "I've got a complaint to lodge, m'lady; a serious complaint."

"If it's about your new home, my sisters and I will be taking care of it first thing in the morning. A little patience . . ."

"Patience? Go preach patience to a rock! I'm in no hurry for *your* crowd to make me a new home; not if it's to be more o' the shoddy spellwork you girls turn out."

"*Shoddy?*" This time there was no need for Basoni to feign anger.

The demon's paw splayed out to make a sign of protection. A faint blue aura arced up crackling around the youngest of the Twelve, a sure sign of temper in certain of the witchborn. Wishing to placate her quickly, he said, "Wrong word, m'lady, wrong word and badly chosen. Not shoddy—I never meant offense—but more like . . . butterflyish. That better?" He gave Basoni his most charming smile.

Basoni's aura subsided. "I don't understand you, friend. Butterflyish? Do you mean . . . pretty?"

"Pretty? Nay, m'lady, more'n that. Glorious! Magnificent! Regal-like!" His paws described vast circles, then folded demurely on his paunch. "And gone faster'n springtime. M'lady, look down."

Basoni looked, and saw—nothing. What was there to see? First Menka's hidden bower, now this . . . whatever it was. For the second time The Demon of the Laidly Marshes had drawn her attention to something whose significance eluded her. How vexing to be consistently less perceptive than a demon! The assorted independent fiends of the Twelve Kingdoms had a universal reputation for being thickwits: fine company to be in. Basoni made a real effort to comprehend what her flame-spitting friend was complaining about before giving up and asking, "What's wrong? It's only ground."

"*Wet* ground, m'lady. Ground as—if you'll permit the sayin' of it—ground as might make a pretty little swamp, given time."

"Our spells . . ." Basoni stooped to grab up a pinch of the soggy earth. It was gritty with sand and smelled of the sea.

"M'lady, I'm not pretendin' to be tellin' you yer trade, but I do know my own. It's not the nature of things t' stand still in this world, not even spells. Oh, some gives the effect o' being permanent. Didn't too many folk believe *that* 'un to be safe in his bonds forever?" He made a guarded gesture in the direction of Helagarde. "Nothing's forever . . . 'cept death; and from what I hear, *that* 'un don't leave death alone when he can help it."

He was near the mark. Basoni promised herself that she would never again underestimate the intelligence of the demon breed.

How strong were the spells we used on these marshes? Basoni thought, bending to plunge her fingers deeper into the watery ground.

The soil was Shama's domain. When Basoni had come to divide the business of changing the Laidly Marshes, some tasks had fallen naturally to certain of the sisters. Shama's ability with gemstones and other minerals made her the perfect one to send spells that pressed the waters from the marshland and left only solid ground behind.

Solid? Not now. Why are the spells slipping, letting the old marsh come back? I'd better find Shama and ask . . .

"Please excuse me," she said to the demon. "I must find one of my sisters."

As she hurried by, the demon called after her, "You won't find her in her tent, if that's where you're minded to seek, m'lady." Basoni stopped and cast a questioning look back at him. "They're in your brother's tent, they are; all of 'em. That's what woke me up, see, all them witchy-girls a-yammer and a-yowl. Don't take on like I come calling on you to do more'n complain about all the gibble-gab those goldy-haired magpies be raising. I wasn't here a-warnin' you, and who says so's a liar!"

Careful not to smile, Basoni said, "Certainly not. Warn me? A monster like you wouldn't warn his own mother of a quicksand patch."

The demon knit his brows. "My mother *was* a quicksand patch," he mumbled before sinking back into the soil—easier going now that the spells making bog into firm earth were coming undone.

Basoni ran to Ayree's tent, a glowing golden lantern of light that rivaled Helagarde's unwholesome radiance. Before she reached the entry, she heard the angry voices. The debate within was stormy, and too fierce for any of the participants to notice when Basoni came in.

In the center of the tent, Ayree sat on his camp stool looking very weary. On faldstools, tabourets, pillows, silk rugs, and the ground itself, eleven of the Twelve sat in two opposing groups before him, five in one, six in the other.

Lavah was speaking from her place on a plump kidskin cushion. With her long, overcurled tresses in a muzzy tangle and her soft, frilly pastel robes, she looked like an enraged pastry. "—inhuman! What can he hope for? Have we saved him merely to cast him out with no true life awaiting him?"

Shama sprang to her feet. Coldly she said, "There are lives enough to choose from in the Twelve Kingdoms. He's not a baby, Lavah, so don't act as if we're tossing him into the River Salmlis in a basket!"

"Why not?" Lavah replied. "If he *were* a baby, I'm sure you'd suggest doing just that with him!"

Basoni gasped. It was the first time she had witnessed Lavah stand up to her immediate elder. Every aspect of Lavah's ancient role as Shama's toady was gone, and from the discomfited look on Shama's face as she sank back onto her tabouret, this obviously wasn't the first time in the discussion that Lavah had slapped her down.

No wonder the ground was affected, Basoni thought. *Shama so angry and hurt. I can feel her drawing all her powers in to shield herself, even if she doesn't know she's doing it. She's called back some of the magic binding the soil. She must be told . . .*

"Look who's here!" Sacchara rose from her place to welcome Basoni. "Come and sit with us, dear one." Her fingers closed around Basoni's wrist a bit more firmly than necessary as she steered her to a green and blue silk rug at Ayree's left.

"Let her choose her own place, Sacchara!" Senja was on her feet, a flash of brilliant Vahrdish satins in the eye-paining combinations those barbarian fighters preferred. Twin swords of her own forging were thrust into the green and yellow sash at her waist, their crimson leather-wrapped hilts protruding.

"What does it matter where I sit?" Basoni pulled out of Sacchara's hold. Standing between the two groups, she grew more alarmed as her eyes went from one face to the next. The feelings she saw were too strong: resentment, hostility, fear. Even gentle Hodah had the look of a woman on the brink of great loss, a face strained with a thousand unsaid prayers.

Ayree was grim. "It matters, Basoni. Your sisters have chosen sides, you see. Take your place with the fools or the idiots." He waved indifferently to left and right.

"Fools?" Zabala sounded hurt. "Brother, we are on your side!"

"The foolishness is that there are two sides to begin with." The Prince of Warlocks glared at the five sisters to his right. Under that look, warlike Senja subsided to her place on the bare ground. Basoni saw her shift uncomfortably. Perplexed, she touched the soil, rubbing damp fingers together.

"Is that what you don't like, Ayree?" Menka was the only one of the five who did not flinch away from her brother's icy blue gaze. She stood to confront him. "That we've taken sides against each other? We've done that before. Practice honesty, for once. Admit what really galls you: we've finally found the courage to stand against *you!*"

Basoni felt her skin chilling as Ayree rose from his stool. He exuded no aura; his emotions now were more secret than the vaults of Tsaretnaidos. Basoni let Sacchara pull her to sit down with the left-hand group.

"Your stupidity galls me." There was hardly any inflection in what he said. "What does it take to bring you to adulthood? Not years alone; if you were all magicless beings, your ages would be more than enough to rank with the village wisewomen."

It was a subtle thrust. One bond the Twelve Kingdoms shared was conferring the delicate title of "wisewoman" to the oldest, least lovesome, longest unpartnered females.

Menka lifted her chin. "If basic kindness is stupid, then I'm proud of it. You can keep your wisdom, Ayree."

Basoni found herself sitting between Sacchara and Zabala. Tugging lightly on Zabala's heart-shaped braids, she asked in a whisper, "Menka defying Ayree? Ambra save us all, what for?"

Zabala bent her head to hiss back, "Galivert, the *sivrith* Hodah freed. He must go back to his mortal life."

"Certainly; why not?"

Sacchara put her oar in. "Because he's lost it, that's why not. Doesn't recall a thing beyond his name—not kin, kith, or Kingdom!"

"Sacchara." Ayree's passionless mask was beginning to slip. "If you have something to say, say it for all of us."

The mistress of fruits and bees smoothed her already wrinkleless skirts. "I was just telling Basoni what the fuss is about."

"Indeed? Stand, Basoni." The youngest of the Twelve obeyed

her brother's order without hesitation. Across the way, Senja made a sly comment in Lavah's curl-hung ear. The two of them stared boldly at Basoni and smirked knowingly.

If Ayree overheard what Senja said, he ignored it. "Now that you know the vital subject we're debating, would you like to know how long this little exercise has been going on?" He didn't wait for an answer. "From an hour before sundown until now, when dawn is coming."

As long as that! Basoni realized that she must have slept a bit after all, and that the awful images of Hodah and the *sivrith* were the product of dreams, not visions.

"The nub of it is this: the mortal Galivert has no place here at the siege of Helagarde. He must go, for his own safety."

"For your convenience, you mean," Menka broke in.

"Yes, if you like to put it that way. I do find his presence here a bother, a distraction." Ayree's pale eyelids lowered halfway. "The time I spent overcoming him in his demon form was time lost from adapting the weird of Morgeld's doom. It was time that would have been better spent on bringing us that much closer to the battle that will end Helagarde and all it contains."

"How does it feel to know that our dear brother found it so tedious to save your life, Basoni?" Senja's taunt ended in hooting laughter.

Hodah slapped the laugh from Senja's face. The wardlady of Vahrd glowered and wheeled from her cross-legged seat to a kneeling position, her hand dropping to the hilt of one sword.

The blade flamed to a hissing drift of steam just as the last shining inch came free of the scabbard, the hilt crumbling between Senja's fingers like crushed clay.

"Draw against your sister again," Ayree said, "and you will fight Morgeld with spells alone; not steel."

To Basoni's amazement, Senja was not at all frightened by Ayree's threat. She brushed the red crumbs from her palm as she ranged herself beside Menka. "I apologize to Hodah," she drawled, "and to Basoni as well. We've had to apologize for telling the truth more and more since you came to camp, brother; I'm used to it. I'll even apologize in advance for what I'm going to say now:

"Basoni, the freed *sivrith* hasn't a memory to bless himself with—no idea of who he is beyond the fact that his name's Galivert, and that's a name I've heard used in more than one of the Twelve Kingdoms. He's too dark to be one of Zabala's Malbens, he's too plainspoken to hail from Vair, and he's got a

sight more manners than I've found among my Vahrdmen, but
that still leaves nine possible lands to claim him, plus Braegerd
Isle. We might send a spell of searching, but that would only
work if he has living bloodkin. Besides, the time wasted on it,
and the power . . ."

Senja shook her head and clucked her tongue like the worst of
ambulant dramatic actresses. "If Ayree thought saving *your* life
was such a nuisance, he'd hardly approve a searching spell for
Galivert's benefit. So! What's to be done with him? Toss him out
to find his own way when he hasn't a chasplat's notion of what it
is? There's the perfect recipe for despair, Zabala! And despair is
how Morgeld got him in the first place."

"We might as well escort him back to the gates of Helagarde
right now and save time," Lavah said. "Ayree seems so preoccupied with saving time."

The witch-king's tent exploded into a wild dispute, all of the
Twelve talking at once. Basoni found herself on her feet with the
rest, all of them behaving as if Ayree were a world away. She
heard Fortunata giving Zabala a lecture detailing endless intelligent reasons why Galivert should remain among them; Resha's
hypnotic drone and Sacchara's shrill arguments alike breaking to
flinders against the wall of Menka's obstinacy; Senja and Lucha
screaming the full-bodied oaths of the southern lands in each
other's faces with no attempt at reasoning at all, and Lavah
taking every bit of Shama's cutting abuse and hurling it back
with interest.

"Well, Basoni, have you chosen me?" Hodah's smile mocked
no one but herself. "You know you never could convince me of
anything when you were little. Perhaps you should get some
help." With her eyes she indicated Asapha, who had pulled
solitude around her like a cloak and held aloof from the fighting.
"She's on your side, all for getting Galivert out of here as soon
as he can stagger. At least she could do her part to persuade the
rest of us."

Basoni looked helpless. "I don't even know which side I'm
on, Hodah. I'm still too confused . . ."

"Confusion never stands in the way of other mortals' deci-
sions. Why should it affect the witchborn? Just close your eyes to
the facts and choose."

"It does seem rather cruel to cast that poor man out when he
doesn't know where he belongs," Basoni admitted.

"Of course it's cruel!" Hodah's eager response was a little

unnerving. Basoni recalled the way her beloved sister had shuddered when the redeemed *sivrith* first opened human eyes.

"But"—Basoni eyed Hodah steadily as she spoke—"Ayree is right, too. There is no place for him in a siege-camp; not this one. He was Morgeld's slave. I don't think Morgeld will give up even one of his prisoners just like that."

"Morgeld is trapped in Helagarde!" Hodah's life-giving hands became raised fists. "Trapped there by our spells! He can't do a thing!"

"But his servants can. They come and go freely, doing his will—Galivert's the proof of it."

"Galivert . . ."

His name brought the magic of sudden silence. The Twelve stopped quarreling, each moving away from her opponent until all stood separate, isolated, twelve islands linked by severed bridges. In that stillness, Ayree extended an open hand and took three steps toward the tent's entryway.

"Galivert. Join us. We were just speaking about you."

He came out of the shadows of false dawn, entering Ayree's tent with unstudied grace. He wore a robe dyed with the juice of yellow crocus, a simple garment that Zabala had quickly stitched together for him from two of Lavah's gowns. Three gowns might have been better. His shoulders were too broad for Zabala's needlework, though the clinging fabric's warm color made his skin shine like rubbed bronze and accented the rich brown of his hair and eyes.

The man made an awkward bow to the witch-king. "I'm sorry, my lord, I didn't mean to intrude. I heard voices—"

"No doubt you did. My sisters were raised in the northern wastes where whispering's a lost art. Stay, Galivert. I'm beginning to think that you're the only one who can put an end to this argument. Tell me, have you remembered who you are and where you're from?"

Galivert looked down and shook his head. "I'm sorry," he repeated. "My lord, I hoped . . . but no."

"Well, if you don't know where you belong, let me offer you the next best thing. Sometimes a man's hopes stay with him even when he loses everything else. Do you have a hope you remember, Galivert? Can you recall whether there is any place in the Twelve Kingdoms you would like to be?"

The man raised his head. A broad, white smile made his dark eyes sparkle. "A hope . . . a dream . . . Ah, my lord, if you only knew how long it's been since I dared to use words like that! Yes, there's a hope I remember, though you may find it strange: I've always fancied seeing the wild places, my lord, like Vahrd or Braegerd Isle. Do you think . . . do you think I might go there?''

"Oh, yes, if you want to die with a sword in you before a week's out!" Menka exclaimed. She turned on Ayree. "Is that your solution, brother? Don't put him where he belongs, put him where he wants to go? Why don't you travel the Twelve Kingdoms and give babies fireballs to play with?''

"I see nothing wrong with Ayree's idea," Lucha declared. "We've given him his life again, and added the most generous offer you'd like, if you weren't such a sheepskull. For all you know, things weren't so wonderful for him back in his own land. Why would he have fallen into Morgeld's snare otherwise? Give him a fresh land to go with a fresh life! Give him Vahrd, if that's what he wants!''

Ayree said, "I intend to. Come here, Galivert."

The man did as he was told. As he passed the Twelve, he shyly smiled at each. Basoni returned his smile just as shyly. "I hope you will fare well."

Her words made him pause, their eyes meeting when he replied, "As well as may be."

A fleck of violet light winked for a moment in the depths of his dark brown eyes, but was gone too swiftly for Basoni to be sure she had seen it at all.

Galivert stood beside Ayree. The witch-king touched his shoulder and his makeshift robe became a short, sleeveless tunic, the cool garb most Vahrdmen preferred when not actively engaged in war.

Ayree was satisfied with the results. "You are a bit smaller than the average man grows where you're going, but you're muscular enough. My advice is that you try to pass for citybred. The women of Vahrd take their fun where they find it, especially in the ports. Children of foreign fathers aren't that rare. Don't rise to any challenges or get the idea that you're a warrior just because you're surrounded by warriors. The barracks' jests would kill you before you made it into battle.''

Galivert took a deep breath and tried to hide any sign of misgiving, unsuccessfully. "I've always wanted to travel. At least . . . I think I have. Will you—will you be sending me there by magic, my lord? Make one of those fly?" He pointed to the abandoned floor-rugs.

"As good a way as any. Stand on that one; it's got a Vairish design. You can sell it for a good price once you reach Vahrd."

"You can sell this, too." Senja removed her sash and remaining sword, pushing them both into Galivert's hands, ignoring his protests. "No one can match the steel I forge, not even in Vahrd. I ought to know; it's my wardland. You'll enjoy living there, Galivert."

"My lady, if it's your land, I hope I shall."

"I know you shall. Because I'm going with you." She linked arms with Galivert and steered him onto the rug Ayree had chosen. "Well, brother? Don't waste time. Fly us to Vahrd, why don't you?"

"Get off the rug, Senja." Ayree's voice was flat as a snake's stare. "He goes alone."

"I don't think so. Oh, you can lift me off this bit of weaving. You can hogtie me with spells or ropes or anything you choose until Galivert's long gone. I'm not questioning your powers, Ayree; I'm well acquainted with them. But you'd better learn something about mine: If you keep me from using them to help this man, I'll never use them to help you."

"You're not that great a fool, Senja," Lucha said. "I know you—you live for battle more than those barbarians you nursemaid. Throw aside the battle of your life for a man? And for *him?*" The lady of Vair laughed. "When this war is done, you can have your pick of any man in Vahrd. I've seen Vahrdmen." The way she said it left no doubt that the look had been long, close, and appreciative. "Would you lose a chance like that for a mortal like this? There's no comparison."

"Stay out of this, Lucha," Ayree said.

"I was only trying to help."

"I said, stay out of it. I have made my decision. He will come to Castle Snowglimmer—"

"Ha!" Senja did a little victory dance on the rug.

"—with the rest of us."

The Prince of Warlocks raised his hands. A cascade of water and sand flowed from his palms, a murky stream apparently without end. The Twelve watched, baffled, as a puddle of brine that smelled of long stagnation seeped up around the witch-king's feet. The tent began to shift place, its deep-driven poles and pegs losing hold in the newly sodden ground. The western side gave way first. Hodah threw up a warding spell to keep it from tumbling down entirely.

Ayree's mouth curved up, briefly. The grainy flow from his

hands ceased. He formed a double star with his hands and the toppling canvas walls disappeared. Salty air blew away the last phantom of his tent and all its furnishings.

Watery pink light clung to the treetops of the Naîmlo Wood, foretelling day. It was light enough for the Twelve to search the full compass of the horizon and mingle their cries with the harsh call of seabirds.

"Our tents are gone!"

"My trees! And where are the hives?"

"My roses grew so near Ayree's tent— Why can't I smell them?"

"I don't even smell my herbery, Lavah; or Zabala's ovens."

"Honeybread! I was baking ten loaves of it. If you can't smell them, and the wind coming from that quarter, then . . . Ayree, what have you done?"

"I had the forge hot, waiting for me." Senja completely forgot about Galivert, who remained standing on rough gray sand instead of a delicate silk rug. "That smell carries farther than any bread. Ayree, by all the gods, I swear—"

Senja did not get to finish her oath. The Prince of Warlocks said again, "To Castle Snowglimmer," and was gone. Galivert was gone with him.

By firstlight the Twelve found themselves staring at all their spellwork gradually sinking back into the strand. From the north came the terrified whickering of floundering horses.

Cursing, Menka soared into the dawn sky to rescue her herd. There was no debate about using magic freely now. One by one the others followed her, departing for the north until only Basoni and Hodah were left.

"Why?" Hodah asked. "Why did he have to destroy everything we'd done? It was like . . . a child's tantrum. From the moment our mother died, Ayree shaped our lives for one thing: Morgeld's unmaking. Look there, Basoni; look at Helagarde. I think I see our sealing spells growing brittle as glass. One touch of Morgeld's hand—even the crippled one—will break them."

For once Basoni resisted the pull of Helagarde, and she kept her eyes averted. "Ayree did nothing but let us see what we've done to ourselves, Hodah. We did it the moment we fell back into our old quarrels. We brought the new land forth together, and when our melded magics came apart, so did what we created. And if we'd made a spell to bind the changes . . . ? No; that, too, would have come undone when we divided against ourselves. We use powers that we don't fully understand, my sister. We created so much . . . and we destroyed it.''

''I am ashamed.'' Hodah turned her face to the north, the direction of Castle Snowglimmer. ''We should all be ashamed. But we can mend this rift. We can unite our powers again, come against Helagarde again—''

''Trap Morgeld napping again? Not likely. Come, Hodah, let's go home.''

The sisters took hands and rose on a seawind that soon took the shape of a skyblue wave. It rolled across the skies, bearing them on its crest, until they were lost beyond the northern horizon.

Where they had been standing, the ground gave a heave and a burp. Leaning what passed for his chin on his paw, The Demon of the Laidly Marshes watched them go. He fingered the muck around him thoughtfully. A company of mists began to seep from the shelter of the Naîmlo Wood and surrounded him before he could put his ruminations into words.

''Not bad,'' he said to the returning vapors. He pulled a flower from the ooze, one of the fast-sinking traces of what the Twelve had wrought before their linked powers frayed and came undone. The blossom, part of Lavah's tenderly cultivated gardens, was scarcely recognizable. He munched the limp stem thoughtfully. ''Not home yet, but near enough. Time'll mend what's lacking.'' He yawned and plunged into miry sleep under the sands.

From Helagarde came the sound of laughter.

Chapter VII

THE MEMORY

"He is gone, thrice gone! Banished, dead, forgotten!"
"Nay, Majesty. You lie poorly, for a queen."

—"The Parlay of Queen Nahrit and the Hetman"
from *The Scroll of Oran*

After ten weeks of silence and isolation from his sisters, Ayree sent for Basoni to come to his apartments. The messenger was one of her brother's soft-pawed winged cats, who presented the witch-king's summons on a tiny rolled strip of parchment held nicely between sharp teeth.

Basoni read the message and said, "I'll come as soon as I can."

She was studying a book about the wilder parts of Sombrunia—the foothills of the Senach Mountains, the broad stretches of the Dunenfels Plain—in the hopes of finding some key word or name that would waken Galivert's memory. The others of the Twelve were supposedly doing the same, each delving into the smallest details of life in her wardland.

Did the swineherds of Paxnon speak a secret argot known only to themselves? Sacchara would learn it, and try some of the phrases on Galivert. Did legend hint that the dour fishermen of Sumnerol worshipped a god whose name had been lost to all the other kingdoms? Resha would ferret it out and speak the hidden name where Galivert could hear. Even Fortunata had been forced to admit that there was more to her wardland of Clarem than the university city of Panomo-Midmists. She now studied book after dust-dry book about the weird hereditary patterns of basket

73

weaving in the villages near the junction of the Rivers Persa and Salmlis.

Even for Fortunata, it was boring work.

But you never knew what would strike a spark of recognition. Basoni closed her book reluctantly. She had learned little about Sombrunia that she didn't already know. Ayree's familiar mewed impatiently, oaring the air with its pied wings, then darted from Basoni's presence, flying eagerly back to its master.

Basoni went to Ayree's chamber at a more circumspect pace. He had made them all wait ten weeks for a word. Now he could wait a little. In the courtyard just outside his bedchamber she paused to circle the fountain, touching each of the silver deer once on the eyes, for luck.

Her fingers came away from the last emerald eye glowing with green light. Before the cry of surprise half left her lips, she heard Ayree's laughter; then the witch-king was beside her, folding his long white hands over her smaller ones.

"Did my jest frighten you? Forgive me." He released her hands from his, and when she opened them, a baby coney was warming her palms.

"How soft . . ." She raised it to her cheek, letting its golden fur caress her skin. She could feel the small nose quivering, never still, and smell clover on its breath. Cradling the little rabbit between her breasts, she followed Ayree into his bedchamber.

He offered her a comfortably cushioned chair and took the stool at her feet. "I have missed you, Basoni; you and the others."

"Then why did you stay away? We thought you were—" She paused, not wanting to repeat what Menka said the first night they were all back in Castle Snowglimmer.

"What did you think I was doing? Sulking?" He laughed at the effect that word had on her.

"Then why did you isolate yourself for ten weeks?"

"I didn't know that so much time had passed. You see, from the minute I returned to Snowglimmer with Galivert, I realized I'd been unjust to him. Anger blinds me too often, Basoni, but not for long. When I reconsidered matters, I saw that the five of you who insisted on keeping Galivert with us were right after all. It's a terrible thing to go into the world with nothing but a name. So at first I sent out many searching spells to try and find our guest's old life. It's easy to lose track of time when you are deep in magic."

Basoni was abashed. She had shared her sisters' sin of misjudging Ayree. At the same time, she felt a rising joy. She could hardly wait to tell the others, and she yearned for the mutual reconciliation that must come.

"And have you learned who Galivert is? Is that why you sent for me?"

Her brother's expression dashed all her hopes away. "I haven't searched every corner of the Twelve Kingdoms yet. You know that there are some places where our magic can't penetrate, but whether Galivert's life lies there or simply somewhere I haven't looked, it doesn't matter. I sent for you, Basoni, to warn you; and to have you warn the others."

"Warn us of what?"

"Of this."

A silver goblet set with red jasper appeared in the witch-king's hand. Red wine rained into it from the air, no sooner filling it than Ayree drained it in a single draught. One last drop gathered on the lip when he held the vessel upside down. It fell, and a blue cat with white wings sprang forward greedily to lap it up.

"Control, Tabrac," Ayree chided his familiar. "If you can't control your own desires, what will become of you?"

His smile was gone. He flung his empty goblet at a wall of air that shattered into silver and red fragments of light and shadow, bits of radiance that swirled into visions. Silver plucked distant, familiar faces into focus; wine flowed into the sleek limbs of galloping horses.

Menka and Galivert: She rode a white mare, unsaddled, unbridled; he rode a roan stallion accoutered like a prince's mount. Wrapped in fur-trimmed capes, they galloped laughing over the sunlit frosty plains.

Lavah and Galivert: In a drift of petal-colored robes she strolled with him through the purely ornamental garden she had planted beside the castle's outer wall. Her spells kept off the cold, made trees and bushes sweetly bloom, their many-colored splendors doubled by reflection in the ice wall of Snowglimmer. She stood under a featherbough and he shook the flowers down on her in a rosy rain.

Senja and Galivert: She spent hours telling him the bold tales of Vahrd, while sparks flew from the sword she hammered out for him, and the forge under Castle Snowglimmer cast sooty shadows over his rapt, handsome face.

Fortunata and Galivert: He questioned her endlessly on the ways of music and minstrels. Fortunata guided him into her treasured library, showed him the scrolls of old songs, taught him the fingering of the lute-minor. The first song that he made, he made for her.

Hodah and Galivert . . . There was no vision of the two of them; only Hodah sitting alone by a high tower window, embroidering her shield-device on a square of midnight blue cloth. It was night, with star and moon to illuminate her work. Her needle stitched the features of Galivert's face as precisely as if the man himself were in the tower chamber with her. And in a way, he was.

"When I emerged from my most recent search, I finally thought to see how long I'd been lost in magic." Ayree's voice was a knife that slashed the vision away. "As soon as I realized that nearly ten weeks had passed, I put on invisibility to see if all was well in Snowglimmer. I hoped to see that one of you had succeeded where I'd failed, for Galivert's sake." Another filled goblet—this one of unadorned glass—materialized in the witch-king's hand. "I saw more than I bargained for."

"They . . . love him." Basoni's voice shook. She saw love in only one guise—a shining god who left death in his wake and never looked back. Nothing in the Twelve Kingdoms or beyond was more terrifying, less comprehensible to her. Basoni feared deeply for her sisters, for her beloved Hodah most of all. And yet, there were times she wondered whether she were again merely fleeing dreamborne fears, Morgeld's handiwork. The distant past grew hazy, her mother's death a shadowplay long over. In Sombrunia she had met a nobleman of King Alban's court whose lips brushed fire from the hand he kissed. She had dreamed other dreams after she met Lord Cafran . . .

Ayree's voice shocked her back into the here-and-now, into the certainty that love was death's undying partner. Lord Cafran's handsome phantom vanished behind a mask of grinning bone.

"Yes, and why shouldn't they? He's a fine-looking man, well mannered, kind, intelligent . . ." Ayree saw Basoni's startled look, and how she hugged the baby coney more closely to her bosom. "What's troubling you?"

"I— This is the first time I've ever heard you speak well of someone who isn't witchborn or wizard."

"You're exaggerating." His fingers strayed up to stroke the little pet he had given her. "You've heard me praise other men without a scrap of magic to them: Mustapha, the animal-trainer who saved your life when you were a child; Alban, your Sombrunian king; that jolly little minstrel friend of his, Lymri

. . . Something else makes you tremble now, Basoni. Will you tell me?''

She shook her head violently.

Ayree did not insist. "Keep your secret, then. Snowglimmer has become a castle of secrets, some of which I have discovered.''

Wanting to change the subject, wanting to keep Ayree's attention diverted from her, Basoni asked, "If you think so highly of Galivert, why must we go through all this useless work to find him his true home? We could let him stay on here. It's been years since we had human servants.''

Her brothers silvery brows shot up. "A servant? Do you think those five would keep him so? Basoni, even for one so young, you are naive. And I . . .'' He sighed deeply. "I am very naive for one so old. Your sisters want a lover: That is why Galivert must go.''

Again love, and again a vision of her mother's death in the darkness. Her fingers knotted in the coney's silky fur until the small beast squirmed and she relaxed her hold. Still she said, "But if they all love him . . . how can he be lover to them all?''

"He can't. But if he remains in Castle Snowglimmer long enough, he will make a choice. He must be gone before then.''

"If he's such a fine man, what would be wrong . . . ?''

"A fine man, capable of begetting many children. You remember the Rule of Loss.''

Basoni did. Witchborn, she might control much, but never herself. Nothing a witchborn man or woman could do would prevent the conception of a witchborn child if the child was fated to be conceived; nothing their lovers could do to prevent it, either. They were only exempt from this law the first time they mated; after that, they had no choice. And if the child they begat or conceived was of a different sex from its witchborn parent, a measure of that parent's power would dissipate, lost forever. It was not even conserved in the child.

Basoni had been taught that lesson long ago, long before Ayree imagined, when her mother conceived a second son who stole the last measure of power keeping Charel alive. So it was fated: his death with hers.

"That is why I've kept such close watch over you and your sisters. No lover is worth the chance of your losing even a shade of your powers. The prophecy of the Tree must be fulfilled! The Twelve must be Morgeld's unmaking!''

He was on his feet suddenly, letting the glass goblet smash on the floor. His attendant familiars took to the air in a cloud of confusion, except for Tabrac who crouched to carefully lick up this unexpected windfall. The Prince of Warlocks strode to his spartan bed, the rude painting of the Tree of Second Light above it. Basoni had to rise from her place to see what he was doing. A touch, and the bed vanished. A second touch, and the heavy wooden panels of the painting swung back on hinges so smooth and discreet that they must have been jeweler's work.

The portrait of Janeela, the Silver One, filled the room with light.

"She gave up her life to put Morgeld in bonds that held him for centuries," Ayree said, his eyes on the mortal woman's painted eyes. "She gave up many things, all for the sake of holding him, buying time for the Twelve Kingdoms. When you hear the songs and legends of Janeela, they tell of her selflessness and her glory, but never of her pain. In one verse she sees what Morgeld will do to the Twelve Kingdoms, in the next she becomes his lover, and in the third she binds him, just like that!"

Ayree was no longer talking to her, Basoni knew. He spoke on, but his thoughts were somewhere else. His hands framed another face, smaller than the generous dimensions of the portrait, the size of life.

"No one ever wonders why she did it," he said. "No one cares what her life was before the decision, what she gave up, or what it would have been like if she had decided another way. No one knows what she went through, all those years that she was Morgeld's lover, the mistress of Helagarde. To the world she is Janeela, the Silver One, almost a goddess. But she was only a girl . . . a brave and lovely girl."

Ayree's face went abruptly cold. "If a mortal could give up so much to delay Morgeld, have I asked so much of the Twelve to unmake him? Why can't they wait, your sisters: Is the oldest of you *that* old? We can outlast time itself with our powers!"

Basoni set the coney down and opened her arms to her brother. He came to her like a rage-spent child. "Why?" he murmured into her hair. "Why can't they wait? Haven't I waited so much longer than they? Don't they know what they're risking? Oh, Basoni, if it weren't such an abominable thought, I could almost kill Galivert to save the Twelve for what they must do."

"But it is abominable, and you won't," Basoni said calmly. "Why don't you just send him away?"

Ayree regained control of himself and resumed his place at her feet, still holding her hand as the two of them sat down. "It wouldn't work. Your five lovestruck sisters would find him and bring him back. A searching spell sent after a specific person always works."

"Then send him away and put the banns of sorcery on him. Their spells can't penetrate that."

Ayree gazed at his youngest sister with deep fondness. "At least I have one ally. But I'm afraid our enemy is too strong for us."

"Galivert?"

"Your father. I discounted his influence, and now he's giving me a hard lesson about underestimating Krisli. I'll never dismiss the power of the human heart again. If I send Galivert away and hide him from all searching spells with the banns, your sisters will leave Castle Snowglimmer to find him without magic. I know they will, and the time lost that way will give Morgeld all the leisure he needs to strengthen himself against us, to try to cut the mortal branches of the Tree, even to attempt destroying ours."

"He couldn't . . ."

"He would only need to kill one of the Twelve to do it. Galivert nearly succeeded in doing that when he was still Morgeld's slave. If the five go seeking Galivert, will they be alert to anything but the search at hand? Five tempting targets, then."

Something moved the folds of Basoni's skirt. The baby coney poked its wiggling nose out into the air and looked up at Ayree with golden-brown eyes. The witch-king picked it up and gave it back to Basoni.

"What can we do?" she asked. The coney's heart beat like spring rain against her fingertips.

"I intend to go back to my searching spells, Basoni. I hope that when I find Galivert's true place there will be a wife or sweetheart waiting there for him. Menka, Lavah, Senja, Fortunata and Hodah can't complain if I settle him back where he belongs. They'll get over their infatuation. But you must help me. You must go back to them and warn them—remind them of the dangers love can bring to our kind. Oh, paint me in as the villain, if you think that will keep them from going too far. Make the worst threats you can imagine, in my name."

"They're already angry with you."

He stood and gave her his hand. She rose to accept a kiss. "Then they might as well fear me, too. Thank you, Basoni."

She left him staring at the portrait of Janeela.

Basoni had only gone as far as the courtyard when she stopped.

Could there be a spell to probe dreams? Galivert's sleeping mind might tell us more than Galivert awake. I'll ask Ayree.

She entered softly. The witch-king's bedchamber was very quiet, unusually so. She wondered whether Ayree were still there, or if he might have left the room by sorcerous means on some mission of his own.

He was there, kneeling on his bed like a worshipper before the fane of a vanished god, contemplating the painting. As Basoni was about to call his name, he raised one hand and traced the line of Janeela's cheek. It glowed, and the light softened to the rippling of water. The ripples filled the frame, washing away the painted face with the surge of a distant sea.

She heard her brother call on Sarai then, Sarai the mother of more than gods. Tears choked this invocation of greatest power, and Basoni was unable to do more than stand witness as her brother summoned vision.

A young man and woman swathed in hooded gray cloaks stood on the shifting sands of the Laidly Marshes. At first they stood so still that Basoni was unsure whether they were rock or flesh. A great darkness lay over all the marshland, shadows of a storm. The waves of the Lyarian Sea threw up huge gouts of spume when they crashed into shoreline rocks—rocks that had long since been ground to pebble and sand.

"Tell me that this is only a jest, Janeela. You cannot mean to seek him . . ."

"I made my decision long ago, Ayree." The woman turned and began to walk away. A haze of purple light shone through the mists, the cold call of Helagarde.

Ayree cried out in despair and seized her hand; he would not let her go. She paused and looked at him. "So you intend to hold me by force?" Her words were full of pity. "I know you can, but will you? For how long, Ayree?

"Until you come to your senses! Janeela, what are you thinking of? The gods? When have they ever thought of you?"

The man's hood fell back, and Basoni saw her brother's face, his starfall hair, and the blue eyes full of pain, pleading. He was not the all-powerful witch-king now. He was helpless, vulnerable, afraid.

The woman's face was still in the shade of her hood, but Basoni was grateful for that. The beauty of Janeela, the Silver One, was legend. A legend was infinite, ever-changing, ideal. Each person who heard the tale might shape Janeela's beauty to his desires, bounded only by his own imagination. But to see the woman as she really was put limits on the legend. She might still be fair to see, but the loveliness of flesh was so much less than the loveliness of a dream.

Janeela's hand caressed Ayree's cheek. "Not for the gods," she said. "The Twelve Kingdoms gird for war with the night-spirit's son. War . . . We mortals have dwelled with the gods, and the peace of the gods. Are we fit for battle with demons? It would be a war of lambs and wolves. It is not yet time to fight Morgeld openly; even I know that." Her hand dropped to her side. "I will buy us time. I cannot strike him down, but I will try to contain him while the Twelve learn war."

Ayree's voice was tender as a boy's. "I won't let you do it . . . Let the Twelve Kingdoms meet their fate! I will take you far from here, to where the stars ride and rule, to where dwell greater beings than the gods! I will take you with me by force if you won't come willingly!" The falseness of the threat made his words shake.

Janeela smiled and kissed him deeply. His long white fingers clutched her to him with desire, and the terror of loss. "You cannot stop anything. You can only delay. The gods have made us alike, Ayree, though you are witchborn and more than witchborn, and I am only mortal. Perhaps that is why I love you; why I always will love you."

He pressed her hands to his face again. His fear was naked in his eyes. "He will kill you. If you succeed, if you make him love you, if you betray him, he will kill you, Janeela! And then I will have to kill him."

"No . . . " The Silver One shook her head gently. "You will not be the one. And you must not endanger your life, for if you die, who will remember me as I truly was?"

The waves of light rushed in to sweep the scene away. They ebbed into a new seeing—brief, grievous: Against the dimmed light of Helagarde, a white-haired man walked across the sands, the body of a woman in his arms.

"Now you know what drives me, Basoni." Ayree's voice was a shock that wrenched her free of the vision. He stood before her, though she had not been conscious of the moment when he left his bed. The moving light in the frame above it settled back into the lines and shades of Janeela's painted face.

"I—I didn't mean to—"

"To spy on me?" He rested his hands on her shoulders. "To

see me as I was then? Does it lessen me in your eyes, little sister?"

Basoni spoke sincerely. "Nothing could do that."

"So you say."

The young witch looked back at the portrait, but the hinges had closed. She saw only the painting of the Tree. "So that is why you are so eager for ours to be the branch that destroys him." Many things made more sense to her now. "Revenge. That was why you sent us against Helagarde so quickly, when the final spell wasn't—"

"Yes." He did not let her finish. "Revenge made me act rashly, I fear; too rashly. May the gods forgive me for it. Now you see why your sisters' infatuation for Galivert concerns me so much: I know how strong a passion can be, how uncontrollable."

His hands slid down her arms and dropped back to his sides. "Do you see how easily I confess it to you, Basoni; all my weakness? My hunger for Morgeld's destruction that sometimes makes me lose sight of good sense. It's a sorry flaw. It's a worse one than having a poor head for wine. It must come from my mortal blood. Oh yes, I have a measure of that, too! Why do you think I mistrust the mortal branches of the tree so much? They are as riddled with human flaws as an old stump with wood-worms. They are too weak, too vulnerable."

Basoni's lips parted to protest, but Ayree laid his cool fingers across them. "Do I speak of mortals too harshly for you? It is only because I am older, and I know what a cruel world this is we have been given. I fear for the magicless. Their defenses seem so frail beside ours!" He lowered his hand. "So. Now that you have seen all this, which of our sisters will be the first to hear?"

"None. I will keep silent, I promise you."

The witch-king smiled. "If any of the Twelve had to learn my secret, I am glad it was you. Now I know that I was not mistaken in loving you best of all." He glanced over his shoulder at the painting. "Sometimes, when I am alone, I summon that vision deliberately."

Basoni held the coney with one hand and slipped the other into her brother's. "Why? It must be painful for you."

"Often we need the memory of pain to urge us on. These past weeks have tired me. When I grow weary of the struggle, I must force myself to remember the cause of it all, recall it in every detail. I open old wounds so that I will never forget who made them. You speak of pain, but you have only seen a little of the story. I pray you never learn more. Please leave me now, little one. I am rested, and must go back to seeking Galivert's past.''

"Ayree, I came back because I had a thought. Could we discover Galivert's past from his dreams? Is there such a spell?''

"You are as clever as you are dear. Yes, there is such a spell. It allows the seeker limited access to a man's dreams. I thank the gods for such limits! If we could not keep some inner corner of ourselves safe from prying eyes, this would be a world of madmen.''

"Then use it on Galivert!''

"I have tried. I have found nothing. He does not dream, or else he is one who guards his inner self well. There are men like that. I will continue to search out our guest's secrets by other means. Don't trouble yourself over it, Basoni.'' He kissed her on the brow and bade her farewell.

As she wandered back to her room, the coney snuggling against her breast, an idea struck her. Galivert was a good man—hadn't Ayree said so himself?—and reasonable. If he knew what was at stake, perhaps he would part from Castle Snowglimmer voluntarily.

I'll promise him refuge at the royal court of Sombrunia, Basoni thought. *He'll be an honored guest. And as soon as possible, I'll use every bit of my power to search out his real life. If he'll only tell my sisters that he's leaving Snowglimmer because he wants to, it will be all right. They can't claim to love him and then stand in the way of his wishes. And they* will *get over it.*

Full of confidence, Basoni went looking for Galivert.

Chapter VIII

THE TRYST

"Do you give me reasons when I give you love?"

—"The Queen's First Plea"
from *The Scroll of Oran*

Snow fell from a murky gray sky over Castle Snowglimmer, and a harsh wind threw darts of ice against the palace's glassy walls. Those who enjoyed such spectacles could watch the storm from a window or from the castle battlements. But for those who sought tranquility, there were the gardens.

Wind, snowfall, and sky alike might as well have existed in another world. The inmost gardens of Castle Snowglimmer were roofed with ancient magic, spells that painted an unending succession of fabulous scenes against the all-encompassing dome—sometimes the loves of the gods, sometimes mortal affairs both comic and serious, sometimes the movements of distant stars and worlds without number or name. The only reality that could seep through the great shield was the sun itself.

These gardens were older than Ayree. The spells that had made them were so old and had endured for so many centuries that credulous men claimed here was proof that magic was eternal.

Magic was not; the source of magic was, and that source had been well used to create a place of mystic beauty where plants of every Kingdom grew in all weathers, ever safe from storm or season. Here the different plants also crossbred into fabulous new forms, frond and flower and fruit to be found nowhere else in the world. When the Twelve had been young, their yearly expedition to call up the spring in their special vale was a weak imitation of

84

what had been begun here, in the gardens of Snowglimmer where Basoni now found Galivert.

He sat on a green malachite bench carved in the shape of three small hedgehogs carrying a smooth golden crescent moon on their prickles. Werejuice vines, heavy with their swollen blue-black berries, found good climbing up and around the hedgehogs. Galivert was alone, a cluster of the ripe fruit in his hand. Basoni came near with a light step, but he heard her.

"My lady Basoni!" He rose happily to welcome her. "I've been lonely here, hoping for someone to come by."

She let him seat her beside him on the hedgehog bench. "I wish I were bringing you better news, Galivert."

"It's good enough news if you're here. I don't see as much of you as I'd like." He plucked a single berry from the cluster in his hand and was on the point of popping it into his mouth.

"Galivert! No!" Basoni struck the fruit away so sharply that her pet coney leaped from her grasp in fright, scampering for cover in the undergrowth. To his shocked stare she replied, "Eat nothing you pick here."

"Why?" Galivert studied the remaining berries in his hand. "Are these poisonous?"

"Those are werejuice berries. They won't kill you, but they affect the muscles, causing convulsions that make you look as if you're becoming a monster. When the fit ends, your face and body will remain frozen in mid-spasm."

"Whew." Galivert dropped the fruit and crushed the juice from it with his foot. "I've had enough of monstrous forms for a lifetime. Is everything that grows here like that? I thought I recognized plain raspberry bushes over there, by the fountain behind the trees."

He pointed off to the left where a stand of slender trees made a parti-colored barricade with their green and silver trunks, their gold and orange leaves. The sound of sweet water splashing in thin streams came from behind that natural screen.

"Well, they may look like ordinary raspberries," Basoni said. "They may even be ordinary raspberries. But don't eat them unless you've spoken to one of us first. Many of the plants growing here have changed. Even I amn't always sure about which are safe and which aren't."

Galivert chuckled. "So all the tales of witches' gardens are true: death—and worse—hidden by pretty flowers and luscious fruits."

Basoni laughed, too. She felt quite at ease with this charming man, and no longer uncertain about making her plea that he leave Castle Snowglimmer for Sombrunia. There was something about the way he looked at her, the innate chivalry of his every gesture that said, *Ask me for anything and I will do it, all for your happiness.*

She pushed a long lock of hair back behind her ear. "It's too bad that those witch-tales seem to run through all the Kingdoms. Otherwise we'd have a clue there to where you come from. I'm sorry, but we still have no idea—"

"Do you think I care?"

Her smile faded. His voice had changed, the transformation leaping out at her. So deep it was, so serious, so intense and unexpected that she was momentarily stunned. He leaned closer to her on the bench, and she felt his hands touch her robes very lightly, biding.

"I don't want to leave," he said. His new voice held her immobile more securely than his hands yet dared. "Whatever my life was out there, I don't want to have it back. I want to stay here, Basoni. With you."

"Galivert, you can't . . ." His hands had come to rest now, one on her shoulder, one on her lap. Their touch was still light, but she sensed that this would change. "We have no place for magicless mortals here," she lied.

"Where, then? The Twelve Kingdoms are wide. You and I can find a place somewhere. Where? Where can we be together? Basoni, why do you turn away from me? Am I still a demon in your eyes? Or have I just frightened you by what I've said? My lady . . . my lovely lady, witchborn eyes don't always see everything. I wanted to speak to you many times, but we were never alone. And now that we are . . . I can't let this chance go by; it's all coming out too fast, but it's true. You must hear the truth of it. I love you, Basoni. Don't be afraid to hear that."

The hand on her shoulder grew heavier, the other stole up to complete the embrace. Basoni stiffened, her first desire to flee, her pride not letting her, and her fear stealing her wits.

This is how it begins . . . Oh, Mother! Mother, help me escape your fate!

"Look at me, my love, my lady. Look at me . . ."

She looked, and saw great power burdening the air around Galivert. His eyes held hers with their dark strength, and all resistance drained from her bones. Her arms encircled him without her consent, her body melted against his. The feeling was too potent, too terrifying. She had seen such power emanating from another figure, but her father wore his force like a warm, fiery shadow. What clung to Galivert was a stormcloud's chill promise of destruction.

And as lightning will suddenly lick from the black cloud holding it, a gleam of amethyst fire blinked in the depths of Galivert's eyes.

"A nice picture!"

Basoni and Galivert sprang away from each other with the force of a bursting milkweed pod. Ten steps away, Menka, Lavah, and Senja stood glaring at the pair of them. The slender trees that concealed the fountain had concealed the three sisters as well. Basoni saw the path they had kicked through the fallen gold and orange leaves.

"You little slut." Senja spoke those words without accusation or surprise, merely realization.

"Should we tell Ayree what his pet does to occupy her free time?" Lavah tittered, covering her mouth with a folded silk fan. "That would roust him out of his den."

"Let him keep to himself. He'd only find some excuse for her. He always does." Menka folded her arms across her chest. "We can handle this ourselves."

"What's there to handle? A whore sets her own prices in Vahrd, and collects what's coming to her. Well, Basoni?" Senja still spoke in that awful, matter-of-fact tone.

"Shut up! I've done nothing—" She tried to stand, but Galivert seized her arm and held her back.

"My ladies, please, you must understand . . ."

For once his entreating eyes missed the mark. "Save your explanations for Fortunata," Menka said. "She's the one who collects fairytales."

Lavah giggled again, a strained, artificial sound.

"You have no right to speak to me like this," Basoni cried. "Sarcasm and name calling when it's all envy! *You* want him! It's made you stupid; it's blinded you to what can happen if this man does become your lover."

"I'm sure you'll tell us all about that," Lavah purred. "From experience."

Menka regarded Basoni with a look of quiet disgust. Lifting her chin, Basoni met that look with defiance.

"You haven't done a thing to find out where Galivert comes from; not in all the time we've been back home." She spoke boldly, backed by the knowledge Ayree's visions had granted her. "You want to keep him here. I'm not your rival: I don't want him! If you do, at least have the wisdom to wait a while— just a little while longer, until . . .''

Menka's backhanded slap took her entirely by surprise. It was a hard blow that made her stumble and snapped her head painfully to the left.

With subdued fierceness, Menka said, ''Don't preach wisdom to me. You don't want Galivert? I see through you, Basoni. You want everything; for Sombrunia, everything. And I know why. Did you so enjoy Sombrunia's lord—that young, handsome man on the throne of your wardland? Not all of us had your good fortune. My land's king, Elberd Far-reach, didn't show much enthusiasm. I had to steal the shape of one of his squires. But Alban of Sombrunia— How many times have you risked the Rule of Loss to share his bed? And would it matter to you if you did conceive a son of his? The Tree of Second Light holds two prophecies. If we fail, the glory of Morgeld's unmaking will go to Sombrunia. What a pretty lover's gift for you to give your Alban.''

''A whore and a traitor, too?'' Senja lifted one brow. ''How ambitious of you, Basoni.''

''Stop it! It's not true!'' In spite of herself, Basoni burst into tears. Between jagged, angry sobs she repeated, ''Not true! It's not true!''

Galivert tried to take her into his arms but Basoni shoved him away. She heard Lavah's grating laugh again, and Senja saying something about how all whores made great actresses. There was an aching hollow in her chest. She covered her face with her hands and turned away from all of them.

She felt Galivert reach for her a second time, but she sidestepped his touch. Menka was saying, ''Poor Galivert. She used you, didn't she?'' Then footsteps came running along the bluestone garden path, slim hands took her by the shoulders, spun her around, and Hodah's scent enveloped her as surely as her beloved elder sister's arms.

''You ought to be ashamed!'' Hodah blazed with rage, keeping herself between Basoni and the rest. ''This is our sister! You'd treat a stranger better than this!''

''Any stranger would deserve better,'' Menka returned. ''Our baby sister's taken a new lover. Surprising; she wasn't a greedy child. Alban Stonesword should be enough for any woman.''

''A *new* lover?'' Hodah blinked in amazement. ''A first lover, you mean.''

"All right, if you want to quibble: her first lover since the Sombrunian king."

Basoni wiped the tears away in time to see Hodah smile. "Her first lover. Her first and only. Menka, my dear, there are some things you don't know."

Menka became confused. "Her *first?* But she came of age years ago. She accepted the wardship of Sombrunia . . ."

"And that is *all* she did." In a softer voice, Hodah asked, "Basoni, you confided in me. Do you mind if I speak of this?"

Basoni shook her head. Her lesser secret didn't seem important now.

"You can't mean she's still a virgin?" Senja was blunt.

"If you have no objections," Hodah replied sweetly.

"But— How can she be wardlady of Sombrunia if . . . ?"

"Oh, come now, Senja. We have been the wardladies of the Twelve Kingdoms from birth. Nothing was needed to seal the pact. We learned the Rule of Loss as soon as Ayree could pound it into our heads, but we also learned that the only time we wouldn't run the risk of conceiving a child was the first time. No law said we had to share that first time with the rulers of our wardlands. Let's thank Menka for that. You've always been fond of the grand, poetic gesture and the fantasies that go with it, haven't you, Menka? The lord of your wardland at your feet, so grateful for the honor you bestow on him. Except it didn't work out that way."

Menka went red but said nothing.

Hodah, still smiling, added, "You had to put a good face on your humiliation, didn't you? You got the satisfaction of misleading the rest of us into sharing your error: all except Basoni." She ran one hand over Basoni's hair.

Menka snorted loudly and stalked off. Senja and Lavah looked at one another and likewise left the gardens.

"They won't apologize," Hodah said, "but they'll have a word or two with Menka, believe me."

Meekly Galivert approached the sisters. "My lady Hodah, I can't thank you enough—"

"Never mind. Basoni is . . . very special to me. Make her happy." A thread of ice seared Basoni's cheek as Hodah disappeared.

"Where did she go?" Galivert wondered. "Why did she take off like that?"

His questions went unanswered. In a murmur of timeworn words, Basoni sent a searching spell after her sister and slid into the plane where witches fly when they bypass the limits of space, following the spell's trajectory. She stepped out of the air into Hodah's room and saw her sister stretched out on her bed, weeping.

Basoni knelt beside her. "You do love him," she breathed. "You love him, too."

Hodah tossed her head. Her face was damp and hot, her sidelocks pressed to flat curls against her cheeks. The motherly mask she had worn in the gardens was gone. "Why do you care? It's you he wants. You—who never speak two words to him!"

"I *don't* want him."

"So you say."

"I mean it."

Hodah didn't seem to hear. "Why you? I'm the one he owes his life to. I freed him from that demon's skin. I nursed him when we brought him back to camp. What have you ever done for him?" She started crying again. "Leave me alone! I gave him to you . . . I gave him the way I always gave everything to you! Now take him and leave me alone!"

Basoni heard Resha's words in her mind. *When the wound's too deep for herbs to cure, that's when the knife's needed.* She rose from Hodah's bedside. "I'm going to fetch Ayree."

Hodah stopped crying at once. "What for?"

"Something's wrong here; something about Galivert. I felt it when I was near him. If he were witchborn or wizard, I'd know what to call it and I wouldn't be afraid, but he's only a man. Hodah, he chills me! I don't want anything to do with him, I never did. And yet . . . when I was with him . . ."

"Why not stop lying to yourself, Basoni? You did want him! What's more, he wants you."

"Can't you understand? Something forced me to want him! It's the same thing that's making you cry for his love. Something I can't name clings to Galivert—" She gave up trying to explain and tried to go for Ayree.

Hodah was out of her bed, standing between Basoni and the door. "And Ayree will remove it? He'll destroy Galivert first! That would please you. You're a cold creature, Basoni, nothing could chill you any colder than you already are. You know nothing of love except that you fear it; you fear it the way you fear anything that would steal a sliver of your precious self-control. You love to command everything, even yourself. You'd give Ayree the excuse he needs to be rid of Galivert—a little accident while he searches the man for this 'something' you

claim clings to him? Spells that probe the mind can be dangerous, and they can slip . . .''

"Hodah, I don't want Galivert harmed.''

"Neither do I. And I will prevent it.''

She was gone in another whisk of ice.

When Basoni attempted to follow her this time, she found the
way barred. The banns of sorcery lay thin across Hodah's track.
Soon they would crumble, but they would be there until the
unseen trail had cooled. Basoni could try to find her sister by
ordinary methods in the meantime, though she could hope for
little luck there. She was not the only one of the Twelve capable
of invisibility.

She decided not to try. Hodah could move swiftly in the planes
where witchly flight shared a cautious border with the realm of
the night spirits. Hodah would not linger in Castle Snowglimmer,
and Basoni had no wish to try following her if she had gone into
the white wastes beyond the castle. Too many old fears haunted
the snow.

Something sleek caught Basoni's eye. It was a square of deep
blue cloth, rumpled in with the blankets on Hodah's bed. She
picked it up and smoothed it out. The warrior infant's insolent
glance met hers, his face the same face it had been in Ayree's
vision.

A point of violet silk showed among the brown threads forming his eyes, a hint of purple light that should not be.

Basoni crumpled up the embroidery work and touched it with
fire. She held it suspended in midair until the last ember was ash,
then went in search of the others.

It was nearly time to dine. She found them in the hall where
the long black table stood. Ayree sat in his proper place, attended
by four of his familiars including the tipsy Tabrac. All her sisters
were present, even Hodah. Their looks were inscrutable. It was
impossible to tell what sort of welcome Ayree had received,
or if he had paused to accept one. Other matters occupied him
now.

"Where has he gone?" Ayree demanded. No one answered.
"The man was a guest in our house. He can't have vanished!"

Basoni looked sharply at Hodah. The wardlady of Glytch gave
her a smug smile.

Ayree pursued the subject of Galivert's whereabouts for a
time, then dropped it. He announced that he had always suspected that mortals who lived without the stabilizing influence of
magic and its fixed laws were flighty as sparrows. Galivert's

abrupt leavetaking confirmed his opinion and should serve as a moral lesson for the Twelve. The meal that followed was served and eaten in silence. Fortunata, Menka, Senja, and Lavah all seemed to have lost their appetites.

When dinner was over, Ayree beckoned for Basoni to stay behind. "Where is he?" he asked quietly.

"I don't know."

"Oh. I thought . . . It doesn't matter. Basoni—" He started to say something, stopped, passed one palm over the other. A small, strangely misshapen object veiled with a bit of brown velvet appeared. Sorrow in his eyes, he removed the coverlet.

Basoni looked, then squeezed her eyes tight shut, but she had seen the horror already. An overwhelming sickness swept over her. Tiny body twisted into an unnatural contortion, eyes wide and nose distended so radically that it was a miracle it could still breathe, the baby coney lay shaking in Ayree's hand. The dark stains of werejuice smeared the fur around its mouth.

"They would never eat such things on their own, the little creatures," the witch-king murmured sadly. "They are wiser than we are at scenting evil. Wisdom isn't always enough."

Basoni took the little creature from him and cradled it to her, speaking words of healing. These ended with a touch: the spasmed limbs relaxed. But the ordeal had been too much for it. Its heart leaped once against her breast, then stopped. She looked to Ayree as grief took her.

"That was why I didn't heal it myself when Tabrac brought it to me. Don't cry, Basoni," he said, hugging her. "We are rid of him now. He won't cross the threshold of Snowglimmer again, I promise. And when I can, I will send a searching after him—"

"No. Don't look for him again. Good riddance to him. Let him be gone forever."

Ayree hugged her more closely. "He is, Basoni; he is."

"Is it done?" Galivert raised himself on one elbow from the pile of skins and made his demand with all the authority of a king.

The caped and hooded woman came into the trapper's lodge and sank to her knees opposite the *lir*, the cookfire blazing up between them. "Done," she said, her voice strangled with misery and shame. "Though why it had to be done at all . . . when I have given you all this . . ." Her arms swept out to include the well-appointed lodge and all it contained.

"Stop crying. We have no use for tears, you and I." He offered no comfort.

Hodah shook her head feebly. "I have betrayed so much for your love, Galivert. I've even betrayed myself. The coney . . . I recall the first time I saw one. I was very young, riding to the stag hunt with King Ottal of Glytch. The king thought I was just another of his court ladies. I chose to hide my identity until I could see what manner of man ruled my wardland. Much was at stake . . . You can never understand how much. There was a stand of bracken. The horses plunged through. The coney sprang from covert. It was under the hooves of the huntsmen's steeds, and I saved it. I dropped my disguise and plucked it to safety by magic. A life . . . a new life . . . nothing more full of promise, more sacred to me, and yet now . . . Why did I listen to you, Galivert? Why did I kill that helpless creature? Is that what love is, in the end? Is it only betrayal?"

In the face of her despair, Galivert changed his tone. Gently, persuasively, he said, "It was hard for you, my dear one. Don't I know how hard? Dry your eyes, love. It pains me to see you so."

"Then why did you make me do it?" she wailed.

Softly he replied, "So that you might blame me for something you would have done anyway."

Hodah was dumbstruck. Galivert gave her a rueful smile. "Love is betrayal, my sweet, just as you say. But its treachery is twofold when love is true. We lose our selves in each other's minds and hearts, fears and desires. I love you, and so I read your soul, and saw how much you longed to strike out at your sister. I could almost hear your spirit shouting its need. I gave you the excuse."

"To—to harm Basoni? I—I never could—"

Hodah stopped her protests. The truth came to her and she was too weary to deny it. "Yes," she said. "Yes, I wanted to hurt her, to make her sorry, to have her pay for my own hurts! When I thought she would be the one to have you, and I wanted you so much, so very much—!"

"Hush." His smile was the most entrancing thing she had ever seen, his voice wine. "No one but you shall ever have me."

Galivert was on his feet. He came around the fire to kneel behind her, his breath warm in her ear, his voice still full of that same hypnotic power that had drawn her to him against her will.

No, that was a lie. If she had wanted to resist him, she could have done so. Her little Basoni had fought away from his spell, but she—she wanted to surrender. She sought it. She was sick inside, hollow for too long, yearning for the promises of love and new life that cried out to her from every living thing she saw. The source of her special power was the source of her weakness, and she had struggled against it for too long.

Let mortals undo Morgeld! They would be the ones to suffer most under his rule, not the witchborn. Why should she sacrifice so much for their sake? She had given away enough of her life, too much. Now she wanted to take, and there was something in Galivert's eyes that urged her on.

He pulled back her hood. His hands were warm on her face, brushing tears aside with smooth fingertips. His lips closed gently on her neck, and all her thoughts were meaningless mind noise as sensation alone commanded.

"Don't cry, my lovely Hodah," he whispered. He pulled her into his embrace, teased the werejuice stains from her fingers and palms with his tongue. Held entranced, Hodah never noticed how the poisonous juice had no effect on him. All that mattered for her was his smile. "Don't cry. You have proved yourself to me, and what is one small life to that? To the proof of love?"

A stranger inside her agreed, consented, and fell into his arms.

Chapter IX

THE SECRET

Love comes unasked to many feasts,
And death to many more,
Yet come when asked they seldom will
Though all the gods implore.

—"The Wandering Infant's Song"
from *The Scroll of Oran*

King Ottal, lord of the small kingdom of Glytch, laid the letter
aside and covered his eyes as most folk will who have seen
something that pains them. His courtiers dared to whisper speculations as to what that letter contained. A man in the livery of
good Duke Emtrans had brought it—that much was no secret—
but matters concerning Duke Emtrans' family were always food
for gossip.

How such a father could have sired such a son . . .

Two such different sons, you mean.

No, for there's no wonder in the duke's elder son. He is the
mirror of his father, and there's not a better man in the kingdom.
But his other son, Tor—

Hush. Tor is long gone from this land. May he never return!

No one returns from serving the master he *chose.*

Hush. To name him is to conjure him.

King Ottal raised his head wearily. "Duke Emtrans is dying,"
he said. The courtiers ceased their muffled gossip. Some mumbled useless hopes that it was not so, others expressed equally
useless wishes that he might have an easy death. The wisest kept
still, knowing that their hopes and wishes for good or ill would
not touch Duke Emtrans' death when it came for him.

"He has made one last request," the king went on. He was no longer young, and thoughts of his good vassal's deathbed put him in mind of his own. He would not deny Duke Emtrans anything now, not for the sake of the kingdom itself.

"He asks that our wardlady, the witch Hodah, be with him when he dies." King Ottal folded the letter and passed it to his steward. He rose from the throne and gave the command dispatching a runner to the turret room where the wardlady of Glytch was housed with honor whenever she deigned to visit her land.

King Ottal forgot his sorrow for a moment when Hodah came into the court. Her beauty was unchanged after all the years that he had known her, but that was often the way with the witchborn. He still recalled that single night of love she had shared with him, never to be repeated, made more precious by its singularity. Every time he looked at her, even dressed in the shapeless blue and silver gown she favored these days, he recalled slender limbs and downcast blue eyes, golden hair and ivory skin that shone like harvest moonlight in the darkness of his curtained bed.

Once, and never again. Other memories were less pleasant: how he had pleaded with her to return; how she had spoken to him like an infinitely patient mother giving her child excellent, hated reasons why he can't have what he desires; how he had offered her all that honor allowed: a throne beside his, a queen's crown, a prince's cradle for their children.

That last had held her for a bit . . . the cradle. There was great longing in her eyes as she gazed into the gemmed and gilded cradle where the kings of Glytch first dreamed of milk and warmth and love, not crown and scepter and power.

But she had said no at last, and explained why, and left him brokenhearted.

Time, which had aged King Ottal and was about to claim Duke Emtrans, had not touched her. She approached the throne with slow grace and settled into a deep curtsey before the king. He told her of the duke's request.

"Of course," Hodah said. "I will go to him at once. Will Your Majesty be kind enough to summon a litter?"

"For you?" The king was puzzled. "Wouldn't it be faster if you flew, my lady?"

"It's not so far to Duke Emtrans' castle, Your Majesty. Flight is faster, yes, when the way is clear. But the paths that we witchborn take are like your roads: we must sometimes share them with other traffic, and that slows us down or holds us up altogether. I'd prefer to attend Duke Emtrans by a more depend-able way. Your men-at-arms can clear the road to his castle for me if they must, but no one can clear the invisible paths of air."

Everything she said was so reasonable. The king called for the finest royal litter and the best horses to bear it. He himself rode beside it all the way to Duke Emtrans' castle.

The good duke lay comfortably in his bed. He did not look particularly ill or unhappy. Only the sight of his wife, his son, and his daughter-in-law weeping beside the great bed gave any sign that an unwelcome guest would soon arrive.

In the corridor outside the death-chamber the duke's three grandsons clung to their nurse, too scared to ask questions. When they saw the royal party come sweeping up the hall toward them, the gloriously beautiful wardlady herself in the van, they pressed themselves to the wall with their nurse's skirts held up around them for shelter.

They were wrong if they thought to avoid notice that way. The nurse tugged her skirts away and plopped to the floor the minute she saw King Ottal and Glytch's lady. The old duke's grandsons were left defenseless. Hodah paused at the door that King Ottal held open for her and turned to stretch out a hand to the cowering children.

"Why do you hide, little ones? Are you afraid of me?"

The eldest of the three found the inner strength to give her a hard look. "We're not afraid, but we aren't stupid. We don't want you to kill us, too."

Gathering courage, the middle boy added, "*Someone* has to rule the dukedom after Grandfather dies. Our father's in there with him. You might take him, too, when you take Grandfather."

Hodah shook her head. "I take no one."

"Yes, you do." The eldest would not be swayed. "I over-heard Father telling Mother so. He said that when a good man dies, one of the Twelve takes his spirit. Otherwise it wanders all over the world, looking for its way home."

"That's partly true," Hodah said. "But we don't take anyone; we guide. In fact, it isn't even necessary for one of us to guide a good man's spirit after death."

"Grandfather thinks so," the youngest piped up. "That's why he sent for you."

Hodah lost a little color. "Such a good man as your grandfa-ther doesn't need me."

"He doesn't think he's *that* good," the eldest said. "*We* do, but he doesn't."

"My lady." King Ottal was mildly urgent. "The duke is waiting."

Hodah's smile was stiff as she took her place by the duke's bedside. His family made way for her, falling back into the shadows as if they had no right to be present. The duke did not look his years, but when she took his hand she felt the weakness there.

"I am here, my lord duke," she said. "King Ottal has come, too."

"It was good of you to come, my lady," Duke Emtrans said. His voice was still firm, though here and there Hodah could detect a slight shiver. He turned his head to smile at King Ottal, who stood at the other side of his bed. "Your Majesty is kinder than I deserve."

Gruffly the king said, "You have always been a good vassal, a fine man—"

The duke cut him off with a sad shake of his head. "I have done great wrongs, Your Majesty. You know as well as I that it's true. And yet . . . death makes me bold enough to ask our dear wardlady for one last favor."

Hodah remained silent, her fingers tightening on Duke Emtrans' hand. The dying man noticed neither the increasing pressure nor the silence.

"I have heard all the teachings of what waits for evil men after death. And Helagarde stands in plain sight beside the Lyarian Sea."

He spoke ruefully, thinking of his lost son who had chosen Helagarde's grim halls while he was still alive. The duke blamed himself for Tor's choice. Surely there must have been something he might have done to prevent his proud-stomached younger boy from taking such an evil path! Some word he might have said, some deed he might have done . . . or not done. He would never be certain, and that was the black phantom which haunted his deathbed, casting all the rest of his life into an abyss of worthlessness. And was Tor yet alive? The duke and his lady wife didn't know.

"It's harder to imagine where the blameless spirits go," he went on. "Oh, we have our tales of ghosts, but even ghosts find a final resting place eventually. And so, my lady"—he tried to return Hodah's handclasp and failed—"if there was ever any merit to my life, now I ask you to take my spirit to whatever home awaits it."

"My lord duke, there's no need for that. A man like you needs no guide but confidence to reach Sarai's realm." She spoke quickly, her smile becoming even more brittle.

"But I am afraid, my lady. I am not confident. I feel responsible for what my son became. My other son." Tears trickled down his cheeks to stain the white lawn pillowslip.

"Nonsense!" Hodah spoke a little too brightly. She felt the incredulous stares of the duke's family and King Ottal as soon as she uttered that fantastic chirp. In desperation she chattered on, trying to cover one wrong word with a score. Her heart ached to give that good man some stronger comfort, but it was that same heart which had betrayed her, robbed her of the power to ease the duke's passing. She had played the fool, and now it was only fitting that she gabbled like one. "You will find your own way to Sarai's realm. You mustn't be afraid, or your spirit will suffer for it. Why should I guide you where you can take yourself? You mustn't think of your son's fate, but only believe—"

She was still babbling when his spirit slipped away.

The old duke's wife stepped forward and took her husband's hand from Hodah's grasp. King Ottal leaned across the bed to close the dead man's eyes. The new duke spoke respectfully but coldly to the wardlady of Glytch.

"I think you had better leave."

In the corridor, the old duke's grandsons watched, astonished, as the regal witchborn lady fled past them, crying like a whipped child.

A mournful ghost lingered beside the the three little boys, misty fingers seeping through their thick, black hair. Then it shuddered and drifted off, seeking a promised path it did not believe it ever deserved to find.

Chapter X

THE UNMASKING

"It is a well-known fact in my land, Your Majesty, that no man may keep a chaste wife and no woman keep a secret."
"Such wisdom merits reward. Take this man out and cut his head off, that his ears need never be offended by overhearing what dolts we are here."

—"The Ambassador's Miscalculation"
from *The Scroll of Oran*

Basoni and Tabrac played at toss-stones in the anteroom of Ayree's minor library. Gambling was the blue-and-white familiar's fourth favorite weakness, and it was hard to find a game at which he didn't cheat. Ever since Ayree had closeted himself in the smaller bookroom with the wizard Paragore-Tren, leaving instructions for Basoni and his familiars to wait outside, the rest of the winged cats had busied themselves with useful little chores to pass the time.

Tabrac had produced a set of toss-stones and an appealing look.

Zabala came in bearing a baker's dozen of seedcakes on a tray. "Don't play with that one," she advised. "He cheats."

"What, this old darling?" Basoni chucked Tabrac's chin and the winged cat put on a guileless expression.

"That old darling rooked me out of five of my best apple loaves, which is why Ayree and our guest will have to make do with these. *And* he ate all five loaves himself! There's nothing worse than a sweet-toothed bandit."

"Why don't you just make some more apple loaves, Zabala?" Basoni asked.

100

The wardlady of Malbenu Isle set her tray down on a small table and wiped her hands on the baker's apron she wore so often. "Just like that. By magic, I suppose you mean. Well, let me tell you, a spell may make a cake faster than a bake-oven, but you'll always taste the difference. Real magic happens nowhere but in kitchens."

Basoni smiled. "Your magic does, Zabala. No one performs more miraculous transformations than you. From a plain brown egg to that glorious golden soufflé of yours, what a wonder!"

Zabala bowed her head modestly.

NOW IF YOU COULD ONLY DO SOMETHING ABOUT YOUR HAIR

Her eyes opened wide in a goggling stare. *"Who wrote this?"* She grabbed one of the seedcakes from the tray and thrust it into Basoni's hand. The rest of the tray followed. Each cake bore a separate word gouged into the top, the letters etched by a claw. Taken together, they formed a most provoking sentence. Only two remained untouched.

Zabala was easygoing until the subject of her hairstyle arose. She had confined her thick blond locks to two horsetails anchored high on the crown, then drawn back and plaited together into a single braid trailing down her back. The whole was always adorned with gems or flowers, in keeping with the occasion. When it came to decorating a cake, a gown, or herself, Zabala did not recognize restraint.

"Tabrac . . ." There was a nasty undertone in her voice.

HAIRY . . . HEART. The words materialized atop the last two cakes. Ayree's roguish familiar cocked his head to one side and purred.

"You shouldn't have insulted him," Basoni said, trying not to laugh.

"Fine." Zabala snatched up the tray again. "Take his side. Play toss-stones with him. You'll learn."

Tabrac flew up from his place, whisked the cakes from her hands, and vanished with a taunting yowl. By the time he reappeared, Zabala had left the room in a huff.

"Did you take those to Ayree and Paragore-Tren or did you eat them yourself?" Basoni demanded, trying to look stern.

Tabrac purred louder, ignored the question, and brought out the toss-stones again.

Basoni laughed, promised him a game, scratched him behind the ears, and lost three bracelets before she discovered that the stones were misweighted. She was giving the shamefaced familiar a lecture on the evils of cheating when Paragore-Tren came out of the library.

"Up to his old tricks, is he?" The wizard's wild black beard, now liberally streaked with gray, hid any improper expression of amusement. "My old mare was the same way—the talking one. She tricked me into buying her a Sombrunian stallion with her winnings at beg-and-lend, but what's a cat going to do with bracelets?"

Basoni shrugged. "I think Ayree gave him a magpie's wings. He collects things."

Tabrac hiccuped.

"Mostly empty wine bottles, I'd say." Paragore-Tren tickled the unrepentant beast between the wings, then asked Basoni, "Will you join us now? Ayree has news for you."

The white-haired Prince of Warlocks sat at a tilt-topped table with three walls of heavily laden floor-to-ceiling bookshelves behind him. He looked like one of Fortunata's pet scholars from Panomo-Midmists. For the first time in months he seemed entirely relaxed and content.

"We have found it, Basoni," he said. "We've found the fruit of the Tree."

She knew which Tree he meant, and she rejoiced with him. The wizard looked on as brother and sister shared their gladness over the long-sought, carefully refined, preciously tested spell that would free the Twelve Kingdoms.

"You're sure?" Basoni couldn't help a small doubt creeping in. It all seemed too good to be true.

"I wasn't; no, not even I. That's why I sent for Paragore-Tren."

"It's a true spell of unmaking," the storm-bearded wizard said. "They are rare—the gods be thanked—but I've studied long enough to know one when I see it. How long did it take you, Ayree?"

The witch-king drummed his fingers on the desk top. "Too long. I had the spell itself for almost a year. But the process of honing it for use took up most of that time; and then, I had other troubles to distract me." He made a wry face at the wizard. "I'm surprised you haven't lost all respect for me, my friend, for being so gullible."

Paragore-Tren waved off Ayree's self-depreation. "Are you still moping about that . . . what was his name?"

"Galivert." Basoni pronounced it almost inaudibly. "It wasn't Ayree's fault about Galivert; it was mine. I should have spoken sooner about the chill I sensed around him, about that unholy light I saw in his eyes . . ."

"And I should have had the foresight to examine him more closely when I brought him here." Ayree made a short sound of self-disgust. "I never should have assumed that disguise has only one skin."

The wizard snapped his fingers. "Yes, that's it; Galivert the *lir*. Ayree, don't punish yourself for it. The *lirim* are spirits of deception incarnate. They share the world of the night-spirits, and you and I both know how powerful and capricious those elemental beings are. A *lir* can put one disguise on top of another the way a man puts a cape over a tunic over a shirt! And in every one of its disguises, the *lir* will be perfect; undetectable unless you know what you're looking for. Basoni, you are both too sensitive and too shy. Once you did tell Ayree about how badly Galivert set you on edge, we had our clue. There's a certain aura that clings to things of the night-spirits' realm and fades slowly. Snowglimmer still holds a little of it, I think. With such an aura, the *lirim* are even more astonishing in their deceit. The only way to see through their disguises is if they want you to."

"The way it wanted us to see through the demon's skin," Ayree said bitterly.

"Well, it's gone now, so stop torturing yourself." Paragore-Tren patted Ayree on the back. "The *lirim* are like the night spirits: creatures of whim and malice. Who knows why it came or why it left? Be grateful that it did no harm while it was here."

Ayree admitted that his friend was right. "It killed Basoni's little pet rabbit and stirred up a lot of mischief among the Twelve, but that's over. Soon after Galivert vanished, they all went back to their separate kingdoms and found other things to think about. I doubt they even remember his name. Only Basoni stayed on at Snowglimmer, to keep me company while I worked on this spell." He looked fondly at his youngest sister.

"Sombrunia gets on well without me," Basoni said. "But someone has to keep order here. I'm glad Zabala came back to visit, though. No one can match her skills in running a kitchen."

"It's not every woman would trade being wardlady of a pleasant kingdom for being an unpaid housekeeper," the wizard said. "Even if the house is a castle and you have a corps of familiars to help you with your tasks. Wouldn't you prefer to be royally entertained in your wardland? I visited Sombrunia recently. King Alban said that you would be more than welcome when you decide to visit them again."

"That visit will have to wait," Ayree said briskly. "Our weapon is ready and the time is still favorable. Morgeld broke the old spells the Twelve placed on Helagarde to keep him within, but he hasn't chosen to come out of his hole yet, and it wouldn't matter if he did. This enchantment will strike him down and turn all his works to nothingness wherever they exist— Helagarde, the Lands Unknown, the places between the stars, anywhere! He cannot hide from it. When the Twelve gather this time, they'll work a spell that will shake all the Kingdoms to their roots and call the gods home."

The witch-king stood and closed his eyes. The silver circlet on his brow began to glow with a diamond light. Basoni heard the summons in her head and knew that her sisters heard it, too: Ayree's voice, mindsent, calling.

The circlet's glow died. Ayree opened his eyes. "When will they be here?" Paragore-Tren asked.

Although no one could guess Ayree's true age from his smooth, high-boned face, his grin made him seem like a carefree boy. "Let them come whenever they like; the results will be the same once they're here. A day or two won't change that. They may have some pressing business to settle up in their wardlands. Let them. We have waited so long that we can afford to wait a little longer."

But Ayree's nonchalant attitude changed as the days passed and by ones and twos the Twelve arrived. Basoni noted this. She was the only one of the sisters who did. The others were too taken up with exchanging greetings and gossip as each new arrival joined their ranks, trading speculations about the great spell of unmaking and the melding of power that lay ahead of them.

"It will be more difficult than any of us dreamed," Menka said. "But we shall do it."

Lucha teased a few good notes out of her latest lute and said, "What's so difficult about a blending of powers? When we were at the Laidly Marshes, didn't we play at braiding our spells until we were cross-eyed?" She tried for a major chord, got a twangle, and the faithless lute met the fate of so many others.

"That was nothing compared to what's ahead of us," Fortunata lectured her. "It's like . . . cookery. There's a difference between the stews of Vahrd and the sugar subtleties of Paxnon. Both are mixtures of many things, but for the stew it doesn't matter if you juggle amounts or substitute ingredients."

"*I* stay out of the kitchen. I don't understand all that pinch-of-this, sniff-of-that fussing," Lucha said, sounding proud of her ignorance.

"Too bad for you," Sacchara said affably. "You're missing out on some very tasty results." She brushed the crumbs of Zabala's latest batch of honey cakes from her robes. No one appreciated the sugar subtleties of Paxnon better than that land's own wardlady, as her serene, round face and rather plump figure testified. A garland of bees streamed from her sleeve and carried off the fallen crumbs.

Menka was her old businesslike self. She commandeered the banquet chamber of Castle Snowglimmer, cleared away the gryphon-trestles where Charel had once feasted with kings of another age, and turned the room into an indoor training ground. Here she took it upon herself to practice minor exercises of harmonic magic with as many of the others as she could catch.

Ayree complimented her tersely when he came to see how the sisters were preparing themselves for the casting of Morgeld's unmaking. Menka dimpled with pride, hungry for her brother's praise, just as she used to be in the days before Galivert had made her turn on Ayree. This show of renewed submission left him unmoved. From her place in the circle of ten, Basoni wondered why. She made an excuse and went after him when he left.

She overtook him in the hall. "Haven't you forgiven Menka yet? I've heard criminals praise their hangmen with more sincerity. I thought we handled that combined spell well. If you found fault, help us with it instead of giving us one-handed applause."

"No, no, you all did very well—all of you that were there."

"Resha wasn't with us, but you know her. As soon as she got here she set up her tent, filled it with dreamsmoke, and went off into one of those trances like a Sumnerol shaman. For her, that's the best way to prepare."

As she spoke, she knew that Ayree was not thinking of Resha. Seven days had passed since the summoning and still Hodah had not arrived.

"What can be keeping her?" Ayree smacked his fist into the palm of his other hand. "Without the Twelve together, we might as well throw sticks at Helagarde," he said grimly.

Basoni slipped her arm through his. "I can send out a searching spell for Hodah right away, brother. Mine will find her faster than another's. That is . . ." She wasn't sure how to explain it.

Ayree spared her the explanation. "She is special to you, and you to her. Love will always call to love."

Basoni murmured, "I didn't think you noticed."

"Oh, I wasn't always the cold taskmaster, Basoni. There were days when I watched my pretty sisters at play and wished that we had all been born in another time and place, free of the burdens that power and prophecy have laid on us. You were all so young! I envied you, but I envied you and Hodah most of all. I wished that I were young again. I wished that there had been room for a second child in her arms."

A hoarse roaring raked the castle hall. "The watchers!" Ayree exclaimed. He had heard the voices of the two ice-carved monsters topping Castle Snowglimmer's gate. Winged lions with the tails of dolphins, their far-seeing eyes were a deeper green than any of the castle's icy walls. When the Twelve were small, they had teased each other with the tale that the watchers' eyes were blind to everything but secrets.

"She's coming!" he added. With Basoni at his heels, he ran to the courtyard just as the great gate of icicles rose high without gear or gatekeeper to lift it. At their posts, the monstrous green-eyed statues continued to roar a welcome and a warning.

The wardlady of Glytch sat wrapped in gray furs on the back of a broad-padded skyel deer, the kuroc's distant northern cousin. Stolid as a man of law, the skyel deer inclined its antlered head slightly at the din the fishtailed stone lions were making, and went back to chewing its cud.

Hodah slid from her high-backed saddle and Basoni was in her arms before she could speak a word. "Hodah! Hodah, thank all the gods that you've come!"

Hodah skillfully fended off Basoni's embrace. "Why are you always bothering the gods?" she asked, laughing while she held her at arm's length. "No, stay there, let me look at you!" Basoni's second attempt at hugging her sister close was also parried. "What fine color in your cheeks! The northland agrees with you."

Ayree waited until Basoni, disconcerted, made a temporary retreat. "You are the last to arrive, Hodah," he said. "Now I see why." He indicated the skyel deer, who launched a perfunctory gob of green spittle at the witch-king's feet.

Hodah regarded him archly. "Don't be silly. From Glytch to Castle Snowglimmer in seven days on skyelback? I only chose to make the last leg of my journey like this. Your call said to come, but not how quickly."

"My error. Come inside." The two sisters fell into step behind Ayree, who led them both back to the huge chamber where

Menka and the rest still wove their separate spells into larger tapestries of magic.

"Hodah's here!" Lucha exclaimed with delight.

"Now if someone will drag Resha out of her reeking tent, we can do something worthwhile." Senja ran a hand through her own short cap of curls. "Just make sure you don't inhale while you're in there, or you'll be seeing dragons climbing out of your boots."

"I am here," Resha said, her voice slurred, her eyes dreamy. "I've been here a while, Senja. Are you sure that *I'm* the one who's been inhaling the wrong things?"

Lavah's sharp giggle was slapped from the air by a hard word from Shama. Toady and mistress had found their proper places again.

"Splendid!" Menka strode through the gathered women, pausing only to seek some look of approval from Ayree. "If we are all together, we can begin our melding spells in earnest, and before a fortnight I predict—"

"What?" Hodah's face was pasty.

"Take your places. Form the circle. We'll make the whirling northlights first. That's one of the easiest weirdings for the twelve of us to work together. Do you remember, Hodah? It was the first one we ever did with our powers linked successfully." Menka took Basoni's arm and reached for Hodah's, but the lady of Glytch backed off. "It will be just like old times!"

"But I just arrived! I haven't even brought my things to my room. Must we do this now?" Hodah's protests were too loud. "At least let me rest a while, remove my coat . . ."

"Yes, but this spell's a short one—"

"Don't waste words persuading her, Menka." Ayree's eyes were slits of silvery blue, the edges of twin swords. "She'll give you nothing in exchange."

The Twelve gave him much room as he came closer to where Hodah stood holding the thick, smoke-colored collar of her coat tightly to her throat with both hands. "By all means, take off your coat, Hodah."

She did as he told her. The fur made a cloud at her feet. Basoni imagined that her sister had grown more beautiful since she'd seen her last. She looked taller and more slender than the youngest witch recalled.

Then Ayree said, "Two skins, one inside the other, deceived me once; not again. Take off your coat, Hodah, or I'll remove it for you. You know the coat I mean." His voice and his look allowed for no stalling or excuse.

She bowed like a parching flower. Illusion bought with weakened powers dissolved easily. Basoni's gasp was only one of many as Hodah stood in her true shape for all of her sisters to see.

The loose robes she had adopted for so many months were not enough to conceal the child she carried.

Chapter XI

THE SUNDERING

Life denies the final sorrow,
Death stands by and laughs at joy,
Hope departs to seek the morrow,
Love is more than passion's toy.

—"The Blind Girl's Grave-Song"
from *The Scroll of Oran*

Basoni knocked timidly at Hodah's door, even though a prisoner did not have the right of privacy. When no one answered her knock, she tried again, again got no response. The two winged cats hovering near the door made soft-pawed motions for her to go in anyway.

There was no lock on the door and no spell to serve a lock's purpose. The room itself was actually a small suite, reserved for guests who seldom came to Snowglimmer these days. It was an altogether luxurious cell, but Basoni knew that most prisons were things of the mind.

She found Hodah in the inner chamber, seated on the edge of the high bed with her slippered feet resting on a stool. Her hands were folded in her lap, her head and shoulders bowed. There was no telling how long she had been sitting there like that.

"Hodah . . ."

The wardlady of Glytch continued to study her hands. When she finally spoke, it was as if she spoke only to herself.

"Why did I think I could deceive him? He would have learned sooner or later. I have lost so much power . . . it must be a boy. And there isn't even the consolation of thinking that he will be witchborn. He may be as magicless as a mouse, for all I know—such things happen. The powers depart, and often never return.''

Basoni clambered up beside her sister and put her arm around Hodah's shoulders. "Don't worry over that. You still have enough of your powers left to bring the child safely into the world. New life has always been your special care. I don't think *that* power will ever leave you, though you forfeit all the others. Your boy will be born healthy and well loved; the rest is meaningless.''

''*Meaningless?*'' Hodah's penetrating look took Basoni aback. "Is that why Ayree has put me here? Because I carry a child who's going to be 'well loved'? I am diseased, foul, worse than the lowest of Morgeld's servants. I have betrayed my kin, betrayed the Tree of Second Light, betrayed the gods themselves!" Her voice dropped; she rested her hands atop her swollen belly. "And I am not sorry.''

"Hodah, what happened wasn't your fault. Ayree will see that with time." Basoni yearned for the right words to banish the terrible apathy that had stolen Hodah's spirit the moment her masquerade was stripped away. "The thing we called Galivert was a *lir,* and the *lirim* are living lies. Even Ayree was fooled. He can't blame you for—''

"For loving Galivert?" Hodah finished. "For making love with Galivert when I knew the risks?''

"For being deceived by him—by it," Basoni said.

Hodah laughed in her face. "Talk about lies! Ayree can blame me for anything he likes. He can even try to make himself feel better about it by lying about Galivert. A *lir,* is it? Where did Ayree dream that one up? Though I suppose it's easier to stomach the idea that his sister betrayed him for the sake of something more than mortal.''

Basoni forced her elder sister to look at her, cradling Hodah's face with her hands just as Hodah had done to her when they were young, playing at mother and child.

"Hodah, Galivert wasn't a mortal; he never was! Paragore-Tren has spent a lifetime studying the beings of the night spirits' realm. Few of the witchborn or wizardly suspect how many dark forms of life dwell there, or know what will draw them out. He's the one who told us that Galivert was . . .''

"Paragore-Tren would say chickens give cheese if Ayree wanted him to. Who should know Galivert's true nature better than I? If Ayree can't stand the fact that I took a magicless mortal for my lover, let him grind his teeth to the gums. I have no regrets.''

Hodah's hands leaped from her belly, kicked away from within.

She smiled and touched the place where small feet pushed. "There is still the second branch of prophecy waiting on the Tree for mortals to reap. There is still hope. Perhaps we Twelve were never meant to be the sword of the prophecy. Perhaps Galivert's son will live to see the waiting fulfilled."

The waiting . . . Basoni thought. *And why couldn't you wait, Hodah? As Ayree has been waiting for more years than you know, and in such pain . . .* She knew the answer. She had felt the force surrounding Galivert, the compelling, overwhelming force that blanked all reason and resistance from the mind. And if the victim gave it the name of love, it was a little easier to surrender.

She wondered whether this force was likewise a natural part of the *lirim*. Paragore-Tren had only spoken of their perfect skill at disguise, not of any additional power to entrap their victims. They all knew so little of the creatures who dwelled in the night spirits' realm!

"Will you walk with me, Hodah? Fresh air would be good for the baby." Basoni slipped from the bed and offered her hands to assist Hodah down.

"Walk where? Pacing up and down on the battlements? With a guard, no less! No, thank you. It might make Ayree nervous to learn I'd strayed from my prison."

"Ayree sent me to visit you! Don't wrong him. He doesn't want to punish you for what's happened."

Hodah's gentle face had grown hard during her brief confinement. Her voice had sharpened, too. "Who does he want to punish, then? Galivert? He'll never find him! The banns of sorcery I cloaked him with still hold!"

A suspicion creased Basoni's brow. "How can you be so sure of that? Unless . . ." Her frown deepened. "Unless he's nearby, under the banns' cloak, and you were with him when you heard Ayree call."

Ayree's youngest sister recalled the uproar in the banqueting hall the moment after Hodah stood unveiled before them all. Ayree had wasted no time in commanding the three oldest sisters to examine her, to learn how much magic the Rule of Loss had left her. They set her the customary tests administered when one of the witchborn claims to have reached maturity: illusion, creation, transport, levitation, more.

She wove illusion easily as other women weave cloth, but that was not a spell requiring much power. She created a seed and with her nurturing magic made it sprout to a fine young shoot, but the tender green stalk soon withered and died.

She could neither fetch nor dispatch small objects from one room to another, nor could she herself leave the ground.

She could not travel by witchly means. She had lost that ability the moment new life—male life—began inside her. She had to go everywhere as mortals do, and yet she had arrived at Castle Snowglimmer on skyelback only seven days after Ayree had sent out his mindcall.

Glytch was much more than seven days' travel from Snowglimmer if the wayfarer came without magic.

Hodah almost smiled when she saw the look of revelation in Basoni's eyes. "Spare yourself the calculations, little sister. I was nowhere near Glytch when Ayree summoned us . . . fortunately for me. At least I was able to present myself to our brother before he thought to come hunting me. He would have found more prey than he bargained for. I couldn't have hidden from him, or I'd have done so."

"You couldn't place the banns on yourself."

"Not now," Hodah replied. "Not with this baby coming. I wish I'd had the wisdom to place the banns on myself while I still had all my powers. They are one of the strongest spells, and no one knows how long they last once cast unless they are deliberately removed. But I miscalculated, and by the time I thought to use them to hide myself, I no longer had the power to do so."

Basoni understood everything now. "If Ayree had gone hunting you by magic, he would have found Galivert with you. The banns don't make your lover invisible. Where is he, Hodah? Why does he linger in the Twelve Kingdoms?"

"You have to ask that? *Here* is the reason!" Hodah clapped both hands to her great belly. "When I rescued him from all the petty squabblings of this house, I gave him a way to make his living and find contentment. Often I went to see how he was faring, because it was a lonely life I'd given him. He was happy, Basoni; happy to see me, and grateful, and . . . and . . . loving. I never knew there was so much love in the world, so much tenderness." Hodah's eyes swam with memories. She hugged herself and longed for other arms to do so. "We're raised to believe our great good fortune in being witchborn, but the consolations of a magicless life are worth more to me now than all the weirdings ever cast in these Twelve Kingdoms."

"Hodah, Galivert is no mortal."

"If he is a *lir*, why didn't he abandon me the moment he knew I'd conceived? The harm was done then. They say the night-spirits and their kin only leave their realm to do mischief. Why was he still waiting for me, his love unchanged, when I fled Glytch to find him? You should have seen his smile when he heard that we would have a child!"

Basoni was unconvinced. "Maybe because he wants the child—"

"Of course he does!"

"—to harm it; or worse, to steal it away into the night-spirits' realm."

Hodah fell speechless. Her skin, pale with pregnancy, went even whiter. When she found her voice, it was a vicious hiss. "Get out. Get out of my sight. You are Ayree's creature, his pet, his slave more than Menka ever was. You wouldn't stand against him if he came to you with a dripping sword in his hand and told you he'd killed my child."

Hodah got down from the great bed and tried to sweep past Basoni. As she did so, her heel caught a small hump in the rug and she fell. Basoni caught her before she could hit the floor and gently helped her to a sling chair.

"You should have let me fall," Hodah said, fingers sinking into the carved oak faces of the dragon armrests. "You would have done Ayree's work for him."

Basoni began to cry. "I would never let any harm come to you, Hodah. Don't you know that? Not for anyone or anything! And if I let anyone hurt your child . . ."

She had been three years old when she took that oath at her unborn brother's bidding, but old enough for oaths to bind. She remembered the lessons of loving and dying that she'd learned in that darkened bedchamber—death and desire forever one in her mind now—and the promise she had made to one small spirit.

Basoni began to cry. She sank down to rest her head on Hodah's knees as she had done when Hodah was all the mother left for her, the special love that gave a child comfort when she cut her illusions against the hard edge of the world.

"Hodah . . . Hodah, I swear to you by Musa's blood and Ambra's runes, I'll never let anything happen to your child."

Hodah's hands were soft on Basoni's trailing hair.

The sisters remained as they were while Basoni's tears subsided. At last Hodah said, "I trust you, my little one. I wish I could trust Ayree, or the others. When I stood exposed before you all, I saw the pity in your eyes, but the rest . . . Those who don't scorn me for what I did, envy me. If they could, they'd throw me out of Castle Snowglimmer and not think twice about it. This isn't my home anymore.''

"It will *always* be your home!" Basoni was ready for a fight. "They haven't the right to deny that!"

The slightest smile warmed Hodah's face. "You are still young enough to believe in rights, and justice, and what's fair. Don't lose that, Basoni; no matter who tries to shake it from you, don't lose that.''

Hodah breathed deeply, as if the short distance from bed to chair had exhausted her. "I think I'd like to rest now. Come and see me again later, if Ayree will let you.''

"Ayree won't say yes or no about it. He's going away on another of his mysterious trips.''

"Is that so?" Hodah looked most interested. "Probably off to warn our kinfolk about mad Hodah, disgracer of all witchborn blood.'' She laughed at Basoni's expression. "My darling! I'm only joking. Don't believe everything you hear.''

She shooed Basoni out of her rooms. Basoni left with the consolation that at least Hodah seemed more cheerful. The promise she had made to her elder sister was a heavy lump in her chest. Still, she knew she couldn't have done otherwise. This promise was only the echo of a pledge already given.

Basoni would have given much to be free of both promises. She dreaded scenes, and there would be plenty of those once this baby was born. At the moment, she felt too weary to think about the taunts and insults her other sisters would level at her for siding with Hodah and the baby, and Ayree might not intervene. Maybe Hodah would regain enough of her old spirit to stand up to Ayree and the other ten after the birth. Or perhaps the two of them would leave Snowglimmer and raise the child elsewhere. King Alban had offered Basoni hospitality. From what she had seen of the Sombrunian rulers, he would not turn away extra guests.

That night, Ayree departed on his unguessed journey. In her bed, Basoni imagined him riding off on a skyel deer of stars to hunt the silver-pelted monsters of the night. He would return from the hunt in a more pleasant mood—sport always cheered him—and then she would suggest that she convey Hodah to Sombrunia. Her head filled with a thousand happy endings, she fell asleep.

Clawless paws prodded her and a small, icy, wet nose dug at

her face. A curious odor of spiced wine and dreamsmoke tickled her awake, and she found Tabrac kneading the bedclothes covering her. The winged cat mewed insistently, then stuck his nose in her ear and purred at top volume when she tried to burrow her way back into dreams.

"What is it, Tabrac? No begging at this hour of—"

Full wakefulness seized her. With Ayree gone, his familiars should also be far from Castle Snowglimmer, happily back in that corner of otherspace where the winged cats lived and bred and tumbled through the air of a world that was their own special paradise. Even Tabrac would not leave the comforts of that place for anything so paltry as a wine cellar raid.

Nor could he. The familiar's realm was Ayree's to open or shut with a word. The winged cats could not nose that door open themselves. Tabrac could *not* be here; yet he was.

Basoni knew that there were many ways of opening a door: a word; a touch; a key. But when these three are lacking, there is always an ax.

An ax, she thought, *in whose hands?*

She leaped from her bed and conjured a large blue glow to fill the chamber with light. Tabrac's pupils contracted to slits. He spread his wings and flew around her head as she ran barefoot from the room, with only her reed-green sleeping gown for cover. Witch and winged familiar sped through the halls of Snowglimmer, not stopping until they reached a certain door.

Hodah's room. None of Ayree's creatures hovered on guard at the doorway. Basoni had not lied: Ayree trusted Hodah. He had installed her in apartments away from the others not to banish her, but to protect her from the jibes he knew would come. His familiars played sentry to keep cruel tongues away, but when he left the castle, he had sent them home.

Basoni's glow cast a comet's long light as it flew a pace ahead of its mistress, making the way clear. Through the outer room of Hodah's suite it went, then plunged through the door to the bedchamber . . . and died.

The jagged tear in the fabric of ordinary light and shadow cracked the wall in a lightning pattern near the head of Hodah's bed. The tear was narrow, but wide enough to devour anything incautious enough to come near. A gale of poisonous heat slim as a knifeblade blew from the break in reality and seared Basoni's hand, then turned to a cold so sudden and so bitter that she felt her skin crack and bleed.

She spoke hasty words of shielding, throwing protection around

herself and Tabrac. The winged cat yowled and clung to the
invisible wall with his claws, his broad blue and white pinions
beating. By the time he calmed enough to perch on her shoulder,
Basoni had managed to heal her hand.

Something purple-black with a citrine eye slipped past the rift,
moaning. There were other shapes and shapeless things as well in
the blackness beyond the tear. At the edges, two threads of
light—one blue, one rose—formed an eerie contrast against the
darkness they bordered.

"The plane of witchflight," Basoni murmured, recognizing
the dawnlight pathway. The blue strand was a glimpse of Tabrac's
home. But the blackness between was a place the young witch
had heard of, but never wished to see: a gateway into the
elemental realm of the night-spirits.

Tabrac bumped her with his wedge-shaped head and dug his
claws into her shoulder. She touched his brow and said a prayer
to Sarai's Messenger—the white bird with a human face who lent
the skill of mindlore to certain mortals. Mindlore, that sometimes
let a human harvest memories from another being's mind.

*Winged cats at play in a world of clear air and exciting smells
. . . a swoop and a pounce of nestling kittens just trying their
weight against their wings while their proud mother looked
on . . .*

*Then madness. Panic. A multicolored cloud of Ayree's loved
pets taking to the endless skies, fleeing a hairline fissure that let
terrifying hints of sound and sight contaminate their lovely world.
Only one of them was curious enough to fly toward the fissure
rather than away.*

"Brave Tabrac," Basoni said, stroking his fur. The big cat
thrummed as his memories continued to pour into her head.

*A passage that was too quickly over to be feared. A landing in
a place familiar to him, yet not entirely. Hide! Hide! The crack
in the world was here, too, and the one who had caused it was
coming. Hide, then peep out and see . . .*

*Hodah alone, asleep, unconscious of the tearing of the wall
between worlds. Darkness seeping into the shadows of her bedchamber, taking the form of a handsome man clad in a trapper's
colorful garb.*

"So that was the life she gave him," Basoni said half-aloud,
gratefully drinking in all that Tabrac had spied from his hiding
place. "No wonder she was near enough when Ayree's call
came."

He roused her from sleep and she gave a glad cry. She never saw the gate by which he'd come, only him. He spoke of how Ayree had found him at last in his hut among the snows, told him to leave, ordered him to forget Hodah forever.

"Or the child will suffer for it, he said." The lir lied so well that even Basoni had almost believed him, and Hodah did without question. He told of dangers passed to breach the walls of Snowglimmer as soon as he knew that Ayree was gone. Hodah accepted all, clinging to him, blind and deaf to everything that was not Galivert.

"I have a sled not far from here, and a boat waiting for us at an inlet on the coast. We'll sail to the southern lands. Your brother will never find us."

Basoni's vision vanished as the lovers threw a few of Hodah's things into a blanket, rolled it up, and departed. Tabrac's memories had served their purpose.

"The coast . . . Tabrac, wake the others. It will take more than one of them to seal the crack that the *lir* made between the planes. Clumsy creature, only haste could've torn it this badly. What was driving him? Go, Tabrac, and I'll go after Hodah."

She released Tabrac from her shield and saw him safely out of the chamber. Still in a skin of protective magic, she stepped into the plane of witchly flight while the horrors of the night-spirits' realm leered perilously close, testing the frayed edges of a passage that tempted them into the mortal world.

There was only one inlet in the northern wastes that wasn't choked with ice at this time of year. A modest alliance of power between Ayree and others of the witchborn kept the waters fairly clear, a convenience for any seagoing witch, warlock, or wizard who sought Ayree's counsel. Hodah had told King Ottal truly when she said that the plane of witchly flight was often too crowded to enter, but the seas of the Twelve Kingdoms were wide, and the way easy when magic filled the sails.

Basoni emerged from her flight on an outcrop of centuries' hardened snow, a frosty buttress that the winds had sculpted into the crude likeness of an eagle's head. From this perch, she could survey the inlet, its waters like rippling coal.

The tracks of sled runners scored the snow. The sled itself stood abandoned, the traces empty, two sets of footprints flying from it. Tabrac had remained in hiding too long after the lovers fled. The corpse of the skyel deer that had drawn the sled lay in the shallows. Rime frosted his coarse hair, white all over except at the throat where a scarlet slash was crusted over with frozen blood.

Basoni shuddered with the cold. No matter how she perfected her spells of shielding, she could not keep the icy northwinds at bay. Old dreams lurked among the snowdrifts—a snow-beast in the skin of a trapper's fairspoken daughter. What had cut the dead skyel deer's throat, and why? Fear chilled deeper than the winds.

She scrambled down from her lookout point and ran through the snow to the water's edge. Woolly fog had set in, gray tinged with violet moving swiftly up from the southwest, but Basoni's spell-keened sight could pierce the banks of cloud. She saw the single-masted ship in the near distance, its sails belling out as if a northeast gust filled them.

The wind's not from that quarter! The ship cast a dull amethystine light that mocked Basoni's sudden understanding. She knew its source and its master . . . too late. Too late she knew why she had seen that selfsame glint of Helagarde's aura in Galivert's eye.

Her warscream split the snowy silence. Bow, quiver, and sword were in their places, her hair streaming in the rival wind that she summoned to carry her after the ship. She straddled air, no longer feeling or fearing the cold, nocking the first shaft to her bow as she flew in pursuit of Morgeld's servant and her sister.

She seared away the topmost layer of fog with words that Hodah had taught her years ago. She wanted a clear field of vision for whatever fight she would now have to wage alone, and she wanted all her powers free for battle.

The mist melted into rain and she was looking down from her height at the deck of the ship. Hodah must have been belowdeck, for there was no one in sight except Galivert manning the tiller. The borders of his disguise were beginning to soften and run, his true self a blot of shadow where he had let his illusion relax.

Ambra's runes poured over Basoni's arrow the moment before she let it fly. The *lir*'s head snapped up, his face still full of human malice as the witch's arrow struck. Light pulsed outward from the point of impact, turning disguise to darkness, darkness into nothing. A second arrow pierced the *lir* where a man would have his heart. Drops of night trickled through the cracks between the planking of the deck and were gone by the time Basoni set foot there. The dark spirit had melted into nothingness.

"Hodah! Hodah!"

The deck groaned beneath her feet, then splintered upward as the ebon wings of a giant bat cracked the ship from prow to keel. The shattered ship went down, splintering out from under Basoni's feet. Only a few pitiful bits of wrack bobbled on the surface or swirled in the white wake behind the batwinged apparition. Hodah was gone, gone too swiftly for Basoni even to cry out her sister's name again.

Framed by the giant wings, a man's mocking face bared dull gray teeth at the young witch, burst into laughter as she mounted the air and loosed an arrow at him. It passed between his eyes and the sea swallowed it with the same lazy gluttony as it devoured the spars and planks of the little ship.

Batwings folded in upon themselves to form a man's limbs, sheathed in ghostly mail. *Seek your sister in my master's halls, lady.* The hollow voice filled sky and sea. *A prize for Morgeld. A double prize, to seize one of the Twelve and know that now your precious Tree is stripped of half its branches! I rejoice that the thing you called Galivert was so swift to answer our lord's summons. A hasty flight leaves a plain trail, and you followed it . . . to your own undoing. Even now I wonder whether Morgeld planned it so: Calling the lir home, commanding him to bring that woman, knowing he would not have time to cover their tracks, knowing it would be you and no other who would follow them . . . Who can know Morgeld?*

Come near, come nearer and fight with me, for I am Tor, Morgeld's most faithful servant, and I would gladly bring my master yet another prize!

The apparition's words cut her to the heart and twisted tears of rage from her eyes. She cast her bow into the sea that had claimed her sister's body and drew her sword. Tor laughed and a shadowy blade materialized in his hand.

Come near, he said, in a lover's sweet persuasive tone. *Oh, come near, my lovely lady.*

Basoni!

Her name rang in her ears, though she did not hear it. Hodah's voice, now no voice, but still there.

Fly, Basoni, fly! Don't stand to fight with Tor unless you must. Ghosts feed on life, on blood! None drink so much power from it as Morgeld's chosen slaves. I did not know what Galivert was until we stood on the shore and he summoned the skyel deer to him. When he cut its throat, when Tor's dark shade came and drank the blood, that was when his glamour on me broke and I knew him for what he was . . . too late! How cold, how dark the air that clings to Galivert! Too late . . . too late for me, but for another— Oh, fly from Tor, my sister!

Hodah? She sought her lost sister with a thought, but spirits speak to the souls of the living, not their minds.

Fasten your magic to the skyel deer's death, draw out one bone and turn it into an arrow, call back your bow, send Sarai All-Mother's words against Morgeld's servant, hurry, hurry!

Basoni did not waste more time in doubts or questions. She arced across the sky to where the skyel deer's bloodless body still lay in the tidewater. She touched one of the great forelegs and with the same words of command that fetched her bow back from the sea, she slivered the heavy shank into thirteen slim darts. Kneeling on the dead beast's belly, she bent her bow and raised it to meet the swooping descent of Tor's warring ghost.

Sarai's words turned creamy bone to gold. The arrow painted a sunlit streak across the gray sky. Tor saw it coming, and knew what it was. His wings clapped out, beat once, and carried him into invisibility seconds before Basoni's arrow would have struck him.

All was quiet in the cove again, with only the muffled sound of small waves washing the shore. Basoni stood beside the skyel deer's corpse, staring out to sea. The waters rushed over her bare feet, but she did not seem to feel them. She gazed into the west as if she expected to see Hodah's ship still afloat, her sister joyful in the arms of Galivert—a true man and not one of Morgeld's minions—but her eyes hungered for the impossible.

Basoni . . . the voice called, and suddenly there was something bobbing on the waves. Eyes searching for a lost ship had overlooked it, dismissing the small, rolling shape as a bit of flotsam. Basoni walked into the water, straining to hear her sister's call, for it seemed to come from that lonely object. She levitated, feet trailing drops of brine, and sailed above the sea to meet it.

Round and round the cockleshell spun, played with by the wavelets, rocked by the seawind. It turned as Basoni approached, and the voice that had been calling to her soul dwindled and thinned into a newborn baby's cry. Red face, red fists, and a coverlet of midnight blue were all that Basoni could see as she plucked the cradle from the waves and hurried it to shore. She knelt beside it on the snowy strand and touched the infant's cheek.

It was warm. The last of Hodah's life had flowed into an embrace of enchantments to shield her son from the cold, to make him a cradle from the ship that doomed her, to set it afloat on the waves. That same special magic, hers alone, which brought forth new life so easily and nurtured it so tenderly, had let her give birth swiftly enough to place her baby far from the reach of evil. Basoni knew then how deeply ran the darkness of Morgeld's servants, to make Hodah risk her infant's life on the northern waves sooner than keep him near her to the end. In this love too, was magic. Now the magic ebbed, and the chill of the northern wastes seeped in past the shieldspell, making the baby yowl.

Basoni lifted him from the cradle and wrapped her own power around him. Comforted by her arms and newfound warmth, he snuggled in against her breast. She stood perfectly still for a time, afraid to break the spell that was more potent than any Ayree had ever cast. When the wonder of the baby's presence finally began to pall, she held him in the crook of one arm and carefully stooped to pick up the remaining arrows of skyel deer bone. Their power would not fade, and instinct told Basoni that this child would need every scrap of protection that wit and magic and love could afford him. When the other ten finally arrived at the cove, they found her holding him near, singing him one of old Rista's songs.

She would not surrender the infant to any of her sisters. She would not tell them what had happened until they were back inside the walls of Castle Snowglimmer. She turned deaf to all their questions, for she thought she heard one last call from Hodah's spirit. It was much weaker now, and it floated at the periphery of perception, but she knew that if she concentrated, she would hear . . .

Hadin . . . Hadin . . .

Silence. Basoni blinked. She was in the great hall of Snowglimmer with her ten living sisters around her, all of them demanding that she speak. In her arms, the baby was stirring and starting to cry for milk. She looked at him and smiled.

"He is Hodah's son," she said. "His name shall be Hadin."

She did not see that she was the only one smiling.

Chapter XII

THE PLEDGE

"Children are born ignorant of the evil in this world, and grown folk must take many pains to teach it to them. They never thank us, ungrateful little beasts that they are."

—"The Fifth Eunuch's Observation"
from *The Scroll of Oran*

"Basoni! If you're looking for Hadin, he's in here!"

Senja's strident voice rose above the uninterrupted, ringing blows of steel on steel, the roar of the smithy fire and the creaking of the great bellows. Stripped down to a sling of plain white cloth, the wardlady of Vahrd cast a diabolical shadow in the orange light of her forge.

On a wooden box, feet dangling three fingers from the floor, a black-haired little boy watched, enraptured, as a warrior's sword took shape under Senja's hand. His huge eyes, colored the deep gold-flecked blue of lapis stones, seemed to grow larger and shine with an inner fire caught from the glowing coals. He didn't look up when Basoni came bustling into the forge, wiping floury hands on her apron.

Basoni was in no mood to be ignored. She had been wrestling with the mysteries of batter and bake-oven all morning, her labors interrupted more times than she liked to think about by Shama's mewlings and Lavah's dutiful echo.

"Ayree won't like this; he won't allow it!"

"No, he won't, and he'll be right!"

"What is there to celebrate anyway?"

"You should be wearing mourning, not baking cakes."

"The way she bakes, Lavah, it's the cakes that come out wearing mourning." The two of them screeched with laughter.

To top that jolly scene, she had had to humble herself beyond belief to Menka and Fortunata, begging them not to shut themselves away from the great hall at dinner time. She had flattered and cajoled, and she would have uttered threats if they'd have done any good. Fortunately, groveling had been enough.

And here was the object of her efforts, unaware of all she had done for him, hanging around Senja's forge and— Basoni saw the streak of soot on his cheek and the sprinklings of charcoal dust smearing the boy's banded tunic, his best one. It was the last straw.

"Hadin, look at you! You're filthy! Soot all over your tunic . . ." Basoni leaned against the doorway to Senja's forge and heard herself begin the old, old lecture. The boy tore his gaze away from the nascent sword, looking every bit the martyr. She sighed. What was the use? Hadin learned his lessons immediately, or not at all.

Keeping his good clothes neat was one of those lessons he had *not* learned immediately.

Senja held the newmade sword up for a final inspection, nodded, then plunged it into the bucket of water beside the anvil where it hissed and burbled like a cranky dragon. She wiped sweat from her face with the back of her arm and gave a signal to the scurrying familiars that worked her bellows—her familiars, not Ayree's, with the shapes of brush-tailed copper foxes whose fur assumed the green patina of that metal as they aged. Their paws were clever to serve, with longer, more flexible toes, and dewclaws that had grown to the proportion and utility of human thumbs. They saw their mistress' signal and released the bellows, then ran off, yipping happily.

"Lazy bastards," Senja remarked. She drank a dipperful of water from the same bucket where the sword still cooled. Basoni made a face, but Senja only grinned and said, "My Vahrdmen drink 'iron tea' all the time, and they're no worse for it. It hardens their guts, they say. Let the boy be, Basoni. Getting dirty's the nature of the beast. What've you got him all prettied like that for anyway? The Malben wedding's not for a week yet." She gave Hadin a long look and added, loud and clear so he could hear it well, "*If* he's allowed to come at all."

It was a mild snub compared to many he'd received. Hadin's face was expressionless. It usually was, seldom showing joy or sadness, anger or hurt. Born magicless, he had still managed to create a shieldspell of his own as soon as his young consciousness understood the way things were for him in Castle Snowglimmer.

Senja laughed. "That doesn't bother you, does it, boy? Nothing bothers you. Your mother gave birth to a block of wood, or a slab of stone. You're one of the men of garnet from the Desert of Thulain, come to life!"

"Senja, stop it!" Basoni hurried over to stand behind Hadin, her arms around him. "He *is* going to the wedding, no question about it. If I go, he goes."

"And you most certainly must go. Mustn't offend the wardlady of Sombrunia, or what would the Malbens do for brandy?" Senja's mouth twitched at the corners. "You look like a lioness, Basoni; a lioness in an apron. What are you protecting that precious cub of yours from? From me? We're the best of friends, Hadin and I. Tell her, boy."

Hadin squirmed free of Basoni's sheltering arms. "The lady Senja told me I could stay and watch her forge that sword," he said, sounding embarrassed to have to go through this explanation. "She's been . . . telling me stories while she works: Stories from the days of the Older Empire."

"The old tales of the Tree, Basoni." Senja grinned. "All nothing but fairy stories now, what once upon a time were prophecy."

"The story of the three swords, too." Hadin's voice sank to a murmur, and he looked away from Senja. "The three that shall be one." His chin dropped to his chest as he mumbled, "I wish I had a sword."

With a venemous glance at Senja, Basoni seized Hadin by the hand and dragged him from the forge. The child ran to keep up with her long stride, but he never complained or asked her to stop. She pulled him with her all the way from Senja's forge, across three courtyards, down a colonnade of amber ice, and through the veiled gate leading to the inner gardens of Castle Snowglimmer.

She urged him into a bluestone niche where flowering ivy clung to the carved rock. The cold feel of the stone seat through his hose and tunic set him wriggling until Basoni's hands on his shoulders stilled him. She stooped before him most uncomfortably, in order to meet him eye to eye.

"Hadin, tell me the truth. Was Senja mean to you?"

And what could I do about it if she was? The thought made sour bile burn the back of Basoni's throat. *You are here on sufferance, pour little soul, and I must play a daily game of beg-and-lend to keep you comfortable.*

The little boy shook his head and kept his eyes down, one of

Hodah's constant mannerisms in the last days. She could hardly stand to look anyone in the eye, then. Basoni's memories of her were mostly of a suddenly averted gaze, a quickly glimpsed blush of shame.

"She was all right. She let me stay, and she did tell me stories about the three great swords. A mortal's going to be the one to forge those three blades into one, a mortal without any magic at all!" The boy's voice rose with excitement and his whole face was transformed.

Basoni's smile answered his. It was a mistake. Hadin realized that he'd showed too much of himself and he wiped all signs of gladness from his face, speaking on in a flat, matter-of-fact tone. "She said that when the gods still walked the Twelve Kingdoms, there were many mortals who served them. Some served the gods so well that they became gods themselves, or nearly. Like . . . like Nailer the smith; or the jeweler Eyndor, who was Janeela's father."

"Eyndor is dead, Hadin." Basoni's mouth became a line. "Morgeld killed him."

The boy's chin thrust out stubbornly. "I said *nearly*. And Eyndor lived years and years before Morgeld touched him. I bet Morgeld couldn't have hurt him at all unless Eyndor himself *wanted* to die." The thought seized Hadin's mind for an instant. "When you're magic, you don't have to die for a long, long time, do you? Only if you want to die, but . . . why would anyone want to die? You're magic, Basoni. You can live forever and ever! Can't you use your magic to make *me* live forever, too?"

Basoni nibbled her lower lip to buy time. She had loved Hodah's son from the moment she held him in her arms, but she'd never dreamed anything so small could burst with so many awkward questions.

To her relief, Hadin's mind flitted to another topic. "Today's my birthday," he said. "I think the lady Senja told me all of those stories and let me stay so long in the forge as a present."

"I'm sure of it," Basoni said hastily. She knew that it was the only present Hadin was likely to get from any of his aunts but herself.

"It was a very good present." The boy sounded satisfied. "Though . . . when I saw the little sword she was making . . ."

"You are too young for swords!"

"Oh, I understand that." Hadin's expression told Basoni that he didn't understand that at all, that he refused to understand it, that it was only to pacify her that he told such a whopping great lie. "So it was even kinder of her to tell me stories about them."

Again Hadin's look was unguarded. His disappointment over the lovely little sword—not to be his—showed very clearly. Basoni did her best to cheer him.

"You are a big boy now, Hadin—six years old today! You're not old enough for a sword of your own yet, but you are old enough to begin accompanying me on my travels."

"Travels? You never go anywhere, Basoni."

She ruffled the child's dark hair—*dark as a night-spirit* were Shama's spiteful words—and said, "I've had a lot to keep me busy in Castle Snowglimmer."

"Oh." The boy's dusk-blue eyes looked elsewhere. "Because of me."

"But I will be making more journeys now—we both will! First we'll go to Malbenu Isle for that grand wedding celebration, and from there . . . Why, from Malbenu it's only a short sail over the Opalza Sea to Sombrunia. I'll take you there with me, and we'll visit King Alban Stonesword, and perhaps he'll let you see—"

"The Black Sword?" Every defense fell. Hadin grabbed Basoni's hands and bounced up and down on the hard stone seat. "The Black Sword, really? Do you think he'd let me touch it, too? Hold it?"

Basoni held in a chuckle. Her heart rejoiced every time she saw Hadin behaving like an ordinary child, daring to have dreams and impossible desires, full of the hope that even the impossible can be fulfilled by the magic of belief. She didn't dare to laugh aloud, for these precious moments were fragile, shattered by the wrong sound, the wrong expression.

"He will let you hold the Black Sword, Hadin. It's made of stone and very heavy, but maybe one of the king's four sons would help you with it."

"I will hold it myself." The stubborn look was back. "I'm strong enough."

"Good." She slapped her knees and straightened up. "Then you're also strong enough to run back to your room, clean your tunic, and scrub off that topsoil you picked up talking to Senja. Don't dawdle! I haven't enough magic to make time stand still, and it will be the dinner hour soon."

"Yes, Basoni!" The boy sprang from his seat and sprinted from the garden. He ran like a boarhound pup, all lolloping feet and willingness but little grace. He hadn't gone six strides before he tripped over a paving slab and sprawled.

"Be careful, Hadin!" she called as he picked himself up. "Watch out, or King Alban won't let you near the Black Sword for fear you'll break it."

"Break a sword made of *stone?*" The boy looked back at his pretty aunt as if she'd lost her wits. With an incredulous shake of his head he ran on.

For herself, Basoni decided to return to the kitchens and see whether the cakes were cool enough to decorate. She'd left a pot of candying syrup bubbling on the hearth, and as she passed through the gardens she plucked tiny sprays of flowers to dip into the sugary brew. She wished she had Zabala's talent for making cakes look like bouquets. Zabala could turn out a dozen cakes, all exquisitely adorned, in the time it took Basoni to bake one.

But Zabala would not bake so much as a crumb if it were meant to honor Hadin's birthday. She would be "busy" with vital, mysterious business the moment Basoni asked her for aid. But at least she was diplomatic. Some of the others saw no need to spare Basoni's feelings, or the boy's. They'd made their attitude clear from the first.

"Get that magicless bastard brat out of my house!" Menka had shouted.

"Snowglimmer's as much my house as it's yours!" Basoni had shouted back. The baby was squalling, very hungry, and it seemed as though his howling was the catalyst that released them all from the double shock of Hodah's death and his birth. "It was his mother's house, too! He has a double right to stay here."

"If we're talking birthrights, then let him go to his father's folk, and the sooner, the better," Senja had snarled.

"Oh, no!" Lucha was jolted from her lazy self-absorption. "He's only a baby! You can't send him off to the night-spirits' realm."

Basoni flung an additional layer of shielding around herself and the child, whose howls for milk rose to shrieks.

"Why not? It's not like those creatures never saw an infant before. Wasn't Morgeld himself born there?"

Fortunata had quickly confirmed Senja's harsh words. "He has bad blood in him, like Morgeld's: night-spirit blood. See what Morgeld became because of it!"

Is that something to be blamed on blood? Basoni asked herself. She knew all the tales of Morgeld's begetting and birth— the battle-god Inota unwillingly trapped into fathering a child whose night-spirit mother later tired of him. *What would he have been if he had been born of love?*

Resha's slurry voice made a marked contrast with Fortunata's crisply clipped condemnation of the infant. "Who here is adept enough to untangle the weavings of blood? We are all the children of the gods, the witchborn, and mortal blood, too. Each taints the other, if taint's the word you choose. Will you send our own blood into the darkness? Will you be the one to tell Ayree what you've done to Hodah's child when he returns?"

There was an uneasy silence. Then Menka said, "Let the creature stay until our brother comes home. He'll decide, and we'll abide by it." She leveled a meaningful look at Basoni. "We will *all* abide by it."

"Good," Resha said. She held out her arms for the infant. "Give him to me, Basoni. I know where there's a skyel deer herd nearby, and I've invited three of their cows to visit Snowglimmer." Basoni slowly released her shieldspell and passed the babe to Resha. Clad in her white leathers and furs, eyes always lost in dreamsmoke visions, the wardlady of Sumnerol smiled vaguely at her youngest sister.

That was the last smile Basoni or Hadin got for some time. Ayree was furious when he returned and heard the tale of Hodah's death. He had lashed out at all of them—eleven not enough to keep watch over one?—then shocked them past help when he turned to Basoni and praised her for having slain the *lir*.

Very modestly, very quietly she took that opportunity to beg her brother to allow the baby to remain. She would take care of him, she swore, and no one else would ever be bothered by the child's presence. It would be as if he had never been born.

"So be it," Ayree had said. "But let it be exactly as you've promised."

At first Basoni was too grateful to comprehend the full meaning of Ayree's words. She was immediately taken up with all the problems and trials of caring for a newborn. But she learned what her brother had meant the minute she tried to summon up her own familiars to help her tend the baby.

Nothing answered her call except Ayree's voice, mindsent, saying, *Those unborn need no familiars to wait upon them. Your servants will still work for you, but not for any task depending on the child. I have seen to that. Honor your word, Basoni.*

It was the same tale when Basoni went looking for Resha to ask her herbwise sister for a cure when the baby had colic. Resha, who had stood up for Hadin willingly, now shook her head.

"We have all given Ayree our word that the baby is yours

alone to care for. Some of us"—she grimaced at the memory—
"were more glad to make that promise than others. In Sumnerol
my fisherfolk say that more ships sink from the weight of envy
than from the gust of storms."

"How could any of them envy Hodah, seeing how she died!"

Resha shrugged her thin shoulders. "When I hold a knife I can
use it to cure and kill, but it's the same knife. Our sisters who
envy Hodah all believe that if they'd been Galivert's lover, the
knife would have cut only one way; they'd have found a way to
take all the good and none of the evil out of sharing his bed.
Maybe they imagine that their love would have broken Morgeld's
hold on him, or cracked his *lir*'s hide open and a god would've
stepped out. And they call me the dreamer!"

"Then you won't help Hadin?"

Resha sighed. "I've given my oath. But of course . . . nothing's stopping you from making a fast flight to Sumnerol. I've
founded a school there to teach my folk the ways of medicine. A
colic cure is simple. There's no reason one of my students
couldn't help you with the child."

"How can Ayree expect things to truly be the same as if Hadin
had never been born?" Basoni cried out in frustration.

"How long can he fool himself, the way that boy yowls? It
fills the whole castle." Resha laughed, but Basoni was too angry
to be comforted by a jest. "Don't lose hope, little sister. Time
will soften much."

Resha's words were prophetic. Gradually the walls of deliberate blindness and silence surrounding the boy began to crumble.
By then the child had built up other walls of his own, but Basoni
believed that these would fall of their own accord, too. Her ten
remaining sisters departed from Castle Snowglimmer to attend to
the affairs of their wardlands, and on their return greeted Basoni
and the boy by name, forgetting that he was supposed to be
invisible among them. Even those who had hated his mother
forgot their promise to Ayree. Such a situation was simply too
unnatural to survive. Ayree took them all to task once or twice,
then gave up. He, too, spoke the name of Hadin.

But that was not enough for Basoni. Today—Hadin's sixth
birthday—she intended to win more for his sake. She decked the
cakes with sugared flowers, washed up, cast off her apron, and
went straight to Ayree's rooms.

Ayree was in his solar, a room high on the southern face of
Castle Snowglimmer's central keep, where he stored an odd
assortment of instruments, musical and scientific. They were all

equally useless to the witch-king, who had only to speak a word and have the most skilled minstrels in the Twelve Kingdoms appear for his delight, or make a gesture and summon visions from farther off than any spyglass could frame. No one knew the reason behind his strange collection.

Ayree was standing at the great round window when Basoni entered. He had his back to her and was bent over something on the sun-drenched stone sill, but Tabrac was with him and saw Basoni right away. With a joyful meow he flew to perch on her shoulder and nuzzle her ear ferociously.

"Ayree?" Basoni skritched the curly white fur on Tabrac's breast. Her white-haired brother motioned for her to join him at the window. Coming around on his left side, she saw what so fascinated him.

It was only a slip of paper. Very cheap, very thin. It lay on the broad stone windowsill, and the Prince of Warlocks bowed over it as if it were a relic of the departed gods. In his hand he held what looked like a good-sized mirror with a jade handle and gold frame. Then Basoni looked again and saw that no silvering backed the glass.

"What's that thing, brother?" she asked.

"Shh! It's about to catch." He changed the angle of the curved glass slightly and with much satisfaction said, "Ah! Look at the paper now."

Basoni looked and saw a spot of strange brightness, a ray of light stronger than the weak northland sunbeams, that fixed itself on the paper and seemed to emanate from the mirror-that-was-not.

"This is a burning-glass, Basoni," Ayree said. "They're common enough in the Twelve Kingdoms, but I never had one till now. Look! The paper's burning."

Basoni saw no great cause for joy in that. The bright spot was indeed beginning to smolder—cheap paper burned readily enough—but she could have consumed a ream of it to ash in less time than her brother had wasted at the solar window. "Was there some curse that wouldn't let you burn that paper up by magic, Ayree? I didn't see any runes written on it, but if they were invisible . . ."

Ayree's thin lips parted in a wide smile. "Morgeld's not sending me love notes, if that's what you mean. I wanted to experiment with what most folk use in place of magic. Isn't it wonderful, if you stop to think of it, that those born without witchly blood or wizardly ability can still create small enchantments of their own? From the mind and heart and hand, the wits and ways of magicless mortals are very clever. Never underestimate them!'' The witch-king shook his head and looked rueful for a moment. ''That was my mistake, and one I clung to for too long. We are born to our magic, and the wizardly come into theirs through study, but our powers have limits. The number of spells in this world is finite. The magicless know no such boundaries. Imagination is all that holds them back or sets them free.''

Basoni folded her arms. ''I know. I've been doing quite a bit without magic these past six years.''

For the first time since she'd joined him, Ayree really looked at his little sister. ''You've got flour on your nose,'' he said. He tried to wipe it off, but she slapped his hand away. Tabrac protested at the sudden move, digging his claws deeper into Basoni's shoulder and oaring with his wings in an attempt to keep his seat.

''I've been baking.'' She made it come out as an accusation. ''Not conjuring up cakes, but baking them by hand. Today is Hadin's birthday and I'm going to cook the entire dinner myself, and it's going to be a feast. You're invited.'' The last two words had the sound of a dare.

Ayree continued to smile. ''Invited to dinner at my own table? Thank you.''

''Invited to stop making that poor child's life miserable! Invited to stop laying blame on him for something he never asked for! I loved Hodah dearly, Ayree. She was more to me than any of the others—yes, even you!—but she behaved like a fool. Even I saw that. If you want someone to bear the blame for what has happened to the Tree of Second Light, blame her for it. No, blame me! If you blame Hodah, your anger goes looking for a living target and lights on her son.''

Ayree's smile was no longer so confident. ''My worst fears are coming true. Haven't I always feared the taint of passion that comes from mortal blood, even my own? Half of the greatest prophecy ever spoken in the Twelve Kingdoms died because Hodah could not curb her desires. Two roads could have brought the gods home again, and now there is only one. If Morgeld's creatures could conspire to defeat the witchborn, what chance will the magicless branches of the Tree have to bear fruit? How will they survive against the lord of Helagarde?''

Basoni snatched the burning-glass from Ayree's hand so fast that Tabrac was spooked from her shoulder. ''You can say that after what you've just been telling me? *Here* is magic!'' She held the jade handle high. ''Here is all that the witchborn and wizardly are: a burning-glass for the gods. We have no powers in us, but we are the focus for powers greater than ourselves. And yet the magicless mortals you scorn *own* their enchantments: They come from no other place but within themselves. They are truer magicians than we will ever be! If Ambra gave the great prophecy the shape of a tree, she had her reason. Let the Tree of Second Light be like other trees—the weakest branches fall first in a storm."

Ayree was no longer smiling. He took the burning-glass firmly from Basoni. "Then I suppose I ought to write Morgeld a letter of thanks for giving us one of these all-powerful mortals to raise up among us. Maybe I should just hand the Blue Sword over to Hadin right now, as a birthday gift."

Basoni's shoulders slumped. "I'm sorry, Ayree. I didn't intend to argue with you."

"You are nothing but arguments these days. What happened to my sweetest sister? Has drudging for Hodah's pup turned you sour?"

Basoni bristled. "It's not drudging, and if you would let me use my magics for Hadin—"

"Please." Ayree held up his hands. "I see my mistake, though it took six years to do it. I should have sent the baby away to a competent nurse somewhere peaceful, pleasant, and damned far from Castle Snowglimmer. I'm surprised you didn't clear out with the boy before this. It can't have been very nice for him, growing up here."

"At last." It was a mocking snarl. "Ayree, prince of hindsight."

Ignoring the insult, Ayree asked, "Then why did you stay? You could have taken him to Sombrunia."

"Yes, I could have. I was tempted to do that many times."

"Why didn't you? I wouldn't have objected."

Basoni spoke like a woman far older and wiser. "Run away? I ran away when I was a child to prove a silly point, and you know the danger I ran into headfirst. Hodah ran away because she was alone, ashamed, and afraid, and see what happened to her! Well, while I live, Hadin has nothing to fear, nothing to be ashamed of, no reason to be alone, and running away proves *nothing!* I decided to stay here with him until you and the rest acknowledged him as kin. That may be his only birthright, but I'll do what I must to secure it for him."

Ayree looked at her long and closely. After a pause he said, "I always thought Senja was the warrior among you. Now I doubt whether she could fight such a long battle, even if she were to forge a thousand swords."

"A long battle, but not a hopeless one." Basoni lifted her chin.

"You seem sure of that."

"I won't trade words with you anymore. I am celebrating Hadin's birthday, and all of the others will be there. I count four hearts that will be elsewhere, but so long as their bodies show up, I don't care. Our sisters have admitted how foolish it's been to ignore a living child as if he were air. Will you do less?"

The witch-king put his arms around his belligerent little sister. She stiffened in his embrace until he said, "I will do more than that. For your sake, my brave Basoni, I will accept Hadin, forget what's past, and— Well, it won't be the Blue Sword, but I think I might come up with a birthday gift he'll enjoy."

"Oh, Ayree! Ambra bless you!" Basoni threw her arms around her brother's neck and kissed him. Tabrac swooped in caterwauling circles around them, demanding to be admitted to the hug. Vexed when they paid him no mind, the blue-and-white familiar flew away, only to return shortly with an offering.

"Oh!" Basoni cupped her hands to receive the black kitten whose baby wings were the same gold-flecked blue as Hadin's eyes. Ayree laughed aloud and praised his wayward familiar.

"Tabrac doesn't want to be outdone. Here's an early gift for Hadin."

"How I wish I'd had the courage to speak to you this way years ago!" Basoni held the winged kitten close as it mewed and kneaded her bosom with soft paws.

"No, Basoni," Ayree said quietly. "You know how hard it is to command a spell of unmaking. All things must be in perfect balance, even the moment chosen to cast it. To undo an old foolishness is the hardest unmaking of all. I needed time to change."

"But you have changed, and that's all that counts. Hadin will be so happy!" She gave him another kiss and ran to show the boy his winged present.

She did not see how Ayree's face hardened soon after she was gone.

Chapter XIII

THE CURSE

"Words? What are words? Blessings, curses, magic spells, promises of love, threats of pain, all these are only words. They have seduced more women than a score of swains, slain more men than a hundred swords, rendered more cities uninhabitable than a thousand plagues, and yet you stand there clothed in smugness and no sense asking me, 'What are words?' You fool! Dolt! Cheesehead! Most manly of eunuchs! Ravisher of chickens and small sheep! There are words for you!"

—"The Condemned Counselor's Last Harangue"
from *The Scroll of Oran*

That night was the worst in Basoni's memory, and no doubt in Hadin's as well.

Yet it began merrily enough. Hadin was delighted with the winged kitten, calling it Midnight and at six years old imagining that he'd come up with a strikingly original name. If he'd had a choice, he would have spend the rest of the evening playing with the little cat.

Basoni wouldn't have it. She was too eager for the grand new future she foresaw for the boy to let him miss the feast.

"This is only the beginning," she told him. "Ayree himself will give you a present tonight, in front of everyone. You know what that will mean!"

Hadin looked at her. His steady gaze made his eyes seem much older, oddly out of place in such a young face. "It must mean something good, or you wouldn't be so happy."

"Of course it means something good. It means that everyone

will be much kinder to you from now on. Where Ayree leads, they'll follow.''

''Always?''

''Always.'' Basoni spoke the word with confidence. It was blind confidence, and confidence that chose to forget how the Twelve had once split ranks against their almighty brother.

Hadin teased Midnight with a wriggle of fingers. The winged kitten pounced without taking flight. It took the newborn generations of Ayree's familiars some time to realize that they were not the same cats their ancestors had been. So, too, the boy Hadin had trouble grasping the full significance of the change about to touch his life.

''I don't remember my lord Ayree being mean to me,'' he said, still watching the kitten's antics. ''He's always so busy with other things . . .''

''He will have time for you now. He'll have more than time. You're his nephew, after all; his blood relation.''

Hadin nodded. ''The way you are Morgeld's niece,'' he said. He did not see Basoni's features freeze at the name, and the memory of the dark man of nightmares. Unaware of anything but his kitten, Hadin continued, ''Maybe someday everything will be all right between you and Morgeld, too.''

''Leave the kitten alone,'' Basoni said tersely. ''It's almost time for dinner. Go wash up.''

Hadin obeyed, making Midnight a snug nest of blankets in a corner of the room that he shared with Basoni. When it was time to go to the great hall, his aunt had nothing to criticize about his appearance.

The ten witches and Ayree were waiting for them. The first course of lightly steamed vegetables in cold lemon and yellow pepper sauce was already on the table. To her pleasure, Basoni saw that Hadin's usual place at the foot of the long table was occupied by Asapha and her own by Zabala. Instead, two seats had been left empty on either side of Ayree's chair. She took the one next to Menka on purpose, leaving Hadin to sit beside Shama. Shama might have an acid tongue, but she didn't have Menka's reasons for hating Hadin. For Menka, the boy represented the folly she herself might have committed for love of Galivert if Hodah had not forestalled her. But Menka did not think of it as folly. She only saw the handsome lover, lost to a younger sister. Hodah had done her a favor, but Menka was incapable of seeing it that way. It was humiliating, and the only salve Menka knew for wounded self-pride was to make someone else pay for her mortification.

"Welcome, Hadin," Ayree said, extending his hand to the boy. "I wish you a good year."

The boy made a stiffly formal bow, and an equally stiff and formal reply. "Thank you, my lord Ayree. The gods grant you many more."

The witch-king raised one brow. "How old did you say he is today, Basoni? Not six! He has the manners of a Malben courtier."

"Better manners than that," Zabala said. "And as wardlady of Melbenu Isle, I ought to know."

"Thank you very much, my lady Zabala." The boy bobbed his dark head awkwardly, then took his place at the table.

Basoni did not enjoy a relaxing meal. She was torn between alternating worries over the reception accorded to her cooking and to Hadin. As the fourth course was cleared away by a flock of Ayree's familiars, she believed she could safely stop worrying about Hadin and concentrate her anxieties on the fact that Lucha had gone a little green over the stew.

She was sure Hadin was going to be fine. His behavior during the entire meal was mannerly, quiet, and above reproach. The six sisters who had never held any grudge against the boy spoke to him frequently, trying to draw him out, giving him encouraging signs and smiles. He was hesitant but polite in his replies. The guarded silences of six years could not be undone in a night.

The four sisters who remained cold toward Hodah's son kept silent. In its minor way, this was a good sign, for they were likeliest to spring on any error the boy might make. They would exploit a weakness if they found one, but they would never make one up out of nothing. Silence was the closest they would come to approval just yet.

The final course was laid on the table. The sugared flowers had melted into blobs of rose and blue, striping the sides of the three cakes. Zabala shook her head, bemoaning the ways of amateurs.

"Basoni, dear," she said, "next year you must permit me to show you how it's done."

Next year! Basoni's heart danced. *He's accepted! Oh, Hodah, let your spirit rest easy now.*

"Three cakes, Hadin!" Ayree rested his hand on the boy's shoulder and pretended to be sad. "On my birthday I only had one. This is a memorable day. Are you having a good time?"

The boy nodded earnestly. "Yes, my lord Ayree, thank you very much."

"Don't thank me yet. All this is Basoni's doing. We must thank her for everything."

"Even the stew?" Lucha whispered hoarsely, her lips very dry.

Resha discreetly pressed one of her herbal pastilles into Lucha's damp palm and just as discreetly whispered, "That stew would sit easier on a stomach not already filled with sweetmeats. Lucha, someday your self-indulgence will kill you."

"Good," Lucha muttered. "I hope it's today."

Ayree stood up. "You may thank me—thank all of us—when you've had your present. Sisters . . ." He motioned for them all to rise.

Lucha demurred with a weak wave of her hand. Resha touched her sister's forehead and said, "Ayree, she must rest awhile."

The witch-king was not perturbed. "Take care of her, Resha. What I have in mind doesn't call for all of you. In fact, I don't want Basoni in this spell. She's done enough for Hadin today. All the rest of you, join me." He fixed his eyes on Menka, Senja, Lavah, and Fortunata in turn, then added, "I know you want to."

They followed him into the middle of the great hall with only a passing show of reluctance—a downcast eye, a slower step, a murmur no one else could catch. Ayree gestured, and eight lozenges of ruby light glowed in a ring on the floor. The witchly sisters took their assigned places, with Ayree in the center.

"Come to me, Hadin," he said. "No, Basoni, let the boy come himself. He's a grown man of six now, and you won't be able to hover over him every minute when we're all at that royal wedding next week. Let him come out from behind your skirts now, for practice. It's his present we're making."

Hadin stood and cast one swift look at Basoni. She caught a flicker of fear in his eyes, but it vanished instantly. She had never really known how good he was at playacting. He went bravely from the table to stand beside the Prince of Warlocks.

"Now, Hadin, can you tell me what you'd like for your birthday?" Ayree asked.

The boy's eyes darted to Basoni, but his head never moved. In a low voice he answered, "I—I don't need anything, my lord Ayree. Thank you very much for asking me," he added so fast that the words tumbled all over themselves.

The witch-king rubbed Hadin's head the way a huntsman roughly caresses his prize hound. "Don't stand on ceremony, lad. We have six years to make up to you. In six years you must have longed for something?"

The dark head bent. "A sword."

"What? I didn't hear you."

"A sword," Hadin said louder. He looked up at his uncle. "But I'm too young for swords."

"Too young?" The red lights whirled themselves into cups at the feet of the eight witches, growing taller and taller as they turned, like clay beakers taking shape under the potter's hand. Strands of white began to lick out from a misty tangle of brightness forming in the air just over Ayree's head. The spiral's center shone with the blue-white radiance of polar stars.

"Too young?" Ayree said again, and he thrust his hand up into the heart of the twirling light. A shaft of cold blue stabbed into being, a blade of ice that only one power in the Twelve Kingdoms could melt: the Blue Sword.

The witch-king lowered the blade so that Hadin could see it. "To young for this sword, perhaps." He chuckled at the way Hadin's normally impassive face gaped at the miracle in front of him. The boy hardly dared to breathe, for fear of waking from what must be a dream.

"But not too young for a different one."

Hadin's head jerked up so abruptly that Basoni was afraid he'd sprained his neck.

"We will make you a sword, Hadin," Ayree said in a kindly voice. "We will make you the sword of your dreams, taking its shape and size and every detail of it directly from those dreams. It will be a sword forged of magic, not steel, but it will last. May you grow up to wield it well."

Hadin was speechless. Too many emotions were trying to get out at once; too many, suppressed for too long. All he could do was shake his head, terrified that if he said what was in his heart—*Yes! Yes! Give me the sword I've dreamed of! The gods bless you forever, give it to me!*—a clown-faced demon would leap out of the shadows and bray that it had all been the cruelest and most carefully planned of jests.

"Hadin! What do you say?" Basoni's reprimand shocked him out of his daze.

"I— Thank you, my lord Ayree. Thank you. Thank you all for—"

"Thank us afterward, Hadin. Now dream. Heat the forge that will make your sword. Close your eyes and dream of it."

Ayree's fingertips barely touched the crown of Hadin's head. The boy closed his eyes, and as soon as he had done so, a feather of golden light whisked into being from his brow, a dream's essence, visible to witchborn eyes. The Prince of Warlocks caught it on the icy point of the Blue Sword and drew it into the waking world the way a spinster's fingers whirl flax to thread. There was never such a spindle as that wondrous blade. The dreamthread snaked down the length of the Blue Sword to circle its hilt, then up Ayree's arm. It hugged the witch-king's shoulders in a gossamer filament of sunlight before returning down his other arm to its creator's bowed head.

"Dream," said the witch-king. The thread of Hadin's dream reversed its course, ran back the way it had come, from Ayree's fingertips, over one arm and the other, shooting up the length of the Blue Sword into the spinning canopy of snowlight overhead. Eight rising scarlet columns of burning power now arced in to meet the luminous whirlpool of Ayree's creation. The spiral arms hooked on to the blazing powers of the eight sorceresses and twisted their essence into a web of linking magics.

"Dream, Hadin." Ayree's voice held the command of unknown centuries. At the center of the vortex doming man and boy, the filament of golden light seemed to be swallowed by a pinpoint of purest black. The dream still spun its thread from Hadin's brow, but the hole devouring it was insatiable.

"What is he doing to the boy?" Lucha asked, still a little groggy. Her color was better, and she was at last able to take more than a casual interest in the weirding being woven before her.

"He's making him a sword, taking the pattern of it from the child's own mind," Resha told her.

"From a child's mind?" Lucha shook her head weakly. "A good thing it's Ayree managing that spell. I'd never dare anything so dangerous."

Basoni was instantly alert. "What danger? To take a shape from dreams and make it real is a common spell."

"Oh yes, when you're dealing with an adult," Lucha said. "When we long for something, it generally takes a fixed shape in our minds and stays that way, the image cut in stone. But children? Their minds change more than an Ishma haggler's prices. The spells of shape-giving can make dreams real, but when there are too many dreams at once, the gods know which one the magic will pounce on. Sarai save us all if a waking nightmare slips in among the waking dreams!"

"Ayree would know all that," Basoni said, trying not to sound too desperate. "He knows more sorcery than all of us."

"Yes." Resha's voice was strangely dry, as if the dreamer had finally awakened to a horrible truth. "Ayree knows exactly what he's doing."

The thread of Hadin's imagination spun on and on; the prick of blackness in the center of nine converging magics continued to suck it in. The light made a tent enclosing the eight sorceresses with Ayree and Hadin. Basoni saw her brother, head back, staring at the twisting, melding powers above, his face inscrutable. Hadin's eyes remained shut, but they were more than merely closed; they were squeezed tightly, not to capture a dream, but to lock out a nightmare. The boy shuddered, and a thin wail broke from his lips.

Flames of gold like a dragon's breath shot from the merging canopy of magics. A figure in shades of ash and bone, long and thin as the deadliest of swordblades, burned into being. A hand deformed by the blow of a legendary sword stretched out in mock blessing to include them all—Ayree, the eight within the spell's ring, the three without—coming to hover high above Hadin's dark head.

Too real to deny or call a vision, Morgeld spoke from the flames.

"The darkness sires beauty: Witchly blood blends well with that of the night spirits! Who can predict the nature of this breeding? I do not trust you, boy. Your birth stole much of your mother's power, brought her her death, yet you are magicless . . . to most seemings. Seemings are deception, and your father was deceit incarnate! Doom and deceit were your parents, but whose doom? I will not wait to see. I will seek, and send my seekers after you, boy. I will buy your death as surely as I bought your mother's."

Morgeld's gaunt figure bent over the child, his face so like an unhealthy parody of Ayree's fine features. Hadin shook harder, and he called Basoni's name.

She ran from the table, but the eight pillars of ruby light had spun themselves into a solid wall to keep out everything not already contained by the ill-fated weirding. She pounded against the barrier with spells of opening, of attack, and when these failed she beat against the shimmering sheet of light with her bare hands. Lucha and Resha flanked her. The wardlady of Vair slashed at the wall with a curved sword dipped in magic, the lady of Sumnerol with long and short knives that stabbed their enchanted blades into the bloody envelope of light to no avail.

Morgeld laughed. *"Do you think you can destroy me even if you can reach me? You had your chance, and it has gone forever. I am Morgeld, and my rule shall spread over all the lands. I will not abandon you so easily as your precious gods!''* His triumphant words rang through the spinning dome. Even when he lowered his voice to a sickeningly sweet cajoling tone, Basoni heard him plainly.

''I want your service more than your death, boy. Serve me, come willingly to me, and I will make you a prince of half my kingdom. Men will tremble at the name of Hadin! They will worship you as a god, as more than a god. We share the blood of dark places, boy. You shall be my heir, my son, my beloved . . . Do not force me to kill what I could love.''

Now Hadin did open his eyes, and the flecks of gold suspended in the depthless blue crackled into diamantine sparks. The atmosphere inside the turning red dome was thick with power, and the boy had witchborn blood. He had no more choice than a dry sponge plunged into water. Never a focus of magic, never a source, his magicless self still could not help but absorb some part of all the enchantments saturating the air around him.

"Go away!" Hadin shrieked, lashing out at Morgeld's floating body. He knocked Ayree's hand from his head and a corona of frosted fire flashed from his skin. "I won't be yours! Basoni, Basoni, save me!" He ran from his place beside the witch-king, ran to where he saw Basoni standing between Resha and Lucha, and clawed at the wall keeping them apart.

On her side, Basoni's hands grabbed for Hadin's, though she knew they could never touch, and both the sisters with her also stretched out their hands for the boy's.

The light was cold, yet as Basoni groped hopelessly for Hadin's hand, she felt it grow warm. Solid magic liquefied, hard scarlet light wavered and slowly dissolved into streams like blood that ran down Basoni's arms as her hands—Resha's hands, Lucha's hands—broke through and touched the child's living flesh. Magic on both sides had breached the dome.

Ayree saw. "We have him!" he cried. "We have Morgeld! Hadin's dreams summoned him, our magic formed him, and now we can seal him away from the Twelve Kingdoms for longer than Janeela ever did! Basoni! Resha! Lucha! Enter the dome, join with us! Hadin, use what's inside you to help us fight him! We'll freeze him inside a shell of power and hold him until the second prophecy of the Tree can safely be fulfilled!"

"Hold me? You dream, Ayree!" Morgeld cried. But fear showed in his pale face, and Basoni had hunted often enough to

recognize the quarry's look when it breaks from cover to find itself ringed by the hunters it thought to elude.

She and her two sisters stepped through the wall of light and took their stations in the ring.

"I will destroy you all!" It was a roar, a threat all sound and no teeth. Basoni felt the building current of strength running from witch to witch, pouring from her body into Ayree, the focus of it all. The Blue Sword pulsed with it.

"Hadin!" she called, exultant in the midst of so much power. If only the boy would attend, the magic he had unwittingly stored would bind with theirs and be the final measure for the sending of the spell to capture Morgeld. "Hadin, join with us now, for Hodah's sake!"

She could not take her gaze from Morgeld or look for Hadin directly, fearful of breaking the great sealing they all worked for now. She could just see him out of the corner of her eye. The magic he had absorbed still haloed him, making the boy into a nimbus of light. He hung back, at the very edge of the dome where she had so lately broken through. She gestured wildly for him to take her hand, eyes still locked on her enemy.

"Hadin!"

All his terror suddenly broke free. The boy moaned and fled, through the portal that he and his three aunts had opened, out of the dome, out of the feasting hall, running so fast that he almost outdistanced the angry words Ayree flung after him:

"Hadin, the gods curse your cowardly blood! You will forever undo the great magics!"

Basoni found him later, in her room. He was sobbing into the pillows on his little bed. She sat beside him and stroked his back. He looked up at her, face streaked and swollen with weeping.

"All's well, dear one," Basoni said. "Morgeld has gone. He escaped soon after you—" She hesitated, not wanting to use any word to describe Hadin's flight that might carry the stigma of cowardice.

"I was so frightened, Basoni." The boy burrowed into her lap and hugged her fiercely. "Morgeld . . . I never knew that was who he was. When I stood with my lord Ayree, I tried to keep my mind on the sword I wanted. I did! But always when I imagined having that sword, I pictured myself using it to . . . to kill evil things."

Basoni smoothed the thick black bangs. "Nightmare things, Hadin? I know. When I was young, Morgeld lived in my worst dreams, too." She embraced him tenderly. "It wasn't your fault, love. It's over now, and it's all right."

Hadin thrust himself out of her arms. "No, it's not!" he protested. "He— Morgeld put a spell on me, a terrible spell! Oh, Basoni, you have to help me. You have to take it off me!"

"A spell? What spell? Hadin, he didn't do anything like that. I would have seen or heard something, or sensed it magically. A lot of magic filled that place, and some of it clung to you for a little while; that's all. You're not used to the feel of sorcery inside you, but I swear, Morgeld cast no spell—"

"Look!" The single word was a wrenching sob. The boy rolled across the bed to hang over the far edge and scoop up something small from the floor underneath it. Basoni recognized Midnight's glossy black fur and she felt sick.

But Tabrac's kitten moved in Hadin's hands, stilling Basoni's worst fears, merely asleep. Hadin placed his pet gently on the bed between them. "I picked her up as soon as I came in, Basoni," he quavered. "I wanted to hold her. I picked her up . . ."

He roused the sleeping kitten with a careful prod under the chin. Her pink mouth yawned daintily and she stood, stretching her wings—

Her wing. Only the left pinion was still there, still attached to the kitten's back. Midnight bent it around, sniffed at it, and assumed a puzzled look when she tried to do the same with the other and it wasn't there.

Hadin produced the missing wing from under his pillows. "It came off in my hand when I touched her there. I don't think it hurt her, but . . . it just came off. I crippled her. Basoni, it's a spell Morgeld put on me! You have to take it off! You have to!"

Basoni took the wing from Hadin. She felt traces of magic still on it. "Touch her again, child," she said calmly.

"Touch her—?"

"On the other wing; it will come off, too. It's cruel to leave her neither one thing nor the other. Once she is an ordinary kitten and not a thing of magic, your touch won't have any effect on her again."

Tentatively Hadin followed Basoni's instructions. The second lapis wing came away. Midnight uttered a mew that was more surprise than discomfort, then leaped onto Hadin's leg and rubbed against his side.

"She's too young to know that she was ever anything but a cat like every other," Basoni said. "She'll be fine."

"What about me? Why did it happen? I did what you said, Basoni! Can't you help me now?"

Basoni shook her head and told the first of many lies.

"I haven't the power to lift any spell Morgeld has cast, my darling. All I can do is help you learn to live with it—as you can. As you shall. You must be more careful in the future is all; when you are near things created by magic, I mean."

"Things . . . ?"

"Like a familiar's wings. Though a thousand generations of winged cats are born, they are still only common cats with wings made of magic. Or if I were to make a gown of ordinary cloth and sew it up with spells, it would fall to pieces when you touched it."

More tears were forming in Hadin's eyes. "Morgeld must hate me very much. He . . . said he was the one who had my mother killed, and he wants to kill me, too. Now he's done this." A sudden hope made him ask, "My lord Ayree is very wise. Do you think he could lift this from me?"

Lies come more naturally with practice. "Ayree can't lift it either, Hadin. But if Morgeld thinks this spell will hurt you, he doesn't know me—or you! You will turn Morgeld's every mouthful bitter when he learns that you've grown into a man who laughs at the worst his spells can do to you. Hope and joy are poison to him, and with them you will win out over him, Hadin. Make me a promise that you will not despair, you will not give up, and that you will always fight!"

Hadin hung his head. "I can't fight. All I do is . . . run away. Maybe it would be different if I had a sword, but— I can never have a sword made by magic now."

Basoni forced him to look at her. "Swords don't make heroes. Magic doesn't, or blood, or anything but you, yourself. Make me that promise I asked for, Hadin. Give me a hero's word."

She heard the boy swear with childish solemnity exactly as she wished. But over and above his treble came the echo of a curse— no spell of Morgeld's casting, but Ayree's:

The gods curse your cowardly blood! You will forever undo the great magics!

Chapter XIV

THE EXILES

"Let the memory of your face be a madman's dream, and the desert drink your footsteps!"

—"Queen Nahrit's Farewell" to the hero Oran
from *The Scroll of Oran*

"What are you worrying about, Basoni?" Fortunata called after her as she tried to leave King Egdred's grand pavilion. "The boy's in his element here, surrounded by magicless things. He can't do any extraordinary harm."

Basoni did not reply. All around her, her ten sisters were enjoying the lavish hospitality of the Malben king and his childlike second wife, Tarada. In the style of Malbenu Isle, every aspect of a formal occasion was lovingly planned, exquisitely executed. The lords of more barbaric kingdoms in both the northern and the southern lands might scoff at the Malbens, calling them white-skinned, water-eyed weaklings, but in their hearts they longed to be asked back to Eddystone Castle so that they might partake of a waking dream. The rulers of more refined and civilized realms likewise longed to attend any function on Malbenu Isle, though envy burned their hearts, and their minds were preoccupied by taking notes on everything they saw, for future reference.

The Malbens knew that they were the aspiration and envy of all other folk—or at least of other folk's rulers. They were too schooled in politeness and politics to show the pride they felt over this.

So they thought. In the Kestrel Mountains one old saying counseled, *If you seek the frozen peaks, take a Malben with you. Prick him once and you'll never lack a source of hot air.* There were other sayings that spoke of Malbens as excellent providers of a certain type of odiferous fuel, but these were tavern matters.

Ayree's eleven sisters were scattered throughout the grand pavilion, each in her finest clothes, each deferentially attended by at least one representative of her wardland. The occasion of a royal wedding draws many kings—or their delegates—if only to measure the childbearing potential of the bride, the manliness of the groom, and so calculate whether the next generation will be conquerors or court fops. Bards still sang of the century-long Wars of Wedding that raged through the northern lands in the fourth century as kings and lesser nobles vied to marry off their heirs to the healthiest, sanest, most fertile mates to be found, purchased, or kidnapped from the clutches of rival rulers.

The resulting hostility between the unwilling marriage partners was never blamed for the rash of bar sinister successions in almost every ruling-class family in the years that followed.

Basoni had been enjoying the Malben hospitality as much as any of her sisters. On the arm of Lord Cafran of Sombrunia, she viewed the pleasures of the grand pavilion, conversing amiably about how things were going in her long-neglected wardland.

"My lady, if you would condescend to visit us, we would make you a holiday such as you've never seen," Lord Cafran said. He was only a little older than Basoni's twenty-eight years, yet he had the serious bearing of a seasoned counselor. His red-shot brown hair and beard made him look older still.

Basoni caught herself staring at him as he spoke, and nothing he said seemed more important to her than the small, simple fact of his presence. The initial joy that seized her heart when she saw him again, the burning blood that coursed from the hand he kissed to flood her whole body with liquid fire, the shuddering chill of fear that followed in its wake, all these became secondary to what she saw when her eyes lost themselves in his. She felt ensnared, yet not afraid, and the wonder of such a contradictory feeling called up a protest from her childhood memories: *This is love, and love is death's own brother! Flee, flee from what you know will follow!* But though she forced herself to look away from him, she would always find herself meeting his eyes again, and each time, the warning of memory grew weaker.

She made herself attend to his words and tried to force her stronger feelings to arm's length. Then she was gazing at him again, and saw an answering fire in his eyes to equal her own. Her heart measured out a dozen beats before either one of them could break the spell and act as if nothing had happened.

Basoni accepted the shrimp tartlet he took for her from a lackey's tray. Between melting bites she said, "I have had grave business in the north to keep me busy for many years, my lord. I could not abandon it. Now, however . . . I'll consider your words." In a softer voice she ventured to add, "It is very good to see you again, my lord, to speak with you like this. It would please me if we could do so more often, and not have to wait for an occasion like this to bring us together."

Lord Cafran remained the perfect diplomat, although his eyes told another story. "Your desires are mine. Please do think about what I have said, my lady; though I am afraid the only thoughts a person could have in this place are fantasies."

Basoni gave him a smile. "King Egdred's pavilion is a wonder, isn't it?" she said as they strolled on.

The grand pavilion was not so vast as Eddystone's great hall, but it was more pleasant. Windows were precious few and dampness was everywhere in that royal keep, with a few outstanding exceptions. The castle had been built for military reasons, not pleasure, and it still conserved much of its old martial aspect. King Egdred's new queen, Tarada, had found it a gloomy home and said so. To please her, King Egdred had brought an enterprising young architect from Cymweh itself, set him loose in the castle, and told him to follow his vision. The architects of that great northern port were justly famed for their ability to cope with transforming the oldest structures in the Twelve Kingdoms so that they might conform to the newest fashions in wood and stone. Let lesser lights build on untouched sites! Where was the challenge in that? Cymweh itself showed their artistry. Being a major trading center, each newfangled fad and fancy from abroad first made itself felt there. Yet for all the seaport's age, her architects made the gracious, elderly queen-city of the north show the world the facade of a fresh young princess. Surely, King Egdred reasoned, one of them could effect the same miracle with Eddystone.

It would not be an easy task. Alterations in the old structure were difficult or awkward at best. It was harder to turn an old warrior into a courtier than many people imagined.

No one thought of the roof. The architect did, and with King Egdred's patronage and help he erected a stone pavilion of silvery-gray marble whose delicately carved pillars and fan-vaulted ceiling looked as though they had been spun by a tougher sort of spider. There were wide, unglazed windows aplenty, and since the grand pavilion was so exposed to the elements and so far removed from the kitchens, it became the perfect place for summer entertainments, all with the obligatory cold buffet.

Cold or hot, the fare was succulent. Basoni was not immune to the attractions of well-prepared food, though as she and Lord Cafran concurred, the Sombrunian cuisine was simpler and just as nourishing. This reception in the grand pavilion had nothing to do with the wedding feasts and rites. It was entirely to honor the king's most cherished guests—those of witchly or wizardly blood who had agreed to attend a double wedding. The marriage gifts that mages can bring are coveted, for good reason. To have one wizard present at a wedding was fine, but to have the great witch-king Ayree and all his sisters was unimaginable good fortune. No expense or attention had been spared.

It felt so good to be welcomed, wanted, and served. Basoni had brought Hadin with her into the pavilion, but soon she told him to run along and enjoy himself. There were so many new people, so many clever people! She savored Lord Cafran's company. She was weary of conversations that ended in taunts or fights or expressions of pity. She was sick to death of having only Ayree and her sisters for companionship, and as for Hadin . . .

The child had changed. The past seven days had been nearly unbearable for Basoni, who was forced to see that this was no passing phase, like nightmare-fears soon forgotten. He'd always been shy, but the curse that had seized him on his birthday had made him more withdrawn than ever. At Castle Snowglimmer he would not come out of Basoni's room even for meals. She had to feed him there, or let him starve. When Resha, Lucha, or one of the other sisters who bore the boy no grudge came to ask after him, he hid. He did not speak—even to Basoni—more than necessary to make modest requests or to answer direct questions.

Once she came into the room veiled in invisibility and heard him talking with great animation. He was spinning a story of how a mighty hero would come out of legends and defeat Morgeld at the very gates of Helagarde. The hero would have a sword torn from the entrails of a dragon, and a ring that let him understand the speech of beasts, and a phoenix for his steed, and on and on in the same vein.

He was telling his tales to Midnight. The little black kitten purred, comprehending nothing, and Basoni stole out of her own room with the feeling of an interloper.

She had hoped the trip to Malbenu Isle would reverse the black change in Hadin. He might feel safer among other magicless mortals. His words would be freer, and he might even lose some of his fear of magic. He had reason to fear the force that had betrayed him, cursed him, then left him to carry the curse forever.

But Hadin hadn't changed on Malbenu; he had vanished. Basoni sensed his absence from the grand pavilion long before her eyes and minor searching spells confirmed it. She did not dare use a major searching, not with so many of the witchborn and wizardly in the room. A great spell would disturb them and disrupt the party as much as if Queen Tarada were to leap naked into the cold salmon and set fire to her hair.

The handsome Sombrunian lord noted how his land's wardlady stiffened suddenly, like a deerhound picking up an unexpected scent. He was too well-schooled a diplomat to show how deeply this perturbed him.

"Do you see Hadin anywhere?" she asked Lord Cafran.

"Hadin?" he echoed. "The little boy who came in with you, my lady?" He made a careful search of the crowd around them, saw no children in it, and shrugged. "If he's eaten his fill, there's little to interest a child at such a gathering as this. I'll sift the pavilion for him, if you like, or I could send one of the servants to fetch up one of my own page boys. Children can't hide from other children."

"Please . . ." Basoni fought to steady her voice. "Do both, my lord. I must find him."

Lord Cafran's tawny eyes rested on the fair young sorceress' face for a time, speculating. Then with a brief bow he went to do her bidding.

Where was Hadin? Where could he be? Basoni knew that she had to leave the party before she could use her magic to locate the boy. Lord Cafran would do what he could, but she knew very well how inadequate mortal means could be when trying to accomplish simple tasks. Magicless beings were forever losing things, and losing things forever. She would have to leave immediately and cast her own nets for the child. There was no mistaking the harried look she wore as she hurried for the door, and it wasn't hard for her sisters to guess what had put it there.

Fortunata saw, began to protest, then decided not to be content with words alone when actions could be so much more annoying. She ran after Basoni and grabbed one of her long blue hanging sleeves, gold pomanders swinging from the trailing cuffs. With Basoni thus in tether, Fortunata said, "If you take off like a headless fowl, you'll insult King Egdred. Behave with a little propriety, for once in your life. What can happen to the brat? Malbenu's an island! He won't get far. Besides, Hadin hasn't the stomach to strike out on his own.''

"Stomach?'' It was Menka. Tall and austere in white, she stood like an accusing ghost, magically summoned by the mention of Hadin's name. It was amazing how the same familial blue eyes that looked so warm and compassionate in Basoni's face dwindled to chips of ice under Menka's thick blond brows. ''The pup hasn't got stomach, backbone, heart, or liver for anything but hiding under beds. A fine creature our sister got in trade for her life! A hero born!''

Basoni shut out the hateful words. Fortunata was right. It wouldn't do to offend King Egdred. She spied the monarch in jovial conversation with her brother and the wizard Paragore-Tren. They stood by one of the large ogive windows from which the keen-eyed observer might discover the distant shimmer of the Opalza Sea. She would excuse herself first, then to go find Hadin.

As she came nearer, she saw that this trio was not interested in the view. The rippling azure radiance of the Blue Sword in Ayree's hands held king and wizard more fascinated than any prospect of the sea.

"So that is one of them,'' King Egdred said. Age had silvered his hair, but stolen none of his strength in voice or limb. Even his murmur of admiration concealed a lion's roar. ''Alban of Sombrunia holds the second, I hear. Someday I must travel to Castle Pibroch to see—''

"Ah, Basoni!'' Paragore-Tren welcomed her with arms wide. ''Your Majesty''—he bowed her to King Egdred's hand—''you have lived to see what few men will, unless they read transcriptions of the bard's tales. Basoni was the finder of the Blue Sword, though she was only a baby at the time.''

"Three years old is hardly infancy,'' Ayree corrected, his cheeks redder than normal. On the nearby windowsill, there were a number of empty winecups which an officious servant was now loading onto a tray. ''And whether she actually *found* it . . .''

"She was in the same room as you and the sword, and she was there first. There have been more casual findings in these Twelve Kingdoms, yet the effects of those discoveries are no less important, quibbles aside.'' The wizard winked affectionately at Basoni through his spectacles.

"Then it's kind of her to let you tote *her* sword around so freely!'' King Egdred roared, laughing. He turned to her with the same charm that in his earlier years had kept his subjects content at home while he hared off to wage useless, costly wars against the barbarians of Vahrd.

"Well, my lady?" Egdred raised an eyebrow. "What rents do you charge your noble brother for the use of the Blue Sword?"

"Your Majesty, if Ayree uses it—"

"—it is only out of Basoni's generosity." Paragore-Tren finished the sentence quite differently than Basoni would have done. "Ayree, you yourself told me it was Krisli's gift, and Basoni is Krisli's daughter. You haven't any claims to what the lord of the human heart bestows."

The wizard, still in a jesting mood, took the Blue Sword from the witch-king's hands and presented it to Basoni with mock ceremony. "Lady, guard your father's gift well. King Egdred will tell you that it's not wise to trust brothers."

The Malben king lost his smile. His brother Prince Phalaxsailyn was long dead, but the memory of his treachery was kept bright in the minstrels' songs. He would have let King Egdred live and die in the Vahrdish prison to which his vain wars brought him, doing nothing to free him, taking his throne. Good fortune alone had made things turn out otherwise, but at a dearer cost than any war.

"Indeed, my lady," King Egdred said, remembering his first queen in all her beauty, bravery, and wisdom. "I would not trust anyone too far on the basis of blood alone."

Basoni mumbled something innocuous, eager to make her excuses and go after Hadin. She tried to pass the Blue Sword back to Ayree, but apparently he, too, was entering into the spirit of jest that had possessed Paragore-Tren. She saw the flush of wine on his face and knew that once more he had let himself dive too deeply into the bottle.

"Keep it, Basoni!" he exclaimed expansively. "Keep it, it's yours! When you fight, don't you prefer to use a sword? Here's one for you, then! A worthy blade. Only this . . ." He laid his lips to her ear, one hand brushing the Blue Sword, and spoke in a whisper all nearby could hear. "Don't let Hadin touch it, or we'll have a puddle of water to fulfill a prophecy."

She yanked the sword away so fast that Ayree staggered, the worse for too much good wine. She spoke in a voice that sounded hard and bitter, alien even to her own ears, and her manner was cold enough to kill the merry atmosphere surrounding king, warlock, and wizard.

"King Egdred of Malbenu Isle." It was no simple naming, but

a formal summons. "Paragore-Tren of the Naîmlo Wood, I call on you in the names of Sarai All-Mother, Lady Ambra, Elaar the sea-witch, and Lord Inota to witness."

Egdred and Paragore-Tren exchanged a puzzled look. The wizard asked, "That's a mighty invocation to lay on friends. What must we witness, Basoni?"

Her eyes and throat felt very dry. Cold rage against Ayree for his cruel joke had come on her with no warning. She was amazed at how detached she felt, demanding oaths of truth from king and wizard, closing her ears to her brother's weak, bewildered protests.

"In the gods' names, witness that Ayree has given me this sword; this, and no other. He himself has called it *mine*, the gift of my father. I accept full charge of it from my brother's hands, with thanks to him for all the years he kept it safe for me." Her eyes rested long on each of the three men near her in a gaze that penetrated skin and flesh to the marrow of the bones. "By the gods I have named in their exile, I call you to witness too that I bequeath this sword, the Blue Sword of my father, to my sister's son, Hadin. Let your eyes record, your ears remember, and your hearts testify to the truth of it from this day on."

The spell of command she had laid over the little group broke. Ayree shook off some of his winey haze. "You can't be serious, Basoni. Do you know what this sword is?"

"Better than you think, brother."

Red-faced, the Prince of Warlocks turned to Paragore-Tren. "Here's where your fooling's led us! Once the brat touches the Blue Sword, it will vanish!"

"The brat." Basoni gave Ayree's words back to him again, saw his face flush even deeper. She gained confidence in the presence of witnesses and knew that now was the moment to demand what she must for Hadin's sake. Before, in Castle Snowglimmer, she did not have the courage to face Ayree as boldly as this. "You tell the truth tardily, Ayree. Was that why you set Hadin up for your curse on him? A witch-king's curse on a six-year-old child?"

"What is she talking about?" Paragore-Tren demanded. "What curse?"

In cool, measured tones, Basoni recounted everything concerning Hadin's ill-fated birthday feast. The wizard's eyes grew round behind his spectacles, his sooty brows rising. King Egdred of Malbenu folded his arms across his broad chest and his lips tightened.

"Ayree . . ." Paragore-Tren shook his head sadly. "You of

all mages in the Twelve Kingdoms should have known that to seek shapes in a child's dreams—''

"I wanted to *please* the boy! Why do you look at me that way? Are you going to listen to Basoni's speculations or the truth? Did I plant a vision of Morgeld in Hadin's brain? Though I might have expected it to be there, yes, seeing what close kin those two are!''

"A child doesn't choose his kin," King Egdred said.

"It was accidental. I swear that's true on Janeela's grave." Ayree stood tall, but a grievous burden of misery weighed down the oath he'd chosen. Only Basoni and Paragore-Tren could know its full measure. Again Basoni saw the vision of a young Ayree—truly young in soul as well as flesh. She saw it all once more, in memory now, but the sight still had the power to grieve the heart.

In Basoni's mind, Ayree trudged across the misty sands of the Laidly Marshes, a slender bundle in his arms, wrapped in a silver cloak. Where wandering ghosts drifted near to stare and wonder, his magic dug his love's grave deep. He left her there, in sight of Helagarde, so that Morgeld, too, would be compelled to remember. He placed his wards of unbreachable sealing over her. The spells flowed not from his hands, but from his heart in a river of red tears that soaked the marshy ground and brought forth a quickly fading breath of blue-gray fare-far, her favorite flowers. Her rest would never be disturbed while he lived, for half the witch-king's heart lay buried with her.

Basoni softened. Some of her old tenderness slipped back into her voice as she said, "I believe you. Only promise to remove the curse on Hadin and I pledge to give you back the Blue Sword at once."

Ayree summoned one of the ever-circulating servants and took a crystal goblet of pale green wine from his tray. He drank half of it with the first draught, drained it on the second.

"Keep the sword, Basoni," he said. With a brief bow to the Malben king, he left them.

Discomfited, King Egdred looked from witch to wizard for an explanation. Basoni was as much at a lost as he, but Paragore-Tren was not. Stroking his thick, chest-length beard, the wizard of the Naîmlo Wood said, "Well, little one, how does it feel to win the game?"

"What game? I wasn't playing—"

"There is your prize"—he pointed to the Blue Sword which Basoni held by the hilt in one hand, its ice blade pillowed on her other palm—"and the old tales all claim that each of the Three must be somehow earned, not given, before their final powers will be manifest. Whether you played fairly or not, you've won."

"Don't give me lectures on fairness!" Several guests in the vicinity of their small group turned involuntarily at the sound of a voice raised in anger. A snap of the Malben king's fingers roused a corps of specially trained servants who lured the eavesdroppers' attention away with offerings of particularly dainty delicacies. Soon there was a girdle of empty floor around king, witch, and wizard.

"Fair." Basoni lowered her voice truculently. "Is it fair that Ayree hates Hodah's son? That show of friendship on Hadin's birthday was false, all false! Was that fair? I didn't ask for the Blue Sword—he gave it to me as a joke. Well, the joke turned sour, but I gave him a chance to redeem it again. I'd call that fair enough."

"Very fair," Paragore-Tren said. "Child's play for Ayree to remove a curse, isn't it?"

"If he wants to," Basoni retorted. "But he wants revenge more."

"Is that so? And can't you think of one time your almighty brother failed to undo a spell?" He gave her a searching look. "Think, Basoni."

The wizard's dark eyes sparkled, held hers in a gaze that drew up the past. Memories returned: childhood memories of another six year old, herself. A snow-beast's captive, terrified to the brink of madness, she had been rescued miraculously by a traveler named Mustapha of Vair and his dog Elcoloq. These two had come so far north because they sought Ayree's help in lifting an enchantment from the dog.

"He couldn't do it," Basoni remembered. "Even owing them my life, he couldn't help them. There were too many spells on the dog, a tangle of magics. I have heard that only the gods may undo such knots of sorcery without killing the subject of the spells."

Paragore-Tren nodded. "From what you've told us of Hadin's unlucky day, there were twelve major founts of power flowing over him when Ayree . . . spoke too rashly: You, your sisters, Ayree himself. We might have to count Morgeld's presence too. Thirteen, then."

"And Hadin." Basoni remembered too well. "He had absorbed some of our joining powers, though he lost it soon."

"As he had to, being born magicless." The wizard threw his hands up helplessly. "There you have it. A skilled sorcerer can undo one part of a complex spell and leave the other layers in place, but only when that spell is cast by one mage, or by many magic-wielders united by a single plan. When different sources of magic come together randomly, there you have a tangle, and not even Ayree, Prince of Warlocks, can unravel it."

King Egdred's huge hand closed over Basoni's on the Blue Sword's hilt. "It is in your charge now, my lady. For good or ill, you hold one of the Three in trust. Guard it. It's all the hope we poor magicless folk have left now."

"No, no, I'll give it back to Ayree, I'll free him from his bargain, I'll—"

The wizard interrupted. "Do you think he'll take it back? You don't know your brother very well. You humiliated him before us, your sworn witnesses."

"He *will* take it back," Basoni insisted. "When he's sober, he'll realize what he's done and he'll take it again. He's too worried about the Tree's second prophecy to let this sword anywhere near Hadin. Oh! Hadin! Your Majesty, I must ask you to excuse me, but the child's missing. I have to find him."

Graciously the Malben king waved her from the grand pavilion, but once more she was detained at the doorway by Fortunata. This time the studious wardlady of Clarem was accompanied by Lord Cafran.

"My lady, what's this?" The Sombrunian peer's eyes grew wide at the sight of the Blue Sword.

"Never mind." She made it a sheath and belt of nothingness and plunged the blade into invisibility at her side. "Have you found him?"

Lord Cafran shook his head.

"Then I have to find him myself."

As she started past them, Lord Cafran grabbed her arm. He answered her indignant glare with the words, "My lady, it seems to me this boy's more to you than just a wayward page. I'm coming with you."

Fortunata giggled like an unskilled coquette. "What a fine way to draw men to your side, little sister! And since it no longer matters what we do with ourselves, thanks to dear, dear Hodah, why not indulge? You are a very handsome man, Lord Cafran. I wish you joy of—"

Basoni smacked her hard across the face and ran, Cafran on her traces. Down and down the winding turret steps from the castle roof they ran until these ended on a round landing. An archer's window cut a gash of light across Basoni's face, and she reached for the outer air, her searching spell a thick wave of magic pouring from her heart, directed partly by her extended fingertips, partly by the force of her desires.

"My lady?" Lord Cafran's breath smelled of honey wine and was very warm on her neck. She felt a hot prickling all over her skin and shook it off irritably.

"I must concentrate . . ."

"My lady, let me help you." His hands were on her shoulders, warm and strong.

"Be still!" She twitched out of his grasp and felt herself shaking inside her skin. The truth was that she could have sent her spell questing for the child with no need for such inviolable silence and separation. It was indeed the simplest of spells. But Lord Cafran's presence was unnerving, and his touch aroused sensations which in their turn aroused ancient fears.

"The gardens," she said after a while. Her arm fell back to her side. "He's safe in the gardens."

"Shall we leave him there, my lady, or . . . ?"

She smiled at him apologetically. "I'd be honored if you'd take me to him, my lord."

Lord Cafran inclined his head. "The honor is mine. I wish I might enjoy it more often, my lady. To serve you is my chief desire."

"You are very gallant, my lord."

"I don't mean it as empty gallantry!" The words came out with force. Lord Cafran looked startled by his own vehemence. Embarrassed, he turned away. "Your pardon, my lady. I didn't mean to shout. I only wanted to say . . . that I would offer anything in my power for your happiness."

It was a courtly compliment like many others, but Basoni knew Lord Cafran well, though this was only their second meeting. She had seen him in Sombrunia, and even then marked him for a man whose nobility was more than an empty birthright. It drew him to her more than any outward attraction. When he spoke of serving her, he uttered it with his soul, and her soul answered. "I believe you," she said softly, and gave his hand a fleeting touch. For the first time, there was no echo of fear.

She wished the moment might endure forever, but Cafran interrupted it. "I will take you to the gardens now, my lady. You want to find the boy."

The gardens of Eddystone were another addition made to

indulge Egdred's new queen. They occupied the southwestern side of the castle and stretched from the River Koly to the royal Port Road. The saplings that the king's gardeners had planted for Tarada were now healthy young trees—apple and peach, plum and pear. In the sea-kissed mildness of Malben summer, some still clung to their spring glory, but most were already showing the small, ripening fruits.

Under a black-limbed apple tree, Hadin lay with his head in the lap of a fair woman. She rested her back against the twisted trunk and sang him a song never heard in the Twelve Kingdoms.

When she saw Basoni and Lord Cafran, she smiled and put a finger to her lips. Very gently she let the boy slip from her lap, pillowing his head on a soft tussock of grass between the apple's roots. Rising to her feet, she came to meet them, her face shining, her gown of apricot and gold, violet and rose. Lord Cafran knelt in homage.

"You must be Basoni," she said, giving both hands to the young witch. Her voice was sweet and cool as a desert spring. "Hadin has been telling me all about you. Poor child, he's very tired, and he wept so much . . ." A cloud of compassion dimmed the brightness of her face for a moment.

Anxiously Basoni asked, "Is he all right now?"

"Oh yes," the Lady said. She seemed to take no notice of Lord Cafran, who remained kneeling, his face averted. "He has a heavy burden to bear, for one so young. Yet that may be best for it will prepare him for what waits. He understands his weakness better now. He told me how he feared to touch anything in Castle Snowglimmer, thinking it would all fall apart under his hand. Every time you came near him, Basoni, he shrank in terror at the thought of what his touch might do to you."

"To me?"

"You are magic, aren't you? You were born to it. But I have read the limits of his curse, and now he rests easy." There was the peace of a calm night on her face as she looked at the sleeping child. "Only those things of magical making will come undone in Hadin's hands. Inborn magic is not affected, nor those things created by a greater force than magic itself."

Unsure, Basoni asked, "What greater force, Lady?"

Eyes of dawnstar light brightened with amusement. "That's your brother talking. You know as well as I that magic is neither be-all nor end-all for these Twelve Kingdoms. Common folk stare when the magician dances, but who is it that plays the tune?"

Basoni understood why Lord Cafran still knelt, not looking at the tall and lovely woman. She herself was beginning to feel giddy from looking at those alien eyes. Her head hurt, and she was in no mood for riddles.

Then the Lady said, "Your sword."

"What?"

A pale hand pointed to the invisible scabbard as if it were plain to see. "The sword your brother just gave you, however unwillingly. The sword that you shall give to Hadin, when the time is right. And so your father wished it to be, when he left the blade in your mother's keeping. Poor burning soul, he thought his son would hold it."

"His son died unborn." Basoni again heard the small soul's plea inside her head, and she knew that she had more than fulfilled her promise to him when she chose to love Hadin.

"In that body, yes," said the Lady. "The gods know too much, so that we mortal beings dream they know all things."

"Lady," Basoni said hoarsely. "Lady, you are no mortal."

The woman laughed, and her hair, whiter even than Ayree's, rippled like a silk mantle from the crown of her head to her heels. "I am . . . now; and now I must leave you. A bride must not be late for any of the wedding festivities, or people begin to chatter. My servants worry if I'm out of their sight too long. Do they think I'll fly away? When Hadin wakes, tell him what I have told you. The Blue Sword is his."

She left Basoni to keep watch over the sleeping child, and as she went back toward the castle, she touched Lord Cafran gently on the shoulder. He rose from bent knee with the blinking, baffled look of an old mastiff who has brought down a kill in dreams and wakes to find himself cheated.

"Where is the Lady?" he asked. Basoni knew that he had heard nothing, been aware of nothing since the moment he first knelt before her.

"She's gone back inside."

Lord Cafran stretched his long limbs and looked at Hadin. "No more need for you to worry," he said. "Shall we rouse him or let him rest? These are pretty gardens."

They strolled across the grass, admiring the myriad greens of stalk and stem, leaf, shrub, and blade. Lord Cafran spoke again of the possibility of her coming to visit Sombrunia when the Malben wedding celebrations were done. This time he did not mention his king, but only himself. Under the rosy snow of a peach tree, he took her into his arms and dared to kiss her.

The suddenness of his embrace gave her no time to think, no time to dredge up her fears. This was nothing like the *lir*'s assault in another castle's garden. Warmth ran through her from bones to skin, and she returned his kiss with all of her mother's old fire. She felt his hands on her neck, a touch that melted past and future, leaving her only *now*. His hands fell back from neck to shoulders with the lazy grace of falling peachblooms, slipping beneath the loose neckline of her robe as if it were the most natural progression in the world. Her own hands wandered, too, and between kisses little sighs of longing escaped their lips.

Belatedly the old fears tried to assert themselves, but it was too late. Something more powerful had taken their place. No longer dreading what she knew would come, Basoni thought, *Fortunata is right. It doesn't matter whether we're chaste or wanton anymore. Now I can give thanks that King Alban never had me. This time, the first time, I am safe from any danger of conceiving a child, perhaps losing my powers if I bear a boy. Yet . . . even if it were not so, I think I might have chanced it anyway to taste your love, my lord.*

Oh, Hodah, now I see what you gained for what you risked! And I am Krisli's daughter, too.

Still, fear warred with reason and desire. She pulled away from Lord Cafran briefly when he tried to undo the golden girdle binding her blue robes and softly protested, "What are you thinking of? Anyone could come into the gardens and find us!"

"Cast your magic over us, then. Make us invisible, sweetest lady." He reached for the fastening of her robe again, then made a wry face when his fingers encountered something decidedly bulky yet decidedly not there.

Basoni laughed with relief, glad for a pause to gather some control of herself. "I've already made one thing invisible today, Lord Cafran."

"By the gods, what are you carrying there?"

"A sword."

His winged brows rose. "I see you came prepared not to trust me, my lady. Still, I don't think you'll use that blade to discourage me . . . will you?"

She told him no, but not with words. Control lost all value when she looked at him. She cast invisibility over them like a morning mist, and in that sanctuary she learned the truth of the teaching that the witchborn, who may control so much through their inborn powers, can never control the whims of their own bodies. The childhood terror of love that had held her captive for so many years was gone, and she knew that her life would never again be the cold, timid little thing it had been.

Cold no longer; never again cold. They were a fire, she and Lord Cafran; a blaze of her father's making. The lord of the human heart was born of the war god Inota and a fire-spirit mother. Now Basoni learned the truth of Krisli's fire, the searing, wondrous battle where victory and surrender melded into one. She laughed aloud, a laugh that became a moan, a moan dying into a sob of purest pleasure. Lord Cafran's lips were on her neck, calling up new sensations of delight even as she felt the old slipping away. Joy renewed itself endlessly, a spell more powerful than any the witchborn might command.

Then Lord Cafran raised his head, and Basoni gasped. A mask had fallen over his features for a moment, a shell of darkness with the sharp, hungering face of Morgeld.

This is well . . . A dry voice trickled through her thoughts, freezing her limbs for a moment—only a moment. Morgeld's mouth came down on her own, but it was Cafran's kiss she tasted. Love banished fear, and the strange seeing faded from her mind.

Lying in Cafran's arms, feeling him drowse by her side, Basoni spared a moment to send a casual searching spell out to check on Hadin. It brought her a peaceful vision of the boy, still asleep beneath the apple tree, the rise and fall of his breath the only moving thing in the whole calm scene. There were no more strollers to disturb his rest, no birds or small creatures to be seen, no wind to ruffle his hair or shake the bright blossoms on the tree above him.

Only the grass moved—a ribbon of movement that came winding through the green, and Basoni caught a glimpse of two tiny, lidless eyes of black ice.

She sat up with a scream. "Cafran, a snake! A snake's creeping up on Hadin!"

The Malben lord was battle-trained, his reflexes formed in reprisal raids against the pirates of Braegerd Isle. He lost no time in groping for his clothes, but leaped naked from the tent of invisibility, a court dagger in his hand. Her robe unfastened around her, Basoni ran after him.

Panic clouded her mind, but not for long. An arrow of spell-summoned fire flew past Lord Cafran's left ear, buried itself in the grass at Hadin's feet. The blades burst into a circle of flame that extinguished itself when its work was done. The boy woke up, startled, rubbing his eyes. A second of Basoni's sendings lifted him from the ground and reeled him to her side as the Sombrunian lord stared down at what was left inside the ashy circle.

"A snake," he said, speaking with the wide-eyed wonder of a village witling.

Hugging Hadin to her, Basoni asked, "Is it dead?"

"Dead enough, for something unnatural. There are no serpents on Malbenu Isle." He picked up the charred body on the point of his dagger and studied the markings not discolored by burning. "A marsh adder," he said. "A deadly rarity in the northern lands. In Clarem they call it Morgeld's Whip."

"Morgeld . . ."

I will seek, and send my seekers after you, boy, the dark one's words echoed.

One memory of horror was enough to banish all recent love and pleasure from Basoni's mind. In the clipped, commanding tones of his land's wardlady, she told Lord Cafran to dress himself properly and accompany her to her brother's presence. Hadin gazed from his adored aunt to the handsome Sombrunian, uncomprehending. When the three of them stood before Ayree in his private suite in Eddystone, Hadin still did not understand half of what was said.

What he did know was that his mighty uncle was wineflown, with a tavern-brawler's temper. He kept close to Basoni, hiding himself in her skirts like a nurseling.

"An attempt on his life? Basoni, you've been sharing Resha's dreamsmoke! He's a brat like a thousand others—yes, I'll call him brat to your face! That's all he is, and beneath anyone's notice. Why should Morgeld bother with him?"

"Wine makes you forget too much, Ayree. Or do you simply *choose* to forget that Morgeld reached for this child in the heart of Snowglimmer itself? You of all people should know that he's not one to accept defeat after a single attempt."

"Helagarde's lord hasn't any liking or need for cowards."

"Helagarde's lord sent a snake to kill him!" Basoni's voice was too shrill. Hadin was glad to have Lord Cafran there, a steady hand on his shoulder, a calmer, confirming voice.

"That's true, my lord prince," he said. "Malbenu Isle has no serpents, let alone marsh adders."

Ayree smirked. "What do you know of hidden things, little Sombrunian lordling? I can see from the realm of the night spirits to the place of the gods in exile, and I tell you that just because none of *your* weak-eyed breed ever saw a snake on Malbenu Isle doesn't mean there are none.''

"We must protect Hadin," Basoni said staunchly.

"From what? Your fancies? You always had lively nightmares when you were a child," Ayree replied. "Taking them into adulthood is tiresome. Go away. Protect him from your own imaginings, but leave me out of it. Besides, how should I protect him? He has a greater weapon than any of mine. Give him his inheritance, Basoni, and let him protect himself!''

Basoni started to reason with Ayree, but the words wouldn't come. She could no longer stomach the thought of pleading with Ayree for favors. Instead she hurled an empty curse at her brother and marched from the room, dragging Hadin with her and taking Lord Cafran in her wake. Ineffectually, he tried to soothe her once they were by themselves in one of the many small anterooms leading to the royal guest suites.

"My lady, your brother spoke rudely, but perhaps he's right. I don't pretend to know the habits of every creature in the Twelve Kingdoms . . .''

"No, Cafran. You are right and Ayree is wrong; wrong because it suits him to be. I must accept the fact that he'll do nothing for Hadin. He boasts to you about how far he can see, but he can't look inside himself. He hates the child, and only now he's coming to admit it.''

"He may . . . not be too fond of the boy." Lord Cafran gentled the words deliberately, for Hadin's sake. He could not know that Hadin had accepted an outcast's lot as his due; that the boy was used to abuse and rejection. "Still, he wouldn't let Morgeld harm him.''

"Not consciously. But he can deny that Morgeld means to harm Hadin—look the other way—so that when another attempt is made—"

"The gods defend him!" Lord Cafran's hand tightened on the child's shoulder.

Basoni gave him a grateful look. "The gods are gone, and for all of Ayree's bragging, no man knows where they dwell now; no, not any more than we know the full reason why they fled these Twelve Kingdoms.''

Lord Cafran shook his head. "I've always left questions about the gods to scholars. My lady, if you believe that Morgeld wants to hurt this boy, you have my word that he must come against me first.''

"Cafran, you wouldn't challenge Helagarde's lord!''

The handsome Sombrunian chuckled. He took her and Hadin into his arms and hugged them both warmly. "My king already has a court fool. I don't want his job. Let's learn from the gods themselves, my lady, and run away."

Basoni's eyes were wide with questions, Hadin's with fear. Lord Cafran knelt to look the boy in the eye when he spoke to him.

"It isn't cowardly to run away, Hadin; not always. Sometimes it's the wisest thing a man can do. The best way to defeat your enemy isn't always a head-on charge; not while he's strong and you're weak. No: evade, sidestep, go to ground, baffle, confuse your foe, lose him, and all the while build up your strength so that when the final battle comes, you're the stronger."

Hadin's voice trembled. "Stronger . . . than Morgeld?"

Lord Cafran's smile was warm and confident. "You're still young. Who knows the shape of your manhood? I have faith in you. Already you've got a loyal swordsman and a lovely lady in your service, my little lord! What won't you have when you're a man?"

Hadin stared at Lord Cafran for three breaths, then wordlessly flung himself into the Sombrunian's arms. Lord Cafran stood up with Hadin still clinging to him and gave Basoni his hand.

"We will take the boy to my lord King Alban," he said. "Morgeld still has a painful memory of what my master's sword can do. He won't dare come against the child there."

Basoni clasped Lord Cafran's hand warmly. "I'll lay the banns of sorcery over us as well," she said. "No seeking spell of Morgeld's will be able to find us then."

"But my lady . . . neither will your family."

She encircled Cafran and Hadin with both arms and serenely kissed man and boy, lover and beloved child. "I have another family now. Cafran, you'll never know how much I thank you for this. I can't repay it."

"You've given me all the reward any man could ask, my sweetest lady. Come, we'll see King Egdred privately and take my ship back to Castle Pibroch on the evening tide."

Still carrying Hadin, Lord Cafran led the way through the corridors of Eddystone. As she walked beside him, Basoni thought, *Your reward . . . At least you will have the memory of that, but never again. And will you understand? Can any mortal truly understand the price we witchborn pay to keep our powers whole? For Hadin's sake, I must guard mine. Oh, my beloved, will you still stand with us against Morgeld? Even when you learn that I can never share your bed again until he is destroyed? This time—the first time—I loved you without risk; impossible, now. And will you pardon me for this? Will you still love me, still know that I love you, with nothing but my words to warm you? A sad reward, my darling. May the gods forgive me.*

She breathed a strand of words, the banns of sorcery descended, and they passed from the sight of every mage in the Twelve Kingdoms.

Chapter XV

THE HUNTED

"Why should I flee my own kin?"

"Ah, my lord, there speaks a man who doesn't know dog-droppings about families!"

"Why should I fly from those who love me dearer than kin or kind?"

"Because they will tear the heart from your breast if you go, and the soul from your body if you bide."

> —*"The Last Dialogue of the Hero Oran and the Queen's Fool"*
> from *The Scroll of Oran*

The first winter rain lashed the stout turrets of Castle Pibroch, stronghold of the kings of Sombrunia. Basoni laid her hand against the diamond-paned window and felt how cold it was outside. Soon the thick glass would not be enough to keep the damp sea-chill at bay. Already servants were hustling from room to room throughout the castle, taking down the thin wall hangings of summery silk and replacing them with the thickest wool tapestries available, freshly unrolled from warm-weather storage.

Basoni inhaled a pleasant odor of mothbane emanating from the newly hung weavings, which coupled agreeably with the bitter aroma of wood burning in the fireplace behind her. She came away from the window to see what scenes were represented in the tapestries now going up in her sittingroom, for she would have to spend a good part of the Sombrunian winter staring at these walls.

One hanging showed a merry scene of Braegerd pirates carrying off a parcel of plump Sombrunian farmers' daughters and nearly perishing under their considerable weight. In the background, one of the farmers' more enterprising sons was toting off a willing Braegerd shieldmaid in trade. She would have to be willing, for her swain carried no weapons, while she was armed with sword, axe, and dagger, all of which she had inexplicably and abruptly forgotten how to use. As the menfolk bore the ladies off in opposite directions, the tapestry weaver had seen fit to include a knowing wink exchanged between the ravished shieldmaid and the heftiest of the Sombrunian farmgirls. Basoni smiled approval and turned to view the next hanging.

Her smile died as soon as she saw the second weaving. It was a fairly innocuous tableau of a hunt, but one look at the quarry made the young witch start.

"That's a bear hunt!" she cried.

The brighter and brawnier of the two men who were redecorating the sorceress' rooms paused over the roll of discarded summer weavings he was binding up. He looked at the hunt tapestry and uttered a low but heartfelt curse. "Come down off'n that stool, Benglin. This 'un won't do. Wrap 'er up again and don't stint the mothbane. Shan't be having this 'un up for a goodly long time."

From his place on a treacherous little stepstool, Benglin glared down at his partner. "What's wrong with 'un? Hangs straight and she's one o' the warmest you'll ever see. Need a warm 'un in the high rooms."

"Take 'er down and stop clapping your jaws. 'Tis a hunt scene, you great jellbones. A *bear* hunt!" he added meaningfully.

Realization dawned. Benglin's eyes opened wide with horror as he stared at the tapestry from an awkward angle. Still, it hadn't been the easiest thing to hump the huge roll of cloth up the turret stairs, unfurl it, sweep it, and then pick it completely clean of dried herbs. Threading its hanging loops over a heavy iron bar and wrestling the whole burden high to suspend it from the wall hooks hadn't been soft going either. Benglin was not lazy, but he hated having to redo a job already well done.

" 'Tisn't such a much of a *big* bear, Vinco. Could a'most pass for a wild pig." He turned to Basoni in appeal. "M'lord King Alban won't be coming up here to call on you *that* much, will he, milady? If you keep the room dark, he mightn't notice . . ."

"Lumpwit!" Vinco bawled, and shot the stepstool out from under Benglin's feet with a furious kick. His partner had hardly hit the flagstones before Vinco was up on the stool and taking down the tapestry himself.

Basoni stooped to ask a stunned Benglin, "Are you all right?"

Benglin closed his mouth and shook his head once, but the negative gesture was more by way of checking to see if neck and head were still partners. A loving touch to his own rear ended in a wince. "Neimar's nuts, that hurts," he groaned.

"*Benglin!*" Vinco let the tapestry fall, iron bar and all. Basoni leaped clear, but Benglin was smothered by the great hanging. He flailed around underneath it, too panicked to be thankful that the iron bar had missed his skull by inches.

As she tried to raise enough of the tapestry to free its captive, Basoni regretted her abdicated powers, and not for the first time since she and her party had arrived in Sombrunia. A touch of levitation would turn the unlucky weaving into a flying carpet out of the old tales, but she could not use even that small dab of magic. Not now.

She had cast the banns of sorcery over herself and the boy, but while these offered great protection, they did not make a flawless shield. The banns sheltered them from the searching spells of wizards and the witchborn, but did not make them invisible to ordinary eyes.

And my magic makes us even more visible, she thought. Each spell she cast was like a fire kindled within a tent: The tent might hide the flame itself from sight, but it could not contain the smoke nor the smell of burning.

Vinco leaped from the stool, grumbling under his breath, and took his place beside Basoni. His muscular arms had their own magic, and one twitch flipped the tapestry off Benglin's head. The unhappy man sat there, gasping for breath, sneezing from dried herb dust, and covered with a greenish powdering of crumbled mothbane.

"You—you—you—*bastard!*" Benglin finally managed to sputter.

"Shut it or it's back under wraps for you, clodnoggin," Vinco said calmly. "Or worse, if'n I make report of the foul language you've been using in our wardlady's presence."

Smiling, Basoni tried to assuage Vinco. "I've heard worse language than that, Vinco, I promise you. We came here on shipboard . . ."

Sniffing disdainfully, Vinco pulled his shoulders back. "Milady, in your wisdom I know you're too bright to go comparing seamen to castle servants. We'll fetch up a better hanging for your walls, double-quick."

"Yes, but . . . I suppose I could hang this one on a darker

wall, or in my bedchamber. I doubt the royal family will be coming all the way up here to visit me."

Still proud, and somewhat condescending, Vinco said, "Milady, with *this* royal family, it's the gods' own guess. We can't have 'un hanging here, and that's that. Roll 'er up, Benglin, and stop your lolling."

Bemused, Basoni watched as the two men trundled off the offensive tapestry, Benglin still sneezing sporadically. They had not been gone more than a few minutes when there was a knock at the door.

Basoni opened it and immediately fell into a profound curtsey. "Welcome, Your Majesties."

Vinco had spoken from experience when he commented on the capricious ways of his royal masters. Arm in arm, more like young lovers than a married couple with four strong sons to their credit, King Alban Stonesword and his bride Queen Ursula the Accursed came sailing into Basoni's rooms.

"I hoped you were going to drop all those formal tags with us, Basoni." Ursula raised the young witch from her reverence, embraced her warmly and planted a sister's kiss on her cheek, then glanced around the chamber. "I *thought* it was a bit cool in here. Where are the rest of the winter hangings? They should be up by now."

"We . . . ran into a little difficulty with one of them," Basoni said. "I didn't care for the design."

"What, the bear hunt again?" King Alban laughed. "Really, Ursula, why won't you let me burn it and be done?"

"It's a good tapestry and it was part of my dowry, that's why. Am I the only one who takes no offense over it?" The queen tossed her honey-colored hair defiantly.

Alban replied, "You are too ready to forgive everyone everything. I often think that your sister Mizriel showed very poor taste in sending you that particular tapestry when she was parceling out your dower-goods. Or what's more likely, she did it on purpose."

Ursula gave her royal husband a patronizing pat on the cheek. "Well, we'll never know, will we? So we might as well make the best of it. Maybe Mizriel *did* choose a bear hunt deliberately, the same way she threw that curse on me when we were children. Yet the curse worked out to our advantage in the end, didn't it, my love?"

King Alban gathered his wife to him fondly. "True. You might have been married and a mother before I ever met you if the curse hadn't kept all your suitors at bay."

Ursula laughed, and Alban looked at her with the same gaze of abiding tenderness that had glowed in his eyes nearly twenty years ago. Their eldest son was now the same age as Ursula had been when she met her beloved lord, yet it seemed no time at all had passed since the moment these two first declared their love. Basoni's heart ached with envy and longing when she watched them together.

"Mizriel's childish curse didn't discourage *all* my suitors, Alban," Ursula said.

The Sombrunian king stopped smiling. "Don't name him, Ursula. They say that to name is to call, especially *that* one."

Ursula touched his cheek again, this time in simple caress. "I don't believe in old wives' tales, and I didn't mean Morgeld. I meant you."

The queen's soft hand continued to stroke her husband's cheek. He took it and pressed it to his lips. Suddenly, with almost no warning, he turned his head aside and spat on the floor.

"Ugh! Ursula, it's almost winter! Haven't you shed your old coat yet?"

The queen of Sombrunia growled at her husband. She growled deep in a throat no longer white and slender but short and brown and covered with fur. Her small hand was a viciously clawed paw the size of a goodly cushion, and her regal robes of silver-shot green had magically vanished to accommodate the change as Ursula's curse turned the lovely woman into the shape of a shambling she-bear.

King Alban ignored his wife's transformation in much the same way as she had come to overlook his sorry habit of nailbiting. He continued to pick and spit loose bits of fur from his lips. "It's always this way," he explained to Basoni. "She won't submit to a good currying when she's in bear-form. She thinks it's enough to comb her human hair, though I keep telling her that the one has no connection with the other."

"I've got better things to do when I'm bearish than have the stable hands groom me," the bear rumbled, shaking her humped shoulders. With a rolling gait she went to the tapestry-bare wall and stood up to rub her back against it, making little pleasure-grunts. "Besides, those currycombs hurt."

Alban sighed and turned to Basoni for support. "Have you any idea of what sort of important business a bear could accomplish that a queen can't?" he appealed to her.

"In truth, I don't know," Basoni said.

From the wall, Ursula snorted. "In truth, you don't think,

Basoni, yet you and I share the same task; I for my son Alaric, you for your boy, Hadin.'' She gave her shoulders a final rub and fell to all fours, satisfied.

"How is that, Ursula?" Alban asked.

The she-bear shuffled over to lean her bulk against Alban's leg, nearly toppling him with affection. "Why, to teach the young ones that to be cursed is not to be doomed. The gods know, they think it's the end of the world. My poor Alaric! I'll never forget how astonished he looked the first time he changed. He was only eight years old and he thought it was Paragore-Tren's doing, because he'd hidden the wizard's spectacles under a chairpad."

"And forgot about it and sat on them afterward," Alban added solemnly.

Basoni stifled a giggle. Paragore-Tren's spectacles were his dearest possession and he was very protective about them. Like the witchborn, the wizard who could alter the outer world in so many ways was powerless to alter his own body's infirmities. The most renowned mage in all the Twelve Kingdoms was moleblind without his spectacles.

"We had to explain to Alaric that Paragore-Tren had nothing to do with it. My curse had descended to him, that was all,'' Ursula said.

"Only to Alaric?" Basoni asked. "None of your other sons?"

The she-bear nodded her heavy head. "He complained that it wasn't fair. Children think that fairness answers everything. But curses are like life: They aren't fair, they're random, and their random nature is what makes them so much more terrible than any other spells. You never know what to expect with a curse. Some can be lifted with a word, others can't be removed by death itself; some vanish in an hour, others cling to the blood. I never knew that Mizriel's temper tantrum would be passed on to one of my sons. Whether his children inherit it too . . .'' The bear tried to shrug, an impossibility.

Quietly Basoni asked, "And has Alaric come to accept his fate?"

Alban replied, "Sometimes I think he has, other times I doubt it. He was an outgoing child, but he's grown up more thoughtful than his brothers. When the change strikes him, he always runs off.''

"He says he doesn't want to affright the ladies," Ursula put in. "The same ladies who see me go bearish so often that a loose mouse gets a louder squeal out of them! Once we had an animal trainer visit the court with a dancing bear in tow. The beast broke its lead and got lost. No one knew where it was until I ran into one of my maids of honor in the hall. She took one look at me and asked how my headache was. 'What headache?' I asked. 'Why, pardon the liberty, Your Majesty,' she said, 'but you grumbled so much and even lashed out with your paw at dear old Lady Sasseel, and not a word could we get out of you, that we all assumed you had a bad headache. So we bathed you and dried you and put you to bed and Lady Sasseel gave you a big dose of her nerve tonic, and—' ''

''That was when Ursula told her that she hadn't been in bear form for days,'' Alban said.

''When we brought the real bear into the great hall—''

''—with Ursula's nightrobe over its shoulders,'' Alban interjected, snickering.

''*When we two brought him in*''—the she-bear glared at her husband—''and told the tale, Lady Sasseel took one look at the beast and fainted.'' Alban's queen made a gruff sound that was ursine laughter. ''And the bear took one look at her and fainted, too. Poor thing, I've dealt with Lady Sasseel *and* that nerve tonic of hers, and I don't blame him.''

Basoni wasn't laughing. ''So Alaric keeps to himself.''

''Sometimes.'' Alban sounded defensive. ''A young man has many good reasons for wanting to be private at his age. It isn't all the curse's fault. Youth brings a few curses of its own.''

Ursula deliberately bumped her shoulder against him so that he fell over onto his back. One paw rested majestically on the king's chest as she inquired, ''And who cursed you with stodginess, my dear husband? 'Youth brings a few curses of its own.' Phaugh! Spoken like a boneyard philosopher. Can't you see that Basoni's worried about her Hadin? Fine comfort you give!''

As Ursula spoke, she dwindled. Fur retreated as ladyfine skin and queenly garments reappeared. Before the last word was out of her mouth, she was a woman again, and very silly her husband looked, pinned to the floor under her hand like that.

Ursula turned a blind eye to Alban's glowering. She stood, smoothed her dress, and blithely said, ''Get up, darling. That floor's a mess of mothbane. As for you, Basoni, feel free to send Hadin to speak with me if you think it will help him learn to cope with his curse. I've come to excellent terms with mine. It's done me more favors than disservices, so far.'' She held one slim hand up for contemplation. ''Who would think that *this* was all the weapon needed to kill Morgeld's ill-famed Captain Tor? Perhaps

Hadin's curse will serve him just as well. Will you and he be dining with us in hall tonight?''

Basoni indicated not. "I hear there are ambassadors from Paxnon and Clarem in court. If they saw me or the boy, they might ask questions and report it when they returned home. Word could get back to Fortunata or Sacchara.''

"And so to your brother and the rest. I understand.'' Ursula clasped Basoni's hand. "They say it's no secret when more than one soul shares it, but we've managed to keep your sanctuary unknown for this long.''

"I am grateful to you both.''

"Be grateful to Lord Cafran. I never knew the man had such a talent for intrigue," Ursula said. "Of course, he has a very special inspiration these days. We'll have your meal sent up here, for the three of you.''

"Thank you.'' Basoni did not think it was necessary to mention that lately these private suppers only included herself and Hadin. Lord Cafran no longer came regularly.

This night, however, he was there. When Basoni opened the door to admit those few servants trustworthy enough to guard the secret of her presence in Castle Pibroch, Lord Cafran was with them. He answered her doubtful greeting with a curt nod, then set to directing the servants as they laid out the evening repast.

Basoni felt her stomach knot painfully. She could read nothing of her lover's thoughts from his expression, where once she had been able to see his every feeling for her in his eyes, offered freely. Now she was locked out, excluded, and the sensation was like walking over knives.

Hadin welcomed Cafran with all the pent-up love a young boy can feel for the first man ever to show him some kindness. From the moment the Sombrunian peer had comforted Hadin in the gardens of Eddystone Castle, the child was his. On board ship, during all of that uneventful voyage from Malbenu Isle to Sombrunia, not a day passed but Hadin spent every moment possible in Lord Cafran's company.

Even now, over dinner, the boy was prattling on to Lord Cafran about what he had been doing all day. Basoni was taken for granted, relegated to second place. Unnoted, she watched Lord Cafran closely. She saw how he still smiled at Hadin's enthusiastic recitation, but it was a cooler smile. Much of the old warmth was gone. Everything about her one-time lover seemed more abstracted, more distant than before, and every day added its share to that growing gulf. She knew what was at the bottom of it, but she wondered whether Cafran himself understood. Silently she prayed that Hadin might not be blamed for this, too.

"You unhorsed Prince Alveiros?" Lord Cafran gave Hadin a speculative look. "He's more than twice your age—fifteen years old, he is! And you claim to have unhorsed him?" A little of the old affectionate light glowed in his heavy-lidded eyes. "Exaggeration isn't a virtue anywhere but Vair and the law courts, Hadin."

"No, no, I'm telling the truth, my lord." Hadin was bouncing in his seat, not touching the food before him. "I was with Prince Alain—he's nearest my age—"

"As near as we stand to Braegerd Isle. There's a vast abyss between six years and thirteen, my boy."

Hadin looked ready to start a fight, even with Lord Cafran. "*He* never acts like we're so distant, my lord. Prince Alain is my friend, he said so, and . . ."

"Hadin, you must eat your greens," Basoni interjected. "I'm sure the story will wait until you've finished the salad. And your meat is growing cold."

Lord Cafran gave a hearty laugh and pounded his empty goblet on the table. "There's a better lesson for you than you'll ever get on the field of arms, Hadin! A man can fight a hundred battles, slay a thousand foes, and when he comes home to tell about how he barely escaped alive, there's always some woman waiting to say, 'Yes, yes, but all that can wait until you've eaten, or until you've washed, or until you've taken off those filthy clothes, or until the world ends.' " Two deep lines showed just above his nose. "A woman is never without an excuse to keep a man waiting."

Hadin did not notice Basoni's retreat into a lasting silence. He seized his chance to recount his wonderful exploit with King Alban's second-born son.

"Prince Alveiros was riding at the standing target, trying to knock a gourd off the post with a cane lance while riding at full gallop. He kept missing, and began to complain that he always did better with the whirler—you know, the mockery man on a pivot. If you don't hit his shield just right, he spins around and gives you a wallop with his sword. The whirler was broken, Prince Alveiros' tutor said, and he was too old to give the prince practice against himself on horseback. So then"—Hadin's voice dropped into a mischievous whisper—"I sneaked away. I ran into the stables and I put on a big padded leather vest and practice helmet, and I mounted one of the smaller horses, and I took a wooden sword from the rack, and I came galloping down the hill from the stable right for Prince Alveiros. I was screaming an awful battle cry . . .''

"What was that?" Lord Cafran asked lazily. " 'Help me stop this damned horse!'?''

Hadin scowled until he realized that his friend was merely jesting. He resumed his tale with no loss of enthusiasm and hardly any pauses for breath.

"Oh, you should've seen the tutor's face! You should've seen Prince Alain's, and if Prince Alveiros wouldn't't've been wearing a barred helm like mine, I'll bet his face was a sight, too! I was kicking the horse to go faster and faster, and I was waving my sword, and just when I thought no one would do anything, Prince Alveiros spurred *his* mount up the hill to meet my charge. Oh, it was wonderful! I saw that he had a lance and all I had was a sword—*much* shorter. He had the—the—''

"The advantage of arms," Lord Cafran supplied.

"Yes, that. But I didn't care! I just kept riding, and he tried to sweep me from the saddle with a sideways blow of the lance, but it struck the top of my helm and went *right* over my head and I gave Prince Alveiros a great big swat with my sword and I got him smack across the chest and he went *flying* off his horse's back and—''

"And that was that. Except for what Prince Alveiros had to say when he found out it was you, I'm sure.''

Hadin shook his head decisively. "Prince Alveiros didn't say anything to me; not anything bad. He laughed as loud as Alain and said that this was the final proof he'd been wanting to show his father that he didn't have the makings of a fighter.''

"That much is very true." Lord Cafran chased the last trace of beef gravy from his plate with a morsel of bread. There was a half-smile on his lips as he contemplated his empty plate in contrast to Hadin's virtually untouched portion. "From the time he was young, our Prince Alveiros showed himself born to the lute and citern more than the sword and spear. His father has Neimar's gift of music, so it's no great wonder to find it in his son. There have been famous bards of royal blood before this in the Twelve Kingdoms.''

"Bards." For a six-year-old, Hadin had developed a fine, adult sense of prejudice. *"Songsters!* If I had to spend my whole life making up songs and tales, I'd be bored out of my skin. I'd rather die!''

"I'm very glad to hear you're so firmly resolved. I've heard you sing. Killing people with a sword is much more merciful.''

Lord Cafran reached across the little table to ruffle Hadin's black hair and the two exchanged a smile of perfect friendship. "Don't discount the bards, my boy. There have been many heroes in these Twelve Kingdoms—more in the olden days than in these sorry times—but we only know the names and deeds of those whom the bards have chosen to honor. For the rest . . ." He scattered invisible ashes. "Heroes have slain countless foes, passed untold perils, won kingdoms and more than kingdoms, yet the bards have defeated countless heroes simply by *not* singing a song."

Hadin looked down at his plate. "I don't sing that badly," he mumbled.

Lord Cafran's crooked smile rose noticeably on one side. "Isn't that just like a child?" he said to Basoni. "He only hears what he wants to hear. Or is that like someone else as well?"

Basoni tried to hold on to the illusion of a pleasant evening meal, though she knew well of whom Lord Cafran spoke. "I'm sure that's like many people at court."

His lordship laughed. "Which court? Not Sombrunia's. We may conserve the formalities, but they are only for show. We are never deaf or blind to the truth, just because it suits us to be so. You must be thinking of Malbenu . . . or perhaps Snowglimmer." He looked at Hadin. "Tell me, my boy, as one ordinary mortal to another: How did you manage to grow up among so many witch-spun lies and still know there's such a thing as truth in the world?"

The boy looked bewildered at his idol. "I . . ."

Basoni stood up and pushed her chair back. "Hadin, you haven't touched your dinner," she said severely. "Perhaps you've been too distracted. Lord Cafran and I will leave you alone until your plate is clean. Then, and only then, will we have dessert. Lord Cafran . . . ?" She offered him her hand in a way that was more order than offer.

He rose, still wearing that enigmatic smile, and, taking the proffered hand, raised it to his lips. Gallantly he threaded her arm through his and let her lead him into the inner room of her turret suite.

The heavy oak door was fitted with a gilded iron latch which Basoni let fall into place. Turning, she saw that Cafran had ignored the two comfortable chairs beside the window. He was sprawled at ease across her bed instead.

"I won't ask you to join me, my lady," he said. His strange smile was gone. "We've had more than enough opportunities to renew our first acquaintance—chances that were more private and favorable than this. Or does it change things to have Hadin so near? He was nearby the first time too, if I recall, but I thought it was an accident, not a necessity."

"Be quiet!" Basoni stalked across the room and flung herself down in one of the chairs Lord Cafran had scorned. A brazier stood close beside her, adding its warmth to the angry heat already bathing her cheeks. The softly glowing metal vessel had the whimsical shape of a bear guzzling honey, though the ravaged hive between his paws held hot coals.

"Quiet, my lady? That's your speciality: silence, and a few tattered excuses now and then for variety's sake." The two small lines between his brows were deeper. "I would have brought you and Hadin to sanctuary in Sombrunia anyway, you know. You are the wardlady of our land, and I could do no less. There was no need for you to *earn* your passage."

He meant to hurt her, and he succeeded. Outrage left Basoni voiceless for an instant, but it could not stop the tears of anger from coming to her eyes. If she lived as many centuries as her brother Ayree, she would never be able to conquer that deplorable reaction.

Of course Lord Cafran misinterpreted her tears as a sign of sorrow. "Do you regret it, my lady?" he asked, with no kindness. "Now that you know it was unnecessary, are you sorry to have bedded me? Use your magic to erase the past, then. Use it to find yourself a worthy lover—a sorcerer, a magician, a god!"

The tears spilled over, but they were no longer angry tears. The small voice of her newfound pride protested weakly, unable to stop their flow. The pain swelling inside her was too great for pride or sense to control.

She heard Cafran speak, his tone softer, and she grimaced. *Do I have to buy kindness with tears?* She fought down the treacherous signs of sorrow, wiping them harshly from her face, only to find her lover kneeling at her feet, her hand in his.

"My lady, don't cry." His lips were soft on her work-roughened palm, the thrilling sensation of his touch made even more acute by long abstinence. She could cup the breath of his life between her fingers.

"I never meant to cry, Cafran. I . . . You hurt me."

"I was hurt myself. It's unnatural not to try striking back when someone hurts you; even someone you love."

"You love me . . . yet you don't believe a word I say."

"Believe you?" The old exasperation came back into his voice like a flood. "Inota be my witness, how do you expect any man to believe the tale you tell?"

"Why not? You know that I am witchborn. I've explained to you many times that the laws ruling my body are different from those governing magicless women. How have I hurt you? By denying you my bed after I took you so readily—so gladly!—as my lover on Malbenu Isle? Oh, Cafran!" She bent over him as he knelt and drew his head to rest on her bosom. "Cafran, if it were in my power, I would never spend another moment out of your arms. Now I can believe the songs they sing of my father's power. Krisli's daughters are also the greatest of Krisli's Fools. I wanted you from the moment I saw you, without knowing I wanted you or how sweet it would be to love you. Now I know, and the pain is so much worse, wanting you, knowing what I want, and knowing I can't have it . . . not now."

He burst free of her arms. "Why not?" he demanded. "Not because of that story you told me about conceiving a boy-child . . . ?"

Basoni was grim. "If you keep calling it a story, as if it weren't true, then a story killed my mother and my sister."

"I didn't mean it that way. Krisli bridle my tongue! Basoni, what I mean to say is, you and Hadin are safe now. My lord King Alban has placed you under his protection. Every fighting man in Sombrunia will defend the child against any harm, if you whisper a word to the king. Besides, you haven't done so much as lift a plate with your powers since you've come here."

"I don't want to do anything that might draw the wrong attention to us. Every time one of the witchborn or wizardly uses magic, it changes things, and some beings are very sensitive to changes."

"Like hunters tracking a deer." Lord Cafran understood. "It's a shadow barely seen in the forest, but a good hunter doesn't have to see his quarry: a broken twig, a pile of leaves disturbed, a little bark rubbed off the trees with its antlers—these are trail enough. You made a wisewoman's choice, holding back your magic."

He did not notice the fleeting look of guilt pass over Basoni's face.

"My lady, you are safe, you don't use your magic, so what difference would it be if you and I did make a son between us?" He rose from his knees and lifted her from her chair into his arms. "*Our* son, my beloved . . . as Hadin is already our son in everything but birth. I will stand as a wall of swords between the two of you and any evil. Believe me, trust in my strength, trust in my love . . . love me.''

She wanted to believe him. She wanted to believe that they were safe, that it didn't matter anymore whether she bore a child or not.

Would it be so bad! she asked herself. *We are not alone, Hadin and I. Cafran is right: He will help us, and Alban, and I could even call upon Paragore-Tren if I lose a measure of my . . . Ah, no. Not the wizard. He would befriend us, but he works too closely with my brother not to return us to him. To be under Ayree's protection is worse than no shelter at all for Hadin.*

Basoni's thoughts spun madly as she gave herself up to Lord Cafran's embrace. She wanted to have a child, his child. He was all she wanted. The bear-shaped brazier held a cold flame compared to the carefully banked fires that now leaped inside her. He was kissing her, and she was returning his kisses with desperate haste, eager to have desire outrun common sense.

A loud crash came from the outer room, a sound of smashing dishes that shattered the moment. Lord Cafran was gone from her arms, leaving Basoni standing entranced. He flicked back the lock and threw the bedroom door wide, a dagger shining in his hand.

''Basoni!'' Horror hoarsened his voice. ''Basoni, quickly!''

She followed, still half dazed, but her head cleared at once when she saw: Sprawled on the floor, small hands knotted in the folds of the tablecloth, Hadin lay lifeless.

She was with him in thought's time. The boy's face was the damp, cold white of ice. His lips were stained with gold. Lord Cafran ran to the outer door and thrust it open, bellowing down the twisting turret stair for servants to fetch the king, the queen, the court physicians. Basoni touched the boy's lips and felt the gentlest stirring of breath. It was fading even as she found it.

She didn't know whether the castle's chief leech was wise enough to save the child, or if so, whether his knowledge would come in time. She didn't know how or by whose hand Hadin had been poisoned. For the moment, she didn't care. She knew what she had to do.

While Lord Cafran continued to call for help, she placed her lips to Hadin's. There was a sugary taste, and the suggestion of pears. She savored it, and traced its presence on his dying breath. Her own breath entered his body, questing like a hound. She was a hound on the track, a golden hound, Ambra's hound. All

Basoni's soul fell from her body into Hadin's and took the shape of Ambra's faithful tracker, the hound of life and light.

Dark corridors opened up before her. Her paws raced over a trail of blood and breath. Her passing left a streak of light in the garnet-colored shadows, and the walls around her pulsed with renewed vigor. She could not stay to see how the glow faded after a time. Ambra's hound had greater quarry to run down.

At the heart's core, she found him. He was a black blot that clung to the scarlet walls and spread tendrils of death that stiffened and stilled the throb of life. Faceless as he was, she knew him. Ambra's hound fell back on her haunches and bayed the quarry's doom.

The hound's belling summoned up a face in that spreading black deathweb. Tor's white leer overshadowed the golden hound's upturned muzzle. Burning, scornful laughter charred Hadin's heart.

You come too late. He is my master's now.

I come in time! A hound's lips could not form human words, but the ferocity of her thoughts struck the dark spirit like a gale. *I come in Ambra's name, and I will burn you without fire, purify what you have spoiled, save what you would steal!*

Save his body. Soon that will be all that's left: his shell. Pour your howling into that, bitch! See, already he comes to my hands.

A slip of shivering whiteness stood in the red shadows. It trembled like a wandering marshlight, floating nearer and nearer to Tor's outstretched midnight wing.

Baying, the hound leaped. She landed cat-light between Hadin's spirit and Captain Tor. Hackles bristling into a sunburst, she dug in her paws and bared her shining teeth at Morgeld's slave.

Hard laughter roiled through the chambers of Hadin's heart. *Do you think you can keep me from my master's own? He is Morgeld's. He will come with me.*

I'll kill you first!

You cannot kill the dead. You cannot bar the path to Helagarde. Those who die in despair come to my master's halls. Even your bloodless gods can never undo Morgeld's workings in this world!

Ambra's golden hound lowered her guard. The radiant fur shimmered and blurred, rising in a pillar of light that took back Basoni's original shape. In a woman's naked skin with only Ambra's runes cast over herself for shielding, the witch called for her bow and twelve weird white arrows.

"Your master won't have my boy!" she shouted. "Not now,

not ever! Let him come himself, if he dares. Do you see these?"
She brandished the fistful of arrows. "You flew from the first,
when I made them from the skyel deer's bone, but I have twelve
shafts left. Each one still holds enough magic to blast you into a
billion scatterings. The world will end before the parts of your
spirit reunite, and not even Morgeld will survive the end of all
things. Masterless spirit, where will you be then?"

Without wasting another word she nocked one arrow to her
bow, drew back the string, and fired. The other eleven swarmed
into a ring of light that kept Hadin's small spirit safe behind her.
Her aim was perfect, and the range too close to miss . . . unless
the target vanished.

He did. The black lines crisscrossing Hadin's inner heart vanished with him, whipping free from their anchorage and streaming away in Tor's wake like the tail of a devil-star. Basoni's
arrow struck the heartwall and was gone, but the power of magic
on it flowed into Hadin, and his witchly blood drank it thirstily.
Basoni could almost hear his body sing as magic stimulated life.
She turned, and the child's wisp of soul flared before her eyes.

The burst of new strength threw her spirit out of Hadin's body
and back into her own. She came to her senses in King Alban's
arms, with Queen Ursula kneeling beside her.

"Thank the gods, you're alive," Alban said.

"Of course she's alive." Ursula sounded out of temper. "She
was never in danger! You'd have done better to look after Hadin,
or set your men after that traitor."

"Hadin!" Basoni seized Ursula's arm.

"Hush, he's fine. You should know. My ladies have put him
to bed in your room."

"Is he really all right?"

"He's well enough to yell the castle down. He didn't want
women undressing him," Alban said.

"He'll learn better as he grows, I'm sure," Ursula remarked
dryly. The queen stood and helped Basoni up. Her husband remained
cross-legged on the floor until she yanked him to his feet. The
whole Sombrunian court knew the queen's impatience with idleness.

"Alban, *will* you go and find something useful to do? You're
the king, there ought to be something that needs your attention.
The servant problem, for instance," she added meaningfully.

"Servants . . ." Basoni could still taste a hint of the rich
dessert that Hadin had taken so greedily while she and Lord
Cafran had been in the other room, a cloying treat such as
children love. Poisoned. "One of the servants did this."

"One of Morgeld's servants." Lord Cafran's voice took her by surprise. She thought that she and the rulers of Sombrunia were the only ones in the outer room of her suite. With Ursula's help she stood and saw her lover in the doorway, his dagger now stained red.

"What have you done, Cafran?" the king demanded. "I gave orders that you were to ask questions, not play executioner."

"I'm afraid I had no choice, Your Majesty." He cleaned the blade with a soft cloth drawn from his belt. "The servant in question was already dead, in any case."

"What?"

"You may rest easy, Your Majesty. Your servants are all loyal to you—too loyal for their health. As I was going down into the kitchens with my men, I was intercepted by one of the scullery maids. She took me aside silently, with tears on her face, out to the lesser midden. There we found his body."

"Whose?" Still dizzy, Basoni leaned against Ursula for support.

"She told me his name was Dalon—her sweetheart, it seems."

"Dalon! He was one of the five servants I chose to share the secret of the lady Basoni's presence here." The king ticked off their names on his fingers: "Dalon, Mersic, Benglin, Sarum, and Vinco. I would have trusted any one of them with my own life. They were strong men, too. Dalon was the strongest."

Lord Cafran sheathed his dagger. "Not strong enough for what found him. Your Majesty, I saw Dalon serve dinner in this very room. I am sure it was Dalon who came later, bringing out desserts. Hadin would have thought nothing of admitting him, or eating what he brought. He knew Dalon."

Ursula spoke slowly: "But you said Dalon is dead."

"And dead before dinner. He had promised his sweetheart to meet her at the very hour when he was supposed to be serving at the lady Basoni's table. The scullery maid told me he'd made a bargain with Benglin to trade jobs, leaving him free for his sweet meeting." Lord Cafran frowned. "Benglin said that he was as surprised as the next man when Dalon showed up and freed him from the bargain, but he assumed that there'd been a lovers' quarrel." His eyes rested on Basoni momentarily. "Such foolish things are common enough."

"But if Dalon was dead . . ." Basoni closed her eyes. She could well imagine what had happened. Illusion was such a simple enchantment! Some of the least adept magicians could trade skins as easily as they changed their names.

A child's whimper made them all turn. Looking very frail, all the confidence drained from him, Hadin came tottering out of Basoni's bedroom. In his loose white gown he reminded her too much of how fragile his naked soul had appeared to her not so long ago.

"Dalon . . . is dead? He was the one who brought me—who brought me—" He began to cry. Basoni felt her spent strength return suddenly, answering the boy's need. She scooped him up from the floor and let him cry into her shoulder. "He told me to eat it!" Hadin sobbed. "Why? Did he know it was poisoned? Why would he want to kill me?"

"It wasn't Dalon," Basoni murmured.

"Morgeld's work. I know the hallmark." King Alban's jaw tightened. "I left too much undone the last time I encountered him. It may be time to correct that oversight."

"No, Your Majesty," Basoni said. "Your sword could only wound him again, or maybe not even that. He's readier now. The Black Sword alone won't kill Morgeld."

"At least plain steel was good enough to kill Morgeld's skin-stealing servant," Lord Cafran said. "After we found the real Dalon's body, I didn't waste words in the kitchen. My men dragged him forward—for questioning, he thought—but I was the one who gave him the final answer."

"How could Morgeld know to send his creatures here?" Ursula asked. She stroked Hadin's dark hair with a mother's loving touch. "The banns of sorcery are on this boy. Can Morgeld see through them?"

"It's my fault." Basoni tried to keep her voice from shaking. "I . . . gave Morgeld a sign to track us by."

"You, Basoni?" Ursula was amazed.

Basoni laid her lips to Hadin's cheek. "You aren't to blame yourself, Hadin. I could have said no to you; I should have, but I didn't. I love you very much, but I should have loved you enough to deny you." To Ursula and the men she said, "Hadin's kitten, Midnight. When we first reached Sombrunia, we realized we'd left him behind in Castle Snowglimmer."

Ursula nodded. "Who would bring a kitten to a royal Malben wedding?"

Basoni continued, "Hadin missed him, and I thought that such a small fetching spell would be overlooked. There are many witchborn and wizardly in the Twelve Kingdoms, and the air is often full of enchantments, even here in Sombrunia. What harm would one more do? I brought along my weapons with the same spell as fetched Midnight."

"But Basoni, couldn't you have asked me to provide you with arms if you felt the need?" Alban asked.

The witch shook her head. "You could not provide me with weapons like these." She thought of her sheaf of enchanted arrows. "Unfortunately, they were as out-of-place at the Malben wedding as poor Midnight. I never expected Morgeld to attempt anything with all of us there, so I came armed with nothing but my spells. Perhaps I should have brought my weapons to me while we were still on the ship, but—"

She glanced at Lord Cafran. He lowered his eyes. The passage from Malbenu to Sombrunia had allowed her little time to think of what she might have left behind in the north. That journey held a mild foreshadowing of the tension that had built between the lovers as the Sombrunian lord grew more and more bewildered by his lady's inexplicable coldness.

"That doesn't matter now," he snapped. "You fetched them, and Morgeld followed; is that it?"

"Don't worry, Basoni." Ursula's hug strained to include the witch and the child she carried in her arms. "Alban and I know Morgeld too well to be afraid of him."

"No, Ursula, I do fear him," Alban said. "But I know how far to fear him, and I will fight him in spite of my fears; or because of them. Our sons will fight him, too."

"The old songs say that a child of ours will be Morgeld's doom. Which child, I don't know." Ursula shrugged. "Maybe Alaric inherited my curse to slay Morgeld the way I slew Captain Tor. Prophecy was the reason Morgeld tried to prevent my marriage to Alban—or to anyone!—by wedding me himself. He came courting me in a disguise he soon dropped, and had a collar for my wedding gift: a silver chain set with an amethyst from Helagarde's walls, cut by the hand of old Eyndor, the jeweler who served the gods. The prophecies demanded such a bride-gift, because nothing else would bind me." She touched the shining diamond set in a gold band at her throat and looked lovingly at her husband. "But I wore another man's bride-gift before Morgeld could have me, and this gem, too, is Eyndor's cutting."

So this branch of the Tree flourishes, Basoni thought. *Morgeld, who undid Ayree's plans so completely, failed against magicless mortals like these. Oh, Ayree, how wrong you are to look down on those without our powers! Yet I have heard you speak kindly to them, as to equals. Who are you fooling, brother? Them or yourself? May the gods grant that they never find out how you truly feel.*

Alban was speaking. "I don't know which son of ours will put an end to Morgeld, but I'm not going to let any of them go racing off to play the hero. Helagarde will fall in its time. My sons must stay safe until then."

"You sound like an old mother hen," Ursula teased.

Alban wasn't in the mood for levity. "I was one of four sons, too. Morgeld and his servants killed my brothers. To this day I don't know why I alone was fortunate enough to escape his deadly plans."

Ursula sensed that her husband needed her. She went to him, wanting to banish his sad memories and his future cares. "They say that not even the gods can read all answers. You did survive, and I'm too grateful for that to question it. Morgeld will never harm our sons." Her eyes flashed boldly. "He will never harm Hadin, either! Rest easy, Basoni. We will protect your boy as one of our own, in every way we can."

Basoni felt Hadin grow limp in her arms. He was exhausted and beginning to nod off to sleep. *Poor child,* she thought. *There won't be rest for you, not for a long while. I must do what is best for all.*

"Thank you, Your Majes—" A sharp look from the queen made her amend this to: "Thank you, Ursula, but we can't allow you to endanger your own family for our sakes. Hadin and I aren't any kin of yours—"

Ursula broke in fiercely, "What does birth have to do with kinship? My sons love Hadin like a fifth brother. We love him too, Alban and I, and as for you . . ."

"I am the wardlady of Sombrunia, but that's only an empty title, I think. I don't see what good comes of the bonding."

"Evil comes when the bond breaks," Lord Cafran said. "That much is common knowledge. Glytch may not have flourished while your sister Hodah lived, but now that she's dead . . ."

Alban drew a deep, sorrowful breath. "I hardly know what to make of all the rumors that reach us concerning that sad land."

Basoni shifted Hadin's sleeping weight to her other shoulder. Quietly but firmly she said, "No harm will ever come to Sombrunia on my account. I'll look after myself at least as well as I take care of Hadin. We'll return to my brother's protection in the north. If you will give me letters witnessing what nearly happened to the boy here at Castle Pibroch, Ayree will *have* to believe that Hadin's life is in danger."

The king looked doubtful. "When you first came here, you

were hiding from your brother just as much as from Morgeld. Will Ayree pay any mind to our testimony?''

"He will. Ayree knows you, Alban, and you have the wizard of Naîmlo Wood to back you. Even my brother values Paragore-Tren's counsel. If he adds his words to yours, Ayree will have to admit that he was wrong, that I wasn't imagining the threat to Hadin's life.''

The lord of Sombrunia sighed. "Very well, we'll see to it. When will you be leaving for the north? I can have a ship put at your disposal almost immediately.''

With a smile the young witch said, "Don't bother. Why should you lose the use of a fine ship when I can spirit us home? There's no need to hold off using my magic now. We'll stay another few days, to let Hadin recover. The letters should be ready by then, I hope?'' She forced herself to keep smiling. She did not like deceit, and liked still less the necessity of having to lie to Alban.

"Yes, of course. And that's all you want me to do? It seems like a poor way to serve the warlady of my kingdom.''

"There is one more thing . . .''

Alban seemed relieved to hear it. "Yes, anything.''

"Hadin's kitten, Midnight: keep him. Give him to your youngest boy as a present from Hadin. I think he was always fondest of Alain. We can't take the kitten back with us to Castle Snowglimmer. The poor thing will feel like a freak if all the cats he sees can fly, while he can't.''

"A kitten!'' The word was hardly out of his mouth before Basoni raised one finger ever so slightly and Midnight materialized in the king's hands. Sound asleep as his master, the black kitten twisted himself into the most comfortable position possible and resumed his dreams.

"That's all I can ask of you, I swear it. And now, I'd like to put Hadin to bed.''

King Alban Stonesword left Basoni's rooms, his expression perplexed, his wife cooing mindless babytalk over the purring ball of black fur. Cafran followed his lord, giving the witch a penetrating look before he went.

Chapter XVI

THE LEAVETAKING

"Do not ask me, Majesty, to tell you if this war of yours will be worth the lives it takes. No war of men lays waste so much as the battle between mind and heart. Yet even that great struggle is as nothing when the heart wars against itself."

—''The Old General's Insight''
from *The Scroll of Oran.*

Alone, Basoni did not carry the sleeping child back into the bedroom. She held him so that his soft cheek brushed her own, and the special smell of his nightwing hair reminded her of the days when he was tiny and new. She could set no limits on the love she felt for him. She loved Lord Cafran, too, yet that passionate love was a fire, and the wildest fire soonest burns itself to ash. She knew which way her choice would go if she were ever called to choose between them.

My own child, she thought. *You've been happy here in Castle Pibroch, haven't you? Happier in these few months than you ever were in all the years at Castle Snowglimmer. But we can't stay here; and we can't go back. Ayree will never care whether you live or die, no matter who tries to persuade him that you are in very real danger. I think the only one who could convince Ayree would be Morgeld himself. There must be something special about you, or why would the lord of despair persecute you so? No, we can't stay here. The Tree of Second Light has been stripped of half her branches. We mustn't focus Morgeld's attention here, where the surviving limbs are still so young, so easily destroyed. I thought we'd found a home, Hadin, but a king's castle is no more permanent shelter for you than a desert-dweller's tent.*

Hadin stirred and made a wordless complaint. Basoni tried to settle him more comfortably, but the boy gave a sudden jerk and came fully awake. "Where's the king?" he asked, rubbing his eyes. "Where's Lord Cafran? I had such a strange dream . . ."

"Never mind, my dear. Do you feel better?" Hadin nodded and she set him down. "Well enough to dress yourself? Your clothing is in the big chest at the foot of my bed. Go and put it on."

"Are you going somewhere? It's so late . . ."

"Do as you're told. Please."

Later, when the boy was ready and she had packed up the few garments that would serve them best, she held out a small traveler's cloak to him. It had been brought to her hands from a closed city shop by a furtive fetching spell, a stack of coins left in its place for the merchant to gawp at. Hadin took it from her and studied the plain, serviceable wool garb, its insides made warm with a laced-in lining of hodgepodge pelts.

"It's lumpy," he complained as she put it on. "And ugly."

"It's warm, though. I didn't know you cared that much for looks. It's not a prince's cape, but you aren't a prince. Never mind, you won't need to wear it once we're out of Sombrunia."

She could not have shocked him more if she'd told him that they were marching on Helegarde in the morning. "We're leaving Sombrunia? Oh, Basoni, why? Why do we have to go? Have I done something wrong again?"

In a cloak whose poor looks and stark utility matched Hadin's, Basoni knelt to review the contents of the two covered backbaskets she had packed. A fighter's bow and a quiver of eleven slim white arrows lay on the floor between the two baskets, the heads and fletches of the bone darts all of a piece with their bodies.

Basoni fingered the arrows thoughtfully. These, too, had been fetched with the same spell that had brought Midnight to Sombrunia. If that spell had been a careless mistake, it had also brought her the one weapon Tor seemed to fear. So many things seemed to balance themselves out well.

"You haven't done anything wrong, Hadin. You never did. We've stayed here long enough, that's all. I have more friends that just King Alban and Queen Ursula in the southern lands; friends who live in kinder climates. Winter is as nasty in Sombrunia as in the north; the other southern realms hardly know it."

"Why not?"

"Sombrunia juts out into the Straits of Mukthar, where the Lyarian Sea mingles with the Opalza. And then there are the mountains, and the Dunenfels Plain, and—"

Hadin wasn't listening. His face had closed, and the old look of retreat from an unkind world had hardened itself back in place. Basoni felt a deep pang. He had been a child in Sombrunia, a real child, free of undeserved hatred, unjust guilt. Now she had to take all that from him, for his own sake.

Oh Morgeld, how I wish I had the power to destroy you in my dreams! How can you hunt a child? How can you even give a child pain? Can't you recall the pain you knew yourself when you were young and no one wanted you or cared what you became? I hate you, but you've earned my hatred. If you could only show this child some mercy . . .

Hadin hitched the smaller backbasket onto his shoulders. The waterproof cover came akew. Basoni secured it before hoisting her own pack, her blue and silver painted bow attached to the withes with a trio of rawhide thongs, her quiver slung over one shoulder.

"Are we going now?" Hadin asked. His eyes and voice were flat and empty. It was all the same to him.

"One thing more."

Basoni raised her hand, palm outward. A gentle radiance emanated from it, the light of a polar star rimmed with warmth from the common fire still burning on the hearth behind them. The light spun itself into a shield, then lengthened to a blade's shape. A flash of brightness carved the Blue Sword into being and left the rest of the chamber dark. The fire on the hearth had been consumed to ashes by the coming of the Sword.

The witch's eyes sought Hadin's over the glowing blade. "This comes with us. It is yours, the Blue Sword that was my father's gift. Your grandfather, Hadin, and one of the gods' blood! Touch it. Take it. You know your curse will have no effect on this. Go on, it's yours." She turned it so that the hilt was toward him.

The boy's hand closed on the god-carved ice. The Blue Sword was nearly as tall, pommel to point, as Hadin himself, yet it was no struggle for him to raise it. Its radiance struck sapphire light from his eyes and made his fair skin look like the watery blue of aquamarine. He was a child-warrior of precious stone, holding an enchanted blade of ice, and the magic of it transformed him inwardly as well. He stood taller with the Blue Sword in his hand, his face alive with joy.

"It is mine," he said, speaking like a dreamer. "Really mine. No matter where we go, I'll have it. I saw King Alban's sword. It's made of black stone instead of steel, like this blade's all blue ice. When I used to watch Senja at her forge, she'd tell me stories of the three great swords that would become one, and the one sword that would destroy Morgeld and all his evil. King Alban's sword is one of the Three, and mine"—he sounded as if he didn't dare say the words, for fear of his curse being strong enough even to unmake the future—"mine is another. I wonder where the third . . ."

Basoni cast invisibility over the Blue Sword while Hadin still held it. He gasped to see it vanish in his grip the instant the spell touched it, and he let it fall. The witch laughed and pulled back a corner of the spell as if it were a cloth, so that the hilt alone showed.

"It's yours and no one else's, Hadin, but we can't travel with it openly. This isn't Braegard Isle, where they let their children teethe on swords. Most boys your age have to be content with rattan blades. I'll carry it for you. Even if we did have a proper scabbard for it, it's too long for you to wear. People would grow suspicious if they saw a big boy like you tripping over nothing every two steps."

Hadin watched her go through the motions of binding the sword to the belt beneath her cloak. Only the hilt was visible, but he never took his eyes from it until the witch disguised that last remnant with empty air. He crept near and timidly tried to touch his unseen inheritance.

A touch was all it took. The Blue Sword leaped back into sight as Hadin's curse unmade Basoni's magic.

"Well," said the witch. She clicked her tongue. "If you're convinced that I haven't destroyed your sword, Hadin, please let me conceal it again. And don't touch it."

The boy looked ashamed. "I'm sorry."

Basoni rewove the spell as she spoke. "Even though you can't see it, the Blue Sword is with us. I should never have kept it anywhere else, but I was afraid that someone would stumble over it by accident if all that protected it was invisibility. Now I think of it, the first misuse I made of my magic was to hide the Blue Sword on another plane. That spell may have been what betrayed our presence here to Morgeld, not the weird of fetching I used on Midnight. What a fool I've been."

"Another what?" The boy had never grasped the many-leaved reality that the witchborn saw and used in some of their spells. In

Castle Snowglimmer, he had always wondered where the witch-king's winged familiars lived when they were not serving him.

"It doesn't matter, you wouldn't undertand. The Blue Sword won't leave us again. Now follow me as quietly as you can." Smilingly ruefully, she added, "I wish I might make us both just as unseen as the Sword."

"I'm sorry," Hadin repeated, sounding truly miserable. "I . . . I wish you could use your spells on me without them coming undone, Basoni."

"Don't fret, my love. If my spells won't take on you, neither will any other magician's. You will always unmake what is made, but only what's made magically, not what *is* magic. I can still take you with me through the plane of witchly flight."

If I am right, she thought, *if the Blue Sword is what drew Morgeld's creatures to us, then it doesn't matter whether I use magical means to flee him. We cannot abandon the Sword. Still . . . I wonder. Why does he pursue us so avidly? In the realm of magic, Hadin is no threat to him; the child is less than nothing, worse than magicless. With Ayree's curse of unmaking on him, Morgeld would not want him for his servant now. And it is only the royal house of Sombrunia that will fulfill the other half of the great prophecy. Is it the Blue Sword, then, that drives Morgeld?*

She shook her head. *Something more than that is spurring Morgeld's hunt. I wish I could know what it is. I wish that I could face Morgeld himself and demand an answer. Too many patterns are at work here. For now, I will risk using my craft to take us far away; flight through the planes is swiftest. Morgeld seems to use his servants to track us, and their powers are limited. Perhaps if we fly from here, it will take them time to find our trail again, and by then we will be among friends, allies . . . if we have any. Oh Tabrac, I wish I had you here to teach me the ways of a wise gambler! We will try our best to run away, to hide from the lord of Helagarde. But if we cannot, then I will fight, and I will die defending this child.*

Aloud she said, "Come, it's time."

She turned to the dead hearth and spread her hands, thumbs and forefingers touching to make a triangle before her face. A gateway in that same shape, but mansized, irised open in the stone wall behind the cold embers, and the frosty black of the wild place between spaces awaited them.

"*No!*" Hadin backed off. "Please, Basoni, I don't want to go in there. *Please*, no!"

"But you'll be safe—"

"I don't want to! I don't want to fly! Not if it means I have to go in there." She scarcely heard his shamed whisper: "I'm afraid."

The child was terrified. Basoni decided not to waste precious time trying to reason him out of his fears. The important thing now was to get away, not the means of escape.

She brought her hands together with a sharp clap and the gateway closed. "Then we will travel another way. It will take longer, but we have time. Only you must promise me to be *very* quiet now, child. Put up your hood, tread softly behind me, and don't speak a word, not even a whisper. No one must see us go."

"Why not? We're only going to see your friends. Won't we even say good-bye to the king? Or to Lord Cafran?"

"I've done that while you slept." Basoni felt no guilt for what she knew was half a lie. "King Alban said that it was best to keep our departure a secret. I am Sombrunia's wardlady, and some good folk here are superstitious. They'd never hear of my going. Is your hood well tied? Fine."

They played at being thieves as they stole down the winding turret stair. They crossed the castle's inner courtyard silently. The cold rain had stopped, leaving the cobbles slick with a glossy skin of ice. Even when he skidded and fell on the stones, Hadin didn't make a sound.

At the guardpost, Basoni motioned for Hadin to hang back while she cast a disguise over herself. The guard thought nothing of passing out a grimy-faced serving wench who claimed that she and her little brother were going off to visit their parents in the city below the keep. By night, guards worried more about who entered Castle Pibroch than who left it.

It was the same story at the outer gate on the far side of the bailey. Fortunately, though the hour was late, it was not late enough for the great bars to have been lowered into place. The guardian soldier at his post unlatched the small door in the huge portal and let them out. He nipped Basoni's thigh as she squeezed past him and got a slap for it.

Outside, with a flatstone road leading down from the castle motte into the city, Hadin asked, "Why did you hit him? He could have stopped us."

"If I'd let him get away with pinching me, he *would* have stopped us. He expected to get smacked, and he'd have suspected at once if I'd done anything else."

"I'm never going to understand grownups."

The capital city of Sombrunia was small in comparison to the chief towns of her neighboring kingdoms. Like many others, she took her name from the castle guarding her: Pibroch. She was small, as cities go, but very old. More than one ancient mystery had been played out in her streets.

If there was a respite from the rain, the famed Sombrunian fog was already rising to harass the travelers. The city lanterns were blurry glows seen through the shifting mists as Basoni and Hadin hurried down the hill to lose themselves in the tangle of streets.

Not many people were abroad that night. The early winter storm had discouraged most wanderers. Even the less respectable Sombrunians—those with a dozen ill-intentioned reasons for roaming the night—had holed up in their favorite taverns in hopes of staying warm, getting drunk, and maybe picking up cardsharps' or pickpockets' gleanings if the gods smiled.

Hadin lagged. The backbasket was not heavy, but the boy had gone through too much in one night, and he hadn't recovered entirely. The fog bewildered him, and Basoni's unexpectedly hasty decision to leave Castle Pibroch confused him past words. He sneezed and snuffled, feeling less and less like the bold knight who had unhorsed Prince Alveiros only that morning.

Basoni stopped at a cross-street, waiting for Hadin to catch up. "Don't dawdle. If I lose you in this fog, it would take a searching spell to find you. We aren't going much farther. There's a waterfront tavern where ships' passengers stay. Lord Cafran showed it to me when we first arrived."

"We're leaving by ship?"

"If I can find one bound for Vair. Otherwise, we might buy horses, or purchase passage on a trade caravan."

Hooves picked an echoing path out of the fog behind them. Lord Cafran emerged from the fog mounted on a blazed bay stallion. "Why waste your money, my lady?" he asked. "In Castle Pibroch I have horses enough for all of us. You only had to ask me. Instead you lied, and fled."

He guided the horse into the range of the lone glass lantern that overhung the junction of two narrow streets. He slid from the saddle, and by that light's scant beam Basoni saw that he had a woman riding pillion.

"You are an ill-suited wardlady for Sombrunia. We are fighters— Oh, not with the blood-and-glory reputation of the Vahrdmen, but good fighters all the same. And we never run away."

He turned to help the woman dismount. Basoni still wore a serving wench's face, and when Lord Cafran brought his passenger forward into the light, she found herself gazing at another of that sisterhood.

"Before you bother with any more lies, here is my witness," he said. "Her duty is to bring refreshment to the men on guard. She saw you at the inner gate and recognized Hadin. At first she thought he was being taken against his will and came to warn me, since she didn't know you for yourself in that skin."

"How would she know me in my own? I never saw her before."

"But she *has* seen the boy before, and she knows he is important, not just one of the puppy-pack that tags after our royal princes. Her lover was Dalon of the loose tongue. You already know the role she played in helping us find Morgeld's skin-stealing assassin. You should thank her, Basoni."

The little wench pulled her shawl up over her head and would not look at the witch.

Basoni's spell of disguise melted away. "All right, you know we've left the castle. We're leaving Sombrunia. We're guests, not prisoners."

"Rude guests."

Basoni wanted to slap Cafran's face the same way she'd slapped the amorous guardsman, but she resisted. This was no time for quarrels. He loved her, he had been hurt before, and he was hurting now. She could understand pain too well. If there had ever been a harsh streak in her soul—harsh enough to foster vengeance over compassion—the years had burned it out of her.

She bowed her head. "I won't bother to answer you, Cafran. You never believe my answers anyway."

His hard laughter rang back from the windowless streetside walls of the houses. "What's so hard to believe? That you love me, but won't let me near you? That you're going north openly, in a few days, but you steal out of Castle Pibroch like a thief, this very night? Go, then. Take your lies with you. I came after you on the chance that you might have something truthful to tell me. I see I've wasted my ride." He turned his back on her.

She had so much that she wanted to say to him—and knew she would say nothing. In her soul, she made a small prayer to Ambra, goddess of the light-in-darkness, that someday she might see Lord Cafran again and have him listen, have him believe.

"Come, Hadin."

The boy gazed from his aunt's face to Lord Cafran's stiff back. Timorously he piped, "Farewell, my lord." Then he scampered after Basoni. The fog swallowed them.

"Aren't we going to follow them, my lord?" the scullery wench asked Lord Cafran.

"Let them go," he said.

"Where, my lord? To Vair? I thought . . . I thought that we would bring them back to Castle Pibroch. She is our wardlady! We can't have her leave Sombrunia."

"She never set foot here for years, and we did well enough. As long as she lives, we'll do just as well, no matter where she goes."

The shawl shadowing the scullery wench's face fell back a little. Her gaze gleamed violet by lantern light. "I think you mean to go after her, my lord."

"I? No, never! I've had enough of that game."

"Oh, but I think you will play it for a little while longer." She sidled nearer to him, letting the shawl drop back entirely. Lord Cafran did not think it worth his while to look a mere servant in the face while addressing her, and so did not see the amethyst fires now smoldering in her eyes.

"Mind your tongue, girl." He whistled for his horse and mounted with ease. "Take hold," he said, giving her his hand. "I'll pull you up behind me."

"My humblest thanks." And she took hold of his arm with more than human strength and pulled him from the saddle into the street. The bay stallion squealed and bolted.

Sharp teeth sank into Lord Cafran's throat before he could utter a cry. He died swiftly, silently.

When the creature had finished her feast, she sat back on her haunches and smiled. "Another skin that may be useful to us someday soon. I am weary of this one. Yes, Lord Cafran, my thanks . . . and my master's."

An essence less palpable than the Sombrunian mists seeped from the serving wench's body into Lord Cafran's corpse.

In the morning, the gossips of Castle Pibroch were caught up in scandalous speculation concerning the double death of Dalon and his sweetheart. Tales of quarrels, curses, and cross-purposed passions dribbled from the mouths of every would-be romancer in the hall. Too few people had known of Basoni's visit to link her departure with the two deaths.

As Lord Cafran commented to King Alban, perhaps it was for

the best. "Maybe she had to leave abruptly, for some reason of her own," he said.

Alban nodded. "Who knows what moves the witchborn?"

"Who indeed?" Lord Cafran mused, and the hidden purple light glinted for a moment in his hooded eyes.

Chapter XVII

REFUGEES

"Friends, like fleas, are always there."

—*"The Philosopher's Third Maxim"*
from *The Scroll of Oran*

"Make way! Make way for the lady Lucha!"

The great bazaar of Ishma was a seething sea of buyers, sellers, cheaters, stealers, gawkers, gapers, and riffraff of various legitimacies. In clothing of the northern and southern kingdoms they thronged the streets of that fabulous marketplace, bellowing prices, oaths, counteroffers, insults, and questions as to the paternity of anyone with whom they had dealings. They argued, jostled, threatened, groaned, and occasionally dropped dead on the spot over a bad deal.

They did not make way.

They never did, they never had, and they weren't about to start now. Tradition was almost as important as sales tax to the bazaar-goers of Ishma.

"Swine and children of swine!" Lucha's herald, a bare-chested giant, bawled abuse at the indifferent crowd. They would not budge. He yanked a whip from the wide leather belt holding up his embroidered pantaloons, menacing them all. It was a laughable spectacle: the whip was only for show, its lash of braided silk, and it made no more sound when cracked than a hummingbird's pucker.

Behind this ineffectual attendant, the lady Lucha's palanquin waited. Broad stripes of green, red, and saffron casheen trimmed with rainbow glass bells hid the palanquin's occupant from sight. At the peak of these rich draperies, a silver panther scintillated in the morning sun, its beryl eyes looking almost alive. Eight generously endowed, sleepy-eyed youths carried the elaborate litter on their shoulders. Although they had been purchased for their endurance, they had their limits. Wisely they chose to set the palanquin down until a path might open.

From behind the curtains a musical voice inquired, "Why have we stopped, Mahbub?"

Instantly the angry giant was transformed. He knelt meekly in the dust beside the litter and said, "O unequaled Daughter of Celestial Loveliness, may the blows of ten thousand sticks break themselves across my unworthy back! The skink-eating sons of leprous mothers refuse to give us room to pass."

"Is that all? We have time," said the voice. "See what you can do, and I will beguile the minutes with my lute."

"Your lute . . ." A cold sweat erupted on the giant's brow. As he had chosen to shave his head completely, this was quite a lot of brow, and the salty drops soon trickled down his thickly muscled neck. Frantically he stammered, "Voice of a Thousand Mysteries, do not—do not waste the delectable notes of your magnificent throat on this market scum! Hold—*please* hold but a moment, and I shall clear us a road if I have to pick these dogs up by the scruff one by one and throw them into the next street!"

Lucha replied, "Don't be silly, Mahbub. I don't mind who listens when I play." A muted plinking sounded from the depths of the palanquin. Mahbub's thick lips moved in prayer.

It was a short prayer and a short song. Lucha hit her melodic nemesis in the fifth bar of "The Nightingale Weeps Pearls," on a tricky chord-change. There was a growl, a twangle, and the guilty lute came flying out of the litter with the witchery-aided speed of a javelin. It exploded into splinters against a shop wall. Inside the curtains, the wardlady of Vair used words that made haggle-hardened merchants up and down the length of the street blush crimson.

"Flee!" moaned Mahbub. "Flee, if you've the sense to get out of the way! Flee, for my lady is losing her temper, and that lute's fate is only a warning!"

The temper of Vair's wardlady in matters musical was already famous in the bazaar. It was a byword and a simile frequently on the lips of merchants who wanted to peddle something hot, sharp, quick, fierce, or beyond rational comprehension.

A market-woman in the horrified crowd screamed. "The panther! The silver panther! May the gods shield us, it comes to life at the witch's bidding! Run! Run! It will tear us to pieces!"

With one mind and one purpose, the crowd blocking the avenue raced away, pouring down sidestreets and slipping into shops with an alacrity that left quicksilver looking like molasses. There was nothing left to hinder Lucha's litter but a few tattered slippers that had not been as fast as the feet wearing them.

The silver panther atop the palanquin did not move—had never shown any sign of moving. Imagination is at least as good an animator as witchcraft.

Lucha stuck her head out between the curtains, making the many-colored bells tinkle. Her long blond lovelocks fell in charmingly calculated disarray from the crown of her head down one side of her face.

"Did it work again, Mahbub?" she asked.

"Yes, Entrancing One. Although, if my lady does not take my poor advice amiss, one day the peasants are going to turn wise. It occurs to me that if you, O Gem Beyond Mortal Value, wish a better way of getting through the bazaar, you might let me carry a real whip."

"What?" Lucha was dismayed. "These are my people, Mahbub. I won't have you whipping them when lutes are so plentiful. Besides . . ." Her blue eyes misted over dreamily as she gazed at the litter-bearer nearest her. "They breed such delightful sons. Carry on, Mahbub, carry on." She drew her head back into the shelter of the litter.

From the haven of a shop selling copperware, two robed figures watched the witch's litter go past. Suddenly the taller of the two dashed out into the street, overtook the lumbering litter, and dropped to a supplicant's posture before the redoubtable Mahbub. Kneeling, head bent, it was impossible for the big man to see the face of the one who dared to intercept his lady's passage—and a passage won by such excruciating means! He was not in the mood for charity.

"Be off with you, Child of a Doorway Dalliance! The lady Lucha is in haste. Seek her with your petitions at the governor's mansion on the appropriate days."

The supplicant remained kneeling. Mahbub cracked his useless whip, then flung it down with a snarl of disgust. "If you will not remove yourself, I shall perform that honor. And if you give me fleas, may the gods rain a thousand curses back upon you for every bite the vermin give me!"

"Mahbub! Touch her, and you'll be bitten by worse things!" Lucha's authoritative voice froze the big man in place. The fire in his eye was extinguished, his bulging muscles flabbed, and all the menace gushed out of him like water from a pricked bladder, leaving a piteous hulk behind.

Near tears, Mahbub flopped down cross-legged in the dust beside the still-unmoving supplicant and whined, "My lady, the gods grant you a thousand years of bliss and a fresh husband for every month therein, but may they grant *me* a speedy death! Why will you never allow me to do my work properly? What did you buy me for in the first place? At that price, too! And where have your vitrics flown? To waste, to shameful waste! You give me a whip that couldn't lay stripes on a tiger, you don't even let me *use* it in your service, and when I want to do something for you with my own feeble arms, you thwart me. Ah, may the gods take my miserable soul! What is worse than a professional man kept from his rightful job?"

"Oh, shut up, Mahbub. If you don't like my service, quit. The moment I gave you your freedom, you gave yourself airs." Lucha had the curtains of her litter pulled all the way back now, and her hand was clasped in the hand of a small black-haired boy in a dusty cape. He had taken advantage of Mahbub's distraction to dash up to the litter and make himself known to Lucha. The wardlady of Vair was all radiant smiles as she yanked the urchin into the lush depths of her palanquin.

"Don't sit there sulking. Help my sister in, too."

"Your sister, my lady!"

At once Mahbub was on his feet, and such was the big man's finesse that he managed to scoop Basoni up with him, sweeping her into his glistening arms as if she weighed no more than a baby. Her golden hair escaped in a cascade from the travelworn wool hood that had contained it and she gave a little shriek of surprise as Lucha's servant lofted her into the litter—gently, yes, but with enough heave-ho to leave her stomach several feet behind the rest of her.

As soon as Lucha had Basoni and Hadin stowed in the litter, she tugged the curtains closed and wriggled back into the downy pillows with the grin of a cream-glutted cat.

"You stink," she said pleasantly. "But I'm glad to see you, smell and all."

"*Aunt Lucha!*" No pride is so easily pricked as that of a male cub. The wardlady of Vair chuckled and smothered Hadin's mortified cries in a hug that all but disintegrated the cobweb of salmon-colored gauze purporting to cover her bosom.

"Of course we smell," Basoni replied, not at all offended.

"We've spent the last few weeks of our lives with horses and camels."

"Well, welcome to Ishma, darling. You can spend the next few weeks solely in the company of jackasses. You ought to feel right at home. Why in Insar's name didn't you fly?"

The sisters reclined facing each other inside the amply wide litter, with Hadin now nestled comfortably under Lucha's right arm. She reached down and tweaked Basoni's toe through the thinning leather of her half boots. Involuntarily, Basoni jerked her foot away, then winced. Lucha was immediately sympathetic. "What hurts?"

"Saddle sores."

Basoni's sister tried to keep a straight face. She didn't do it well. "What were you trying to prove, doing things the hard way? And that little play-acting stint you put poor Mahbub through in the street . . . Why didn't you just transport yourself and the boy directly to my palace?"

Basoni accommodated her aching bones to the mild swaying of the palanquin. "I didn't want to shock you."

"Really, Basoni, it's just an old wives' tale that pregnant women can't stand surprises."

"*What?* Lucha, you aren't . . ."

The wardlady of Vair laughed with soul and body. "There, my secret's out. Indeed I am pregnant, Basoni. My luck couldn't hold out forever . . . and neither could I. However, I have reason to guess it's a girl-child. My powers seem unchanged." She caused a jade bowl of ripe pomegranates to materialize in the jasmined shade of the litter just to prove her point.

While Hadin wrestled with one of those succulent, frustrating fruits, spraying droplets of crimson juice everywhere, Basoni told her sister of all the trials that she and Hadin had passed through since the weddings on Malbenu Isle. She did not finish her tale until the palanquin came to a halt in the tiled courtyard of Lucha's palace.

Lucha was not smiling when her porter draped back the bejingled curtains and offered to hand his mistress out of her palanquin. She waved him aside with a harsh gesture and swung her gold-sandaled feet over the side.

"Two ghosts travel with me, Zalaan," she said tersely. "Show them all honor, and tell the rest of my servants—"

"Alas, my lady." The handsome young porter touched his breast with the fingertips of both hands as he bowed. "This very moment your entire household has been smitten with a fearful plague. It leaves them one and all blind, deaf, and most particularly mute when two most honored ghosts are the matter in question."

"Good. See that they remain so afflicted."

The porter bowed again and helped Basoni and Hadin from the litter. They followed Lucha up a broad flight of steps with risers of purest rock crystal. Helianthin fishes cruised behind the glassy stairs, indifferent to everything but their own beauty. Their fins and trailing tails were the verdant veils of dreamsmoke dancers. Twin statues of winged firedrakes cast of bronze overlaid with copper flanked the great door at the top of the steps: Their outspread wings formed an arch of blue and green enamelwork that dazzled the eyes by sun or moonlight. Hollow inside, their gilded nostrils gave off the dizzying fragrance of sweetwood and myrrh burning in their bellies.

Lucha's palace was no less extravagant inside than out. Regal halls were nothing new to Basoni and Hadin—the boy hardly knew what it was like *not* to sleep in a castle—but Lucha's home spilled its delights and excesses over all their senses until they were stunned and gaping. By the time they reached the lady's favorite reception chamber, they were dumbfounded . . . and a little nauseated.

When Basoni recognized the crocodile divan, she felt as if she had met an old, beloved friend. The poor thing, once the splendor of Lucha's battle-tent, looked shabby in its new home, a tin pearl in the heart of a golden oyster. Lucha's shield hung on the wall directly above it—on a sable field, a man's severed head sat enthroned on a pile of gold pieces. Her panther banner was displayed on the opposite wall.

Lucha scorned the mountain of floor pillows, the furred mattresses plumped full of scented cas-cas fluff, the ruby glass couch lined with swansdown cushions, and laid herself across the eternally grinning divan before summoning her familiars: butterflies the size of small dogs, with human faces, whose wings left a trail of stigia-essence. It was a fragrance distilled from what was also called the poet's flower, and its musky perfume filled the heads of susceptible souls with dreams of quiet laughter, beckoning glances, impossible love. At Lucha's command, her magical servants fluttered off to fetch refreshments for her and her guests.

"Take off your cloaks, make yourselves comfortable," Lucha told her guests. "No, no, Hadin, don't sit on the glass sofa! I made that myself, magically, and—"

Hadin jumped away from the glittering creation and stood

beside Basoni, looking awkward. Not even Lucha's assurances that he could safely sprawl on the fat floor pillows would convince him to relax. He only came out of his shell when the servants arrived, bearing trays of spun-honey cake, fruit, and flowerpetal sorbet.

While the child gorged on the many delicacies of Lucha's kitchens, the two sisters talked.

"You were wise to leave Sombrunia, Basoni. Morgeld will look there soon enough, but if we are all lucky, his attention will be diverted until the Tree's mortal branches grow strong." She took a mouthful of sorbet with an amber spoon and added casually, "Ayree's been half off his head looking for you and the boy. He made us all promise to tell him if anyone in our lands heard of you." She smiled away the look of apprehension in Basoni's eyes. "I promised, but I did not swear. Pregnancy plays hob with a woman's memory, as is well known."

Basoni had not touched the cup of wine on the footed tray beside her. "Ayree doesn't care about us; he's after something that we have." She gave Lucha a wink's view of her unseen burden. "The Blue Sword."

"Ah?" The lift of Lucha's perfectly penciled brow betrayed her indifference. "If you care enough about the prophecy of the Tree to protect King Alban's sons, you certainly won't let any harm come to the Blue Sword. Does Ayree think we're not to be trusted with anything? No, *he* is the only intelligent one in the family. *He* never made a mistake in his life." She sucked up the last spoonful of sorbet and licked her lips, then stood, all briskness.

"You two shall be bathed, given new clothes, and provided with horses. I have some nice Sombrunian mounts in my stable . . . my other stable," she added slyly. "After we dine, you will leave."

"Leave . . . ?"

"Well, you can't stay here. I feel the banns of sorcery on the boy, but the banns don't steal out ordinary vision. What if Ayree decides to pay an unexpected call on me? He does, you know. My servants are trustworthy, and they have the Vairish gift for keeping secrets, but Ayree has his little ways . . ."

Weary and still aching from her journey, Basoni asked, "Where shall we go, Lucha? I haven't the strength to run much farther."

"Pigslop! You're the strongest of us all, little sister. You're just tired. Oh, and look at Hadin!" The child had given in to exhaustion and was sleeping curled up one one of the huge floor pillows, one arm thrown over his dirty face, looking very much like his lost kitten.

"I won't send you far, Basoni," Lucha said softly. "Stay here in Ishma, stay near, it pleases me to see you again; but stay elsewhere than in my palace."

Basoni saw sound reasoning behind Lucha's words. "If you could send us to a decent inn . . ."

"And have news of your presence spread to all corners of the Twelve Kingdoms on travelers' tongues? No, I will send you to an old friend of our family . . . a great friend of yours, Basoni, if you will remember."

Silky paper and an inked quill appeared at Lucha's bidding. She scrawled a name and gave it to Basoni. The young witch read: "Mustapha of Vair."

"When you were a child, he saved you from the snow-beast."

"Mustapha . . ." The name stirred memories. "He had a shape-changing dog named Elcoloq." She smiled, recalling the special love and warmth a little girl had given wholeheartedly to a very naughty, instantly adored dog.

"I will speak to Mustapha privately while you and Hadin rest and bathe. He remembers his time in Castle Snowglimmer well, and he is a good man. He will shelter you and Hadin against any peril."

"He would never call Ayree's finding us a peril."

"We won't tell him about that, only of Morgeld. And Ayree has no cause to come visiting Mustapha; only me. You don't know how brave Mustapha is, Basoni, or of all the adventures and dangers he experienced after he left us. He will fight for you with his life."

The snow-beast's hungering face loomed over Basoni again, the years stealing none of its horror. She forced it away. "He has already risked himself for me once. Ambra grant that he won't have to do so again."

Chapter XVIII

THE INTERLUDE

"You never know when your past will leap out and bite you in the ankle."

—"The Comment of the Enchanted Hound"
from *The Scroll of Oran*

Hadin sat at Basoni's feet—the proper place for children during formal family banquets—and wondered why she wept to hear that a dog was dead.

At the head of the low table, Mustapha's face showed how deeply he shared the fair young witch's sorrow. "To this day I cannot believe it myself that he is gone," he said. "Nothing consoles me for his loss. It is ever thus, though I tell myself what a good life he had, and how he relished the escapades of his latter years." He heaved a deep sigh. "He even got to bite the governor's rump. It was his triumph."

Mustapha's beauteous wife Nahraina passed a handkerchief dampened with orange flower water across the table to Basoni. "You would have enjoyed it, my lady. One moment he came flying into the governor's presence chamber as a mat-furred market cur, baying madness. He scattered the guards, bit the governor—"

"I brushed the foam onto his lips myself," Mustapha's son Beglash put in proudly. "Apricot soap; he preferred it."

"—and the next thing anyone knew, the dog was gone. Only a very respectable old gentleman was left mingling with the crowd, looking just as upset as everyone else."

"The governor took to his bed and waited to die," Beglash said. He had Basoni's eyes on him and proceeded to embroider the tale to sustain that delicious sensation. "He moaned like a camel in torment for two days and nights. He freed all of his slaves and made them gifts besides, granted seventy-four pardons to prisoners, and unconditionally repealed the entrance tax on the Nightingale Houses. When he survived the ordeal, he was almost disappointed."

"Elcoloq was born to be a player," Mustapha said. "Alas! That was his last scene. He died in his sleep a week later and was interred with fitting pomp by his devoted wife and thirty-six daughters."

"He had six daughters?" Basoni asked, wiping away her tears for a vanished playfellow.

Mustapha cleared his throat and repeated, "Thirty-six. Six births, six daughters at a time . . ." He tried to change the subject. "Ah, may Sarai herself scratch his ears throughout eternity. He was a faithful friend who always—"

"Thirty-six daughters?"

Mustapha's lips twitched with chagrin. "My lady, he was born a dog and he aged like a dog. And so, when it came time for him to sire children, why should it astonish you that he fathered six . . . litters?"

"Yes, but his wife—"

Nahraina smiled demurely. "Our dear Elcoloq's wife was Patience, who is half mortal and half peri. From what I know of peris—I was raised among them, you know—they usually accommodate the desires of their lovers, and from what I have come to learn of mortals, they usually adapt to most circumstances. If Patience was accommodating and adaptable enough to bear children by the clutch, why does everyone who hears of it react as if now they shall have to breed their young in squadrons, too?"

Beglash leaned daringly close to his father's entrancing guest and murmured, "And why does it always embarrass Father so much to discuss it?" The smile he coaxed from her made him grin even more.

Bored by all this talk he did not understand, Hadin yawned. Basoni rose to take the child to bed.

"Young ones need sleep," Mustapha said, growing sentimental. "I remember when you were that age, my son."

Beglash blushed. "That was a long time ago, Father." He stole an anxious glance at Basoni to see whether she had heard all this talk of age, but she was speaking to Hadin.

"Hadin is very tired," Basoni said. "We will retire now, if you don't mind."

"Both of you?" Nahraina seemed distressed. "We had hoped you would linger with us a while longer. Liligi can put the boy to bed."

Before Basoni could object, Mustapha made a sign to one of the servants in attendance. He dashed away and returned almost at once, accompanied by a squat, bow-legged man in the distinctive dress of Mustapha's household guard: crimson trousers, a gold-shot ivory vest, and a thin, curved sword whose silk-wrapped hilt protruded from a green scabbard.

Basoni had seen many men in these same trappings when she and Hadin passed through the gorgeous halls of Mustapha's house; many men, but none so unlikely a guardsman as this Liligi. To top his unprepossessing looks, he wore an embroidered smallpoint patch over his left eye. The remaining orb was murky, bloodshot, and inspired absolutely no confidence.

"My friends," Basoni began. "My friends, in view of what you know about Hadin, I would feel better if I—"

"Liligi, the mirror," Mustapha said calmly.

Liligi bowed to his master, then made a dove-shape of his hands. Basoni felt herself reduced from one of the witchborn to a market-day bumpkin staring at shell-and-pea miracles. An oval blob of silver the size of a child's face had appeared, floating masklike before Liligi's eye.

"A wizard's mirror." Basoni recognized it at once.

"Ah, no!" Mustapha stroked his beard—once dark, now liberally banded with gray. "It would not do if our beloved governor heard that a man of my humble rank had engaged the services of a private wizard. No, Liligi is merely another of my guards . . . one who has better ways than most of overseeing what happens in my house."

"You may trust Hadin with him completely," Beglash reassured her. "He lost his eye in a tussle with an unruly night-spirit, but he won the fight."

"Stay with us and let him take Hadin to his room," Nahraina urged her guest. "An evening without long talk among good friends is time lost forever."

"I'd like that," Basoni replied. "I'd like to hear more of Elcoloq and his daughters." She looked at the boy. "Would you mind, Hadin?"

"You'll hear plenty of them soon," Mustapha growled. "The law courts meet next week." Basoni didn't catch his words.

"I'll be fine," Hadin told her. He put his hand in the wizard's and as they left the room he pertly asked, "Will you tell me about your battle with the night-spirit? Please?"

Sweet, strong coffee was poured and served with thimble-glasses of *nevra*, the potent liquor of distant Sumnerol. Mustapha's family and Basoni passed much of that night in companionable talk, comfortable silences. When they finally agreed to retire, the air drifting in through the richly curtained windows bore the moist freshness of dawn.

Basoni hardly dared to believe that she and Hadin were safe at last. After a surprisingly short period of adjustment, the boy took to his new surroundings with as much joy as he had last shown in Sombrunia. Basoni scarcely saw him except at meals, and sometimes not even then. He and the one-eyed wizard Liligi had struck up a strange friendship.

"Mhispan be my witness," Liligi said, calling upon the divine Trickster, patron god of all magicians. "I shall outwit the tangle of magics upon him if I die for it!" He touched his single eye knowingly and confided in Basoni, "I could never resist a challenge, which is why I view the world as flat, these days. I won that battle, and I will win this. Hadin! Here!"

Liligi snatched a ball of fire out of nothingness and flung it at the boy without more warning. Hadin's arms crossed reflexively across his face, but when the fire struck, it vanished. Liligi sighed.

"Truly a formidable curse. But I am not so insignificant myself. At least the boy seems to enjoy our games. They keep him from longing for the outside."

Basoni knew that the one-eyed wizard spoke truly. Hadin was safe in Mustapha's house, but it was a safety guaranteed only as long as he remained behind the stone wall surrounding the great estate. For the time being, he was content with his captivity—the parklands attached to the house were still an unknown wilderness to be explored. But how long until the boy came to know every leaf and shoot of those lawns and gardens? What would she do when he began hungering for what lay beyond the wall?

She spoke of her worries to Beglash. Mustapha's son was more handsome than his father, having inherited much of Nahraina's tawny beauty, and he had had that special charm all Vairish mothers wish upon their newborn sons when they smear honey on the infant's lips. From the time they had first met, he had been attentive. She supposed it was only part of the southern tradition of graciousness.

Beglash spoke soothingly. "Why fret over tomorrow? So many things change between sun and sun! Hadin has said nothing about wanting to leave our house; he might never have such yearnings, for all you know. Will you bless me with a smile, my lady? There! I think it's not Hadin who wants to explore Ishma. I will call for horses and we shall see the sights, if that pleases you.''

It pleased her more than she realized. Something in her nature rebelled against confinement. Stone walls pressed down upon her spirit, even the icy walls of Snowglimmer. In the free-flowing robes of a Vairish woman, she rode beside Beglash and was happy.

They rode through the outermost streets of Ishma, keeping far from the bazaar and its impossible traffic. Beglash refused to say where he was taking her. When he reined in his mount before a towering building of basalt and red marble, its sculpted portico upheld by alabaster pillars, she knew that journey's end had been worth the ride.

"Behold!" His expansive gesture made her a gift of the sight. "The Tomb of Elcoloq!"

Mustapha had understated matters when he said that the wise dog's family had buried him suitably. Even Lucha found the tomb excessive. Beglash left their horses in the care of four grubby streetboys and led Basoni through the gates. Sweet roses twined their thorny stems over the fence of twisted brass encircling the grounds. Closer inspection proved the flowering vines to be metal, too, skillfully painted.

The entrance to the building proper was a brass-sheathed door at the top of a flight of red marble steps. Scenes of Elcoloq's heroic deeds were cast in bas relief. One panel showed him as a boy with a dog's head embroidered on his tunic, playing cutpurse in a northern land. Basoni cast a backward glance at the shabby boys minding the horses.

"Don't worry, my lady, they won't steal them," Beglash said cheerfully. "There are so many of those market-rats around that they work in pairs for protection, but shy away from forming larger gangs for fear that the governor will notice and suppress them. Each trusts his partner not to betray him, but no one else. Those four will watch our horses *and* each other, never fear."

"I wasn't afraid of that," Basoni replied. "I was only thinking . . . how much was spent to raise a tomb like this when there are children who must steal to live."

Beglash lost his jollity and lowered his eyes, ashamed. "There are so many of them, my lady," he mumbled. "We can't care for all the children."

"Did you learn that lesson from your father, Beglash? I don't think so." She was suddenly much, much older than he, although only eight years lay between them. "He calls you Beglash the Scribe because of all the hours you spend poring over ancient books. Perhaps you would do better to spend your time learning about life."

That riled him. "I have learned more from a single scroll than my father ever knew, for all his journeys! A scroll that he himself brought out of the desert by chance, never knowing the treasure he carried! The riches of Queen Nahrit are nothing beside it. I—I alone!—have begun to translate it from the Old Tongue. The mysteries I have read in the *Scroll of Oran* will one day—"

"I have heard worse justifications for letting children grow up like animals," Basoni retorted.

From the shadows of the portico just behind them a sweet, mischievous voice added, "Or for letting animals grow up like children. Welcome, pilgrims. Welcome to my father's tomb. No arguing within the precincts; it annoys Mother."

The shadows gave up their secret as a young woman with golden brown hair and huge, limpid eyes came out to greet them, placing her daintily pointed feet with a dancer's precise grace. Her abundant waves of hair were held back from her high-boned face with a pair of richly jewelled combs. More gems glittered from her ears, her wrists, her ankles, her neck, and her tiny waist. This profusion of glitter was fortunate, for the lady did not seem as fond of clothing as she was of jewels. A suggestion of silk hung fore and aft from her sapphire-studded girdle—a very slight suggestion—and that was the sum of her attire.

Beglash began making noises like a beached tuna.

The lady appreciated this inarticulate tribute. "Beglash! How nice to see you again. Is this pretty woman your bedmate? About time you got one! You will find everything in that precious scroll of yours but the cure for virginity. Tell me, are there any good parts in it?" She draped her arms around his neck and let her body explain what she meant by good parts.

Beglash made a valiant effort to remove her. It failed. Making the best of things, he tried to act as if this adhesive lady were standing at a proper distance for formal introductions. "My lady Basoni, may I present Mayhem, fourteenth daughter of Elcoloq."

"Fifteenth," said Mayhem. "Plunder was born ahead of me. May I show you the beauties of my father's tomb?" She removed herself from Beglash reluctantly and walked ahead of them into the cool interior, her hips outlining a lesson in advanced geometry.

Totally bemused by Elcoloq's daughter, Basoni followed. Beyond the entrance, the edifice held a vast emptiness, except for a blocklike structure resembling a tester bed. This was Elcoloq's actual resting place. Basoni admired the larger-than-life statue of the little dog carved from milkstone, resting on a bed of serpentine. The dog was represented sleeping with his muzzle on his forepaws. The visitor making a careful circuit of the tomb would find the tiny effigy of an armed man, kneeling in eternal vigil at the foot of the stone dog's bed. Atop the flat canopy was a conventional mourning statue of a winged woman, obviously painted to life-tones with the same care as the false roses outside. Her feathered shafts trailed low and her face was hidden in her hands, the accepted way to convey grief.

"That's my mother," Mayhem said.

"She is buried with your father?"

"Buried?" The lady's sputtering laughter was woefully out of keeping with the surroundings. "In Vair, our custom is only to bury the dead!" Mayhem grinned up at the winged figure. "Mother! Turmoil and Devilry send you their best and say you're not to worry about Chaos any more. She was bought by a very young and stupid master."

The left wing shifted a handspan. Basoni gasped. "What evil spell is this?"

"Sheer selfishness, if you ask me," Mayhem sniffed. "When Father died, Mother was distraught. Well, we all were, but she got carried away! She's half-peri, you know." For Mayhem, this seemed to explain everything. "She spent almost all of Father's fortune on this stupid tomb, then flew up there and announced she was going to mourn him forever. And she's capable of it. Peris are immortal, and her name *is* Patience. She can come down any time she likes, but it's easier to hide in here."

"What does she have to hide from?"

Mayhem had an enchanting smile. "Why, from her daughters, of course! Thirty-six dowries is a mighty sum, she doesn't have it after building this monstrosity, she's too proud to borrow it from Beglash's father, and she disapproves of our methods for earning it ourselves."

"Petty thievery and hiring yourselves out to the Nightingale Houses are not exactly achievements for a mother to be proud of," Beglash lectured.

Mayhem stuck her tongue out at him. She managed to make it belittling and provocative at the same time. "If Father were alive, he'd cheer us on! So what if a few of us have been caught playing my-coin-your-coin in the bazaar? They sell convicted thieves in the slave market, and we've yet to get a buyer we can't

. . . reason with.'' Seeing Beglash's censuring glare, she added, ''In Vair, all things have a price, and you don't wed dowerless. Can you blame a girl for wanting to be a bride?'' She snuggled up to him again and breathed, ''I hear the benefits of married life are *soooo* much more restful than the Nightingale House trade.''

Beglash choked on an invisible bone.

Mayhem escorted them to the door. ''Thank you for visiting the soon-to-be-legendary Tomb of Elcoloq. The wonders within are maintained solely at the expense of generous visitors.'' She stuck out her hand with less ambiguity than she'd stuck out her tongue. Beglash counted out several vitrics, then several more when she started questioning his virility.

She slipped the coins into a mesh pouch depending from her girdle and bowed prettily. ''A thousand thanks. May the gods walk with— Ambra's sweet shimmy! *There's* a juicy man. Why did you leave him outside? The boys would've watched the horses.''

''Lord Cafran . . .'' Basoni whispered.

The Sombrunian lord saw her and flashed his strange smile. He was hemmed in by a small army of market-boys, and he was paying out vitrics into their filthy hands. Only when the last pair had run off to examine their windfall did he go partway up the steps to meet her.

At the dinner Mustapha gave in honor of Lord Cafran, Beglash was silent and moody. His truculence had no apparent cause; Cafran was the trusted agent of his father's friend, King Alban Stonesword. More than once Mustapha murmured loudly enough for Beglash to hear (in the tongue of Vair, and not the Common, so that Lord Cafran might not know) how glad he was that Hadin was not there to learn manners from a bad example. The boy found the adult dinners too longdrawn and boring. He preferred to take his meals with his newfound friend, Liligi. He would come to this feast later on, if at all.

Basoni watched Beglash uneasily. It was as if a stranger had slipped into the young man's skin. He had been like this ever since the Sombrunian lord made his unexpected appearance outside Elcoloq's tomb and she, almost without thinking, ran into his arms.

''A simple stratagem, really,'' Lord Cafran said, making light of how miraculously fast he had managed to locate Basoni in a city the size of Ishma. ''First I sought the governor, who referred me to the wardlady of Vair. It was a cold trail. Whatever your reasons for not contacting your own sister, I am sure they were sound.''

Basoni grew more nervous under her lover's mocking eyes, but she volunteered nothing. To their credit, Mustapha and his wife remained unruffled throughout Lord Cafran's recitation. They did not give away their part in Lucha's pact of secrecy by either word or sign.

Only Beglash refused to play cards well. "Whatever the reasons my lady had, sound or not, they are her own,'' he snapped.

"Beglash! Apologize to our guest!'' Mustapha could not stay calm when the fame of Vairish hospitality was in danger. Beglash made the proper excuses; they were only words. Cafran accepted them just as formally and insincerely.

He continued: "Having come up against two blind alleys, I described the lady Basoni to as many of the market-boys as I could catch. We must praise their sharp eyes for finding you, my dearest lady.''

Beglash glowered. At the feasting table, Cafran had the place of honor on the host's right, Basoni seated beside him. Nahraina occupied the wife's traditional place when guests were present, on Mustapha's other hand, an arrangement which put their son directly opposite Basoni. She missed none of the hatred he directed at Lord Cafran.

Mustapha poured wine for his guest with his own hands, a signal favor. "Fate advanced your journey, my lord. To find one person in all of Ishma is no easy task, but to settle upon Ishma, out of all the cities in Vair—''

"That was a trifle. Ishma is your chief city, and my lady Basoni has kin here. What better place to hide than among crowds?''

"Clearly your footsteps were guided by a happy star. My lord, may we hope that your reason for seeking out our lady is likewise happy?''

"No,'' said Lord Cafran. He sipped the rare cavriti wine lightly, scarcely seeming to swallow. "It is not.''

Nahraina left off making subtle signs to Beglash, signs that bid him smile now or perish later. "The gods keep it far from us, my lord, then what sorrow has brought you?''

"King Alban, his family, they're well?'' Basoni asked anxiously, laying her hand on Lord Cafran's arm.

He lowered his wineglass to cover her hand with his own. "No greater sorrow than loneliness for one I love more than my life.'' Now there was nothing ambiguous about his smile. He gazed fondly at them all, one by one, even Beglash. "I am unfamiliar with the customs of Vair. If I offend by a public confession of love, forgive me. I cannot do otherwise. My friends, I was wrong once, and my error might have lost me this sweet lady forever. The last time I saw her, we parted with anger, because I could not control my tongue. Now I have come to humble myself before her, to implore her pardon, and to ask for her promise. You are my witnesses."

Not even the burden of the Blue Sword, skillfully concealed by the double blind of invisibility and Basoni's voluminous skirts, put such a weight on her as Lord Cafran's words. "My promise . . . My lord, you know I cannot—"

His hand pressed hers more strongly. "I know, and I accept that. Give me your promise, accept my bride-gift on any terms you like, and I swear by all that I serve and worship, I will abide by your wishes. I will not demand any more from you than you can willingly give."

She lost consciousness of everything but her lover. His words placed their own spell of invisibility on everything and everyone in the room but her and him. She was his again, wholly his as she had always wished to be. *Oh my beloved!* Her thoughts sang louder than the beating of her heart. *My dearest, Hadin will not be a child forever. When he is old enough to shield himself, then I can be yours in body again, as in soul. I feared love, I fled love, yet I have found love. How foolish was I to fear!*

Basoni spoke her consent and her promise.

The room burst into cries of congratulation and rejoicing. Even the attendants could not restrain themselves from offering the couple many good wishes. Mustapha was beside himself. He gave a hundred orders for special wines to be brought from the cellars, rarer delicacies from the kitchens, more perfumed oil to replenish the lamps, Hadin to witness his aunt's happiness, musicians to add Insar's blessing to the unexpected festivities. Nahraina was overcome with emotion and used her scent-dampened handkerchief on her own eyes.

Beglash alone sat unmoved and unmoving.

When the table was relaid as befit such a merry occasion, and the tumult of scampering servants had subsided, Lord Cafran reached inside his brocaded tunic for a small pouch of soft black leather. "I have been lucky," he said, holding the pouch in one palm. "But I was bold enough to hope that I would be favored with your promise. I have come prepared: your bride-gift, my dear."

Basoni and the rest watched as Lord Cafran turned the pouch over in his hand. A silver necklace set with amethysts sparkled so brightly by the light of scented lamps that the stones appeared to lend their purple glitter to Lord Cafran's eyes. He held up the strand for her inspection.

"Let this seal our bond."

She hesitated slightly. She did not care for those stones, for excellent reasons. But then she looked at her lover again, and told herself that there were many folk in the Twelve Kingdoms who wore amethysts without a thought of Helagarde. One evil association could not rob the gem of its beauty. She turned from him and lowered her head so that he might fasten his gift around her neck.

"Basoni! Basoni!" Hadin came running into the room, all his lessons on Vairish manners forgotten. His face beamed with joy when he saw Cafran. "You did come! You really are back! Oh, I'm so glad!" While Liligi stood in the doorway, shaking his head over the ways of children, Hadin leaped to embrace his friend.

Nahraina screamed. She was the only one who found a voice to give to the horror before her.

Frozen and wide-eyed, Hadin clutched the skin of a dead man. Basoni turned back in time to see what that gruesome chrysalis had birthed.

Out of the disgusting shell that a boy's strange curse had torn away, Morgeld's creature reared up among them, the necklace in its claws. Its true form was a skinless commingling of human and demon, blood-red, blood-wet, its eyes full of Helagarde's grim powers. Basoni stood, grabbed Hadin and pushed him behind her. She touched the hilt of the Blue Sword through her skirts and the blade slashed up to meet her hand. At her back she sensed a gathering of power. She would not fight this being alone. The wizard Liligi was with her, and the strength flowing into him was great, tapped from hidden sources of magic only the highest of mortal wizards knew. It was as if a wave of fire rose up behind her, a wall of sorcery securing her. From the corner of her eye she caught the hint of its golden glow. Her ally's power was great.

It was great, but so were the powers of Morgeld's creature. Raw destruction rippled from Liligi's hands and came up against a shielding spell that fit the monster better than Cafran's purloined skin. It looked at him, laughed with yellow fangs stained rust, and swelled to three times its first size.

Mustapha's guards pounded into the hall, answering their mistress' screams. They attacked the creature with swords and spears which snapped and shattered against it. Its three-clawed paw swept down to snap and shatter men as well as weapons. Basoni's desperate cries for them to stand aside—to let her reach the monster—went unheeded, or were heard too late. Beglash fled.

Witch and child of witches! The being's roar dinned in Basoni's ears. It spoke with the same voice Morgeld had used in her earliest nightmares, and the memory of helpless infant terror froze her, immobilized her sword. *Give my master what he desires and we shall depart. Fight me, and I shall slay every soul in this house! Your powers are nothing beside those of Morgeld. Behold!*

The monster thrust the silver necklace over Basoni's head. A thin ray of violet light stabbed from the heart of the foremost jewel and transfixed Liligi in the midst of his enchantments. Fire shot from the wizard's one remaining eye as he was consumed to a seething pool of scarlet.

The Blue Sword lashed out in the witch's hand. Liligi's death had broken the spell of fear, dear payment to undo such a small enchantment. She wielded bow and arrow better, but she could use a sword. Her father's blade struck the shield around Morgeld's creature and did not break as ordinary swords did.

Neither did it make a mark.

The creature laughed again so that the walls shook and the little oil lamps tumbled from their niches. They turned the sumptuous rugs to carpets of flame. Mustapha seized his wife and fumbled for the small dagger all Vairish men wore everywhere, for show. With this paltry weapon he dared the monstrous invader of his home.

You cannot harm me with that, the creature taunted. Its paw closed around the Blue Sword's blade and squeezed, then released it to show that the enchanted edge did not even leave a scratch. *Yours are not the hands. Submit! Or watch me sow more death.*

Basoni called down her own powers, first in a whirlwind to extinguish the blazing rugs, next in an explosion of silver fire to ring the demon. "Run! Run!" she shouted at Mustapha.

"Like that cowardly son of mine? Never! I have faced worse foes than this. I will not run away."

"Then save Nahraina! Go!"

Mustapha shook his head decisively, and Nahraina fought the fear out of her face. She made a grab for one of the tableknives and stood beside her husband, determined but laughably ill-armed.

Hadin still crouched, shaking, behind Basoni. She let her magic coat the Blue Sword's own layer of enchantment and swung it again. Again it glanced off Morgeld's creature. Now the monster did not laugh, but its hairless brows came together in a terrifying grimace. It spat on the unearthly flames surrounding it and they died.

Foolish woman. Now these shall also perish.

It turned its back on her and Hadin as if there would be plenty of time afterward to see to them. Mustapha and Nahraina were its objects. Basoni lowered the Blue Sword and cast curse after curse at the apparition. These had as little effect as the Sword. The triple claw drew back to smash Mustapha and his wife from existence.

A word was spoken.

Morgeld's creature stopped.

More words followed, words in a tongue not heard in the Twelve Kingdoms for many centuries. From the far doorway, Beglash read out a spell of long-lost might, the scroll trembling in his hands. The ancient weirding washed over the monster, skinning it of any shielding spell, shrinking it back down. It wailed like the wind of desolation that twined the towers of Helagarde, and when it was only as big as a man, Mustapha stabbed it.

Fools! The monster's roar was a hiss of death-pain. *I am not my master's only slave. Morgeld will find what he seeks—and he will have it! While gold buys men in the Twelve Kingdoms, he will have it* . . . The being died, and the stench of its blood forced them all to escape the room.

In the small garden courtyard outside, Mustapha embraced his wife and son passionately, as if he had not expected to hold them close again. Basoni watched them, the Blue Sword blazing in one hand, her other arm sheltering Hadin.

He will be back, she thought. The dead guards and Liligi's awful end took all the beauty from the flowers around her. *Morgeld won't give up. As long as men may be bought for gold in the Twelve Kingdoms, our presence anywhere will never be a secret. We can't stay here anymore. I won't put these good people to any further risk. Where can we go? Ah, Sarai! Perhaps I must go back to my brother's house after all.*

Mustapha was still lavishing praise on his son, kissing the antique scroll the young man showed him, laughing like a mooncalf, when Basoni made the sign of opening and slipped away with Hadin into the plane of witchly flight.

Chapter XIX

THE DESERT

"What miracle can bring salvation to a stone?"

—"The Cry of the Hermit of Thulain"
from *The Scroll of Oran*.

What memories would have stirred in Mustapha's heart had he
seen the place where Basoni and Hadin emerged! And yet these
would not have been memories of the icy pleasures of Castle
Snowglimmer. They would be harsher memories, memories of a
place that bordered death: memories of the Desert of Thulain.

On the great causeway where a young player and his wise dog
had marched as prisoners, a woman in Vairish robes cradled a
small boy and tried to stop his nightmare cries. Low knobs of
deep red stone stuck up out of the sand at regular intervals beside
the road. The woman was too taken up with comforting the child
to notice that although time and the sands had worn the stones so
small, they were still recognizable as figures of men. Garnet eyes
in garnet faces impassively beheld the marvelous sword of blue
ice that did not melt even under the pitiless desert sun as it lay on
the sand-covered paving beside the travelers.

"Hush, Hadin; hush, my love. We are safe now." The words
were bitter in Basoni's mouth. She had uttered them wrongly too
many times before.

Hadin's fingers turned to grappling hooks in Basoni's robes.
"Did you see them, Basoni? Did you *feel* them? They touched
me! I never felt anything so—so—"

"Don't speak of it." She hugged him closer. The thought of
what they had endured on the plane of witchly flight would haunt
her for many nights. In that place where night spirits shared a

kind of truce with the witchborn, all the rules had vanished the moment she and Hadin went in, seeking the road to Castle Snowglimmer.

The road had been filled, blocked with a host of hideous shapes that surged forward to pluck and stroke their harried prey with the old, cold touch of dread. They shied away from the clean gleam of the Blue Sword, but there was no footing for a fight on that dark plane.

And what good would a fight do? The night-spirits feared the Blue Sword, yet the witch knew it would not harm them any more than it had hurt Morgeld's skin-stealing servant. What had the creature said to her? *Yours are not the hands.* The Blue Sword was a hollow threat; it would not keep them at bay forever. Basoni could only wheel about and drag Hadin away, back down the route to Vair.

This path, too, was blocked, and the way to Sombrunia, and every way that the young witch turned. The night-spirits beset them all around, herding them toward a faint glow. Wingless they flew toward the light, having no other way to go, but when the light was near, Basoni saw Helagarde's amethyst spell in the brightness. She choked back a scream that would never have been heard and with a desperate slash of the Blue Sword managed to lurch away from that awful goal.

She did not select the way they took. She only fought to escape the pull of Helagarde. When she saw a path materialize at the edge of the plane, she dove for it and felt the last scrabbling touch of the night-spirits as she and Hadin came back into the world.

Into the desert.

Even as they escaped the night spirits, Basoni imagined she could hear Morgeld's dry laughter. The path into the desert had been his choice for them, and no one else's. He would not need to hunt them there, for the land itself would destroy them.

And though her conscious mind was unaware of it, the young witch's gallant soul then and there resolved to cheat the lord of Helagarde of his sport.

The boy was calming down. For a while she had been afraid that his ordeal had cost him his reason. Gradually he sat up and moved away from her. The fierce desert sun made him shade his eyes. "Where are we, Basoni?"

Lost, Hadin. I can't take you out of this wilderness by flight, not again! And if I use magic to summon all that we'd need to leave this place by mortal means—camels, food, water, tents—I will alert Morgeld. Perhaps he may not leave our deaths to the desert after all. Who can know how his mind works? He is more capricious than death itself. I cannot risk attracting his attention, if that's the case; for Hadin's sake. I learned the error of that in Ishma, and here we are far from friends. He has narrowed his watch. He has called on his mother's kin to help him. How can I protect you from that? I couldn't even overcome the creature who stole Lord Cafran's skin . . .

Then she fully realized that Cafran was dead. The thought had been shoved out of mind—she had too much to deal with in the minutes after Hadin's curse revealed Morgeld's servant in its true form. One moment she had been so happy, and the next . . . Reality came back with the force of a warrior's blow, and she doubled over with tearing sobs for the man she had loved.

"Basoni, Basoni, don't cry!" Hadin had never seen her weep like this before. He was so upset by it that he forgot his own recent ordeal. "We'll be all right! Please, please don't cry!" Frantic, he looked all around for something he could do, something he might bring to comfort her. He sprang up to survey their surroundings, but all he saw was desert beyond the stones that lined the road.

He was helpless. There was nothing he could do for the woman who had done everything for him for as long as he could remember. It galled him to the point of tears, but he hardened himself against them. He could not cry now. He must not. It was his turn to be strong.

The Blue Sword gleamed at his feet. He picked it up, felt its heartening weight in his hand, and knew that while he held it, he did not need to fear anything. It gave him new determination as well. He would find a way to help Basoni; he only had to think of it.

Hadin thought. He tried to regain all he had ever heard, read, or learned about deserts. In the old collections of travelers' tales, many spoke of being surprised by ill fortune in the wasteland. Water was the chief worry; all else was useless if there was no water. The traveler made haste to find the nearest oasis, of course; failing that, there were undiscovered oases to be found, hidden springs that waited just below the surface of the sand. It was always most exciting when the traveler described how his feverish excavations yielded sweet water amid barrenness.

"Don't cry, Basoni," Hadin said, imagining that she wept for their plight. "I'll find us water." She was too taken up in her grief to answer him.

Hadin did not know where to begin his search. He looked around again and was struck by the broad smoothness of the highway where they had landed. He was sure that great wealth and power had gone into its making, and when he took a closer look at the deep red boundary stones, he saw that they were the most extraordinary miniatures of men. They barely came up to the boy's waist.

"Garnet," Hadin said to himself. "Garnet . . . I think." He knelt to study one of them at close range, his nose a thumbspan from the carved stone face. The sculptor had been as malicious as he was skilled. Anguish and misery were chiseled into every line.

Hadin leaned back, not wanting to look too long at so much pain, even if it was only stone. He reasoned half-aloud, "These statues are a costly way to mark the boundaries of the road. And such a grand highway! There would have to be many waterholes for all the people who used it, and for their animals. Maybe these aren't just here to bound the road. Maybe some of them show where water is—something written on the base of each statue. But the sand's covered them now."

Resting one hand on top of the little statue for balance, Hadin used the other to scrape away the sand covering the plinth. With a child's optimism, it never occurred to him that even if he did uncover writing, it would be in a tongue and script he could not read.

His optimism ended when he found the base smooth. He repeated the operation on the next statue, and the next, and found the same. Basoni's sobs were grating on his nerves. If he could find water quickly she would stop crying—she would have to! He chose a plot of sand at random behind the first statue he had touched and began digging madly, using the Blue Sword like a spade. The desert sands hissed back into the hole almost as soon as he cleared them out, which made him dig harder, until his breath came in jagged gasps and he no longer bothered to fight the tears of frustration.

"That is a poor way to use a good blade, my master."

Ruddy hands dug into the sand beside Hadin. The boy jumped up, the Blue Sword ready, and saw a red-faced man on hands and knees paddling sand out of the hole dog-fashion. He had dark hair and eyes, and a face somehow keener than any Hadin had seen. His outlandish clothes were too fancy to be meant for daily wear anyplace in the Twelve Kingdoms, too shabby to be court costume.

The man sat back on his haunches and met Hadin's frightened

eyes with a look of peace. "If my master would tell me what it is we're looking for, I might serve him better. So might the others."

"Others?" Even with a sword in his hands, Hadin was still a little awed by grownups. When such an odd stranger also called him "my master," he was thunderstruck.

"Ghiran and— Well, I never did know that man's name. I am called Escondi. See, my master, they are waiting for your word." The first man motioned down the line of statues. The two other plinths Hadin had touched, seeking inscriptions, were empty. Two men dressed in the same style as Escondi stood in the road, heads bowed and garnet-colored arms stretched out low in an exotic attitude of patient anticipation.

Hadin was aware of a familiar pressure on his shoulder. Basoni was with him, no longer weeping. He sagged with relief as he heard her say, "The vision . . . the vision my unborn brother sent . . . Hadin, you have freed them! Freed them and restored them to the proper size of men! Your touch—your curse of unmaking—has become their blessing. You can free them all!"

They knew where water was because they had known the Desert of Thulain far longer than any man. They had known it in the days of the Older Empire and before. They pointed out the right place to dig, then did the digging themselves, using limbs that had been frozen into stone ages ago. They were men again, and they gloried in the work, and the aches and pains which reminded them that they were alive.

Once they had been foolish men, rebels too stiff-necked to ask their lord's pardon when their evilly counseled rebellion failed. As they marched through the desert with Basoni and Hadin, Escondi spoke of those wicked times.

"He gave us a chance to make amends and we scorned it. We knew his powers, but pride is a stronger master than any king! So he laid his spell upon us, turning us to stone." He regarded his hands, still the rich color of garnet. "I see that the spell left a token behind, to remind us. To think I once had the finest, fairest skin in Sagra!"

"Hadin's touch undid that spell," Basoni said. She and Escondi walked in the van of the newly freed men of garnet, and a glance behind her showed Hadin riding on Ghiran's shoulders. They were a hundred men, and their pleasure was to take turns bearing the boy they all called "master."

"There must be much love in him, then," Escondi said, "for it was decreed that love alone would be the touch to free us." In a more sober voice he added, "The gods grant that this land has not changed too greatly since our captivity began. If we cannot find one oasis, it will take more than love to get us out of this desert."

Basoni kept her secrets. She had not told Escondi and the rest that she was a witch, and they were too overwhelmed by new liberty to question how a woman and a boy without any mounts or supplies had penetrated so deep into the unforgiving desert. For all she knew, such feats had been common in their day. She was just thankful that the same mysterious king who had locked their souls in stone had possessed the kindness to grant them use of the Common tongue as a gift on their awakening.

What a moil if we could not understand them, nor they us! Basoni thought. *Although . . . what good will all this understanding do any of us? Ambra, let us find an oasis soon! The desert has changed since these men were imprisoned, but let luck guide us. I don't want to have to use my magic and bring Morgeld down on us.*

She looked back at Hadin again, and the men whose boots devoured the desert. They had been fighters, and their swords were still with them. They had been soldiers, though rebels, and many of them still carried useful pieces of their kit. Filled waterbags swung from many belts, but how long would their contents last among so many? And could even so many ordinary swords be enough to fend off the lord of Helagarde?

"My lady!" Escondi's shout startled her. "My lady, I think I see something!"

"An oasis, Escondi?" She strained to see the telltale strip of green on the horizon. All she saw was the rolling dunes, and a distant cloud of windblown sand.

"No." He stopped and made a gesture that caused the straggling crowd of men behind him to form into the tight ranks of seasoned fighters. Swords made a squared silver hedge around Hadin. "Horsemen."

They came out of the north, riding hard and filling the sun-blasted sky with a confusion of wild, joyous cries. Three riders led the pack, their robes streaming out behind them. They rode so fast and so well that the horses following them could not even touch their noses to the whipping hems of the frontriders' garments.

The distance between the horsemen and the men of garnet was great enough to let the race resolve itself before the riders reached the armed square. The three fastest pulled well away from their followers and were nearly on top of Escondi's men before they reined their horses to a canter, then a trot, a walk, and a halt.

The foremost of the three raised one hand, a sign of peace, but Escondi's troop remained wary. Slowly the rider lowered his hand and spoke a few words to the two others with him. With one accord they unfastened the thick cloths that veiled their lower faces and kept the sand from mouth and nostrils.

"I am Lord Olian of the Desert Hordes," the leader said. "These are my favorite daughters, Shara and Sheena." Some of the Men of Garnet goggled to see the two red-haired women who had ridden hard enough to keep up with the desert lord, but Olian had other matters to discuss than his daughters' prowess. He jerked his bearded chin back over one shoulder. "Those are my men and this is our land. They have as many swords as you, and they are mounted. Speak quickly, before they interrupt you forever. Who are you? Why are you here?"

Escondi made a curt bow. "I am the servant of my master."

"Then let your master speak. Where is he?"

The wall of swords parted grudgingly and Hadin emerged, the Blue Sword on guard. Now it was Lord Olian's turn to stare. Gruffly he commanded, "Shara, Sheena, ride back and bid them wait."

"Father—"

"*Wait*, I said!" The women turned their horses without further argument. Basoni saw them intercept the galloping mass of riders.

Lord Olian dropped from his horse's back. Basoni did not interfere as he approached Hadin. A tug of her hand kept Escondi in check, too. There was something in the desert chieftain's eyes when he gazed at Hadin that told her not to be afraid. When Lord Olian went down on one knee and bowed his head to the boy, she knew she had been right.

"Hail, child of magic."

Chapter XX

THE BARGAIN

"What do you seek, mighty king?
"What I have found in thee; let no man take you from me.
Let death alone try, if death would risk so much."

—''The King's Encounter''
from *The Scroll of Oran*

"This is worse than Snowglimmer!" Basoni shouted in exasperation. She stood over the fragments of a broken waterjug and did her best not to scream. Not that it mattered: No one would have noticed if she'd slit her throat right there among the crowded tents. The camp of Lord Olian of the Desert Hordes had enough chaos to go around without borrowing any from newcomers.

The young witch stooped to recover the pieces, grumbling curses that had no magic to them at all. All around her, the vast encampment went about its daily routine: small boys chased small dogs into places neither of them belonged; young girls fought over whose marksmanship with the long spear was better; mothers cuffed sons and daughters equally and called on strange gods to witness that it was all the fault of their fathers' bad blood; young men stepped slyly into tents not their own and were welcomed or rejected, both noisily; elders slouched through the camp, debating the defects of the new generation, reminiscing over the merits of the old, and trying to look unapproachably wise.

Amid all this, Basoni had tried to balance a painted waterjug on top of her headdress the way she saw the other women do, and had learned much of practice, posture, overconfidence, and gravity.

224

"A little help wouldn't kill any of them," she fumed. When she cut her finger on one of the sharp edges, she added color to her curses, but still no magic.

"Here, friend, use this." One of Lord Olian's red-haired daughters stood over Basoni and tossed her a sweat-soaked head-cloth. "Wrap the bits in that before you slash your fingers to dogmeat."

"Many thanks," Basoni said, not at all thankfully.

"What do you want me to do? Pick that mess up for you?" the horsewoman asked. Her broad face broke into a smile. "Our customs state that all must take the consequences of their actions and no one else may interfere."

"Then if you don't mind, move your boots." Basoni was not normally so grumpy, but her sudden translation from the luxuries of Vair to the spartan life of the desert dwellers had been a rude shock. "You're interfering with my cleanup."

"Is that so?" The chief's daughter looked down and saw that she stood splay-legged over most of the broken crockery. Her long riding robes covered many of the shards, making it impossible for Basoni to reach them without lifting her hem and rummaging underneath. Without more ado, she raised her heavily booted foot and smashed one large fragment into several smaller ones.

"What do you think you're—"

Basoni's outrage met a sudden death when the woman tied up her sleeves, hoisted the skirt of her robe up between her legs, tucked it into her belt, and knelt beside Basoni where she proceeded to shovel bits of shattered waterjug into the outspread headcloth.

"See, now *I* have made a mess, so *I* must take the consequences," she said gaily. A wayward shard nicked her hand, too, and Basoni learned some new words in the tribe's language.

The witch was thoroughly ashamed. "My lady, I apologize for my bad manners. Your custom is right: I should have taken the consequences and cleaned up without complaining."

"Bah! If we didn't complain, we'd burst. There, that's the last piece. Wrap them up and I'll show you where the middens are." The two women got to their feet.

"Thank you very much, my lady," Basoni said. "I know where the middens are, and you have helped me enough."

"Forget that. I want to talk with you. And stop calling me 'my lady' before one of Father's men hears and starts teasing me to death!"

"Then what am I to call you?"

The redhead touched her lips in her tribe's gesture of self-introduction. "Sheena, daughter of Lord Olian, is pleased to call you friend."

Basoni mimicked the gesture. "Basoni, daughter of . . . Charel, is also pleased to call you friend."

As they walked, Olian's daughter cocked her head to one side so that the webwork of braids holding back her hair dangled in loops. "I think we must be of an age, Basoni. I am twenty-seven, by the Great Reckoning. Father claims they use the same system in the northlands, too, but what about where you come from? How do you reckon time among the gods?"

"Gods?" Basoni's grip on the laden headcloth slipped. She had purposely not introduced herself as her father's daughter just to avoid the undesired fame of divine kinship. "Why would you think—?"

"Well, if you and your lad aren't gods, you must be near neighbors, to hear Father tell it. He thinks that the boy is something special, the fulfillment of a great, ancient prophecy. Something about a magical sword and that sort of nonsense. My sister Shara pays more attention than I when he spins out the old tales." Sheena had a hearty laugh. "I prefer the rider's spear to any sword."

"Sheena, what is this prophecy?"

Basoni looked so disturbed that Sheena subdued her mirth immediately. "I didn't mean to offend your beliefs by mocking prophecy, Basoni. I just have a lightsome nature. Shara's always frowning at me, always urging me to become sober-minded. So many folk believe in the old tales out of Vair, but they get them so garbled in the telling and retelling that the same prophecy can sound like twenty different ones. It's hard to take them seriously."

"Please, Sheena . . ."

The chieftain's daughter paused to let down her upkilted robes, then said, "I guess that if anyone has the tales nearest to right, it would be Father. Our tribe was founded through his bloodline some six generations past, by Ashin the Wise. He was a scholar as well as a fighter, but he was exiled from Vair for a crime of which he was guiltless."

"What crime was that?"

Sheena shrugged. "Who knows? But we are sure that he didn't do it, whatever it was. He escaped the wicked justice of Ishma with all his family and a band of honest friends and founded the Desert Hordes."

By this time they had reached the middens, where Basoni emptied the headcloth onto a pile of rubbish. The women did not linger, for the middens had a certain air. Even though the encampment's more odiferous wastes were disposed of by special collectors who took the mess some distance away from the tents for burial, there would always be the inconsiderate cur dog or senile hen who would burrow into the mound of trash and expire anonymously.

On their way back, Basoni prodded Sheena. "You were speaking of the prophecy?"

"Oh, yes. As I said, Ashin the Wise was a scholar. He brought the old tales with him out of Ishma."

"And Hadin fulfills one of the promises made in those legends?"

"If he doesn't, he ought to! What conclusions would *you* draw if you found a hundred armed men ramping through the desert, all of them redskinned as newborn babies, and when you ask them their business they say a child is their master? A child with a sword stranger than any we've ever had in this camp, believe me. It's cold to the touch!" Sheena gave Basoni a steady look. "He isn't a godling, is he." It was not a question.

"No, he's not."

Sheena was satisfied. "I didn't think so; not from the moment I caught him showing off that sword of his to the children and charging them a sweetmeat fee for touching it. He's just a little boy."

Basoni stopped Sheena with a hand on her arm. Speaking very softly, she asked, "Will you tell your father?"

The redhead was surprised. "What for? You don't look like the sort of folk who'd take advantage of him through his beliefs. He's happy with his dreams, and now he can actually get the men to listen when he tells the old tales." She stroked her chin in thought. "You need my father's belief, don't you? You and the boy are in trouble of some kind. Don't tell me of it! You have enough fear in your eyes to infect the whole camp. Well, get rid of it. Father and the rest of us will stand by you against anything. He would do that even if he didn't believe the child to be twice god and once hero. It's not Father's way to let children grow up afraid. Anyhow, the boy brought us a fine troop of new men who seem to know what to do with a sword."

Impulsively, Basoni embraced Sheena. "I believe you, my friend. I actually believe that Hadin and I are safe now."

Sheena pushed her away gently. "Don't make a grain into a sandstorm. Now go get yourself a new jug. You'll need lots of water soon. I saw that boy of yours heading for the middens with his friends just as we were coming away.''

"Why, that little—!" Basoni hastened off to borrow another waterjug.

She heard Sheena's laughter behind her, and the redhead's jolly advice: "Hurry back! A dragonwind's coming up out of the south and it may blow hard!"

It took Basoni longer than she thought to get the new jug. The woman from whom she'd borrowed the first was reluctant to lose another. Before she handed over a second, she made Basoni swear endless oaths that she would not try showing off with this one. More than an hour passed before Basoni set out across the sands for the oasis well.

It was a good distance to cover. Oases were sacred areas of truce in the Desert of Thulain. Lord Olian's riders might sometimes harvest the passing caravans—by open force or quiet cunning—but they swore that they never would attack one when it was stopped for water. If the caravan merchants were skeptical of the Desert Horde's ethics, that was natural. Therefore, to keep skittish caravans from bolting waterless into the wasteland, the tribe never pitched camp within sight of an oasis, as a courtesy.

Basoni could have done without so much courtesy. Sheena's weather prediction was correct. A strong blow came out of the south and caught up with her when she was in sight of her goal. It carried stinging blasts of sand and filled the sky with the hollow roar that gave it the name dragonwind.

Basoni pulled her neckcloth up to protect her face from the sand. She did not know that the born desert dweller's tactic for dealing with such storms was to lie down and wait it out instead of fighting it and becoming exhausted. She shifted her waterjug from one hip to the other and pressed on, imagining that she could still reach the oasis.

The dragonwind blew harder. A shielding spell would have cut its fury off from her as effectively as if they belonged to different worlds; she did not dare to use it. In the increasing gust of the wind she closed her eyes and trusted that she was still heading in the right direction.

The sand underfoot grew less reliable, flowing away on the desert's hottest breath. She stumbled many times, and finally fell sprawling. The waterjug rolled away. She made a vain grab for it, flailing blindly with both arms, but she encountered only damp and gritty sand. Her fingers closed on a limp strand of ocean weed, and through the fading bellow of the dragonwind she heard a seabird call.

Basoni sat up and yanked the neckcloth from her face, rubbing her eyes. Gray waves beat upon gray sands. Mists clung to the beach where she sat astounded. A bank of steely clouds stood in battlements against the sky.

A stonecast away, the tall, dark, somber man of nightmare rested one foot on her waterjug and brought its rolling flight to a stop.

"My lady . . ."

"Morgeld. I should have known."

He made a reverence to her with that peculiar artistry that only the very tall may master. His long bones moved with an elegance learned over centuries. In black and gray and steel he greeted her, his voice powdery dry.

"How did you find us?" she asked. His gaze locked to hers when she spoke. Those eyes were not so frightening in reality as in her dreams.

"Us?" The lord of Helagarde lifted one hand. It was twisted and crippled, but still able to command. A black hawk fell from the cloud-blinded sky to grasp its master's wrist. Tor's face topped the bird's body. Morgeld stroked the creature's breast feathers with gloved hands. "I had sharp eyes to serve me, and this minion of mine was so eager to help find you. He took your scent from the blood of my dead skin-stealer and tracked you down.

"There is so much you do not know of magic, my lady; so much I long to teach you. I have watched you, Basoni. I have seen you dart this way and that, like a swallow pursued by a hawk, trying to escape me. I let you fly because it pleased me to do so. Now I am tired of the game."

Morgeld noticed Basoni's hands working furiously, tracing frantic signs in her lap. "Spells, Basoni? Against me? Here, save your energies."

He gestured, and her bow and arrows were in her hands, one of the enchanted bone shafts already nocked to the string. She scrambled to her knees and fired at him. The arrow would have pierced any other target at that close range; it pierced Morgeld, too, uselessly. The witch's magic trickled from the white shaft and was gone. Morgeld's good hand plucked it from his heart and crushed it.

"You see? Don't waste your time. We have much to speak of, you and I. Shall we do so here . . . or there?"

Green fire climbed the sky, burning the clouds away. Helagarde's amethyst keep emerged in splendor.

"I will not go there." Basoni flung down her weapons and clenched her hands so that he would not see them shaking. "If you have anything to say to me, say it here, Morgeld. Say anything you like, but before you say a word I want you to know that I will never let you harm Hadin. Not even if you threaten to kill me!"

Morgeld's thin mouth curved up. "I could not hurt the boy now if I wanted to. He is more powerfully armed against me than you are, since you put that sword into his grasp." Morgeld gazed at his warped hand bitterly. "I have had some experience with swords of that nature."

He drew the hand back under his cape, out of sight. "No, I will not harm Hadin, Basoni. He no longer interests me. Oh, at first I did think to kill him; there is a little matter touching the bearer of the Blue Sword that concerns me. His must be the hands to forge the three into one. But after the attack in Sombrunia I realized that I could ask for no better guardian of that cursed blade than Hadin! His very touch unmakes what is made by magic. He serves me best alive."

Basoni didn't believe what she was hearing. "Then why did you send your monster after us in Vair? Why did the night-spirits pursue us? Why—?"

"My lady, all I sought was you."

A length of silver set with twinkling amethysts dangled from Morgeld's crippled hand. "Your brother hates me more than any thing in these Twelve Kingdoms, yet he loves you. Your father and I shared a father, yet Krisli and Inota both turn from me. You ward the land of Alban Stonesword, who also cares much for you, who dared to do *this* to me!"

He tried to clutch the wounded fingers shut around the silver necklace, but they would not close completely. Morgeld would not hold a sword in that hand again.

A wind came from the dismal western ocean. It was no colder than Morgeld's voice, or the truths he told. "I do not need to kill in order to do them all the greatest harm. I am called the master of despair, and I will teach them my lessons. What trail did you think I followed to find you, Basoni? The little lights of your spells? The cold glow of the Blue Sword? The hatred for me you nourished in your heart? I think you knew that I would find you in the end, whether you played the magicless mortal or set a blaze of sorcery to consume the Twelve Kingdoms. When you laid aside your magic, you baffled my servants for a time, but you could never lose me; not for long. I am not bound by the constraints of witch, warlock, or wizard. I am more than mortal, more than witchborn! I hold the blood of the night-spirits in my veins. So shall my son—our son. I will have a son of your body, my lady. I will hold you as my bride and wife, mistress of Helagarde by your own consent! Your brother shall know of it, and your friend Alban, and your precious father. *His* daughter will bear my son, and my son will bring an end to every hope of the gods' return.''

''By my consent, you say?'' Basoni laughed. ''You have strange dreams, too, Morgeld. You admit to me that you can't hurt my boy. That was poor strategy. Why should I fear you anymore?''

''A woman should not fear her lover.'' There was something almost warm in Morgeld's words. ''Even if she cannot love, she should not fear. Janeela did not fear me; she betrayed me, but she did not fear me. Janeela, whom men called the Silver One . . .'' His eyes sought the sea.

It was a fool's gamble, but Basoni turned and ran. Morgeld let her run. He remained more motionless than the men of garnet, his back to her, her hushing footsteps across the sands ignored.

A fool's gamble, but Basoni was no fool. Even as she ran, she knew that he would not let her go so easily. She felt Morgeld's hunter circling overhead before she looked up and saw him. Tor leered down, hawk's wings spread wide, a wolf's smile on a face of darkness. He stooped, talons of black and silver reaching for her, and his laughter rang through the gray vault of the sky.

Her sword was in her hand, conjured there. She turned to meet his attack, slashing at Morgeld's servant of shadow with a blade hastily rune-blessed. The edge glowed faintly blue, but the young witch's strengthening spells were enough to make the hawk-bodied phantom veer off, climbing to a prudent height out of Basoni's reach.

Still Morgeld stood gazing out to sea. Tor circled in the air above her, ready to dive the moment she made a move to escape. If she tried to run to the east or south, he was there, putting her on the defensive, harrying her like a sheepdog. Only if she moved west, seaward, he let her go; west . . . or north, back to Helagarde and Morgeld.

The amethyst palace burned with a fire only Basoni could feel. She backed away from it, keeping her guard up, wondering whether she should shift her tactics to assault. She might mount the wind herself, fly straight for Tor, cut him from the sky . . .

Morgeld turned and looked at her steadily. Even from a distance, she could feel his thoughts entering her own mind when their eyes met.

He is not my only servant, my lady. Bring him down, and I will only summon more. Why do you struggle? I will have you. I have sought you from times that are blurred memory to you. I have followed you by many roads. Do not think you will escape me now.

"You don't have me, Morgeld, and you never will!" Basoni cried aloud. Her shout sounded thin and hollow against the boom and rush of the Lyarian Sea. She wheeled and fled again, wrapping invisibility around her, plunging from Tor's sight into the plane of witchly flight.

Gates of fire and night opened. A hawk with a man's head swooped past her, his powers rupturing the slender border between the plane she sought and the plane she dreaded. Captain Tor's mocking laugh shattered in her ears. She fell through the ultimate blackness where the night-spirits dwelled.

Insanity took the form of weird shapes, the sound of manic laughter without a human throat to voice it. A skin of ebon fell across her eyes, a cool, terrifying web where fiery yellow eyes winked back at her from distances that were all within her own head. If she closed her eyes, they were still there. She screamed and struck into the darkness with her sword, but the hilt melted to yielding clamminess in her hand. The twinkling eyes swirled nearer.

She could feel the mockingly soft touch of fingers that became needles of ice. They slipped beneath her skin, lancing her with fiery cold. The spirits laughed and took shapes that had names in the living world: Writhing creatures like giant worms made all of blood, the dancing fire-crackled bones of children, the gaping red mouths of rats that scampered up Basoni's skirts, skittered around her neck, clung to her cheeks with chill paws and gnashed their teeth a hairsbreadth from her eyes. Lord Cafran's face was there, flesh melting from the skull. Hodah's death was there, alone in the darkness of a sinking ship, birth-blood seeping through her clothes, her last anguished cry stifled by the black northern waters filling her lungs.

And through it all a carol of exulting cruelty dinned into Basoni's reeling mind: *This realm is your eternity, child of witchcraft! Forever we shall have you for our own!*

Begone! She will not be yours! By my father's blood, I swear it!

Morgeld was there, his body shining with the hard light of a sword white-hot from the forge. Basoni heard herself call his name, saw her hands—now visible—reach out for his, felt all her terrors vanish as his good hand closed on her wrist and together they fled the realm of final night.

Spindrift blew over Basoni's skin, cleansed the last traces of the night spirits from her. She was kneeling in the sand at Morgeld's feet and Helagarde loomed above them.

"You saved me." Her voice was a murmur, but he heard it. "You might have let them have me. Why didn't you?"

His face was stiff with ancient hate. "Why didn't I?" he repeated her words. "That would be true demon's work, wouldn't it, my lady? To let my mother's kin have you, to be worthy of her blood . . ." The sound he made was almost laughter. "What would the bards of these Twelve Kingdoms make of it if they knew that Morgeld cannot match his mother's art for throwing away a life . . . a life too brave, too strong, too fair . . . a life that should be . . ."

All the fears she had ever had of Helagarde's lord now tumbled into confusion. Her earliest certainty had been that Morgeld was nothing but evil given human form, the child of night and war. But she heard pain in his voice: pain for love lost—Janeela's; pain for love never given—his mother's; pain for love desired . . . hers.

For an instant, by some trick of the half-light clinging to Helagarde, she looked up into Morgeld's face and saw Hadin's.

Suddenly, he clenched his good hand so tightly that the nails must have driven themselves into his palm. Basoni winced in sympathy. "We waste words." He was the bards' Morgeld again, harsh and hard, who only knew pain because he dealt it. "You will be my bride, lady—be sure of it!—and I will have your consent to it. Now."

Even the memory of fear was gone. Basoni stood up slowly, alone on the Laidly Marshes with the lord of Helagarde. She had heard his hatred, his bitterness, and his anger, but his sorrow was something she understood. She came near him and was not afraid to touch his shoulder.

"I cannot consent, Morgeld," she said softly.

His eyes were aged and empty, drinking in all of her compassion and giving nothing in return. "Consent," he said. "I can't harm Hadin, but I can do more."

And all at once she was drawn into the depths of his vision, falling down the roads of flight until she came to Lord Olian's camp again. The tents were silent. The dead lay everywhere, the marks of plague on them. The only sound of life in all that desolation was a little boy's tears. Hadin sat alone, hugging the Blue Sword to him and weeping.

Plague will not touch him, Morgeld's thoughts declared. *The sword defends him, but wherever he goes, I will send sickness on the wings of night-spirits to destroy any and all that he loves. It is not an easy thing, to control my mother's kin. The effort of it may drain me of so much power that it will be centuries before I can hope to conquer all that must be mine. It doesn't matter; I will spend my strength gladly. Death will be this child's lone companion, and despair will take him at the last. That . . . or your consent, my lady.*

The seeing vanished. Hadin's misery was gone; Basoni saw only Morgeld's face—and in a revelation more stirring than any sorcerous vision, she read his starving soul.

Child . . . child . . . And have they hurt you so much, to make your life all hate? She thought what she could not say aloud. *I will work my own spells of unmaking on you. I will undo the lonely years, the rage, the sadness. Show me some hope, lord of despair. Show me that you can feel compassion for a child, and I will heal you.*

She did not back away. She lifted her hands to his face and drew his mouth to hers. His kiss was not the icy caress she had expected, and an answering fire inside herself took her by surprise. When their lips parted, she lowered her head and Morgeld set his collar on her.

"Hadin . . ." she breathed.

"I will never harm him," the lord of Helagarde said when the silver clasp was closed. "I promise this by a vow even I can never break. I swear it to you by the blood of the night-spirits, my lady."

So quietly, so secretly that it was a whisper of the heart, Basoni replied, "And I will love you for this—for only this—my lord."

She raised Morgeld's ruined hand to her lips, and knew that in time she might come to love him for more.

EPILOGUE IN DREAMS

"Who shall name or number all of this world's wonders?"

—*"The Dying Words of the Hero Oran"*
from *The Scroll of Oran*

Hadin, just turned seven, awoke from dreamless slumber to see the shining lady bending over his bed. He cried out and groped for the sword that hung from a pole near his head, but his hand never reached the hilt. He recognized a face he had not seen for months.

"Basoni!" He started up from his bed, but she retreated from his outstretched arms.

You cannot touch me, my love.

He was suddenly chilled through. "Are you . . . dead?"

Oh no, dear heart, I am alive! But I can only travel this way, now, and I did so want to see you again.

"Basoni, where are you? What happened to you? Why did you go away? Why did you leave me?" The words came faster and more raggedly as he spoke, and the tears came with them.

She said, as she had used to say many times before, *Hush, my love; hush, my darling. I went where I had to go. I went gladly, because I knew that you were with good people who would take care of you for me. You are happy here, with Lord Olian's tribe, aren't you?*

The boy wiped away the tears and nodded.

And I am happy with Morgeld.

She saw what a harsh reaction that name evoked in her beloved boy, and she wished she had time enough to explain to him how

235

much he did not know about the lord of Helagarde. She could only repeat, *I am happy with him,* and hope it would be enough.

"But Morgeld—Morgeld is evil! He is—"

He is the one who sent me to you, Hadin. He saw how much I missed you, and he used his magic to bring me here. I could not use my own . . .

The lady turned so that her form was outlined by the dying moonlight spilling in through the open flap of Hadin's tent. Her figure had grown fuller, and her dress pushed out in the sweet curve of pregnancy.

I bear a boy. He must be a very greedy one—her smile was still entrancing—*because he's taken all my witchly powers from me.*

"Why did you let him take your magic, Basoni?" Hadin could not understand why she smiled over it. "If you had your powers, you wouldn't have to wait on Morgeld's charity. You could come to see me any time you wanted to!" His small face contracted with anger. "I hate him! I hate his father for taking you and I hate him more for stealing your magic!"

Oh no, Hadin, no! Basoni's image fluttered mothlike to the boy's bedside and he saw the pain in her face. *Don't hate without cause, don't hate a child you don't know! Hatred is too plentiful in these Twelve Kingdoms; it has already done too much harm, and love . . .* She looked down at her swelling gown. *I have healed much with love. May the gods grant that I live to give this child all that I could never give his father. There are the loveless centuries to erase, and I have had so little time to work my spells of unmaking. My lord learns slowly, but Ambra sheds light in the blackest darkness of the heart. The lord of despair learns hope . . . If I live, I will teach him more.*

A second figure stepped into the vision, a tall man in robes as soft and gray as smoke. His arms encircled Basoni from behind, and Hadin could see that one of the hands resting on her belly was badly twisted and scarred. The boy gave a low cry and reached for the Blue Sword again.

Instantly he felt his hand seized in a grip unbreakable as the grave's. Morgeld's face was so close to his own that he could see every curve and line of skin and bone, every flicker of cold fire in those empty eyes. Morgeld was no dream-borne vision: He was real.

"Basoni!" Hadin tried to jerk his hand away. He was not the master of the men of garnet, Lord Olian's respected guest, the child of magic born of prophecy and legend—he was only a frightened boy, calling out to the one soul he loved best in all the world. "Basoni, help me!"

But she could not help him. She was only a vision, and all but magicless. Morgeld's son grew in her, sapping her strength with her powers, and now she would stand helplessly by as Morgeld himself killed Hadin. The boy knew it, just as he knew it was useless to struggle. Still, he had the soul of a witchborn warrior even if he had no magic in him. He would never surrender without a fight.

Hadin . . . Basoni's image drifted to stand with Morgeld at the boy's bedside. *He only wants to protect himself from your sword. Promise not to take it up against him now and he will release you. Hadin, he will not harm you.*

Hadin shot her a hard stare of doubt and betrayal. *Why should I believe you?* that look seemed to demand. *You, who left me, who abandoned me like all the rest. And I loved you!*

"Hadin." Morgeld spoke to the child's unuttered thoughts. "Hadin, make no mistake: she loves you well. I envied you that love . . . once. There is no need for envy between us now. She has love enough for us both, boy, or so she says. My brother's gifts are strange in the giving. I have suffered more than you, and I can almost believe her. Can you do less?"

Hadin glared at Morgeld and Basoni equally, as unwilling to surrender his suspicions as himself. Helagarde's master released Hadin's hand and stood up with a sigh. "Believe what you will, then. Hate me, hate her, end by hating yourself as well. But know this, Hadin: I gave her the word of blood, swearing by the oath that binds even me. I vowed never to harm you. Here I stand, your life within my reach, and do nothing, though the gods know if you would do the same for me. A mortal's oath is only air. I made my vow to her for the sake of bargain. I renew it freely for the sake of love."

Morgeld was gone. The hour of visions was slipping away as well. Hadin could still feel where the dark one's fingers had closed around his flesh. "Basoni . . . ?"

Yes, my love. Morgeld was truly here, and he spared you. For me. Now will you believe?

Her hands hovered about his face and he imagined she was trying to touch him as before. Hadin said, "I will not hate anyone without cause, Basoni. I promise you."

Swear also, said the vision, fading with the coming dawn.

Swear that you will do as I have done. Swear that no child who lives shall have to live without love. Swear . . .

Hadin took down the Blue Sword from its sheath. Basoni's image smiled, although soon the time of visions would be past. She blessed Hadin, who did not mark the moment when she vanished. His eyes were on the shining blade of his inheritance. He held it high, and in the inmost chamber of his soul, the hero swore.

ON THE BANNS OF SORCERY

by Randu Eluman of Clarem (Notes for an unpublished monograph)

The Banns of Sorcery are one of the most misunderstood magics in all the Twelve Kingdoms. Frequently the layman confuses them with spells of invisibility and other weirds of veiling. Many of these exist, effective to varying degrees in accordance with the learned or inborn powers of the spellcaster, and each vulnerable to penetration according to its own limitations, as with any spell.

The layman's chiefest error in comprehending the Banns springs from the misapprehension that any wielder of magic—witchborn or wizardly—must be all-powerful. This is not so. Even the witchborn, who are gifted from birth with their magics, have limits set to their powers, as the Rule of Loss proves. It is always well to recall that *all magic has limits*, and only dreams have none.

The Banns of Sorcery may be cast by any magic wielder with sufficient power, knowledge, and training. They may be cast over the mage himself, over another living being, or group of same. The only limitation on how many will lie beneath the protection of the Banns is the spellcaster's own complement of power.

The purpose of the Banns is to render the subject immune to searching spells. A searching spell does precisely what its name indicates: It searches out a specific individual. Mages of great strength may use many searching spells at once. There is no-where to hide from a searching spell, save under the Banns.

The Banns are very durable simply because of the great amount of power necessary to invoke them. They can endure even after the original spellcaster has lost his powers or his life. Some places—the homes of the greatest mages, for example—are rumored to have their very walls imbued with the Banns of Sorcery, sheltering all within the walls from magical perception. This remains to be conclusively proven, the very mages who are the subject of this rumor being understandably reluctant to part with either their professional secrets or their privacy. As no wise man would willingly court their wrath, experiments in the holy name of knowledge for knowledge's sake have not yet been undertaken.

The Banns do *not* render the subject invisible. He still remains perceptible to all the senses, save that of sorcerous seeking. Experiments by the magefolk of the Twelve Kingdoms to combine spells of invisibility with the Banns of Sorcery have met with nothing remotely resembling success. This in itself should serve as further proof to the magicless who envy the witchborn and wizardly that there is no such thing as the limitless power of magic.

As in the life of magicless mortals, so in that of mages: There is no act that does not leave some mark on the world. Fire consumes wood, but leaves ash on the earth and smoke on the air, traces of the wood that was. So, too, with spells.

The casting of a spell involves the summoning and utilizing of power. Some refer to this as the "aura of magic," and claim that certain objects of supernatural provenance give off this aura even when their inherent powers are not being actively utilized. This point must remain moot, pending further scholarly investigation. There are many more mages in these Twelve Kingdoms who use their powers than there are those who understand them fully.

The more perceptive of mages claim that they can sense when one of their brethren is casting a spell. This is not a constant state of awareness, but a happenstance occurrence, often peripheral to the preparations for the casting of a formal searching spell. This would explain the high incidence of wizards who "just happened to be passing by" when a feast is being conjured rather than cooked.

The traces that spellcasting creates have been likened to the striking of a single spark on a moonless night. It may pass unperceived, but then again it may not. All depends on whether there is someone present who happens to be looking in the region of the spark at the moment it is struck. The more powerful the spell, the greater the spark.

It is further argued that even after a spark is extinguished, dwindling traces of heat remain, as does a lingering smell of burning. If hounds, which are magicless beasts, may track a long-gone quarry by scent, might there not be some way to track a spellcaster by the diminishing traces of his spell's aura?

The wizardly deny this is possible. The witchborn will not comment. But there is much about magic in the Twelve Kingdoms of which wizardly and witchborn are ignorant, and more beings than they who possess sorcerous powers. This will require further research.

About the Author: Randu Eluman of Clarem graduated with honors from the University of Panomo-Midmists, taking doctoral degrees in Arts, Sciences, and Theoretical Wizardry. He was the youngest professor of Comparative Magics ever granted tenure by the faculty.

It is the sorrow of the great University City that Randu Eluman left so much of his work unfinished. He departed from Panomo-Midmists in the Jubilee Year of King Dalex, heading west. As he confided in his friends and personal secretary, he intended to make a "pilgrimage of wisdom," braving the River Salmlis, the Lands Unknown, the toll-takers of the Leyaeli roads, and the trackless reaches of the Naîmlo Wood, all in hopes of finding the legendary Vaults of Tsaretnaidos, repository of untold erudition. He did not return.

This fragment and others have been prepared for publication with the aid of a grant from the Randu Eluman Memorial Fund.

Esther M. Friesner was born in Brooklyn but left to attend Vassar and later Yale, where she earned a Ph.D. in Spanish. After teaching at Yale for some years, she quit to write fantasy and science fiction full-time. Her short stories have appeared in *Isaac Asimov's Science Fiction Magazine*, *Amazing*, and *Fantasy Book*, as well as in several paperback anthologies.

Currently, Ms. Friesner lives in Madison, CT, with her husband and two children. She writes, "I'm a member of the local Society for Creative Anachronism group, where my pseudo-medieval plays enjoy frequent nonprofessional production. I am also a camp follower of the Fifth Connecticut Regiment, a colonial re-creation military group for which my husband is company drummer. The drummer used to have to bury the dead. So far we've been lucky."

The CHRONICLES OF THE TWELVE KINGDOMS

include

The Books of Prophecy
In which the Scroll of Oran is found, and a great evil is unloosed
Mustapha and His Wise Dog
Spells of Mortal Weaving
The Witchwood Cradle

The Books of Initiation
In which the White Sword and the Green Sword are discovered, and dynasties founded

The Books of Inheritance
In which the Companions are bonded, and sinister Beasts are conjured

and

The Books of Fulfillment
In which the secrets of the Scroll of Oran are revealed